Richard Paul Russo is on
talents to arrive on the sc
compared to that of su
Shepard and George R.R.

By the same author

Inner Eclipse

RICHARD PAUL RUSSO

Subterranean Gallery

Grafton

An Imprint of HarperCollins*Publishers*

Grafton
An Imprint of HarperCollins*Publishers*
77–85 Fulham Palace Road,
Hammersmith, London W6 8JB

Published by Grafton 1991
9 8 7 6 5 4 3 2 1

First published by
Tom Doherty Associates, Inc. 1989

The words from the song 'Cities in Dust' have
been reproduced by kind permission of
Dreamhouse/Chappell Music Ltd,
written and recorded by
Siouxsie and the Banshees © 1985

ISBN 0 586 21229 9

Set in Times

Printed in Great Britain by
HarperCollins Manufacturing Glasgow

This one, too, is for Sally

Acknowledgments

I'd like to express special thanks to Pat Murphy, who read the manuscript and made many invaluable suggestions. I'd also like to thank Karen Joy Fowler, for her comments on the earliest version of this book, and, more importantly, for her friendship and support through some of the hard times. And finally I'd like to thank Wayne Wightman, who didn't read any of the manuscript at any stage, but whose friendship made it a lot easier for me to write this book.

PART ONE

DEPARTURE

Initial Departure

One

Rheinhardt twisted violently in the bed, made a loud, inhaling cry; head and shoulders rose abruptly as he pulled himself out of the nightmare, an arm flailing at the darkness. His hand struck someone's face, and he cried out again, twisted out of the bed and onto his feet.

He ran into the wall, pounded at it with his fists, swearing, then pushed away and dropped to the floor, rolled up against the bed. He grabbed the bed frame, began shaking it. "Fuckin' son of a bitch . . . god damn fucking . . ." He rolled away from the bed, pounded several more times on the wall, trying to drive the images from his head, then was still.

"Rheinhardt, it's me, Terry. It's all right, we're in my apartment, my bedroom." He didn't answer her, his face pressed against the cool metal angle iron of the frame. He knew where he was. "Rheinhardt?"

He was breathing heavily, trying to get air, slow down his heart, and he didn't move.

"Rheinhardt?"

Rheinhardt put a hand on the bed, slowly rose to his feet, nodding. "Yeah," he whispered. "I'm . . ." He turned and staggered out of the room, across the hall and into the bathroom.

Leaving the light off, Rheinhardt dropped to his knees in front of the toilet, raised lid and seat, and vomited into the bowl. His stomach cramped tightly on him, and the retching kept on for several minutes as he pounded slowly on the linoleum floor with his fist. Sweat broke out across his body.

The vomiting gradually eased, then ceased. When he thought it might be finally over, he flushed the toilet and sat back on his haunches for a moment. The floor creaked as he got to his feet and went to the sink. He turned on the cold water, cupped his hands under it, and rinsed his mouth several times. The bad taste gone, he splashed water onto his face, over and over.

Rheinhardt was tall and thin, his dark hair short and stiff except for a narrow, foot-long tail at the back of his neck that had been bleached white. *Twenty years out-of-date,* Terry had said once, fondling the white tail. *I'm not interested in fashion,* he'd told her. *It's what I want.* He took hold of the tail now, held tightly onto it until he felt somewhat steady.

Rheinhardt turned off the water, then walked slowly back across the hall and into Terry's bedroom. He could see her dim form, sitting up on the bed, looking at him. She probably didn't know what to say or do; the nightmares were too infrequent for her, or him, to get used to them.

"I hit you?"

She nodded.

"Sorry."

"You okay?" she asked.

He stood at the foot of the bed, still breathing heavily, looking out the window. He brushed at the water still dripping from his face. "I guess," he said. "Not really." He shrugged. "No, I'm okay." He breathed very deeply. "Fuck."

"Come on back to bed, Rheinhardt. Get some sleep."

Rheinhardt turned to look at her. "You can't be serious."

"What are you going to do, stay awake the rest of the night?"

"Hell yes."

"That bad."

"That bad."

"You want to talk about it?"

"No." He went to the chair, fumbled through his clothes for his cigarettes, lit one. After taking a couple of hits, he began dressing. When he was done, he went to the bedroom door, stopped and looked back at her. "I'm going out," he said.

"It's three-thirty," she said. "Bad time of night to be on the streets." When he didn't say anything in response, she asked, "Will you be back?"

"I don't know." He turned away and left.

The cold, damp air outside felt soothing. Rheinhardt started up the hill, the street deserted, the streetlights pale, casting misting cones of silver through the fog.

A dog barked on his right, startling him for a moment, and he picked up his pace. He tried not to think at all about the nightmares, but the hot white flames kept exploding in his mind, like strobe flashes in the night.

A chopping sound cut the quiet air, approaching, and Rheinhardt dashed toward the nearest building, crashed into it, pressing his body flat against the cold brick. Sweat popped out on his forehead, under his arms, and his heartbeat stepped up, pounded painfully against his ribs. Jesus Christ, he thought, I don't need this kind of shit. He *knew* there was no danger from the helicopter overhead, invisible in the fog, his mind knew that; but his body had reacted as if . . . Christ, as if the dream was coming true.

The chopping sound faded in the distance and he pushed away from the wall, forced himself forward again, walking quickly up the hill. Too much energy, the adrenaline was racing through him, he couldn't stop it. His pulse was still too strong and rapid, the sweat continued to pour from him. He kept walking.

Rheinhardt didn't know where he was going, and he didn't care; he just had to keep moving. The street leveled off for a few blocks, but the sidewalk grew darker as thick trees blocked the light from the streetlamps. He passed in and out of dark, heavy shadows, outlines irregular with the shape of leaves, shifting slightly with the occasional gentle breeze.

A cat ran across the sidewalk, yowled as it leaped onto a windowsill, and he jerked back, another shot of adrenaline slamming into his heart. When headlights appeared from behind him a moment later, followed by the rumble of an engine, Rheinhardt instinctively broke into a run.

He tried to stop himself, but his legs and arms were running on instinct, would not obey his commands. It was as if his mind and body had become separated, with only a fragile, passive link remaining between them. All he could do was watch himself react and run.

He ran up a porch and into shadows as the car passed, then a few moments later began running again, down the porch steps and across the street, watching the red taillights grow smaller. At the next corner he turned, still jogging, headed uphill once more.

At the top of the hill, his breath ragged and fast, he paused for a minute, looking in all directions, then started jogging down the street to his right, which sloped gently downhill for a block before leveling out.

The chopping of a helicopter sounded once more, and Rheinhardt lost all control. He shifted to a full-out run, hardly seeing where he was going. Dogs barked all around him, it seemed, and the city night seemed to grow louder with crashing sounds, windows being slammed shut, cars roaring, wheels squealing. His vision flared on him, the white flash bursting behind his eyes the way it had on night patrols from the uppers they gave him, and new lines of silver clarity appeared around everything.

He came around a corner, crashed into a man walking along the sidewalk, almost fell, dashed across the street as the man yelled something after him. Headlights came at him from two cars, he reversed directions, cut to the side, plunged through bushes and over a low fence into a small yard of cement and thick, dark trees. He stumbled over a garbage can, knocked down a bicycle, and a small dog emerged from the side of the house, yelping furiously. Rheinhardt kicked at it without making contact, stumbled toward another section of fence, scrambled over it into a narrow alley between two buildings. Weaving back and forth, he emerged back onto the street, and kept on running.

Rheinhardt lost all sense of where he was, or where he was headed. He ran down one street after another, his body reacting to traffic, animals, people, unidentifiable sounds. Several times he ran into parked cars he didn't see; he pushed through bushes with branches scraping his arms; he tripped over cracks in the sidewalks or tree roots or sprinklers. He ran.

The streets and buildings changed, grew darker and even more deserted. Houses and apartments gave way to silent machine shops, warehouses, grilled-over bars and stores. Finally, slowing down to a half jog, incredibly tired, Rheinhardt realized he was only a few blocks from the Warehouse. The night seemed to have calmed, quieted, tension in the air dissipated. The sparkling in his vision faded. Rheinhardt managed to slow down to a walk, made it to the cyclone fencing without breaking into another run.

Rheinhardt stood outside the fence for several minutes, his breath and pulse still rapid. His vision blurred with each beat of his heart, his lungs scraped with pain at each breath. He felt sick to his stomach, thought he might start retching again.

The Warehouse buildings were dark, but they weren't empty. Close to a hundred and fifty people were inside, "fellow" artists. Shit, most of them were hacks or frauds. His own studio was inside the building, high in the rafters, but he couldn't go there yet—it was still too dark, he didn't dare go to sleep. He had to do something else. Anything else.

When his breathing had eased, he unlocked the gate with his magnetic key card and code, went through, and crossed the lot of cracked and potholed pavement. He

circled the main building to the steel ladder built into
the back wall, leading up to the roof thirty feet above.
He started up.

He was out of breath again by the time he pulled up
onto the roof, but it didn't matter; there was still too
much energy inside him. He walked across the tar and
gravel surface to Kate's lean-to and all her scrap metal
and welding equipment. It had been years since he'd
done any welding, but he couldn't even think about
going inside and working with the clay. He wasn't
trying to create anything worth a damn anyway. He just
needed something to *do*.

Rheinhardt donned the protective gear, hauled out
the welding equipment and the crates of metal. He
positioned the goggles over his eyes, fired up the torch,
stared at the cool blue-white flame. Then he started
melting filler rods and welding metal to metal with
hardly a thought, aware only enough to perform the
necessary movements. He worked steadily, without
pause.

At dawn, as the sun began to rise, the fog gone and the
sky clear, Rheinhardt cut the flame. He removed the
goggles, put all the welding equipment away, then
looked at what he had done. On the workbench was a
shapeless mass of bent and twisted metal, nothing more
than a pile of junk. Good. That's all he wanted.

He could hardly move, could barely stay on his feet.
All his muscles trembled with exhaustion. Still wearing
gloves and work apron, Rheinhardt walked out along
the roof toward the far edge, where the sun was
beginning to shine. He lay down on the gravel in a
narrow strip of light and warmth, body pressed against
the ridge. Then he closed his eyes, and slept.

Two

Inside Cafe Olivia it was warm. It was a tiny place just off Lombard, half a block from the Presidio, with five tables and no counter. The tip of one of the Golden Gate Bridge towers was just barely visible through the window. Rheinhardt, the only customer, sat at the window table eating breakfast, reading the newspaper and feeling depressed.

Africa had regained prominence in the news the last few weeks, with U.S. troops now in Namibia and in the Sahara—in Chad, he thought, Ethiopia, and the Sudan. It never seemed to change much, it only moved from one country to another, and sometimes back again. Rheinhardt seriously doubted whether anyone knew exactly what the hell was going on anymore, or what the reasons were.

Namibia was in the headlines today, and Rheinhardt skimmed the stories—riots in a township outside Windhoek, quelled by government forces aided by U.S. troops; an American diplomatic aide and his wife and children burned to death in their car at a roadblock. He read most of an article on the Congressional debate over increasing military aid to the right-wing dictatorship in Nicaragua in the face of reports of severe human rights abuses (we put them there, we'll keep them there, he thought). There was another bad toxic spill on a highway in the East Bay, nearly a hundred people hospitalized with skin and eye burns and irritations, half a dozen in critical condition. The city's board of supervisors was debating another raise of

Muni fares, only six months after the last increase. Rheinhardt folded over the front page, lit a cigarette, and started through the inside pages. He was halfway through the front section when the bell above the front door jingled.

Stoke stepped into the cafe, grinning—thin and gangly, he wore a tight, dark green nylon jumpsuit and heavy-soled, red leather boots. He waved at Martin in the back. "Heya, Martin. I'll have a cup of coffee." He sat across from Rheinhardt, gestured at the newspaper. "You just won't quit, will you? Look at your hands."

Rheinhardt glanced at his hands, saw them trembling slightly. At the same time he became more acutely aware of the anger and frustration swirling around inside him. Nothing new, really. He closed the newspaper, carefully folded it, and put it on the floor beside him.

"We both know the world is fucked up," Stoke went on. "Why do you have to keep reminding yourself every day, read the god damn newspaper? That, and what's that weekly one you get?"

"*The Nation.*"

"Right. Every fucking day, Rheinhardt. Why? You aren't going to change anything, so what's the point, getting worked up all the time?"

Rheinhardt didn't answer. He took a final hit on his cigarette, then crushed it out.

Martin, the big, bearded man who ran the cafe, came by the table with coffee for Stoke, took Rheinhardt's plate, then retreated without a word to the back of the cafe where he sat with a mug of tea, reading. Something by Kafka, was all Rheinhardt could make out.

"Hey," Stoke said. Grinning again. "You know what we should call you? The Watcher. Sure, the way you keep up with things all the time, the news and stuff, and the way you're always looking at people, watching them. Even at parties, you don't talk or do much, just hang out and watch. I've seen you, Rheinhardt. Sure, we should start calling you the Watcher."

"It's what they called me down in the 'mericas," Rheinhardt said.

"Really?"

Rheinhardt nodded. "Same reason, I guess. I didn't say much, kept my eyes open all the time, looking everywhere, watching everything. If I was going to get killed, I wanted to see it coming. No search and destroy, just fucking search and search. So they started calling me the Watcher. It's from some old comic book character, Catanzaro said." Rheinhardt shrugged.

"Who was Catanzaro?"

"A guy." A dead guy, Rheinhardt thought. But he didn't say it.

There was a long pause, Stoke looking away, then he said, "I've registered."

"To vote?" Rheinhardt asked, knowing that wasn't what Stoke meant.

Stoke sighed heavily, shaking his head. "You know, Rheinhardt."

"For the draft."

"Yeah, for the fucking draft." He shrugged. "Had a hell of a time getting through all those protesters, thought they were going to beat me to death with their signs." He dug around in one of the jumpsuit's deep pockets, withdrew his hand, then popped something into his mouth, swallowed. Rheinhardt lit a cigarette, waited for Stoke to go on.

"How long has it been since you were in the army?" Stoke asked. "Since you were fighting?"

Rheinhardt had to think about it for a minute, try to reestablish a temporary connection to that time. "About seven years," he said.

"You don't talk much about it."

"No."

"Fact, you don't talk about it at all."

"No."

Stoke nodded, wrapped his arms around himself, looked out at the street. "I don't know what to do," he said. "Why I finally registered. Buys me time, more time to think, to make a decision." He paused, looked at Rheinhardt as if expecting a response. When Rheinhardt didn't say anything, Stoke went on. "What do *you* think?"

Rheinhardt shook his head. "Don't ask me for advice, not about that."

"Will you at least talk about it, then? Tell me what it was like so I know what the hell I'd be gliding into?"

Rheinhardt looked at his cigarette, watched the ash glow, red through gray. He pressed the cigarette into the ashtray, slowly ground it out. "I don't know." He continued to stare at the crushed cigarette, the fresh spot of charred black. "It's not that easy."

"I need to know."

Rheinhardt smiled to himself; he'd said just that to someone once, years ago; it was part of the reason he'd gone. Well, now he knew. He stopped smiling, looked up at Stoke. "Maybe. But not now."

Stoke nodded slowly, said, "All right, but I don't have too damn long." He drank down his coffee, held up his cup for Martin to see. "Don't forget tonight, Wendy's photo exhibit at Deever's. I'll come by the Warehouse and get you."

Rheinhardt nodded, and was about to ask Stoke what time he'd be by when an explosion sounded outside, followed by the scattered cracking of gunfire as dozens of soldiers in fatigues poured out of the Presidio and started down the street, hugging building walls on both sides, moving in coordinated teams. They carried automatic rifles, wore charge-packs strapped to the sides of their light rucksacks; their faces were swathed in dust-colored strips of fabric holding nose filters in place. Teams provided cover fire while other teams, in ones and twos, moved down a building or two. Rheinhardt hoped to Christ they were shooting blanks. Or was something *real* happening out there?

Rheinhardt's gut tightened, and he could feel the adrenaline hit, jacking up his heartbeat. People on the street dropped to the ground or huddled into doorways, or simply stood transfixed, confused and lost as their heads jerked from side to side. An old man couldn't get out of the way and a soldier plowed into him, knocked him sprawling into the gutter. None of the soldiers stopped to help the old man, who was having trouble raising his head.

Stoke had frozen across the table from him, stared with partially open mouth out the window. He glanced at Rheinhardt, said, "What the fuck is going on?" then turned back to the street.

Rheinhardt couldn't answer; he felt paralyzed himself. One of the soldiers shattered the cafe's glass door with his rifle and boot, then dove through it, rolling across the floor and up to his feet, sweeping the barrel of his weapon back and forth.

Martin came running out of the back, shouting, then stopped abruptly when he saw the soldier and gun. After the slightest pause, he asked, "What the hell is going on? What have you done to my door?"

The soldier spoke, voice muffled by the strips of cloth. "This is just an exercise. You will be reimbursed for any damages." He pulled a card and folded packet from his shirt pocket, stepped forward and handed the items to Martin. "The United States regrets any convenience."

"The United States?" Martin cried. "Where the hell are we, Burma?"

The soldier stuck the rifle barrel into Martin's chest, said, "Don't want any shit from you, got it?" He quickly backed out the hole in the door, gaze flicking rapidly in all directions, then a moment later signaled at someone and took off down the street and was gone.

Stoke looked at Rheinhardt with what appeared to be confusion, perhaps fear.

"So this is maybe what I have to look forward to?" he said.

Rheinhardt didn't reply; there was really nothing he could say.

* * *

The clay would not do what he wanted.

Rheinhardt stared at the misshapen block on the worktable; the wire carving tool in his hand trembled slightly, poised a few inches from the clay. His eyes burned, his head ached, and he wanted to throw the carving tool across the room, wanted to heave the block of clay against the studio wall.

Christ.

He dropped the tool onto the table and leaned back on his stool. He held out his hand, tried to stop the shaking, couldn't quite manage it. Didn't even have drugs to blame. Rheinhardt clenched the fingers into a fist, slowly lowered fist to thigh.

For weeks now the damn clay had fought against his fingers, his hands, his vision; or he had fought against the clay. He did not know which was the case. The distinction was probably important.

He pushed back from the table and stood, knocking over his stool. Rheinhardt bent down, picked up the stool, started to set it upright, then twisted, swung the stool and let it fly. It crashed against the wall, bounced undamaged to the floor.

"Feel better?" he said aloud. He stood looking at the worktable, the clay, the stool lying on its side. "No," he answered himself.

Rheinhardt rubbed at his neck, the muscles tight and knotted, slivers of pain arcing along the base of his skull. The studio was quiet, hardly a sound filtering through the walls or floor from the Warehouse below him. Rheinhardt got up, went over to the cot in the dark, far corner, picked up a pack of cigarettes. He lit a cigarette and for several minutes stood unmoving, smoking and staring at the block of clay, not really thinking of anything at all.

The studio was small, about eight feet square, with little open space. His worktable and the piles of tools and materials—blocks of clay, bags of plaster, boxed sets of tools, bundles of thick wire for structural armatures, wood and nails and chunks of metal—

occupied half the room. In one corner was an overflowing bookcase, haphazard stacks of books and magazines stuffed into the shelves, piled on the floor beside it. In another corner was a cot, and under the cot were two fruit crates filled with his clothes—T-shirts, jeans and sweatshirts, faded black or gray or denim blue. Next to the crates were his portable tape player and two boxes of cassettes; lightweight headphones hung from a nail in the cot leg.

Rheinhardt stepped to the table, jammed his cigarette into the clay. Today was hopeless.

Rheinhardt backed away from the table, began pacing, back and forth in front of the worktable and the shapeless mass of clay, the shapeless piece of *shit* that was going nowhere, back and forth, back and forth, frustration rapidly building up, driving him. He clenched and unclenched his fingers, forming and unforming fists he used to pound at his thighs.

Why? he asked himself. What was happening to him, why wasn't it working anymore? Anger and frustration swelled and twisted inside him, pressuring for release. Why, god damn it, why?

Rheinhardt went to the table, swung his closed fist down and into the clay, denting it. He pulled his fist back, swung again, began pounding at the clay, over and over, smashing it one way, then another. Bits of the wire armature poked through from beneath the clay, and he pounded at them as well, deforming them, hardly noticing the pain in his hand.

Breathing heavily, Rheinhardt stared at the deformed mass of clay and wire, hardly recognizing it, barely registering the fact that he had been working on it for days, for weeks.

He had to get out of the Warehouse, permanently. There was no other option, not if he was to have any hope of producing anything worthwhile again.

Trying to calm down, he lit another cigarette, opened the studio door and stepped out onto the narrow wooden landing; he leaned on the rail and, trying to breathe slowly and deeply, looked out over the Warehouse laid out below him.

He had built the room himself in the upper reaches of the old building, in a back corner above the packed-in ground-floor studios and lighting networks, a haven of relative quiet and soothing darkness. A half dozen other small rooms and cubicles had been built in the rafters following his example, all distanced from each other, accessed by pegpoles, rope ladders, makeshift stairways attached to the walls. Slashes of light cut the upper darkness from some of them, leaking out from under doorways, through gaps in warped plywood and irregular holes and patches. All the other rooms were on the ground floor or in the basement; mutelights marked the passageways among them, an irregular maze crisscrossed by jagged shadows. A few people moved along the passages, entering or leaving rooms; the faint sounds of music drifted up from the basement studios.

All these people—a revolving core of artists whose work supposedly pushed at the cutting edges; who were considered to be too radical for public consumption; and who were surreptitiously provided with living/work space in the Warehouse, materials and supplies, a subsistence living, and sometimes public forums and exhibitions.

Rheinhardt shook his head. Radical artists, shit. Not anymore. Terry wouldn't admit it, but the Warehouse was going to hell, and most of the so-called artists in it weren't doing shit anymore.

The landing began to vibrate sporadically under his feet; someone was climbing the rope and wood-slat ladder anchored to the building floor twenty-five feet below. A minute later, in the light from the open doorway, Stoke rose up from the darkness. The unkempt hair appeared first, followed by his thin, grinning face, then the rest of his gangly body enveloped in the dark green jumpsuit. Stoke pulled himself up onto the landing, stomped once with his boots.

"Hey, Stoke," Rheinhardt said.

"Hey yourself." Still grinning. Rheinhardt recognized that grin, wondered what Stoke was on. "You ready to go?" Stoke asked.

"Go where?"

"We're supposed to meet Terry, remember? At Deever's. For Wendy's exhibit. C'mon, we're already late."

"How can we be late for a photography exhibition?"

"My band's playing the back room. *I* need to be there."

Rheinhardt nodded, pushed away from the railing. "Which band?"

"Pilate Error. I've quit the Lude Dudes."

"Well, at least that'll be tolerable." He smiled. "All right, let me get my jacket."

They went into the studio and Rheinhardt stopped beside the blob of clay, crushed his cigarette into it, next to the first butt.

"Your new masterwork?" Stoke asked.

"Yeah." Rheinhardt walked to the cot, picked up his worn black leather jacket from under a blanket. He put on the jacket, stuffed cigarettes into one of the pockets.

"I've got a title for it," Stoke said. " 'Cigarette Butts in Dogshit.' "

Rheinhardt stood beside him, looking at the clay. Again the frustration rose in him, and he wanted to pick up the clay and throw it against the wall, or throw it out the studio door so it would plummet to the floor below. "Good a title as any," he said.

Stoke turned to him, expression serious now. "Having trouble working again?"

Rheinhardt nodded slightly, reached up and pulled the chain to turn off the light. In the darkness, a momentary afterimage of the clay remained before his eyes, deformed and unyielding. "Let's go to Deever's," he said.

They left the studio and descended.

Three

From halfway up the first flight of stairs, Terry looked down on the front room of Deever's Place, which was normally the main bar. At least a dozen people, most in T-shirts and jeans, worked at getting the exhibition ready, shouting above the music blaring from speakers mounted in the ceiling corners, moving tables and chairs, setting out food and beer and wine. Wendy moved along the edges of the room, straightening her photos on the walls, making last minute changes with the layout.

Terry smiled. The damn thing was going to come off, and Wendy was finally going to get some of the exposure she deserved. Terry had even managed a promise from Fowler at the *Chronicle* to cover the exhibition, though they both knew the story would be killed before it ever went to press, or be cut down to a single graph with no pictures.

Wendy turned and looked up at Terry, smiled and mimed a heavy sigh, then turned back to her photos. Wendy had been one of the first Warehouse artists, coming in around the same time as Rheinhardt, and was probably the best photographer that had ever worked there. She couldn't get the galleries to carry her work, though; the owners either said it was awful, or were honest enough to say they felt it was too controversial. But Wendy kept on, not changing anything to make it more acceptable, and, as far as Terry was concerned, was doing brilliant work. And the best of it was being displayed here tonight.

The exhibition was called Tomorrow's War, and all the photographs were black and white. In the center of the longest wall, across from the stairway, was Terry's favorite, a twenty by thirty photo, matted on white, titled "Placebo Effect." The picture was an overhead shot, taken from above the middle of Market Street (how had she done that?), of an electric trolley coach. Sprawled face up across the roof of the coach was the body of a young man, his bare chest a mess of torn flesh, bone, and blood. A strange helmet covered his head, the smoky faceplate shattered. He wore a pair of neatly pressed white pants spattered with a dark liquid (blood? oil?), and dark polished shoes reflecting disks of pale light. A pair of wire cables emerged from beneath the man's body (connected to his spine?) and looped up to connect with the trolley's electrical pickups which were in turn connected to the overhead wires.

Terry pulled her gaze from the photo, glanced over the room again. There really wasn't much more for her to do right now, so she continued up the stairs, looking for Deever. The old man had disappeared an hour ago, soon after Terry had arrived, and she hadn't seen him since.

The second floor had once been a residential flat, but now, connected to the main bar downstairs, was open to customers, with music piped into the rooms. One of the rooms had a large-screen monitor and video decks; video artists could bring in their own tapes and arrange showings. Two of the rooms, plus the bathroom and hallway, were free art zones—artists who dated their work on the walls were given a month before other artists could paint or draw over it.

Now, though, most of the rooms were empty. Two people were asleep on the couch in front of the video monitor, the screen showing nothing but video snow, a loud hiss issuing from the speakers. Deever wasn't anywhere on the second floor, so Terry went out back and climbed the wooden stairs to his flat on the third floor.

The apartment was quiet inside, the music and chaos faint from below, muted by walls and floor. Terry moved quietly through the back kitchen, then along the hall, the hardwood floor squeaking.

She found Deever in the front bedroom, sitting by the bay window looking out into the night. The old man, tall and big-boned with a large belly, was wearing baggy, black pants and a dark green overshirt with the black and red Lazarus patch on the shoulder. A cigarette was held in one hand, a tall, half-filled glass in the other, and a bottle of generic vodka stood on the end table beside him. An empty bottle lay on the floor at his feet. He did not look at her as she entered the room.

"Fog's coming in," he said.

Terry approached the chair, looked out the window. The fog was pouring slowly over the nearby hills and drifting down toward the building. Deever reeked of alcohol. Why did anyone say you couldn't smell vodka on the breath? She sat on the edge of the bed, watching him.

"Between the booze and the cigarettes, you're going to kill yourself," Terry said.

Deever laughed, loud and harsh. "Don't mother me, for Christ's sake. Save it for Rheinhardt."

"Rheinhardt doesn't need it."

He turned and looked at her. "No?" He drank deeply from his glass, refilled it.

"No," Terry said. "You coming down when we open the doors?"

Deever slowly shook his head. "I'll be fine right here, watching the fucking fog." He grinned. "I like the fog, you know. In the air, in my head."

Terry nodded. "Yes, Deever, I know." She stood up from the bed. "Take care of yourself, and I'll see you later."

Deever nodded and turned back to the window, bringing the cigarette to his mouth with shaking fingers. Terry stood watching him for a few moments, then left.

* * *

An hour later, both floors of Deever's Place were crammed with people standing or moving slowly about, the air filled with babbling voices and taped music. All of the second-floor rooms were full, the staircase was a constant, two-directional river of people, and Terry had a hard time moving from one part of the club to another. In the ground-floor back room, Stoke's band was setting up, but Stoke and Rheinhardt hadn't yet arrived.

Terry climbed onto a chair, scanned the main room, looking for familiar faces. She saw Fowler across the room, talking to Wendy, two cameras hanging from his neck. There were supposed to be other journalists covering the exhibition as well, including someone from one of the NewsHawker networks, but she wouldn't recognize any of them.

The large number of people should have been encouraging, but it wasn't. Most people were completely oblivious to the photos on the walls, far more interested in drinking and eating and talking and listening to music and doing more drinking. The wine and beer were disappearing rapidly, and the food wasn't holding up much better. Even people standing directly in front of the photographs didn't pay them any attention. People were here for a party. Big fucking surprise.

Disheartened, Terry got down from the chair and pushed her way into the back room. The band looked like it was ready to go, but Stoke still hadn't shown, and the band members were sitting on the stage, drinking beer. Terry stepped up onto the low stage, sat next to Pace, the drummer. Pace was playing the stage floor with his drumsticks, grinning, dreadlocks shaking, wire-rim glasses flashing light reflections at her.

"Hell of a crowd," Pace said. "More'n we've played to in months." He paused with the sticks, took a long draw on his beer, then resumed playing the stage.

"But no Stoke," Terry said.

Pace grinned and shrugged. "Stoke's always late. He just a kid."

"Yeah? And how old are you?"

"Twenty-eight." Pace laughed. "I the old man of the band. Just call me Ancient One." He crashed the drumsticks twice on the floor, tossed them spinning high into the air. He caught one as it came down, missed the other; it clattered across the stage. "Shit." Pace finished off the beer, started tapping at the empty bottle with the one stick.

"Is Will going to be here?" Terry asked.

Pace slowly shook his head. "He won't be doing the socializing for a while." He breathed deeply. "He talking about moving out, living alone." He paused. "Dying alone."

Terry didn't say anything. She put her hand on Pace's shoulder, squeezed. Then she stood, was about to press back into the crowd when Stoke's voice broke over the noise from the rear of the building.

"The Kid is here!" Stoke shouted.

Stoke and Rheinhardt came in through the back porch, Stoke in green, Rheinhardt two inches taller and all in black except for the bleached tail of hair. Stoke waved at Terry, grinning, jumped up onto the stage and danced about for a minute, clapping a hand on the shoulders of the other band members—his movements were so frenetic she knew he was speeded out again.

By this time Rheinhardt had worked his way to her side, touched her arm. Terry kissed him on the cheek.

"We couldn't get through the front at all, so we went up to Deever's, stopped in to see him, then came down the back."

"How's Deever doing?"

Rheinhardt shrugged. "Passed out in the front bedroom."

Terry sighed. "I worry about him."

"He'll be all right."

"I suppose." She paused. "So you haven't seen Wendy's photos yet."

"Not tonight . . ." A blast of feedback, followed by

Stoke's laughter, cut him off for a moment. "But I've seen most of them already," he resumed. "She's one of the few people in the Warehouse who's still doing anything worthwhile."

"God damn it, Rheinhardt, you're always talking the place down. There's *lots* of good work being done in the place. Christ, you work in it yourself. You think it's so bad, why don't you get out?"

Rheinhardt sighed, shook his head, but didn't say any more. He leaned toward her, spoke quietly into her ear. "Happy Birthday."

Terry smiled. "You remembered."

"Five minutes ago, but yeah. Thirty, right?" Terry nodded. "Still just a kid," he said.

Terry motioned toward Stoke, who was adjusting his guitar shoulder strap. "*There's* the Kid."

"Yeah." Rheinhardt nodded, looking at Stoke. His expression went blank, as if suddenly preoccupied with something, something to do with Stoke.

"Rheinhardt?"

He turned to her, but the taped music ceased, dropping a sudden quiet over the club, and they looked at the stage. Stoke stepped up to the microphone, banged out a minor chord.

"Hey, out there," Stoke began. "Hope you're all having a hell of a time tonight. But quit drinking so much and take a look at the fucking pictures, will you? That's what this is supposed to be about." Quiet laughter through the club. "Okay, we're Pilate Error, and we're going to play for a while. If you have any requests, forget 'em. We don't do requests, we do what we want. And the first thing we want to play is a song called 'Death of White Monkeys.' Listen up." Stoke stepped away from the mike, looked at Pace, and counted off. Pace started the beat, and a few moments later the rest of the band came in, loud and crashing through the rooms.

Terry turned back to Rheinhardt to ask if something

was bothering him, but he was already moving away
from her, pushing into the crowd of the front room. A
minute later he was gone from sight.

Terry thought she heard sirens.

Stoke's band was still playing, people were shouting
over the music (most of them drunk, now, or hammered), but still she thought she heard sirens, getting
closer. Fire trucks? Ambulances? Sounded like several,
converging on Deever's. She moved into the front
room, grabbed the railing and pulled herself up onto
one of the lower stairs, looked out the open front door.
People had spilled out into the front yard, thirty or
forty standing or sitting on the grass, drinking and
talking and smoking.

Two cop cars, sirens wailing and lights flashing,
pulled in from the right, drove up onto the sidewalk.
Two others drove in from the left, also onto the
sidewalk, front wheels in Deever's flower bed.

The sirens cut off abruptly, but the lights continued
to flash, rotating in the darkness. There was no movement at first from the cars, just still, dark shadows
behind tinted glass. People out front had stopped
talking, stared at the cars, waiting. Inside, the band
played on.

Eight doors opened, not quite in unison, eight cops
emerged in black and blue and disks of reflecting metal.
The doors closed. Six of the cops, two women and four
men, approached the front door; two, donning riot
helmets and hefting stunclubs, stayed with the cars.

Terry remained on the stairs, watching, waiting. The
cops didn't seem upset, didn't seem in any hurry. They
nodded and smiled at people as they passed, then
formed a line and started casually in through the front
door. People inside quieted and moved aside as much
as was possible, but the cops' progress was still slow.

Terry dropped from the stairs and worked through
the crowd to intercept the cops as the first one reached
the wide opening to the back room. The cop at the head

of the line was big, nearly six and half feet tall, with a thick graying moustache, and he smiled as Terry stepped in front of him.

"Can I help you with something?" she asked, shouting over the music.

"You the owner?"

"No, but I'm kind of in charge here tonight. Is there a problem?"

The big cop nodded. "Noise complaints from the neighborhood. A lot of them."

"This is a nightclub. Bands always play here. We don't get complaints."

"Doesn't matter, you've got complaints tonight. It's a weeknight. The band's going to have to shut down."

"Christ, you can't be . . ." The band brought a song to a close, and there was a sudden quiet in the club. Terry turned toward the stage, shouted. "Cut it for a few minutes, all right? And Stoke, Pace, come on down here." She turned back to the cop, fighting down the urge to yell at him. When she spoke again, her voice was quiet and calm. "You can't really be serious," she said.

"I'm afraid so." The big cop shrugged. "We don't have any choice, see. We received complaints, so many we have to act on them. No more music tonight."

Stoke and Pace came up to them, and Stoke put his hand on Terry's shoulder, staring at the cop. "What's the load here?" he asked.

The quiet, which had been almost complete when the band stopped playing, gradually gave way to a vague rumble as people resumed talking.

"Noise complaints," the cop said again. "Your band's going to have to pack it for tonight."

"You're shitting us, right?" The cop shook his head, and Stoke went on. "Hey, you want us to crank down the volume, fine, we'll do it. No reason to clamp it down completely."

"Look," the cop said. "We don't want any hassles. Just cooperate here, and everything will be fine. Play again some other night, some other place."

"But shit . . ."

"Stoke . . ." Terry tried to cut him off.

"You want us to conf all your equipment?" the cop said. "We can do it that way, we have to."

Terry gripped Stoke's upper arm, squeezed, pulled him back a step. Stoke opened his mouth, but Pace grabbed him as well, pulled him back another step, and Stoke shut his mouth without saying a word.

The cop grinned. "That's better. Now we can all . . ."

He was cut off by shouts from the front room, and Terry recognized Wendy's voice, screaming above it all.

"God damn it, put that back, motherfucker! And that too! Hey! Hey! Those are my fucking pictures, you can't . . . Hey, sonuvabitch . . .!"

Terry looked around the cop, saw uniformed arms reaching for Wendy's photographs on the walls, saw Wendy screaming and grabbing at one of the cops, trying to retrieve one of her photos.

"What the hell is going on?" Terry said. She pushed into the front room, toward Wendy, but the big cop took hold of her arm, held her back.

"Just wait a minute, miss. Don't get so upset, we'll see what the line is." He kept his grip on her, though she tried to pull away, and guided her slowly toward Wendy.

"MOTHERFUCKERS!" Wendy screamed. One of the women cops cracked Wendy across the face, grabbed Wendy's arms and pinned them behind her back while pushing her face into the wall. "MOTHER-FUCKERS! MOTHERFUCKERS!" Wendy kept on screaming it, over and over.

The other cops were collecting the photographs, piling them onto one of the tables. Glass cracked; one of the stacks tilted, photos sliding to the floor with a clatter. Terry and the big moustached cop neared the table, and one of the other cops held up a framed photograph.

"See, Sarge? I think we've got an obscenity problem here." The photograph was of a naked woman splayed out on the hood of a demolished car, the windshield shattered. The woman's eyes were closed, her flesh dotted with bits of the windshield glass and crossed with long strips of twisted metal. "We decided we'd better confiscate the pictures, see what the D.A. has to say about them."

"These are works of art," Terry protested. "They aren't . . ." She stopped, sagging slightly. There was no point in saying any more. She jerked her arm once more. "Let me go," she said, quiet but deliberate.

The big cop released her arm. "Look," he said. "This is just a formality. I'm sure there won't be a problem, you'll get the pictures back soon enough. But we do have to take them in. DeGraza has a point. We'll just have to see."

Wendy had stopped screaming, but still had her face pressed against the wall, her wrists now strapped together; the woman cop was Cooperizing her.

Terry grabbed a napkin, pulled a pen from the big cop's pocket, wrote down a name and two phone numbers. She handed the pen back to the cop, said "Thank you very much," then walked over to Wendy and shoved the napkin into her front jeans pocket.

"Name of an attorney," Terry said. "With his home and office numbers. Got that, Wendy?" Wendy nodded. "Lou Bernhardt is his name. Remember that in case they take the note away. Lou Bernhardt."

"Lou Bernhardt," Wendy whispered.

"Right. He's a good man, he'll take care of you."

Wendy nodded. All the photographs were off the walls now, and the cops started taking them out to the cars.

"HEY!" someone shouted. "Mr. Police Officer!"

Terry and the big cop turned toward the stairs. Someone halfway up the stairs dropped his pants and shorts, thrust out his genitals. "Eat me, Mr. Cop!"

The big, moustached cop smiled. "I *can* arrest you too, if you want," he said calmly. "But we're really not here to cause any problems."

"My ass!"

"No, your tiny cock."

A few people laughed, but the guy on the stairs remained motionless, naked from waist to ankles. The cop turned to Terry.

"Good night," he said.

Terry remained silent. The big man shrugged, then turned and followed the other cops out the front door.

As the cars started to pull away, red and blue lights still flashing, Terry walked to the back room, stepped onto the stage and up to Stoke's microphone.

"Is this still on?" she said. She heard her voice reverberate through the speakers. "All right." She looked out over the crowd. "Everyone can go home now. This fucking party is over."

Four

The fog obscured the moon, blocked out all the stars. Rheinhardt sat on the third-floor rear porch, his back against the wall; the lights of the city gave the underside of the fog a pale, bluish glow. Quiet, irregular sounds drifted up from below—Terry and Stoke going through Deever's Place, closing down, locking up. Deever was still passed out inside.

Rheinhardt lit a cigarette, took a couple of hits, then crushed it out on the wood flooring beside him. The cops had been, in some ways, so damned polite; except the woman who had rattled Wendy. Smiles and calm voices. Civilized oppression. He wondered if that might be worse than if they'd come barging into the place, tearing things apart, popping stunclubs, smashing the photos, hauling off a dozen or so people after cracking them across the head.

He looked up at the half moon which glowed through the fog in distorted, shifting shapes. Moonlight, Rheinhardt thought. *Mondlicht*. Who had said that? Someone down in the 'mericas. He could not remember who, or when, and wanted to keep it that way.

A cold, damp breeze curled around the corner of the building, cut in under his jacket. Rheinhardt shivered. A door opened and closed below him, footsteps sounded on the wooden stairs, ascending. Stoke came up the steps, up onto the porch, stood next to Rheinhardt, looking down at him.

"It's cold out here," Stoke said.

"Yeah." Rheinhardt shrugged. "Finished up downstairs?"

"Just about. The place is a fucking mess, Terry says we'll clean up in the morning. She's giving it another run-through, locking up." Stoke stuffed his hands deep into the jumpsuit pockets, shook his arms.

"Have you told her?"

Stoke shook his head. "Keep it, will you?"

"Sure, but you'll have to tell her sometime." When Stoke didn't reply, Rheinhardt went on. "You realize she only gets on you about it because she cares a hell of a lot about you."

Stoke nodded. "Shit, I know. Guess I appreciate it. But I don't need it right now, you know?"

Rheinhardt nodded.

Stoke shrugged. "I'm going in, make some coffee. You coming?"

"I'll wait for Terry."

Stoke nodded, opened the door and went inside.

When Terry came up the stairs, footsteps slow and regular, she sat beside Rheinhardt, her shoulder against his. He listened to her breathing, smelled the faint odor of her sweat cooling in the night air.

"Stoke says it's a mess down there," Rheinhardt said.

"Worse than usual. Did you see what they did after the cops left, when I told everybody to leave?" Rheinhardt shook his head. "They cleaned out the place. Grabbed up every last bottle of wine and beer, stuffed them into coats or bags, took all the food. Fucking animals. I wonder if anyone was there to see Wendy's photos."

"A lot of them were Warehouse people."

"I know. You'd think you could expect more from them."

"I don't, Terry. Not anymore. Too many people there are . . ." He shrugged. "I don't know."

"There you go with that shit again. There's still good work being done by Warehouse artists, Rheinhardt.

Look at Wendy. And Dougall. Velasquez. Fuentes. You. Even T'Chang, now."

Rheinhardt didn't say anything. If he got into it with her now he'd end up telling her he'd almost decided on moving out of the Warehouse. He wasn't ready for that yet; the Warehouse still meant too much to her. But the place, and the so-called artists living in it, were stagnating, and Rheinhardt sometimes felt as if the stagnation had leaked into his own studio, was beginning to touch him, seep into his body, his hands, his mind.

A hollow thrump sounded from nearby, above them and to the north, and a dragoncub appeared, flying toward them. The sleek, black and silver vehicle pulsed a vibrating glow, as if it were flickering in and out of existence, and shot past them leaving a trail of hollow thrumps and a wash of oscillating heat. Within seconds it was gone from sight except for a distant flicker of shiny light.

"Those damn things scare me," Terry said.

"They're supposed to. That's why the cops use them." He touched her thigh. "Let's go inside. Stoke's making coffee."

He stood, pulled Terry to her feet. An explosion sounded toward the southeast, and Rheinhardt saw the red tongues of flame several blocks away. They stood watching for two or three minutes, the flashes of red and orange growing larger, spreading. When they heard the first sirens, they turned away and went inside.

Stoke sat at the kitchen table staring into a cup. A glass pot of steaming dark coffee rested on the stove, two empty cups beside it. Stoke looked up as they walked in; his pupils were dilated, and he seemed to have trouble focusing on Rheinhardt and Terry. Rheinhardt went to the stove, poured two cups of coffee, brought them to the table.

"What are you on now, Stoke?" Terry asked.

"Oh, man, don't bark in on me, Terry. It's *my* fucking business."

"I just hate that shit," Terry said. "I've had too many friends . . ."

"I know, I know, too many friends go down the hole. You ought to be more worried about who I sleep with and how I do it than fucking drugs. And did you ever consider the possibility that that's what they wanted, your friends? Going down the hole? That it's what *I* want?"

Terry didn't respond. Rheinhardt sat back, watching them. He'd seen Stoke's anger, his bitterness, before, but never so much with Terry around.

Stoke sighed heavily, and smiled. "Okay, forget I said that. It's *not* what I want, I just . . ." He shrugged, smile fading. "I guess I'm just pissed off because of what happened tonight. I mean, why didn't we do anything? We just let them haul her away, all her pictures."

Neither Terry nor Rheinhardt said anything. Stoke put his cup down, stood up from the chair, and started pacing around the kitchen. "Some exhibition, a couple of hours and then gone. She deserves more than that, doesn't she?"

"She'll get more than that," Terry said. "We've got extra prints of everything, materials ready to do the framing and matting. You come by the Warehouse tomorrow, you can help us with it. By Saturday morning, whether Wendy's out or not, the pictures will be back up on the walls."

Stoke stopped pacing, looked back and forth between Terry and Rheinhardt. "Really?"

Terry nodded.

Stoke grinned. "You had this all planned, didn't you? You knew the cops were going to come down on it, haul off the pictures."

"No. But we knew it *could* happen. Kind of thing happens a lot more than most people realize."

"Sure, I'll be there tomorrow, help out." He sat back down, looking satisfied.

"Speaking of tomorrow," Terry said. "Isn't that your registration deadline?"

Stoke's satisfied expression twisted from his face, and he turned away. "Yeah, tomorrow's the deadline."

"What are you going to do, Stoke?"

He wrapped his arms around himself, looked at Rheinhardt. Rheinhardt didn't say anything, didn't move. It's yours, Stoke, he thought.

"I don't know," Stoke said.

"You'd better know soon," Terry said. "You don't register, we're going to have to start working out what you're going to do, go underground, leave the country, whatever. You won't have that much time before . . ."

Stoke turned back to face her, cut her off. "All right, look, I've already registered, okay?"

Terry hesitated, glanced at Rheinhardt. Accusation, he thought. *Why didn't you tell me?* she was asking. Looking back at Stoke, she said, "When?"

"Yesterday." He was looking away from her again.

"I thought you weren't going to register."

Stoke banged a fist on the table, stared hard at her. "Exactly. *You* thought I wasn't going to. *I* never said. I didn't know what I was going to do, not until yesterday. And now we all know."

Terry slowly nodded. She picked up her coffee cup, didn't drink from it, set it back on the table. When she spoke, her voice was quiet. "Does this mean you'll go into the army?"

"I don't know what it means," Stoke said. "Like I told Rheinhardt, I'm buying time. Buying . . . time." He gave her a halfhearted smile. "Who knows? Maybe I won't get drafted at all, then I won't have to worry about it."

Terry just shook her head. "You'll be drafted, Stoke. Count on it."

Stoke didn't answer. Rheinhardt watched them both, feeling removed and distant, not quite connected to them. Terry was right, of course. Stoke would be drafted. He had everything against him. Wasn't in college, wasn't married, wasn't a member of any of the right churches, didn't have friends or relatives in the right places, didn't have wealthy parents who could buy his way free. Stoke was draft meat, dead and helpless. Rheinhardt knew what *that* felt like.

"I've gotta go," Stoke said. "It's late."

"I'll drop you off," Terry said. "I've got the Warehouse van."

Stoke shook his head. "I'll walk. I can use it."

Terry looked like she was about to say something else, but just nodded instead.

Stoke got up, breathed deeply once. "I'll see you two around." He dug something out of his pocket, put it in his mouth, swallowed, then turned and quickly left through the back door, closing it quietly behind him.

Terry looked at Rheinhardt. "Is it me? Am I being too hard on him?"

Rheinhardt shrugged. "For Stoke right now, probably. But I think he understands."

Terry sighed, nodded. "What about you? Give you a ride?"

"I'm not going back to the Warehouse tonight."

"My place?"

He shook his head. "I think I'll crash on Deever's couch."

"You want me to stay?"

She needed something tonight, he saw that. But he couldn't give her anything; he needed to be alone. "No," he finally said.

Terry nodded, stood. "Will I see you tomorrow? To work on Wendy's stuff."

"I don't know." He was looking at her, but was unable to focus completely on her features.

"Rheinhardt?"

"What?"

Terry breathed deeply, then shook her head. "Nothing. Good night."

"Good night."

She left through the back, as Stoke had, and Rheinhardt listened to her footsteps descend, growing fainter until he could not hear them at all. He remained motionless at the table, still disconnected somehow, and content to stay that way.

In his mind, the image of clay.

A picture of the misshapen block that now rested on the work table two miles away took hold. Rheinhardt had once had a vague idea of where he wanted to go with the clay, of what structure he wanted to form. But, just as he'd had difficulty working with the clay, molding it to what he wanted, he now had difficulty picturing that form in his mind—each time the image began to clarify at all, to focus and stabilize, it crumbled completely, melted down to the image of the misshapen block of clay that now existed in the studio with two crushed cigarette butts disfiguring, or perhaps defining it.

The sound of creaking floorboards jerked Rheinhardt out of his trance. He opened his eyes to dim light, reoriented himself. He was still in Deever's kitchen, the room lit only by the outside porch light angling in through the window, casting narrow, elongated shadows. Rheinhardt heard the floorboards creak again, from the other end of the apartment. Then came the sound of trickling water, the flushing of a toilet, then floorboards again as the flushing sounds faded.

A hulking shadow appeared at the far end of the hallway, staggered toward him. Deever. Coughing, Deever made his way along the hall; stopped in the entrance to the kitchen; leaned against the door jamb.

"Rheinhardt?"

"Yes, it's me."

"It's *I*," Deever corrected. He stumbled forward, pulled a chair from the table, dropped into it. "Got a cigarette?"

Rheinhardt lit two, handed one to Deever. "Want a drink?"

The big man coughed, shook his head. Part of his arm was in the light from the porch, but the rest of his body was in shadow. "The opening over?"

"Oh yeah. Cops came, closed it down. Noise complaints, they said. Came in to stop the music, they said. While inside they saw Wendy's photographs, just coincidence you understand, decided the pictures might be obscene. Confiscated them all, took in Wendy."

"Nice evening."

They smoked awhile in silence. Rheinhardt looked for patterns in the smoke that drifted in and out of shadow from their cigarettes. It seemed to him that patterns did exist in the smoke, but that he could not quite recognize them. He was tired; concentration was difficult.

"Stoke's registered for the draft," Rheinhardt said.

Deever didn't reply immediately, but then asked, "Do you think he'll end up going in?"

Rheinhardt nodded. "Yes. He doesn't know it yet, but he'll go. And Terry will want me to talk him out of it. Because I know what it's like."

"Will you?"

"How can I tell him what to do?" Rheinhardt said. He gestured toward Deever's Lazarus patch. "What about you? You fought in Vietnam, would you try to tell him what to do?"

"I don't know. That was more than forty years ago. I'm an old man, Rheinhardt. If he asked, I'd probably tell him not to go."

"I can't do that, Deever. I can't advise him one way or another."

"I understand."

The light outside shifted, cast new, moving shadows into the kitchen for a moment. Someone knocked at the back porch door.

"I'll get it." Rheinhardt went to the door, opened it.

Justinian stood on the back porch, half his face in light, half in shadow. His long, gray hair glistened with moisture from the fog.

"Hello, Rheinhardt," the short old man said. "You going to ask me in?"

"It's not my place, Justinian."

"Deever is an old, old friend, and I'm certain . . ."

"Let the little bastard in," Deever called.

"Thank you, Walter," Justinian said.

Rheinhardt stepped aside, and Justinian stepped in, went to the table and sat. Rheinhardt closed the door, returned to the table.

"How about cigarettes all around?" Justinian asked. As Rheinhardt passed out cigarettes, Justinian went on. "How have you been, Walter?"

Deever shrugged, took a cigarette from Rheinhardt. "I'm doing all right."

"So you two know each other," Rheinhardt said.

Deever and Justinian both nodded. "We fought in the Nam together," Deever said. "I think I will get a drink." He got up from the table, went to a cabinet above the sink, came back to the table with three glasses and a bottle of vodka. He poured some for himself, drank half the glass and refilled it, then sat. "Help yourselves." When neither Rheinhardt nor Justinian did, Deever said, "All right, why are you here, Justinian?"

"I'm here to help Rheinhardt."

"Help me with what?" Rheinhardt asked.

Justinian smiled, said nothing.

"Christ, that's it," Deever said. He drank down his vodka, pushed back from the table. "I'm going to bed." He stood, looked at Rheinhardt. "You staying here tonight?"

"Thought I would, yeah."

Deever nodded. "Just make damn sure you lock up securely after he leaves. I don't want to have to worry about strange creatures roaming around in here at night." He turned and shuffled down the long, dark hall.

Rheinhardt turned to Justinian, who was still smiling without a word. "So you're a Namvet," Rheinhardt said.

Justinian nodded.

Rheinhardt pointed toward Justinian's shoulder. "I've never seen you wear a Lazarus patch."

"Don't have one."

"You've never been cleared?"

"Never cleared, never even screened. I didn't come back. Not the traditional way. I'm still listed MIA, presumed dead. The V.A. doesn't even know I exist." He held up his cigarette, stared at it. "Do you remember the first time we met?"

"Not really."

"Neither do I." Justinian smiled.

"Why *are* you here tonight, Justinian? I don't need any help. I don't want any."

"Let's go outside for a bit, talk out there." Justinian put out his cigarette, got up and started for the back door. Rheinhardt remained seated for a minute, uncertain, then got up and followed.

When Rheinhardt stepped out onto the back porch, it was empty. He looked up, saw Justinian at the top of the wooden ladder attached to the building and leading up to the roof. The old man disappeared over the top, and Rheinhardt started up after him.

As Rheinhardt came up over the edge of the roof, he saw a flash of metal, saw Justinian's face rushing toward him, then felt hot pain slashing along his left arm. Rheinhardt released his grip on the ladder, started to fall back and away. He reached out with his right hand, grabbed the ladder, then swung back in and crashed back into the building. He nearly let go again, but hung on, scrambled to get his feet back onto the rungs. Teeth clenched against the pain, he grabbed the ladder with his left hand, pulled himself back securely onto it, and quickly dropped a few rungs before settling into a crouch, gazing up at the roof.

Blood dripped along his arm; somehow Justinian had run the knife in under Rheinhardt's jacket, sliced along his forearm. What the fuck was going on?

Justinian's face appeared over the edge of the roof, looking down at him. Rheinhardt could not manage to get out even one of the questions waiting to be asked, to be shouted at the old man.

"You've grown lax, Rheinhardt," Justinian said.

"What?"

"Coming up onto the roof like that, blind. If you'd have done something like that down in the 'mericas, you would have been dead."

"This isn't the 'mericas."

"Not yet. But it's getting close."

Rheinhardt didn't say more, fighting down anger and confusion. He could feel his heartbeat pulsing in his neck, and his fingers were slick with blood; the pain was a long, steady throb.

"You need waking up," Justinian said. "You see it, all right, but you don't do anything about it. You stay in that stupid fucking place, the Warehouse, and you're going to go right down the hole with everyone else."

I already know that, Rheinhardt thought. I *am* getting out, you crazy old man. But he didn't say anything. He slowly climbed down to the porch, staring up at Justinian. Breathing heavily, he leaned back against the railing, still watching the old man.

Justinian held out the knife. "Remember this, Rheinhardt," he said.

Rheinhardt moved quickly into the apartment, locked the door, threw the dead bolts. He stayed near the door and listened for a minute, then went through the apartment and checked the front door locks. Finally he went into the bathroom to take care of his arm.

The cut was clean, about seven inches long and nearly half an inch deep, but the bleeding didn't seem to be too bad. Deever's med cabinet was well stocked, and Rheinhardt cleaned the cut thoroughly with antibac soap, ran it with an antibiotic coag ointment, then pulled the cut together with butterflies. He gauzed and taped the arm to protect it.

Rheinhardt went into the living room, sat on the couch, and looked out the window, half expecting Justinian's face to appear. He was cold, his arms and hands shaking, and he wrapped himself in a blanket. He smoked half a cigarette, then lay out on the couch and tried to sleep. For a long time he remained awake in the darkness, listening to the ceiling noises as Justinian moved about on the roof above him.

Justinian

Justinian dances.

He moves about on the roof of Deever's building, no smile, eyes open, eyes closed. Shoes scrape across gravel, arms swing out, in, out again. He faces the sky, eyes closed, then tips his head down, facing the roof, slowly turns on one foot, digging at gravel with the other.

The fog is thinning, shifting with a slight breeze. The moon, already far along its downward arc, momentarily shines through the fog, then is obscured again, a pale half disk.

Justinian stops. He holds his arms away from his side, opens hands so the fingers do not touch one another. He stands motionless, eyes still closed. His thick gray hair is damp, dusted with tiny beads of moisture reflecting nearby streetlights.

Justinian flexes his fingers, in, out, in, out, now with a regular rhythm. He raises one foot, lowers it, raises and lowers it again, in synch with the flexing of fingers. After two or three minutes of this, Justinian crouches, then leaps into the air, one leg swinging wide, arms out. When he touches down, knees bending, he springs again. He leaps and slides and spins about the roof, eyes open, eyes closed, open, closed. The steam of breath and sweat rises all around him.

Justinian dances.

Near dawn, Justinian walked along dark, quiet streets. The fog was gone, stars visible in the sky above. Buildings on both sides of the street were dark, most in disrepair, some partially demolished; not a single streetlight worked for blocks in all directions.

A grinding sound drifted through the air, faint but growing louder. Justinian stopped, turned his head a moment, then began looking at the buildings on either side of the street. He jogged across to a brick building, quickly climbed up its side using window frames and holes broken out of the brick as handholds and footholds. When he reached the fire escape at the bottom of the third floor, he pulled himself onto it and crouched against the brick, nearly hidden in shadow.

A minute or two later, a police growler came around the corner a few blocks away, started up the street in Justinian's direction. The blue and green light atop the police transport vehicle pulsed steadily as bulb-tipped rods vibrated through the air on all sides; the grinding sound was loud now, emerging from beneath the growler with steam around the wheels. Nothing was visible through the darkened windows.

Just as it passed below Justinian, the growler spun quickly on its wheels, drove into a dark alley across the street. It disappeared from view, then stopped, engines idling. There were sounds of doors opening, grunting and scraping noises, then doors closing. A few minutes later the growler emerged from the alley, turned up the street, and continued on.

When the growler was out of sight, Justinian descended from the fire escape, crossed the street, and entered the alley. The alley was short and dark, ended in a rotting wood fence and a jumble of crates, tires, and pieces of rusting metal. A muffled snort sounded from within the jumble, and Justinian stepped closer.

Behind a stack of old tires, huddled on the ground, were three people wrapped in dark coats and trousers, tagged with police markers. All three were unconscious, the bodies rising and falling with irregular breathing. Another snort sounded, from the person on the right.

Justinian pulled a thin roll of money from his pocket, peeled off three tens. He knelt in front of the three dark figures, reached forward, and tucked a bill into each coat. For a minute or two he remained kneeling in front of the sleepers, motionless. Then he stood and walked out of the alley and continued along the street.

At the next corner he stopped over a storm drain, unzipped his pants, and urinated through the grate. His gaze seemed fixed on the steam rising from the grate, and he blew the smoke of his own breath into the steam, watched it swirl and mingle and rise and quickly disappear. He zipped his pants, resumed walking.

A few blocks farther on, Justinian turned down an alley between two buildings—one brick, the other cement. Metal fire escapes, wooden platforms and beams, strings of metal chain and strips of curling plastic all combined to block out most of the stars, and the alley was far darker than the street, nothing visible except black shadows against other shadows. Justinian stopped in front of a metal door on his right. He withdrew a block of keys from his coat, unlocked both door bolts, pushed the door open and stepped inside, relocked the bolts.

Inside was just as dark as the alley. To his left was the entrance to a dark corridor, and to his right was a descending flight of stairs. Justinian started down the stairs, one hand on the round metal railing. About ten steps down he made a quarter turn, then a few steps later made another. A pale blue glow rose from the bottom of the stairs, another full flight below.

Justinian descended, entered the corridor at the foot of the stairs, and started along it. Pale blue mutelights, spaced irregularly along the ceiling, illuminated the corridor. The walls and floor were smooth, soot-stained cement, the ceiling a dimly reflecting metal. His footsteps echoed quietly, punctuating a faint hiss that seemed to slide along the walls.

He stopped in front of another metal door, unlocked and opened it. Inside, more darkness. Justinian flipped a wall switch, and a bright overhead light came on. He stepped into the room, closed and locked the door.

The room was long and narrow, the ceiling and far wall strung with pipes of different sizes, some coming out of the walls, some elbowing out from the ceiling and running along it. In one corner was a mattress on the cement, with rumpled sheets, a blanket, two pillows. Directly above the bed, emerging from the network of pipe, was a ceiling fan; a long silver chain hung from it.

At the far end of the room was a small, two-burner gas stove atop a metal cabinet. Next to it was a chipped and stained porcelain sink, a set of wooden cupboards, a tiny refrigerator. In the corner stood a dark wooden table and two chairs. Barnwood bookcases, all full, lined the wall next to the door.

Justinian went to the metal cabinet, took out a bottle of bourbon and a glass, set them on the table. He turned to look at the small, round white clock on the nearest bookcase, the ticking sound quiet and regular. Ten to five. He picked up the clock, wound it, set it back on the bookcase. On the wall just behind the clock was a pen and ink drawing of a nude Asian woman sitting on a wooden crate in an otherwise empty room, her back against a cracked plaster wall; narrow shadows slashed across her body and face. Justinian stood gazing at the picture for a long time, then turned away and returned to the table.

For the next half hour, Justinian smoked one cigarette after another, slowly drank four short glasses of bourbon, and wandered back and forth between the bookcases and the table, picking up books and magazines from the shelves, glancing through them.

At five-twenty-five, Justinian put away the bottle and glass, then undressed. Though he was a short man, he was well-muscled, his legs and arms thick, his chest large. The gray hair on his chest and limbs was thick and curly.

Several scars crisscrossed his broad back; the longest began at his left shoulder, ran down along his side, then just above his waist cut over to the base of his spine where it split into several short, thinner scars. Barely discernible beneath the hair of his left arm and both legs were strings of needle marks, a few of them fresh.

Justinian switched on a partially hidden light in the corner farthest from the bed, double-checked the door locks, then turned off the overhead light. The corner light, obscured by pipes and bands of metal, threw patternless shadows through the room. No direct light fell on the bed. Justinian stood on the mattress, pulled the chain above him, and the ceiling fan began to slowly rotate.

He sat on the bed, his back against the cement wall, watched the clock. Just past five-thirty a grinding roar of heavy machinery rumbled from the walls, and everything in the room began to vibrate, including the shadows. A squealing sound cut through some of the ceiling pipes, and a second rumbling joined the first, accompanied by loud hissing.

Justinian breathed deeply once, lay down with his head on one pillow, the second pillow stuffed between his back and the vibrating wall. He covered himself with the single white sheet, and closed his eyes.

Five

The studio was empty.

Rheinhardt swung the rucksack with the last of his books over his shoulder, adjusted the strap. He'd already moved everything else earlier in the day— books and tapes and clothes to Deever's, cot and worktable and supplies to the rafters in Stoke's parents' garage. He could have stored a lot of it at Terry's, probably could have moved in with her for a while until he found a place of his own, but he'd wanted to put off telling her as long as possible. Why, he didn't really know; he'd have to face her sometime. She still didn't know he was leaving.

He shifted position, the scrape of boot against floor loud now in the empty room. He reached up for the light chain, then stopped, fingers an inch or two away from it, when he felt vibrations under his feet. Someone was climbing the ladder. Terry? Rheinhardt breathed in deeply, took the chain and pulled it. He turned and sat on the floor in the darkness, waiting for her.

She appeared a few minutes later in the doorway, a dim silhouette in the pale light leaking up from the Warehouse below. She didn't step inside; instead, she leaned against the door jamb, looking almost directly at him.

"I hear you're leaving," she said.

Rheinhardt nodded, then realized she probably couldn't see it. "Yes."

"Why didn't you tell me?"

Trying to avoid this scene, he thought. Then said, "I don't know," which he knew was a crappy answer. Better to have said nothing.

"Why are you leaving, Rheinhardt?"

Now, when he probably *should* have an answer for her, he had nothing to say. He had answers, he thought, plenty of them, and some were probably near the truth, but he just didn't have the energy to start.

"Why, Rheinhardt?"

"I can't answer that, Terry. Not now."

There was silence for a while, then he saw her slowly shake her head.

"All I've ever really asked of you is that you be up-front with me," she said. Her voice was quiet, but he sensed the restrained anger, the controlled tension. "Now you haven't even given me that." She straightened, took a step back. "Fuck you, Rheinhardt." Voice still quiet, controlled.

Before he could answer her (what the hell could he have said anyway?), Terry turned away from him and started down the ladder.

Rheinhardt remained seated in the dark, motionless, listening to the fading sounds of her descent until he could hear nothing, could only feel the faint vibrations of the floor beneath him . . . and then even that was gone.

A few days later, he went to a party at Pace's apartment, looking for Kit. When he arrived, the party was already spilling out into the hall stairs leading up to Pace's flat. The deep, rhythmic bass of dub rastaka shook the walls, vibrated the air around him. Rheinhardt made his way up the stairs, stepping carefully between talking people, avoiding hands and feet, cigarettes and drinks. Smoke drifted in thick clouds, seemed to pulse with the music, aroma thick and sweet. If he stayed long, he'd get high just breathing the air.

Inside Pace's apartment there was dim, glowing

orange light that cast wavering shadows on the walls, floor, ceiling. There were no electric lights, just dozens of squat candles distributed throughout the flat. Dreadlocks, double-tails, and short tight curls were the dominant hairstyles, bobbing with the music or nodding with conversation; a few people wore blinking, electronic shirts or pants, shoes with spark-heels, but they were out of place here, and they seemed to know it.

He wandered through the hallway and rooms, saying hello to people he knew, declining offers of joints and poppers, beer and wine, flips and curls. Pace was in the kitchen, sitting on the counter, the tip of a water pipe hose in his mouth. His small, round glasses reflected candle flames at Rheinhardt, flashing and shifting as he moved his head. Through some quirk in the acoustics, the music didn't carry well into the kitchen, and conversation was much easier. A dozen people stood or sat in the room, talking without raising their voices. Pace held out the hose to Rheinhardt, but Rheinhardt declined.

"How's Will doing?" Rheinhardt asked.

Pace shook his head. "Not so good. Back in hospital again. And says when he get out he'll be moving, go live alone somewhere. Don' know if I can change his mind."

"How are *you* doing?"

"I'm okay." He shrugged. "I'm not the one dying."

Rheinhardt said nothing for a while; he and Pace looked at each other in silence, some wordless understanding in the air between them. Rheinhardt finally spoke. "Has Stoke been here tonight?" he asked.

Pace nodded. "Yeah, you know the Kid, slicked onto some girl, fifteen, sixteen years old, left with her. Don't expect him back tonight, no." He passed the hose to someone else. "How 'bout you, you going to stay for a while?"

Rheinhardt shook his head. "Not tonight. I don't even know why I'm here."

Pace grinned. "Same problem we all got."

"Actually, I'm trying to find Kit," Rheinhardt said. "Heard she might be here."

Pace nodded, gestured back into the rear kitchen extension, pointing to the door leading into the pantry. Rheinhardt went into the extension, opened the pantry door, stepped inside.

More candles flickered in the narrow room, illuminated the dark, shadowed forms of two people. Even in the dim candlelight he recognized Kit in her standard faded blue jeans and T-shirt, dark blonde hair falling across her face, head bent forward; the other person, a thin, gaunt-faced man with heavy-lidded eyes, looked vaguely familiar, but Rheinhardt couldn't place him. They were hunched over a squat candle atop a cardboard box, and Rheinhardt caught glimpses of a squirt-bottle, glass and metal syringe, reflections of a small round metal dish, white powder, cotton balls.

"Sorry," Rheinhardt said. He started to back out.

Kit looked up, quickly shook her head. "No, don't, Rheinhardt. Stay. Just close the door."

He reluctantly closed the door, remaining inside. He really didn't want to watch. "Kit," he said, "why don't I just talk to you later, I'll stick around the party 'til I see you."

"Heyo, Rheinhardt, it's just coke, it's not the big thoroughbred."

Rheinhardt nodded, leaned back against the door. "When did you start mainlining?"

Kit shrugged. "It's just a thing, once in a while." She turned away from him, watched the other guy squirt water onto the fine powder. "I haven't seen you in a while. You still in the Warehouse?"

"No."

Kit glanced at him, grinning. The guy across from her stopped what he was doing, looked up at Rheinhardt, squinting.

"Rheinhardt?" he said. "Watcher?"

The voice, that word, and something about the guy's

eyes all came together in Rheinhardt's mind. But . . . the body didn't match. "Speedo?" he said.

The thin man nodded, smiled. Rheinhardt felt disoriented, trying to reconcile . . . The Speedo he'd known had been big and strong, muscular from lifting weights; this Speedo was way too thin, almost skeletal.

"You know each other?" Kit said.

"Fought together," Speedo said.

"Bet I know why they called you Speedo, Manny."

Speedo laughed. "Bet you don't."

Rheinhardt tried to smile, couldn't quite manage it. "He was hung up on his tan," he told Kit. "Every chance he got he'd strip down to this tiny Speedo swimsuit and lay in the sun. Middle of the god damn jungle, out on patrol, whenever. A fucking lunatic."

"Yeah?" Kit said. "Well he's still a fucking lunatic. But where the hell's your tan, Manny? Now you're a ghost."

Manny shrugged, returned his attention to his task. Cotton ball was wadded, dipped into liquid; needle was stuck into cotton. Rheinhardt looked up, out the tiny window in the far wall. All he could see were dark leaves shifting slightly with a breeze. He should leave, he thought. But how many times, in how many places, did he tell himself that? Somehow, for some reason, he always stayed.

"I could use a place to crash tonight, Kit," he finally said. "I've been staying with Deever, but the old man needs to live alone. Any chance you can help out?"

"Sure, I suppose. I don't have an apartment anymore, I've been living . . ." She paused, and Rheinhardt heard three slaps of flesh against flesh. ". . . in a corner of this studio space I'm sharing with a painter. You're . . ." Another long pause, intake of breath. ". . . welcome to join me."

Rheinhardt glanced down long enough to see the needle in her arm, blood in the syringe, then looked back out the window. After a short silence, Kit murmured, "Fuuuuuck. Yeah."

Nobody said anything for a minute. Rheinhardt turned, put his hand on the door. "Find me before you leave, then," he said.

Kit coughed, said, "Sure thing, Rheinhardt." Her voice was quiet, harsh.

Rheinhardt opened the door, stepped out into the kitchen, and quickly closed the door behind him.

Kit led the way up wooden stairs on the outside of the concrete building, her footsteps slow and dragging. The heavy fog muffled most sound, but Rheinhardt could hear the distant moan of a foghorn, and the odd, arrhythmic wail of a malfunctioning ambulance siren from nearby. A single orange light burned above the second-floor door at the top of the stairs.

Kit had trouble with the lock. She jiggled the key, shook the door by the knob, kicked it twice. Finally the key clicked and turned; she pushed the door open, hinges and bottom metal strip squealing.

"Fucking piece of shit door," Kit said. "Someday I'm going to get locked out." She ran her hand along the inner wall, switched on the overhead lights, and they went in.

The studio was cold, a long, rectangular room, maybe twenty feet by forty, the walls white-painted cinder block except the longest wall, which was all large windows. The far half of the room was filled with huge painted canvases leaning against walls or crates, a few on easels. Some were tornadolike abstracts in muted colors, others were dark urban landscapes, and a few were portraits that were just slightly out of focus, slightly out of proportion.

Dominating the front half of the room was what Rheinhardt assumed was Kit's current project. Ten vertical metal pipes, heights varying from four to six feet and mounted in round cement blocks, were arranged in a circle about twelve or fourteen feet in diameter. Strands of copper wire, varying in thickness and tension (some tight, some slack and looping) were strung from one pipe to another, most across the circle, forming a complicated, apparently patternless network. From the wires hung bits of clear glass partially painted in bright, reflective colors; strips of shiny, unpainted metal; dripping strings of burnt, melted plastic. Triangular mirrors were mounted on the poles, facing inward, reflecting sections of the work among each other.

In the nearest corner was Kit's bed, a mattress on a layer of fruit drying boxes, piled with blankets and pillows; two folding chairs lay on the floor at the foot of the bed. Near the center of the room was a small alcove with a large sink, a countertop with a hot plate, and a wooden cupboard on the wall above.

"You want some tea?" Kit asked. "Warm you up a bit. There's no heat in here."

"No shit. Sure, tea sounds great." When he breathed in deeply and exhaled, his breath was like smoke.

Kit put a pot of water on the hot plate. While she was making the tea, Rheinhardt walked slowly around the circle of poles, watching colors, reflections, and patterns slowly shift as his viewpoint changed.

"It's not finished yet," Kit said. "But you're circling it in the right direction. Also, there's going to be some kind of light source at the center. I haven't figured out just what yet. Tried a few things, nothing's really worked well enough."

Rheinhardt completed the circuit—he *had* noticed "dead spots" where the integrity had disintegrated momentarily, then came back into sharp focus as he continued—then picked up one of the folding chairs, set it up near the bed. Kit brought over the tea, handed him a mug, sat on the edge of the mattress with her own. Rheinhardt tipped back against the wall, drank. The tea was hot and strong.

"You got a cigarette?" Kit asked. "I'm out again as usual."

Rheinhardt got out cigarettes, handed one to her, took one for himself; he lit them both with a match.

"Thanks." Kit drank from her tea, moved back

against the wall. "No cigarettes, no food. Money's a
problem for me, going to get worse. I lost my job last
week."

"Yeah? Why?"

"Missed too many days, showed up late all the time.
Shit, Rheinhardt, I couldn't do anything about it. I'd
get involved working on that . . ." She waved at the
poles and wires and reflecting glass. "I lose my whole
fucking sense of time." She shrugged. "I admit it
probably never would have made any difference if I *had*
known the time, I wouldn't cut off a good working
session just to go to some job." Kit laughed quietly and
shook her head. "I know, shit work ethic. Well, I'm
paying for it."

"Could you do with a few bucks, guide you through a
bit?"

Kit looked at him. "I won't say no, but I wouldn't
want to call it a loan. I don't know that I'd ever be able
to pay you back, so it better be money you can
permanently do without."

Rheinhardt dug into his front pocket, pulled out a
crumpled wad of bills. He sorted through it, took out
two tens and a five, keeping half a dozen ones for
himself. He handed her the five and tens. "I'll see what
else I can do."

"Thanks. I know you don't have money to dump."

Rheinhardt shrugged.

"So you've finally moved out of the Warehouse."

Rheinhardt nodded. "I didn't much like it anymore.
There's something . . . I don't know. Stifling."

"You'll be better off, Rheinhardt. You know how I've
always felt about that place."

"Yeah."

"How did Terry take it, you leaving?"

"Not too well," he said. What a fucking understate-
ment. They hadn't talked to each other once since the
confrontation in the empty studio.

They finished the tea and cigarettes in silence. Kit
crushed her cigarette against the cinder block, adding

one more scorch mark to the dozens already scattered above the bed, dropped the butt into a clay pot beside the bed.

"I've got to get to sleep," she said. "If you need to use a toilet, there's one on the other side of the building, ground floor. I can give you the key."

Rheinhardt shook his head. He stood and took Kit's cup, brought both to the sink and rinsed them. Kit turned off the overhead light, and the room filled with motionless shadows; light came in through the large windows from streetlamps, building security lights.

They undressed amid the slanting shadows and broad waves of light. Rheinhardt shivered with the cold, but the cold didn't seem to bother Kit much at first, though she was so thin. Looking at her, he noticed a couple of bruises on her right thigh, another on her left shin, several on her arms.

"Jesus, Kit. All the bruises."

She grimaced, sat on the bed and crawled under the sheets and blankets, shivering now. "I know," she said. "Don't worry, no one's beating me. I bang myself around a lot, and I really bruise easy. The acupuncturist I used to see told me it had to do with weak blood, something like that. My gums bleed a lot, too. He had me taking this stuff called Tan Kwe Gin, a Chinese herbal liquid." She laughed. "He called it the Geritol of the East." Rheinhardt crawled into bed beside her, squeezed between her and the wall. They pulled several blankets over themselves. "The damn stuff worked, that's the crazy part. While I was taking it I hardly ever bruised, and my gums stopped bleeding completely. Great stuff."

"Why'd you stop taking it? Money?"

"Yeah. Crappy reason, isn't it? It's not even that expensive. Shit, I don't know about myself sometimes."

They huddled together for warmth, the bed crossed with slashes of shadow and light. Rheinhardt's hand was cupped over her breast, but he felt no desire for her. She was twenty-six and still a virgin, would be one until she died if she had anything to say about it. She was the only truly asexual person he knew.

Lying in the cold and the crisscross of light and shadow, Rheinhardt thought of Terry, saw her outline in the darkness of the empty studio, heard her say once more, "Fuck you, Rheinhardt." Christ. Rheinhardt pulled Kit closer to him, her skin warm now against his, and waited for sleep.

The Winter Gantry

Six

Rheinhardt had not touched clay in nearly three weeks, not once since he'd left the Warehouse. Now he sat on his stool in front of his worktable, several blocks of moist clay laid out before him. Light entered the room from the large window to his right and from the skylight above.

The room sat atop the flat roof of a three-story apartment building in the lower Haight, and when he looked out the window he could see the tar and gravel surface of the roof, stove chimneys, the foot-high ridge that ran along the roof's perimeter. Farther, he looked over and through other rooftops, and had a broken view of the upper treetops of Golden Gate Park.

A few feet from the room was a trapdoor in the roof, and a wooden stairway that ended just outside the top apartment's kitchen door. Rheinhardt was allowed access to the kitchen and bathroom, but the rest of the split-level unit was off limits.

The room itself was set up much like his old studio in the Warehouse—cot and bookcases on one wall, worktable and supplies and tools filling the rest of the room. But everything was different here. He had natural light much of the time, and he liked the sounds of the city that had been either nonexistent or greatly muffled within the Warehouse. Most important, though, he was no longer surrounded by hacks and frauds, he no longer had to breathe the atmosphere of stagnating talent.

Still, he had not been able to start working again. Part of it was the job in Bear's machine shop, both the time and energy it took from him. And there had been the move, the adjustment, settling in. Even the tension between him and Terry, which had not really eased much, was draining. Mostly, though, he had simply avoided the clay, and he knew it. He'd spent hours *thinking* about the clay, about starting again, resuming work on the project he had aborted in the Warehouse, but he had not been able to make himself do it.

Rheinhardt sat without moving, looking at the clay. He was afraid. Yes, there it was. Afraid of being unable to sustain the concentration he knew he would need; afraid of losing control over the clay, over his hands; afraid of producing crap.

Christ.

He wanted to get up, walk away from the table again, smoke a cigarette or take a nap, read a book, maybe go for a walk. Anything but pick up that damned clay.

Rheinhardt looked out over the rooftops, tried to call up the vague image he'd had in mind back in the Warehouse, the seed of an idea for his next work, and got almost nowhere—a tall, undefined block structure, but nothing more. Forget it for now, he told himself. It'll come later. Just get the feel of the clay.

He shifted on the stool, reached forward, picked up the nearest block of clay. It was cold and stiff to the touch, clammy almost, and he slowly turned it in his hands, moving his fingers over it, squeezing gently, pressing. Then he dug his fingers into the cold, resisting substance, twisted, and began changing its shape.

Without anything specific in mind, Rheinhardt manipulated the clay with his fingers, his palms, pulling away chunks only to press them back into the clay in another spot. He squeezed, prodded, twisted and tore at it, and as he worked the clay it grew softer, easier to mold and shape. And it grew warmer.

For an hour, two hours, maybe longer, Rheinhardt sat at the table and worked with the clay, forming nothing, constructing no specific shapes, but slowly and steadily regaining the feel of the clay, and infusing it once again with life.

* * *

Terry was depressed.

She sat at her desk in Monterey House, looking across it at the thirteen-year-old girl in front of her. The girl, Macy, was crying, staring down at her twisting, tugging hands. She was almost five months pregnant, and had no place to live. Terry looked down at the dark, grained desktop, put her head in her hands for a few moments. Macy's story was just too damn familiar.

Four days a week Terry worked as one of the administrators of Monterey House, a kind of halfway home for underage pregnant girls—girls who had no families, or whose families had abandoned them, or who were runaways. Five years ago, just before *Roe* v. *Wade* had been effectively overturned, Monterey House hadn't existed. In the last few years, though, the need had drastically increased, and dozens of similar halfway houses had sprung up in urban areas across the country, funded patchwork from federal, state, and local funds, private donations. Terry had worked at Monterey House since its founding; it was a job she wished she didn't have, a job she wished did not exist.

She looked up again at Macy, who was still crying. *I feel trapped*, Macy had said a few minutes before. *I felt trapped from the start*. No shit, thought Terry. No access to family planning clinics without her parents ("There was no way I could ask them, they wouldn't have taken me."), no access to contraceptives, and practically no access to sex education of any real value. And then, when Macy *had* become pregnant, there were now no longer any viable options for her—abortion had once again become far too dangerous unless you had plenty of money and the right connections, neither of which Macy had.

Goddamn repressive, Terry thought. It was what she thought every time another of these girls walked into the House asking for a place to stay.

Terry came from around the desk and sat beside the young girl. "What about your parents?" she asked again.

"They kicked me out when I told them. Last week. My father screamed and yelled, he called me . . . he called me a slut, a sleazy . . . a . . ." She started crying again for a minute, then calmed enough to keep talking. "They changed the locks on the doors, they wouldn't let me in."

"Where have you been staying?"

"With my boyfriend. But he says I can't stay with him anymore, not if I'm pregnant, and he has a new girlfriend."

"How old is he, Macy?"

"Twenty-four, I think."

Jesus Christ. They'd probably never be able to stick the bastard, either. Or her parents. The paperwork and the bureaucracy would kill the whole damn thing. She put her arm around the thin girl's shoulders. "All right. Listen, we'll find a bed to put you in for tonight, and have a room ready by tomorrow, okay? You met Rebecca out front?" Macy nodded. "Okay, Rebecca will take care of you. She'll have some things to talk to you about, ask you some questions, but for now she'll just show you around, introduce you to some of the other girls. Sound okay?"

Macy nodded again, and Terry led her back out to the front desk. Rebecca looked up from a stack of files she was sorting, and Terry nodded to her.

"So we're going to have a new guest," Rebecca said.

"Yes. Show Macy around, where she'll sleep tonight. Run the paperwork later, when she's settled."

"Right." Rebecca got up from the desk, smiled at Macy. "Let's go."

Macy nodded slowly one more time, and followed Rebecca down the hall without a word.

Terry poured a cup of coffee for herself and dropped into Rebecca's chair. The radio was on, some station playing soothe-pop. Wallpaper music, Terry thought. She reached over, switched off the radio, sat listening to the quiet sounds of the building.

She tried to imagine what it would feel like if

something went wrong and she became pregnant. No choices, no options. For most of her life, abortion *had* been an option, and she had come to take it for granted that she did have options. Even now, five years later, she sometimes found it difficult to believe that choices had been taken away. Well, she supposed abortion was still an option of sorts, but she didn't think she'd be willing to risk her life—she knew of too many women who had been scarred or maimed or killed on some butcher's operating table, even by doctors who were supposed to be legit. Maybe it just hadn't been long enough for things to sort out.

Trapped, Macy had said. Terry felt trapped just thinking about it. She sat motionless at the desk as a strange, hollow sensation fluttered in her chest and would not leave.

Trapped.

She met Stoke in Buena Vista Park just after one for lunch. The air was cool, but the morning fog had burned off, and the sun gave a pale warmth to their unshaded bench. Next to the bench was Stoke's red messenger's bike; he was buzzed out again, could hardly keep still as they ate sandwiches she'd brought. She wanted to talk to him about the draft, about his options (options, that word again), about what he really felt. But she sensed it wasn't a good time. Probably it never would be, and eventually she'd have to broach it herself anyway; but for now she could let it drift.

"Are you still pissed at Rheinhardt?" Stoke asked. The sandwiches were gone and they were drinking tea from Terry's thermos. "For leaving the Warehouse."

"Not for leaving. For not telling me. For not talking about it. But that's between me and Rheinhardt."

"So you *are* still pissed."

Terry shook her head, looking away from Stoke. She wasn't going to be drawn into that with him. It was hard enough as it was. She'd hardly seen Rheinhardt since he'd left, and they'd hardly spoken to each other, the strain still silencing them.

Neither said anything for a long time. Stoke wiped out his cup, put it in Terry's bag, sat with his legs bouncing constantly. She turned to face him. "I'm sorry about that night a few weeks ago," she said. "At Deever's."

"Sorry about what?"

"Ragging on you about the draft, the drugs. I *am* sorry, I know I probably sounded like your goddamn mother or something, but I just . . . I don't know. I worry about you, I guess. Don't want bad things happening to you, like getting killed." She paused, smiled. "I care about you, is what it is."

Stoke turned away. "I know." He didn't say anything for a few moments, gazing across the street. "I just don't know how to handle that sometimes." He stood, paced back and forth for a minute, hands jammed into his jumpsuit pockets. "I should get back to work," he said. "Thanks for the lunch." He smiled at her, shrugged again. "I'm okay. I'm always okay." He leaned over, kissed her quickly on the cheek. Then he turned, stepped to the big bike, mounted it, and without looking back at her pushed off down the street, pedaling faster and faster as he wheeled down the hill.

Seven

Stoke and his parents lived in a small, one-story house in the Excelsior district—white paint peeling, blue trim faded, lawn gone to weeds, shingles missing from the roof, empty driveway of cracked cement, a broken kitchen window that hadn't been replaced in over a year. Stoke and Rheinhardt approached, stopped across the street from it. Rheinhardt remembered how the house had looked two years ago—the lawn lush and green, blooming flowers in well-kept beds, a nearly new car in the driveway.

"Last night was an anniversary," Stoke said.

"Yeah?"

"Yeah. Two years since my father lost his job. Two years of being *un*gainfully *un*employed. He celebrated with half a fifth of cheap scotch and a fistfight with my mother. Lost the fight, but still gave her a few bruises."

Rheinhardt said nothing for a while, then asked, "Your mother still have that job with the Windhover family?"

Stoke nodded. "Why I stopped here. They should be by in a minute to pick her up, I'd rather wait 'til she's gone."

The house seemed empty and quiet, as did most of the houses nearby. There was no street traffic, just a few people hanging out on the sidewalk half a block away. Then a huge, dark gray luxlimo came around the corner, pulled into the curb in front of the house, and the shouting began.

It was Stoke's father, yelling from inside the house,

but Rheinhardt couldn't make out any of the words. Stoke's mother emerged from the front door, closed it, then walked quickly toward the limo, trying not to run. Stoke's father put his head out the front window, shouted after her.

"Yeah, you go do it, bitch! You just go do it!"

The limo door swung open, Stoke's mother slipped inside, the door swung closed. From around the corner, a group of kids appeared, hurled trash and rotting fruit at the limo, then quickly disappeared. The limo slowly pulled away from the curb and started down the street. Stoke's father yelled once more, then pulled his head back in.

"Old man Windhover is putting it to her, that's the word," Stoke said. "My father sure as hell is convinced. But I don't know . . ." He breathed in deeply, slowly exhaled. "We need the money, and my father drinks so much he can't get it up anymore anyway. They do what they can, I guess." He shrugged. "I figure I'll need to start worrying if my father *stops* getting angry about it all."

They crossed the street, walked up the dirt path to the porch, went into the house. The house was quiet again, except for the faint sound of a television voice. In the front room, Stoke's father was sitting on the floor in front of a television set, his eyes closed. The TV was slotted to an all-news station; on the screen was a newsman standing in front of cyclone fencing, low buildings, sleek vehicles, and a rocket gantry in the background. Early next morning was going to be the launch of a team that was supposed to be investigating the accident at the second space station, and the newsman was complaining that he had been unable to interview any of the team members, nor had anyone in authority been forthcoming about the nature of the accident itself.

"Hey, Mr. B.," Rheinhardt said.

Stoke's father nodded, said, "Hello, you two." He opened his eyes, looked at them. "They think twenty-five or thirty people may be dead," he went on, "but still no word on why, or what happened. Military's managed to keep this one tight."

"I've heard that it might be sabotage," Rheinhardt said.

Stoke's father nodded. "Wouldn't be surprised. Wouldn't be surprised if it was our own people."

"I've also read that some people think it might have been something else." Rheinhardt paused, then went on. "That the military is doing biological weapons research at the station, that something went wrong, and they caused the explosion themselves to cover it up."

Stoke's father looked at him. "That wouldn't surprise me either. The bastards." On the screen, the newsman was still complaining, and Stoke's father pointed at him, shaking his head. "This so-called newsguy is a fuckin' idiot." He closed his eyes again, tilted his head back.

Stoke motioned to Rheinhardt, and they left the room. Out in the garage, Stoke took a flashlight from one of the shelves above the wall-length workbench, handed it to Rheinhardt.

"You sure you don't need any help?"

"Yeah. It's just a set of clayworking tools. I don't know how I left them behind when we moved everything out."

"Okay. I'll be up in my room." Stoke went back into the house.

Rheinhardt went to the front of the garage, swung the spring-back ladder down from the garage rafters, locked it into place. He climbed up into the darkness, ladder shaking slightly with each step. Sheets of thick plywood and two by fours had been laid across the ceiling beams, forming the floor of an open air attic which was half-filled with cardboard boxes, wooden crates, bags of paper or plastic tied off with wire or taped closed.

He turned on the flashlight, moved toward the back, where he had stored his supplies until he'd found the place in the Haight. The boxes and bags were covered with a layer of dust, and Rheinhardt moved carefully past them.

It didn't take long to find the box of tools. It was wedged on its side between two crates, tilted at an angle. Rheinhardt pulled it free, opened it, saw that all the tools were snapped into place, closed it again. Then he set the box beside him, sat with his back against a stack of heavy crates, and turned off the flashlight.

Rheinhardt closed his eyes and breathed deeply, a strange ache in his chest. The smell and the darkness twisted the ache, intensified it, bringing flashes of memory—feelings more than images. Memories of when he was a kid and would climb into the attic of his family's house, up through the trapdoor entrance in his closet ceiling, careful to set the door back into place so his parents would not know where he was. Just sitting there in the darkness, doing nothing, breathing in the smells, trying not to think about anything at all.

He opened his eyes at the sound of the door opening, closing, the shuffle of heavy footsteps across the garage floor. Had to be Stoke's father. Rheinhardt remained motionless, waiting for him to leave.

But Stoke's father didn't leave. For two or three minutes there were quiet sounds of rummaging along the workbench—the scrape of metal against wood, slosh of liquid, brushing strokes, shower of small particles onto the cement floor. Then a loud banging began, of metal against metal.

The banging went on and on, almost regular, and seemed to grow gradually louder. Rheinhardt crept forward on hands and knees until he could see below him through a wide gap between the boards laid over the cross-beams.

Stoke's father stood in front of the workbench with a ball-peen hammer, pounding away with the hammer at a large section of dented sheet metal. He seemed to be pounding without purpose, swinging the hammer without caring where it struck the metal. On the shelf built into the wall was a bottle of generic whiskey, and as Rheinhardt watched, Stoke's father reached for the bottle with his left hand, drank from it, set it back on the shelf without breaking the rhythm of his pounding. His shirt was already soaked with sweat, and the sweat on his forehead and arms glistened in the bright overhead light. His face was flushed, muscles in his neck tensed and straining.

The pounding went on for a long time, and Rheinhardt continued watching, fascinated, unable to pull back. Sometime later, though, Stoke's father finally did stop. He dropped the hammer onto the sheet of metal, staggered to a tall, round stool in front of the old, bulky bench vise, and sat. For a minute or so he didn't move, breathing heavily; then he leaned forward, laid his face on top of the metal vise, and began to cry.

Rheinhardt leaned back against the crates, closed his eyes again, and waited for silence to return.

Later that afternoon, headed back to his apartment, Rheinhardt saw a newshawker setting up on Market Street; the bright headline boards shimmered as glowing letters and words moved across their shiny black surfaces, headlines intended to sell evening TV news slots. Rheinhardt stopped to read the boards as people began to crowd around the newshawker.

EXCLUSIVE! the board flashed at him. FILM OF SPACE STATION DISASTER. Then below that, running across in somewhat smaller letters, was a more detailed description.

GLOBENET'S OWN FILM/COM SATELLITE HAS PUNCHED UP ITS ORBIT TO MATCH THAT OF THE SECRECY-BOUND SPACE STATION WHICH LAST WEEK EXPERIENCED A STILL UNEXPLAINED MAJOR ACCIDENT. ALTHOUGH NO NEWS HAS YET BEEN RELEASED, AND NO PICTURES OR FILMS BY THE AUTHORITIES, GLOBENET'S FILM/COM SATELLITE CAMERAS HAVE PICKED UP THE STATION ITSELF, REVEALING DETAILS OF BLACKENED HOLES IN THE STRUCTURE, JAGGED METAL, LOOSE DEBRIS, AND CONTROL CREWS WORKING ALL

AROUND IT. BUY YOUR SLOT NOW FOR TONIGHT'S NEWS, OR
SCHEDULE NOW FOR THE NEXT WEEK, MONTH, OR YEAR AT
SPECIAL RATES.

One of the other boards was running a steady stream
of varied story headlines: SUPREME COURT JUS-
TICE INDICTED FOR BRIBERY ... LOCH NESS
MONSTER FOUND, KILLED, EATEN ... U.S.
MILITARY   CASUALTY   RATES   SOAR ...
LYNCHINGS IN CHINATOWN PARK ...

Rheinhardt shook his head and worked his way
through the crowds; for the newshawker, business was
brisk.

The machine shop was quiet and dark, flooded with
shadows from two small lights on the side walls. All the
machinery—drills, routers and grinders, mold presses
and polishers—was motionless and silent, individual
machines almost unrecognizable in the riot of crossing
shadows. Rheinhardt had just shut down the hydraulic
molding press he'd been using after hours, and now
stood beside it, gazing through the jagged, statuelike
forms all about him. Somehow, with all the shadows
and the high ceiling twenty-five feet above, the shop
reminded him of the Warehouse, though it was much
smaller. Even Bear's office, in the far corner twelve feet
above the shop floor, reminded him of his old studio.
Narrow slats of light leaked through the blinds of the
office window. There was something else, though, that
seemed familiar about the shadows and images of the
shop, but he couldn't quite pin down what it was.

Exhausted, Rheinhardt worked his way through the
maze of machinery toward the office, boots crunching
metal shavings and plastic regrind, rustling bits of
paper and dried leaves that had blown in through the
large doors during the day. Newton hadn't swept up
before leaving, for some reason. Knocking the worst of
it free of his boots, Rheinhardt climbed the creaking
wooden staircase, knocked on the office door.

"Come in," Bear called.

Rheinhardt opened the door, stepped inside. A small

fan whirred above the desk where Bear sat. Bear was a
big man, about six feet four and nearly 300 pounds;
some of that was fat, but most was muscle and bone.
Hair and beard blended together on his face, thick and
curly. Wearing wire-rim glasses now, he was working on
a rough sketch of something. He looked up.

"Pay day," he said.

Rheinhardt nodded.

Bear opened the top desk drawer, took out a thick
white envelope filled with tens and twenties, handed it
to Rheinhardt. "Took out fifty again. Three more
weeks, the advance will be paid off."

Rheinhardt rolled the envelope, stuffed it into his
jacket pocket. "Thanks."

"You're doing good work, Rheinhardt. You want to
come in and work this weekend, more overtime? I can
use you on the big injection molder."

"No, but thanks anyway. I wanted to talk to you
about that, about hours. I want to cut out the overtime.
I'm okay with money now, and I need the time more.
You know I'm a sculptor." Bear nodded. "I need to get
back to it. I need the time. I may even want to cut back
on my regular hours a bit once I get going."

Bear didn't say anything for a few moments, then
nodded. "Okay, just let me know. Like I said, you do
good work. However much you want is fine, as long as
you can give me at least thirty hours a week."

"I can do that."

"Okay. Anything else?"

"No."

"Fine. See you Monday, then." Bear put his glasses
back on, turned to the pencil sketch.

"Good night, Bear." Rheinhardt left the office, stood
at the top of the stairs looking out over the shop. Light,
shadow. The machines looked vaguely like ruined
buildings of a city, still reaching for the sky as they
slowly disintegrating. Aftermath of war? Of a natural
disaster, the big quake that hadn't yet arrived? Civiliza-

tion's collapse? He was struck by a strong urge to hurry back to his room and begin working.

Rheinhardt turned and started down the stairs.

Night, and Rheinhardt started once again on the base. A mound of rubble, something like that. The rest of the piece would rise from it. The image wasn't at all clear. An Indian burial mound? The ruins of older buildings (he thought of the dark and silent machines in the shop)? A garbage heap? It almost didn't matter; he would learn what it was as he built it.

A different approach this time. He began with a two-foot by three-foot section of inch-thick plywood, bundles of thick wire, pieces of wood and scrap metal, piles of screws and nails and rock, gravel from the rooftop, bits of broken glass. He didn't know how much of it he'd use, or if he'd need other materials, but it was a start.

He sat on the stool, hands on the table, regarding the bare plywood and everything laid out around it, picturing his work for at least the next several days. He would gradually build the understructure of the mound, a detailed armature upon which he would later apply the clay. He would hammer nails into the plywood, bend them, run wire from one to another. He would glue rocks together, or to the plywood base, form rough piles and mounds with the rock and wood, string wire over and through them. With hammer, saw, or chisel he would split or crack pieces of wood, readjust and reapply the fragments, file and sand them to varying shapes and textures. With tin snips he would cut jagged strips of metal, bend and form them in among the wood and nails and rock, curling, jutting in all directions.

Rheinhardt could feel energy rising with the anticipation, and he set the first nail on the plywood, raised the hammer, and struck the head.

Eight

The police were nearly done hauling people out of the circled vehicles chained together in front of City Hall. A recorded speech, in deep bass tones, boomed from large speakers surrounded by barbed wire in the center of the circle. Rheinhardt sat on the top step in front of the Opera House across the street and watched the cops drag the protesters out of the cars and vans—their homes, probably—cuff or strap them, then push them toward the police vans lined up near the corner.

The recorded speech, though loud, was practically unintelligible, and Rheinhardt could make out only an occasional single word, but he knew what the protest was all about. The people were protesting the most recent crackdowns on street people and people living in abandoned cars. The cops had recently begun stunning people into unconsciousness—those living in abandoned cars or sleeping in doorways in exclusive areas of the city—carrying them off, then dumping them in seedier parts of the city. Nearly twenty cars and vans, most of them apparently used as homes, had been driven or pushed or towed up onto the plaza in front of the City Hall building, moved into a circle, then chained together. Rheinhardt could see make-shift curtains in some of the windows, battered suitcases, bottles and glasses, and even a few potted plants.

Two cops pulled a screaming, struggling woman out of a battered, primer-gray Buick—apparently the last person left in any of the vehicles. The woman continued to shout and struggle until one of the cops popped

her with a stunclub. She crumpled, and they dragged
her toward the street.

Spectators had been closing in on the vehicles, the
crowd steadily growing, but now the cops pushed them
back, clearing out a large area around the chained cars.
A kind of stasis settled in—the cops keeping everyone
back, the spectators remaining to watch, the unintelligible voice booming from the speakers, everyone waiting
for something else to happen.

Rheinhardt wondered how they were going to move
all the cars and vans; it would take a long time to cut
through all the huge chains that linked them together.
Then he stopped wondering when he heard the thrump
of an approaching dragoncub.

For several moments Rheinhardt couldn't see it—
there was only the regular thrump, approaching from
the north. Then Rheinhardt saw the shifting glitter of
silver, the wash of twisting blue sky in its wake. The
dragoncub came in fast and low, its dark, translucent
shell shimmering. Within seconds it was over the group
of chained vehicles; it expelled a burst of flashing
missiles, then shot off as the cars and vans exploded.

Metal and glass shattered, erupted up and inward,
engulfed temporarily in flames, then showered to the
ground in a small area within the ruins of the vehicles.
None of the debris scattered far enough to strike any of
the spectators or cops.

The booming, recorded voice had ceased. The flames
died almost immediately, leaving a smoking, charred
mass of twisted, broken metal, shattered glass, melted
rubber, fused plastic, and crumbled tile and concrete.

Rheinhardt stared at the rubble, strongly reminded
of the mound understructure he was building. Remember this, he told himself, lock in this image so you can
use it. He wished he had a camera. But he didn't, and so
as the smoke rose, Rheinhardt continued to stare,
impressing the picture in his mind.

Terry descended into the Warehouse basement,
walked along the dim, serpentine corridors searching

for Latiffe or Rosalind. Neither was in their room or in the sound studio they usually used. The basement was unusually quiet; no music played over the sound system, and only the faintest of vibrations from a few of the studios were perceptible. She checked the studios one by one (none had SESSION signs lit), but most were empty, and Latiffe and Rosalind weren't in any of them.

She opened the last door, looked inside, and when she saw Giles sitting in front of the 16-track, headphones over his ears and guitar in hand, she started to back out—not quickly enough.

"Terry, wait," Giles called, voice too loud. "I need to talk to you." His thick Fu Manchu moustache, beaded with moisture, quivered as he spoke.

She almost pulled the door shut on him, but she knew he'd come after her, track her down. With a deep breath, she came back into the room. Giles pulled off the headphones, dropped them onto the floor. On top of the unprotected recording equipment was a bottle of Tanqueray, an ice bucket, and a full glass. Terry wondered if the gin had been paid for out of the Warehouse food budget. Probably. Too much of that crap had been going on recently; she'd have to talk to Richmond and Belsen about it, see if she could get them to come down on it a little tighter.

"What is it, Giles?"

He scowled, flipped a couple of switches, banged out a minor chord which reverberated through the small room. He turned up the volume, hit the chord again, so loud this time it was almost painful.

"Giles." She tried to keep her voice calm, just loud enough to be heard over the tremolo he maintained. "What do you want?"

He finally turned to her, watched her through lowered eyelids as the sound slowly faded. When the room was silent, he set the guitar against the counter, took a long drink from his glass.

"I hear you got a gig for Latiffe and Rosalind at Club Ex."

Terry breathed in deeply, nodded; she knew what was coming. "Yes," she said. "Fact, I'm trying to find them right now. You seen either of them?"

"No, and I don't give a tuber's fuck about Latiffe and Rosalind. What I want to know is why you haven't nailed down a gig for *me* and *my* band."

Terry closed the door, leaned back against it. "I got one for you last month, Giles, at the Subway. You didn't show."

"Yeah, the fucking Subway, dance club for teeny-dips, a place that has nothing but shit bands."

And that's exactly what your band is, she thought at him. Shit. As far as she was concerned, Giles should never have been given a slot in the Warehouse in the first place.

Giles snorted, drained his glass (ice cubes rattling), refilled it. He swirled the gin, staring at it, then drank some more.

"How about it, Terry? When are you going to get something decent for me?"

"You've got to do some of the work yourself, Giles. Put in some legwork of your own, clean up your demos, get them to the club owners. You can't expect us to do it all for you."

"I've tried."

"So have I."

"Not hard enough!" he shouted. "I've been here six months, and you haven't done shit for me."

"I'm not the only one here, Giles. Have you talked to Richmond or Belsen?"

Giles stood up from his chair and threw his glass across the room; it shattered against the far wall, spraying glass and gin and ice across sound equipment, wall, and floor. "*Nobody's* done shit for me!"

"Settle down, Giles."

"Settle down? Listen, you guys have rented halls

before, put on shows with musicians from the Warehouse. It's time you did that for me." ·

"I'm sorry, Giles. We don't have unlimited resources, the budget's extremely tight. We just can't do that for everyone."

"I'm not asking you to do it for everyone, I'm telling you to do it for *me*! For *me*!"

"Your request was reviewed, Giles, and . . ."

"And turned down!" He grabbed his guitar, banged at the strings, held it against the amp, producing painful feedback squealing through the room.

"Giles, cut it, will you?"

He held the guitar by the neck, swung it round, catching the Tanqueray bottle, shattering it and sending the fragments spraying across the room with the splash of clear liquid. A piece of green glass bounced from the wall and into Terry's hair.

Her heart pounding now, Terry quickly opened the door, stepped out into the hall and swung the door shut. More feedback screamed from inside, guitar strings were banged on, scraped, followed by other loud crashes, and Terry wondered if he was destroying the equipment. God damn asshole. She hurried down the corridors, now to find Richmond and Belsen. That was it, Giles was gone.

"Now don't overreact," Richmond said, holding up a hand to Terry. "Just cool down a little."

"Cool down? Tell that to Giles. That guy has got to go."

Richmond smiled. "Nice alliteration, Terry."

They were in Richmond's office, a large room on the ground floor in the back of the Warehouse. Richmond sat at his desk, relaxed, looking at Terry and smiling. Belsen was in the back corner, chair tipped back against the wall, his legs in the light slanting in through the window, his body and face obscured by shadows. Belsen had not said a word, which didn't surprise Terry. He was older than anyone at the Warehouse, with dark hair half gone to gray but thick and curly, and shadowed eyes that usually made Terry uncomfortable. He never said much, and she never trusted the bastard.

"Is he gone or not?" Terry finally asked. "I didn't think there would be any question. He's probably destroyed everything in the studio by now."

Richmond glanced at Belsen, then shrugged, looking back at Terry. "I don't see that we can make an immediate decision here, a *rash* decision." He paused a moment. "For now, Giles will be temporarily barred from the sound studios. Give us a few days, let things settle down, we'll talk to him, get his side of things, then we can make a final decision."

"*Temporarily*?" Terry said.

"Temporarily." Belsen spoke at last, voice deep and firm. Terry looked at him, but he didn't say any more.

"We'll resolve the situation," Richmond said. "Don't worry about it."

Terry looked back and forth between the two men. "You're not going to kick him out, are you?"

"We'll take care of it." Belsen again. "I understand your concerns, but we'll take care of it."

There it was, she thought. Belsen's tone made it clear that the discussion was over. She stood up and left without another word.

It was dusk as she finally left the Warehouse. Outside the gate, Terry looked over the building in the darkness. Everything appeared quiet, no lights, no noise, the building apparently empty for the night, though of course it wasn't.

She'd expected Giles's eviction to be automatic. Temporarily barred from the sound studios. Terry didn't like that word, "temporarily." No, she didn't like it at all.

It was shit like this that sometimes made her want to quit working for the Warehouse. Terry took hold of the chain link fence, then pressed her face gently against the cool metal, looking sideways at the dark buildings.

Quit? What would she be giving up if she did? Too much . . . far too much.

No more photo exhibitions like Wendy's. Or the gig she had in a couple of weeks for Latiffe and Rosalind, recording off the sound board with some local indy label execs in the audience—L&R were at their best live. Or the performance/display she was trying to put together for Fuentes.

Sure, there were a lot of crappy artists in the Warehouse now, quite a few hacks, but there were still too many good artists, she couldn't just give up on all of them. Rheinhardt was gone, but he'd done some of his best work here. Wendy still did, along with a lot of others. And Terry thought of all the displays and performances and exhibits she'd helped put together over the last few years—Carla Rivera flying across Union Square at night in late December, circling the giant Christmas tree, swooping over the crowds, her wings in flames and trailing tiny flaming birds that spiraled to the ground; Dougall's exhibition of "Melting Portraits," a series of portraits of politicians, painted with a specially designed wax formula substance on canvases he kept heated at a specific temperature so that over the length of the two-week exhibit the features very slowly melted, becoming gradually more and more distorted; Tina Wey's all-female band, Three Imaginary Boys, performing for nine continuous hours under an echoing stretch of freeway overpasses, the roads blocked off to cars by phony construction barriers.

There had been others, many others, and there would be more in the future. Without her help, some things would still get done, but not all of them. And even those that did . . . *she* wouldn't be a part of them. That was important, too. She had helped to get the Warehouse started in the first place.

No, quitting would mean giving up too much. Take the bad with the good, wasn't that the expression? That meant dealing with Richmond and Belsen, and putting up with assholes like Giles. All right, then, she could deal with all that.

Terry smiled to herself, still tired and depressed, but feeling better about it all. She pushed back from the fence, turned away from the Warehouse, and started for home.

As Terry came up the porch steps of her apartment building, she saw the glow of a cigarette in the dark corner shadows, saw smoke drifting into the yellow porch light, saw the black of Rheinhardt's boots. He sat in the back corner of the porch, arms resting on knees. Terry stopped on the last step, looked at him.

"Hello, Rheinhardt."

"Hello, Terry."

She took the final step, put her key in the front door, then leaned against it, looking at him.

"I've had a shitty day," she said. "Fact, I've had a shitty week."

"Yeah." He got to his feet, put out the cigarette.

"You going to come in?"

"If you don't mind the company."

She tried smiling, turned the key, then the knob, pushed open the door.

Inside, they climbed the long, carpeted stairway to the third floor and the apartment proper. The apartment was dark; her roommate, Ann, was out (probably for the night), and Terry turned on lights as they went along, small, low-wattage bulbs in the ceiling. The living room was cold, wind blowing in through two windows opened wide. Terry pulled both windows down, leaving them open a couple of inches. Rheinhardt took off his jacket and sat on the couch, his eyes closed.

"How about a fire?" Terry asked.

"Sure." Eyes still closed. "Tea?"

"Please."

Rheinhardt nodded, got up from the couch and went into the kitchen, and Terry knelt in front of the fireplace. By the time he came back with two steaming mugs, she had the fire going, and the living room was warmer.

She sat beside Rheinhardt on the floor in front of the fire, their backs against the sofa. For a long time neither of them said anything, and Terry began to slowly relax. Rheinhardt got up, sat behind her on the sofa, one leg on either side of her, and massaged her neck and shoulders. A sculptor's hands, she thought, fingers strong, moving in the right places.

"You're tight," he said. "Like cable."

She nodded, and told him about Macy, about Giles and her talk with Richmond and Belsen, and as she spoke, as Rheinhardt continued to massage her knotted muscles, the tension slowly leaked out of her, slowly but steadily, leaving her drained, yet relaxed, and almost content.

"I'm sorry," Rheinhardt finally said.

Terry didn't respond, just gazed into the fire, waiting for Rheinhardt to go on.

"I should have told you," he resumed. "Even if I couldn't talk to you about it, or try to explain, I should have told you, and I'm sorry."

She wanted to tell him it was all right, because in a way it was, but it wasn't that simple. Instead, she remained silent.

"That place was killing me," Rheinhardt said.

Terry nodded slightly. "I know."

Neither said any more, and Rheinhardt reached down along her side, took her hand in his and squeezed. Terry returned the pressure, and they remained in front of the fire, silent and unmoving for a long time.

When the fire died, the tea long gone and the room gradually cooling off, they left the room and went to bed. They did not make love, but lay in each other's arms, warmed by one another, cooled by the breeze that gusted in periodically through the open window. Rheinhardt turned and lay with his back to her, facing the window and the night sky. Terry lay with her face at his neck, an arm across his chest.

The room was quiet, the only sounds their breathing and the occasional rustle of papers on her desk from the breeze. Outside was more rustling—of leaves, of insects, of loose trash. A dog barked several times, stopped when someone yelled at it to shut the fuck up. Terry ran her fingers lightly across his face, traced the curve of his ear.

"I love you, Rheinhardt." Quiet, soft.

"I know," he said.

And she wondered if that made him unhappy.

He had never told her he loved her, but she felt certain he did, at least as much as he was able.

"You just can't say it, can you, Rheinhardt?"

He breathed deeply, and she felt his head turn slowly from side to side. "No," he whispered.

"It's all right," she said, and it was. She thought she understood, and so she accepted.

As they lay in the cool darkness, she listened to his breath, felt the heartbeat at his neck, and as both slowed and deepened, remained steady and calm, she knew that tonight, at least, he would not have nightmares.

Nine

Rheinhardt woke one morning to discover that the understructure of the mound was essentially complete. He'd worked on it until two or three in the morning, then collapsed into an exhausted sleep, not realizing it was done. Now he sat on the edge of his cot, looking at the base in the morning light. Without any clay, it looked a mess, a haphazard jumble of scrap, but he knew, somehow, that it was ready.

He checked his wall calender (Friday, wasn't it?), saw he'd scheduled the day off from the shop. Good. That meant the whole day to start applying the clay. He lit a cigarette, smoked it while he dressed.

Rheinhardt went downstairs and into the apartment. In the bathroom, a sign was taped on the shower door: SHOWERS ON TUES., THURS., SAT. ONLY. KEEP TO TEN MIN. GAS BILL'S BEEN TOO HIGH. Friday. Fuck it, he thought. He'd been so preoccupied he hadn't taken a shower in three or four days, and he needed one, deserved one. He undressed and showered, but kept it short.

In the kitchen, Rheinhardt went to the fridge, took eggs, cheese, onion, and tomato from his shelf. As he cooked an omelette, he thought about the sculpture, the base. He thought about leaving it as it was, forget the clay, forget casting it in bronze, just build some kind of structure atop it with other materials. Piece it together with scrap. Wasn't what he intended, but it'd be a hell of a lot easier, quicker. He'd finish it, at least. If he kept on as he'd planned—clay, plaster, bronze—he wasn't sure he *would* be able to finish. It was taking too much energy that he didn't seem to have anymore.

Rheinhardt sat at the table with omelette, coffee, and newspaper. He started reading as he ate, but after he read a story about two fourteen-year-old girls who died together, hemorrhaging to death minutes apart after trying to give each other abortions, Rheinhardt pushed the paper away.

Rheinhardt continued eating, and tried not to even look at the newspaper across the table. But though he did not pull it back to read, he kept glancing at it as he ate, picking up pieces of the headlines—street riots in Germany, something about car bombs somewhere, homeless statistics. Finally he reached across and pushed the paper off the table and onto the floor where he couldn't see it.

Rheinhardt finished eating, then sat and stared out the kitchen window, smoking a cigarette. He thought about the sculpture again, the skeletal base upstairs waiting for him. Sure, he thought. Do it the easier way, simplify, forget the clay, the bronze, forget the quality. Give up on it; give up on the world. What was the point? Futility, that was the point.

Shit. That futility, or its potential, was why he *couldn't* take the easy route, god damn it. If he was going to do that, then there was no point in doing it at all, and that wasn't an option for him yet. Not yet.

Rheinhardt made himself another cup of coffee, climbed back up the stairs to his room, sat at the worktable with a fresh cigarette, and began applying the clay.

Near midnight, Rheinhardt picked his way along the yacht harbor jetty, guided by the boat and pier lights to his right, and light from the moon. The sky was clear, just a low bank of fog drifting in under the Golden Gate Bridge, and the sound of water breaking and sliding against the jagged rocks was sharp and crisp.

As he neared the tip of the jetty, he began to hear the faint, lapping sounds of the Wave Organ, fading in and out with the swells of the bay. He could see the tips of a few of the long, plastic pipes buried in the granite slabs

of old Victorian tombs. There was a plaque, somewhere, which told how and when the Wave Organ had
been built. Mid-eighties, he thought.

Rheinhardt climbed onto a large mound of stone,
pulled himself up with his hands. At the top of the
mound he wedged himself between two tilted sections
of granite, gazed out onto the dark reflecting waters of
the bay. The breathlike sounds of the Wave Organ were
faint, only barely audible over the water breaking
against stone.

Above and to his left the gold and red lights of the
Golden Gate Bridge delineated the sweeping curve of
cable, the tall, erect tower structures. Rheinhardt
thought of his sculpture, of the buildinglike structure he
thought would rise from the mound. He tried to
imagine it now, holding the image of the bridge towers
for support, to add upon, but he could see nothing in
his mind except the towers themselves, and lights
trailing from them in both directions.

The muffled sound of a boat motor broke through his
thoughts, and Rheinhardt sat up, scanned the chopping
water of the bay. A minute or two later the dark form of
a long aluminum boat, low in the water, approached
slowly from the east, bouncing sluggishly over the
swells.

Rheinhardt stood, and when the boat was almost
directly in front of him, only fifteen or twenty feet out
from the rocks, he took a hand-clicker from his pocket,
punched out a series of clicks in a repeating pattern.
Three loud clicks from the boat answered him, and the
boat turned toward shore.

A hushed quiet fell as the motor stopped. The boat
drifted in the last few feet and Rheinhardt made his
way to the water's edge to meet it. Metal scraped
against stone. Rheinhardt grabbed the prow and held it,
halting the boat's movement. A dark figure nodded to
him from the stern.

"Hello, Rheinhardt."

"Hello, Gollancz." In the light of the moon he could

see the scar on his old friend's chin. Gollancz had been wounded the same day Rheinhardt had taken the shrapnel in his wrist.

The boat was loaded with crates and packages wrapped in seal-tight and lashed to the sides and seats, filling the entire boat. Rheinhardt pushed the boat away from the rocks, kicking off the jetty with one leg and, in the same motion, lunging aboard. He sat on the metal bow seat, facing Gollancz, managed to find spots for his feet, and tightly zipped up his jacket. When they were a few feet from the rocks, Gollancz dropped the prop back into the water and restarted the motor. He let it quietly idle, and they drifted for a minute, moving slowly up and down with the swells.

"There's a life jacket under that seat," Gollancz said. "I hope to Christ you won't need it." He coughed, spit over the side of the boat. "You still sure you don't want to know what this is all about? You don't want to know how high the risk, or why?"

"I don't want to know anything," Rheinhardt answered.

"Ignorance won't protect you if we're caught," Gollancz said. "Won't protect you from either jail or a bullet in the head."

"I know. That's the way I want it. You said you needed help, I'm helping. That's all that matters."

"All right. And thanks." Gollancz engaged the prop, twisted the handle, and the boat gradually accelerated, arcing away from the rocks and out into the bay.

The wind picked up as they moved farther away from land, and Rheinhardt kept his eyes nearly closed against it, kept his hands in jacket pockets. Occasionally, when the boat dipped over or into a swell, cold water would splash across his face.

It wasn't long before he realized they were heading for Alcatraz. He'd heard a lot of things about the Rock in the last few years, since they shut down all the tours: that someone—the city or the feds—was using the cells again, locking away people they didn't want to bring to trial, people they wanted to rot away; that medical experimentation on human subjects was being performed on the island, the cells converted to ORs and wards; that the military was using it for experiments of its own; that groups of survivalists had taken it over, worked out a deal to be left alone. Rheinhardt hadn't believed *any* of the stories were true, had thought of the Rock as simply deserted, gradually crumbling in disrepair. But they were taking something out to it tonight, for someone.

They had motored just past the island, then Gollancz had cut the motor, and now they drifted in with the tide toward the dark, towering rock. Fog was thicker now, blowing past them, sometimes obscuring the island completely. As they neared, Rheinhardt could hear the waves crashing against the rocks, or swirling with loud sucking noises.

"Don't worry about the rocks," Gollancz said, voice low. "We've got a way in."

When they were thirty or forty feet away, Gollancz started the motor again and, scanning the steep rock faces in front of them, began skirting along the island.

"There," Gollancz said, not pointing at anything. He cut the motor again. "Start looking for a section of cable, angling up out of the water toward shore. If you see it, there's a piece of chain there on the prow, with a flip-hook, latch it onto the cable."

They continued to drift in toward the rocks for a few moments, then Rheinhardt spotted the cable, ahead and to the right, emerging from the water at an extremely shallow angle.

"I see it," he said, pointing.

"Will you be able to reach it?"

"I think so."

A swell raised the boat for a moment, Rheinhardt lost sight of the cable, but when the swell passed they dropped back down almost right onto it. Rheinhardt reached out, grabbed the cable, then pulled the boat to it, latching the flip-hook. The stern of the boat began swinging toward shore, and when it had swung completely around, Gollancz latched on a rear flip-hook.

From there it was easy. They pulled their way to shore by hand along the cable, the cable rising so gradually it never got more than two feet above the water. The boat rose and fell, tried to drift from side to side as the water swirled around it, sucking at it, but there was little leeway in the flip-hook chains, and their course remained straight, as if on a track.

The cable ended, tied to a metal spike embedded on shore. As the boat banged against the rocks, Gollancz tied it off on two other hooks embedded in the stone, then clambered onto the wet rocks. Keeping flat against the rock, Gollancz climbed a few feet up a steep face, using cracks and outcroppings for handholds and toeholds, then pulled himself onto a narrow ledge about six feet above the boat.

"This is where we leave it," he called down. "There's a small cave back here. Hand the stuff up to me, and I'll pack it in."

It took them about half an hour to unload the boat. Rheinhardt had to unleash the packages and crates one at a time and then, keeping his balance as the boat rocked and rose and fell, stand and hand the packages up to Gollancz. Most of the packages, though not overly large, were heavy, and a couple were so heavy he had to lean them against the rock and push them up along the face, and keep pushing as Gollancz pulled them up and onto the ledge.

When the last of the packages was taken up and put away, Gollancz scrambled back down to the boat, nearly slipping into the water before Rheinhardt caught him, pulled him aboard. Gollancz sat beside the motor, and pulled a small wad of bills from his coat pocket.

"Sometimes they can leave something for me, sometimes they can't. This time they could." He stripped off two twenties, held them out to Rheinhardt. "I know it's not much, but it's something."

Rheinhardt shook his head. "You never said anything about money. Keep it."

Gollancz shook his head in return. "Didn't say anything because I didn't know if there would be any. Take it, Rheinhardt. You worked for it."

Rheinhardt looked at Gollancz, saw that the man was determined, and took the money. "Thanks."

They pulled their way out along the cable, until it ran back underwater, then unhooked the boat from it. Gollancz started the motor, engaged the prop, and they shot away from the island, the boat light and riding high in the water. Rheinhardt looked back at the rocks, and for just a moment he thought he saw the face and gray hair of Justinian appear in the cave mouth, watching them as they pulled away from the island.

Justinian

Justinian stands on the edge of the rocks, motionless, his eyes closed, the toes of his boots protruding over the edge. He holds his arms out away from his sides, stretching fingers and hands. For two or three minutes he remains in that position, unmoving but for a slight swaying with the wind.

Slowly, Justinian raises his right leg and foot, then sticks his foot out away from the edge of the rocks, straightening the leg. His eyes remain closed, now tightly clamped. A shudder rolls through his body, and the muscles around his eyes relax, though the eyes remain shut. Again, for several minutes he stands poised and motionless, his leg suspended over empty air.

Finally, his movements still slow and deliberate and smooth, Justinian brings the leg and foot back in, stands on both feet again, and lowers his arms to his sides. Following another minute of immobility, Justinian steps back from the edge. Another shudder rolls through him.

Slowly, Justinian opens his eyes.

Justinian paced quietly about the rooftop, pausing occasionally and gazing out over the nearby streets and buildings. Heavy, irregular sounds rose from the direction of the ladder, and Justinian turned to face it. Deever appeared, pulled himself onto the roof, stumbled once. He was breathing heavily, coughing and wheezing. Justinian walked over to him, and Deever took out cigarettes, lit one for each of them between coughs.

"You're in terrible shape, old man," Justinian said. "What's the half-life now on your liver and lungs?"

"Shit down your throat, you crazy fucker. Least I'm not doing it with needles."

Justinian sighed once. "Unfair, old friend. Sometimes it's the only way I can get through the pain."

Deever nodded. "I know."

Neither spoke for a while, then Deever said, "What do you think his chances are?"

"Rheinhardt's?"

"Yeah."

"Don't know. At least he's out of the Warehouse. But it may have been too late. Or it might not have been enough. That place isn't the only thing dragging him down."

"Shit, I'd hate to see him go down the tubes, lose it all."

"If he does, he won't be the first, he sure as hell won't be the last."

"You're an encouraging son of a bitch, Justinian."

"And I suppose you're the optimist, drinking yourself into a stupor day after day. Where's *your* fucking hope?"

Deever turned away, didn't respond. He tossed his cigarette to the roof, crushed it with his shoe.

"I'm sorry," Justinian said.

Deever still didn't say anything. He took an envelope from inside his shirt, handed it to Justinian. Justinian tucked it into his jacket.

"Thanks, Walter," he said.

Deever nodded. "Anything I can do with Rheinhardt, let me know."

Justinian shrugged. "Same story, old man. He's got to do most of it himself."

"Yeah."

They were silent again. The wind had died down, and now the fog drifted slowly among the rooftops.

"I've got to go," Justinian said.

Deever nodded, but didn't move. Justinian touched him on the shoulder, then went to the ladder, and climbed down from the roof.

Justinian sat at the wooden table, opened the envelope and took out seven small glassine packets. Each packet was embossed with a pair of intertwined red and green dragons. Under the dragons was a small lattice of Oriental ideograms, and in the lower right-hand corner of each packet was the figure: 98.2%.

He left one packet on the table, put the others back in the envelope, and went to one of the bookcases. Justinian put the envelope in the back of a hardcover book called *Cancerqueen,* by Tommaso Landolfi. He returned to the table, but didn't sit. He wandered about the room for several minutes, then turned off the overhead light and switched on the corner bulb up among the pipes.

Moving in and out of shadow, he went to the cupboard, withdrew a box, opened it. Inside was a syringe, a coil of surgical tubing, eyedropper, cotton balls, metal dish and stand, votive candle and matches. Justinian laid the box beside the glassine packet, sat in the wooden chair, and closed his eyes.

* * *

Naked, Justinian stumbled across the room, shifting in and out of the shadows, bumped against one of the bookcases. For a moment he stared at the pen and ink drawing on the wall, then moaned and pushed away. He staggered to the bed, fell facedown across it, then rolled over onto his back, moaned again.

"Birdland," he whispered, holding one hand in the air. "Flying in to fucking Birdland."

He reached higher with the one hand, grasped at empty air, then let the hand fall back; as he closed his eyes, the tears began.

Ten

The mound was finished. Rheinhardt took off the headphones and pulled his hands back from the clay (they were shaking again; from exhaustion?). Vertigo struck him for a moment, light seemed to whirl in a cone around him, and he nearly tipped over from the stool, grabbed at the table edge for support. He felt sick to his stomach, and his ears felt hot and flushed. How long had it been since he'd eaten? He looked at the clock across the room, but the hands and numbers wouldn't focus. Outside it was dark, but what did that mean?

Rheinhardt slid from the stool, stood with one hand on the table, still slightly dizzy. He walked to the foot of the cot, picked up a plastic water jug which was half full, raised it to his mouth and drank, water spilling across his cheeks and shoulders. Then he raised the jug, poured the rest of the water over his head and face and ears. When he looked at the clock again, he could just make out the time—quarter of five. Jesus, almost dawn. He picked up cigarettes from the cot, took one and lit it, tossed the pack back onto the cot. He started to sit, then stopped and straightened, knowing he wouldn't be able to get up again if he did. He walked back to the table, looked at the clay.

It *was* a mound of rubble, like partially exposed ruins of a destroyed building, contents scattered randomly about, disintegrating. Near the center, though, at its peak, the mound was nearly flat and featureless. From this would rise the upper two sections of the sculpture

—the more intact ruin of another building, perhaps, capped by . . . by what? A strange network of metal, something like that. He didn't have a clear idea yet.

The mound, though, was complete. It was good work, he thought. Hard to be objective, but he was mostly satisfied. There was something both real and unreal about it, and he thought that was exactly what he wanted, the impression that something was slightly askew, was not quite right.

Rheinhardt put out his cigarette, turned off the overhead lights. When his eyes adjusted to the darkness, he could see faint traces of gray now coming in through the skylight and window. First signs of dawn.

He stumbled to the cot, collapsed across it, shifted onto his side. The cot seemed to spin, and maybe the room, too, he wasn't sure. He closed his eyes, and as dream images began to flicker through his mind, a spinning mound of rubble appeared. The plateau cracked, split open, and the blackened, jagged walls of a derelict building emerged, slowly rising toward gray sky.

On a Sunday afternoon, Monterey House celebrated its fourth anniversary with a barbecue in the building's backyard. Past residents were invited, were asked to bring their children and/or other guests, and by one o'clock the backyard was filled with young women, babies and young children, and a few men. They had lucked into a bright warm day with hardly a cloud in the sky, only a bit of high white overcast, no signs of fog, and for the first time in days, or weeks, Terry felt happy, and content.

Even Rheinhardt seemed to be enjoying himself, and she knew it was because he was working again. On exactly what, she didn't know; Rheinhardt never talked about a project while he was working on it, and with this one he hadn't even asked her to look at it. At this moment, though, he was wearing a huge white apron and tending the coals in one of the three barbecue kettles, talking and laughing with Rebecca and Winton, who were taking care of the other two. He looked over at Terry and smiled.

Tables were set up around the yard, laid out with bottled drinks, stacks of paper plates and plastic cups, bowls of chips and dips and other snacks. Before long, the coals would be ready, and they could cook the meat.

Terry went into the house to see how the rest of the food was coming. The kitchen, too, was filled with young women, some little more than girls—but women enough to get pregnant. Macy was at the big wooden table, slicing cucumbers and green onions for the salads. Terry sat beside her, picked up another knife, and started helping.

"How are you feeling?" Terry asked. She smiled down at Macy's huge belly. "What are we, couple months away now?"

Macy smiled, then winced. "Yeah," she said. "Something like that, but I think he wants out *now*, the way he's been kicking lately." She grinned again. "It's a boy, I'm sure of it."

"You won't be disappointed if he turns out to be a 'she'?"

"No." Macy shook her head. "But it's a boy."

Rheinhardt called in through the kitchen window, said the coals were ready. The women in the kitchen broke into a new flurry of activity, finishing up the salads, taking garlic bread out of the ovens, stirring and tasting the chili. Terry got up and helped as they started carrying the food out to the tables, the plates of hot dogs, hamburgers, and chicken out to the three chefs. Sizzling sounds and wonderfully warm smells rose as Rheinhardt, Winton, and Rebecca put the first batches on the grills.

"Is Rheinhardt your boyfriend?" Macy asked as they carried salads out to a table. Macy carried a large wooden bowl, resting it on her belly, and waddled more than walked.

"Sort of," Terry said. "I guess you could say he is."

"I like him. He's a funny guy."

Terry smiled. She had never heard Rheinhardt called funny before.

For the next hour and a half, people ate and drank and talked and laughed and ate some more. Rheinhardt, Winton, and Rebecca managed to keep a steady stream of grilled meat coming, and the pots and bowls of other food steadily emptied. Next door, a dog barked constantly until Rheinhardt finally threw a hot dog over the fence, to the delight of the kids. The dog shut up for about forty-five seconds, then started in again. The children who could talk pleaded with Rheinhardt to throw another hot dog over the fence. A couple of minutes later he finally gave in, tossed one over, with the same results. When the dog started barking again, the kids yelled at Rheinhardt to throw still another hot dog over, but this time he refused. Eventually the kids quit pestering him, but the dog continued to bark.

When the meal was eaten (and Terry was surprised at how little food remained), they brought out large pots of coffee and hot water, bags of black and herbal teas, jugs of milk and juice, and finally an enormous carrot cake, half plain, half topped with whipped cream.

Everyone but the kids seemed to settle down and relax, sitting at the tables or on lawn chairs or on the cement porch, eating the cake, drinking coffee or tea, smoking cigarettes, talking. The kids ran or crawled around the crowded yard, under tables and chairs and people's legs, through bushes and behind trees. It seemed that one cup after another of milk or juice or water was spilled, along with half a dozen dropped pieces of cake.

Back in a corner of the yard, Rheinhardt was set up at a table with several blocks of modeling plasticene, and was making tiny clay animals for the children. Macy

was sitting beside him, watching and helping keep the
kids under control. Terry smiled to herself. It was
obvious Macy was developing a crush on him.

Terry was talking to Sika, one of the first residents at
Monterey House, twenty-one years old now, though she
seemed older to Terry. Older and tired.

"How are things going with the jobs?" Terry asked.

Sika shook her head. "They last about two weeks,
sometimes three, then I go five or six weeks before the
next one. In between, trying to get money from Social
Services or that asshole, George, is practically impossible, so money is all the time just fucked. Sometimes I
think I'd be better off not working at all. The money
would be steady, and maybe more than what I manage
now." She gave an unhappy smile. "I just can't run it
that way, though. I don't know, we get by."

Sika's four-year-old daughter, Lindy, trotted up to
them and tugged at Sika's shirttail.

"What is it, Lindy?"

Lindy whispered something neither Terry nor Sika
could make out. Sika leaned over and Lindy whispered
again, this time into her ear, then Sika straightened and
smiled.

"She's kind of shy. She wants one of the clay toys
Rheinhardt's making, but she's afraid to go over there
by herself."

"Then let's take her," Terry said.

They worked their way through the tables and chairs
and spilled food, Lindy hanging onto Sika's hand.
When they reached Rheinhardt, Lindy scuttled behind
Sika's legs and buried her face between them.

"She's shy around men," Sika said. "But she'd like
one of the clay toys."

Rheinhardt smiled, tried to catch Lindy's eye, but
she remained well hidden. Rheinhardt whispered
something to Sika, she whispered back, and Rheinhardt
nodded. He picked up a chunk of plasticene and began
shaping it.

While Rheinhardt worked, Lindy would poke her

head out from behind her mother's legs to watch, but
whenever he turned to glance at her, she retreated.

When he finished, he held out a small figure of a cat
with its head cocked to one side. Lindy put her head out
and looked at it, but didn't come forward.

"Here," Rheinhardt said. "It's for you. A nice, cute
dog."

Lindy squeaked out a giggle, then started laughing
hard. She stopped, then said, very quietly and still
smiling, "That's not a dog, it's a cat."

"It is?"

"Yes."

Rheinhardt stared at the cat. "You're right, it is. Well,
I'd better change it, then, I thought I was making a dog,
and you want a dog, don't you?"

Lindy's eyes widened, and she quickly shook her
head. "No, I want a cat, I want . . ." She didn't finish,
but reached out with her hand.

Rheinhardt held the cat back out toward her. "You
want this one, then?"

Lindy nodded, stepped forward and took it gently
from his hand. "Thank you," she whispered. This time
she did not retreat behind her mother's legs.

"You're good with kids," Sika told him.

Rheinhardt shrugged and smiled. "It's easier when
they're not your own, I think," he said.

Terry stood a few feet back, watching them all—
Rheinhardt, Lindy, Sika, Macy. For some reason, just
seeing them all together made her feel quite happy.

Late that night Rheinhardt lay on the rug in front of
Terry's fireplace, basking in the heat from the fire; Terry
was curled up on the couch. The fog had come in after
the barbecue was over, but Terry had built the fire and
the room was warm. The apartment was quiet now.
Ann and some guy she'd met at the beach were in her
bedroom, apparently asleep or worn out; earlier, they
had been making a lot of noise that came through the
walls—bed bucking up against the wall, Ann's laughter

and high-pitched squeals, grunting from her newfound friend. Now, though, they weren't making a sound.

Rheinhardt was tired, but content, feeling more comfortable with Terry than he had in a long time. Heat from the fire induced a warm, heavy sensation in his arms and legs, and he could hardly keep his eyes open.

"It was a nice day," Terry said.

"Mmm."

"You awake?"

"Sort of. Yes, it *was* a nice day, Terry."

"You seemed to enjoy yourself, for a change."

"Yeah, I guess I did. Had fun with the kids."

"I've never seen you around children before. I was surprised at how well you got along with them."

"I like kids, for the most part. Like I said to Sika, it's a hell of a lot easier when they're not your own." He paused, looking into the fire. "I don't know, I guess I look at young kids as people who aren't fucked up yet."

"Terrific outlook," Terry said.

Rheinhardt breathed deeply. "Come on, Terry, what do you expect from me? It was a nice day, and I enjoyed myself, and I feel very relaxed and kind of peaceful right now, but you can't expect that to change my view of life."

Terry didn't say anything. Rheinhardt closed his eyes, breathed in deeply the scent of burning wood. With eyes closed, the snapping and hissing sounds of the fire seemed to grow louder, more distinct.

He felt hands on his ankles, opened his eyes and raised his head to see Terry untying his boots. She had completely undressed and, naked and kneeling at the foot of the rug, she eased off first one boot, then the other. She paused, looking at him, then slowly removed his socks.

On hands and knees, straddling him, she moved up to his waist, unbuckled his belt. Rheinhardt lay back, gazing up at the ceiling, and didn't move. He felt the buttons of his fly come loose, one after another, then

Terry began gently tugging at his jeans, pulled them over his hips, turned back to his feet to tug at the pant legs and work them over his ankles, pulled until the jeans came free. She moved back to his waist, slipped off his shorts.

Then Terry returned to his waist, pushed his T-shirt up to his chest. Rheinhardt didn't resist as she moved his arms up over his head, circled around and stripped the T-shirt off over his face, his arms, his hands. She slid his arms back to his sides, rose, then walked back to his feet and stood, looking down at him. She smiled; Rheinhardt smiled back, but still did not move.

Terry knelt again, kissed the top of each foot, his ankles, ran her fingers lightly through the hair on his calves. Slowly she moved up along his legs, sometimes kissing his skin, sometimes just brushing it lightly with her fingertips.

Up near his waist again, she bit at a clump of his pubic hair, tugged it lightly several times, released it, then blew her warm breath through the hair. Already he was fully aroused, though she had not once touched any part of his genitals.

Still on her hands and knees, straddling him again and holding her body about a foot above his, she worked her way up toward his face, kissing his belly, biting his skin gently, his nipples, his neck, kissing his cheek. She stopped for a moment, her face above his, still holding herself above⁴ him, then began moving forward again, much more slowly now.

Rheinhardt gazed straight upward, watched her chin, then her neck slowly move past overhead, her body now flickering with light and shadow from the fire. Her breasts came into view, and he wanted to raise his head to them, kiss her dark nipples, touch them with his tongue, nip at them, but he resisted the temptation, and remained motionless beneath her.

Her breasts moved past, then her taut belly, and finally, as the dark tangle of pubic hair moved directly above him, Terry stopped. She remained poised above him, swaying slightly from side to side, the hair dotted with several tiny droplets of moisture.

"Rheinhardt," she whispered.

"Terry," he whispered in return.

Then slowly, slowly, the dark tangle of hair began to descend toward him, and he opened his mouth to receive it.

Eleven

To start the building armature, Rheinhardt drove several long, thin steel rods into the clay plateau, working them through the mound armature below. Once in place, the rods extended nearly three feet above the mound, which seemed about right. Next he took lengths of thick, stiff wire and webbed it between the rods, giving him both a structure to work on, and added stability.

Rheinhardt sat back and gazed at the armature for a long time before deciding it was ready, then went to the covered tub beside the table and took out a large chunk of clay.

Rheinhardt walked along the crowded sidewalk on Stockton Street, through the heart of Chinatown. A block over on Grant, the main tourist run, he might have blended in, but here he was one of the few non-Chinese in sight. Traffic was heavy in the street, even heavier on the sidewalks, and as he worked his way through the noisy throng, he felt quite tall. And then, seeing hostile stares from almost everyone around him, he began to feel uncomfortable as well.

Yes, they were definitely staring at *him*, and a strange feeling came over Rheinhardt as he realized he should know why they were staring, why there was so much tension on the street, but he could not quite think of what it was.

Ahead of him, a group of teenage girls blocked the sidewalk. They were dressed in black leather pants and red leather jackets, all wearing silver metal headbands studded with jade and ivory. As Rheinhardt approached they spread out to form a solid barrier across the sidewalk, linking arms and staring at him. Other pedestrians moved away, clearing out an area around him.

Rheinhardt stopped a few feet away from the line of girls. They didn't move, and they didn't speak, but they began to make an eerie hissing sound. He started out into the street to go around them, glanced up at the building facade across the way, and saw it.

Mounted on the building was an enormous reproduction of a photograph of the six lynched Asians—two Japanese and four Chinese. All six had been hung by their feet, hands bound behind their backs and weighted down by enormous lead balls so that arms had been wrenched out of the shoulder sockets. All six had had their throats cut.

Christ, how could he have forgotten? Rheinhardt looked away from the picture, looked out at all the people staring at him. *I* didn't do it, he wanted to shout at them, which he knew was absurd. He doubted a single person on the street actually thought he had, but *somebody* had, and that somebody had almost certainly been white. Two different white supremacist groups had claimed responsibility.

Rheinhardt thought of turning back, but he was close to the address Deever had given him (why hadn't Deever warned him?), and so he decided to go on. He skirted the group of girls, stepped back onto the sidewalk, and continued on. When he glanced back, the girls had all turned around and were staring at him, still hissing, but they didn't follow.

Deever had given him an address, but no name, just said it was a kind of Chinese pharmacy. Rheinhardt found it between Jackson and Washington streets, the storefront windows covered with Chinese ideographs; the only word of English was IMPORTERS in small print on the left window. Rheinhardt walked in.

The shop went suddenly quiet. Along the left wall were a number of chairs, and several Chinese women sat in them, most with large plastic bags at their feet. All the women now stared at him, faces nearly expressionless. Along the right wall was a long counter; behind the counter were two small, thin men wearing tailored suits and ties. Each had a long sheet of paper filled with Chinese characters in front of him, and large sections of white butcher paper beside the written text with small piles of dried plants, seeds, mushrooms, and other things Rheinhardt didn't recognize. Behind the men, the wall was a floor-to-ceiling bank of square wooden drawers.

Rheinhardt watched for several minutes as the two men worked. The men would look at the sheet of paper (were they prescriptions?), then open one of the drawers behind them and withdraw some plant or herb, or scoop out some seeds, then weigh them in a hand balance—a long thin stick of wood marked with notches at regular intervals, a metal receptacle hanging from string at one end, and tiny round metal weights at the other. They would hold the stick at a notch, add the plants or seeds to the receptacle until it balanced, then empty the receptacle onto the butcher paper. Rheinhardt was amazed at what emerged from the wooden drawers—dark seeds, light seeds, strips of seaweed, strangely formed black mushrooms, pieces of different roots, a string of tubelike things connected with webbed plant material, dried leaves of different shapes and colors.

One of the men finished, twisted the butcher paper into a cone open at the top, then slipped the cone into a brown paper bag along with the prescription. He said something in Chinese, and one of the women got up from her chair, came to the counter. The man handed the bag to her, and they spoke a few words to each other, then she handed him money. He rang up the sale on an old manual cash register, said a few more words, smiling, and the woman broke into laughter, exposing brown-stained teeth, several of them capped with gold. She said something else, then looked at Rheinhardt, the laugh stopping, mouth closing. She gripped her bag and walked out. The man turned to Rheinhardt, hesitated a moment, then said, "Can I help you?"

"Yes. Do you have . . . Tan Kwe Gin?" He pronounced it as *don kway gin*.

The man nodded, went to a glass case next to the bank of drawers, slid the door aside, reached in and took out a red, green and white box covered with ideographs and the words TAN KWE GIN. "Five dollar," the man said, holding up the box.

"I'll take two. No . . ." He hesitated. How long would one last? No idea. He didn't want to have to come back any sooner than necessary. "Make it three," he said.

The man nodded again, took two more boxes out, closed the case. As the man put the boxes in a brown paper bag, Rheinhardt could hear the swish of liquid. "Fifteen dollar."

Rheinhardt paid him, said, "Thank you." The man nodded, but said nothing in return.

Rheinhardt went to the door, paused, then opened it and stepped out into the crowded street.

Rheinhardt stopped by Kit's place three times before he caught her in the building. It was early afternoon, and when he knocked, Kit answered the door immediately. She let him in, said she had water boiling on the hot plate, and hurried back to it.

"You want tea?" she called. "Or I think there's some shit instant coffee around here somewhere. Olden drinks it."

"Tea," Rheinhardt answered.

"Good choice."

Rheinhardt set the bag with the Tan Kwe Gin on a chair and walked over to Kit's project of poles, wire, mirrors, and painted glass. Something looked different, and he slowly circled it, unsure of what had changed. Then he saw it, or part of it.

"There aren't as many strands of wire," he said.

"Right," Kit said. "It was getting too cluttered. Overkill. I was losing the effect I wanted. So I've been gradually subtracting strands, like maybe add one, take off three, add another, take off two, like that. I've still a fucking lot of work left."

Rheinhardt gazed at the crisscrossing wires strung between the poles, like delicate crossbars of an elegant building under construction, and an image of his own sculpture rose in his mind—the base, the mound of rubble completed, the derelict, roofless building (he was fairly certain now that there would be no roof, and only remnants of the floors within) almost half completed, rising above the mound. There was going to be something more, a skeletal structure of some kind that would rise atop the derelict building, though he still didn't know what it was, or how he could construct it. Clay was going to be a real problem, with what he envisioned.

Abruptly he thought of the welding equipment back in the shop, the old stuff Bear was talking about selling, and just as abruptly the image of the skeletal construction rising above the building seemed to snap closer into focus—thin metal rods, lateral pieces coated with something, dripping something . . . splinters of metal . . . twisted and jagged . . . a lattice structure . . . Yes, he'd have to go talk to Bear.

Kit came up to him carrying two ceramic mugs of tea, breaking his concentration. He took one, sipped at it. Hot and strong, like before. Rheinhardt pointed to the brown paper bag on the chair.

"For you," he said. He stood against the wall, one foot up on the cinder block.

"Really?" Kit picked up the bag, sat on the edge of her bed, opened it. "Rheinhardt! My Tan Kwe!" She took out one of the boxes, ripped off the top and withdrew the dark brown bottle. There was a small, stained white label poorly glued onto the bottle, edges curling, with faded green text. "This is it. Maybe now my gums will stop bleeding so much." She looked up at Rheinhardt. "Thanks, Rheinhardt, thanks a lot, this is great. Hard to believe you remembered. How much was it?"

"Five dollars a bottle."

"Oh, that's pretty cheap, it must be legit right now." She unscrewed the red plastic top, worked at peeling off the metal seal. "The price always fluctuates. David, my acupuncturist, says the government's always changing the regulations, sometimes classifying it a drug, sometimes just a . . . I don't know, something to add to tea or something, I can't remember. When it's a drug, they can't import it, so they have to smuggle it in, and then it gets more expensive. Either way, it's always around, and plenty of it, because so many people here in the city depend on it. Well, the Chinese, anyway. Where did you get it?"

"Chinatown."

Kit stopped working at the bottle, looked at him. "Jesus."

Rheinhardt nodded. "Yeah."

Kit returned her attention to the bottle, managed to get the metal seal off, pulled out the rubber plug, sniffed deeply. "God, it's horrible smelling stuff. Tastes even worse, but it works." She put the plug back in, screwed on the plastic top. "Fifteen dollars, then. I can't pay you back right now, Rheinhardt, I haven't . . ."

Rheinhardt shook his head, cut her off. "Forget it, Kit. It's a gift. I've got a job now, making some money, I'm okay financially."

"Oh shit, that's right, I meant to ask you about that. I heard you got a place in the Haight, right?"

"Yeah, I've been there a couple of months now."

"What kind of job do you have?"

"Working in a machine shop, running some machine with a mold that makes rubber parts. Pretty fucking monotonous, but the guy who runs the shop, Bear, he pays me under the table. What I'm making are some kind of rubber insulators for medical instruments in hospitals."

"Hospitals reminds me, I've got a new job myself." Kit set the bottle beside her on the bed. "Part-time in a hospital. I've only been doing it about two or three weeks, so money's not too terrific, but it'll get better."

"Hospital? What, you a nurse now?" He smiled.

"Right. I clean fucking toilets at S.F. General, is what I do. But it's a job. It's also been . . . what? Enlightening. I see people come in dead, or dying, usually fucked over by other people—knives, guns, pipes, shit, you name it." Then Kit grimaced, closed her eyes and said, "Oh, fuck. I forgot. What time is it, you know?"

"No, don't have a watch."

Kit leaped up from the bed, hurried across the room toward Olden's paintings. "Where's that goddamn clock, I know he's got one here somewhere." She found it on the floor in the far corner, picked it up and looked at it. "Ah, shit, I was supposed to be at work an hour and a half ago." Kit dropped the clock and ran back to the bed, grabbed a coat from under the blankets. "Let's go, I've got to get out of here."

Kit followed Rheinhardt out the door, locked it, and she started down the stairs ahead of him, two steps at a time. At the bottom, she turned and looked back up at him.

"Can you spare me a cigarette?"

Rheinhardt took out his pack, stuck a book of matches inside the cellophane, and tossed it down to her.

"Thanks Rheinhardt. I'll see you around."

He nodded and sat on the top step, watched her run to the sidewalk, head down the street, and disappear around the corner.

Twelve

Through the tinted goggles, the torch flame looked small and cool, blue cone within white. Rheinhardt watched it for a long time, adjusting it slightly, gently turning the oxygen valve on the mixer. The flame was beautiful.

Bear had given him all the equipment for nothing, then had helped him get it cleaned up and working smoothly, helped him haul everything out of the shop and up onto the roof outside his apartment, even found Rheinhardt a steel worktable and huge wooden bench at the junkyard, which they lined with asbestos. Stoke had helped him build a lean-to against the back wall of his room, with locking cabinets, shelves, sets of crates. Two weeks of work, and he was ready.

The sculpture, though, wasn't ready, the derelict building not yet complete, but Rheinhardt was going to need time to practice. He'd done oxyacetylene welding before, but that had been years ago, and he was going to be awkward, clumsy—his stint up on the Warehouse roof had hardly been a refresher course. Maybe by the time he was ready to start on the next stage of the sculpture, he'd know what he was doing again.

Rheinhardt had two pieces of steel tacked together at right angles, set up against brick. He picked up a length of welding rod in his left hand, brought the flame to the near corners of the steel, moving it in a circular motion until the metal started to pool, then began to feed the welding rod into the seam and flame.

Fifteen minutes later, Rheinhardt cut the flame, set

the remainder of the rod aside, raised the goggles from his eyes. The weld was awful. He picked up the two joined pieces of metal, rapped twice at one side with his gloved fist, and the weld broke.

Rheinhardt smiled, pulled the goggles back over his eyes, and prepared to try again.

Latiffe and Rosalind and the two other musicians that worked with them were setting up on stage, and Terry wandered among the full tables in Club Ex, checking to see if there was anything else she needed to do. But it looked like everything was set—it was up to Latiffe and Rosalind now.

She waved at Zege Roget, the owner of Camouflage Recordings, a local independent label. The owners of two other indys were supposed to be here as well, but she didn't see them. No, there was Tristan, from Black Ship, back in the darkest corner. Figured.

Terry drifted to the back, started toward Mick at the sound board, who was talking to a recording engineer. As she approached, Mick looked up and shook his head, smiling.

"Go away," he said. "Sit down and have a drink, you're driving us all crazy. We've got everything under control, Terry, you can't do anything more."

Terry looked at him. "Am I that bad?"

Mick nodded, grinning.

Terry shrugged. "All right. Everything's okay then?"

"Everything's *fine*, for Christ's sake."

Terry nodded, and finally went to her table near the front, where she sat alone, wishing Rheinhardt had been able to come. She was glad, though, that he was working so hard again.

Belsen approached the table, sat in the chair beside her. "Hello, Terry," he said.

"Belsen. I'm surprised to see you here."

"Why? These are Warehouse musicians. Or at least two of them are."

"I didn't know you cared."

"Of course I do. Why else would I be working with you at the Warehouse?"

"I don't know."

Belsen didn't say any more for a while. On stage, it looked like the band was just about done tuning and was ready to begin.

"Richmond and I have decided to go ahead and rent a hall for Giles."

Terry breathed in deeply, then nodded. "I'm not surprised."

Belsen cocked his head. "You don't seem too upset about it. Thought you would be."

Terry shrugged, smiled. "I'm not crazy about it, Belsen. But I don't really care that much right now. Want to know why?"

"Sure."

She pointed at the stage. "Because of them." Her smile broadened. "Listen to them tonight, Belsen. Just listen."

Almost on cue, Rosalind stepped up to the microphone, said simply, "This first piece is called 'A Tropical Night in the Natatorium.' " Then she brought the saxophone to her mouth, glanced at Latiffe, and they began to play.

Pounding at the door dragged his attention away from the sculpture, and Rheinhardt pulled back, reorienting himself. His vision blurred for a moment, as if the sculpture was fading in and out of existence, then snapped back into focus. Christ, why is someone here now? The ruined building was nearly complete, he needed to just keep at it awhile longer, a few hours, a few days, maybe. The pounding resumed, and Rheinhardt finally got up from the stool, went to the door, opened it.

Stoke stood there in his dark green jumpsuit, eyes glassy, pupils fully dilated, sweat on his forehead. Abruptly he grinned, pushed into the room without a word, dropped onto the cot with his back against the wall.

"Hardly see you anymore, asshole," Stoke said. Still grinning. "You're turning into a fucking hermit."

"I'm busy, Stoke. I'm trying to work." Rheinhardt remained by the door, left it open.

Stoke looked at the table. "Oh, shit, man, look at that, a lot better than the dogshit cigarettes or whatever that was." His grin faded, and he twisted, lay out on the cot, staring up at the ceiling. He tapped on the wall with his knuckles.

"What is it, Stoke?"

"The band's going to L.A. for a couple of weeks, play in some of the clubs. Our La-La Tour. Closest we'll ever get to a world tour. Want to come along, get away from the city for a while?"

Rheinhardt closed the door, sat in the wooden chair beside it, lit a cigarette. Something was bothering Stoke, and it wasn't the L.A. trip.

"No, I don't want to come along," he said. "I told you, I'm busy. I can't take time off from the shop, I can't take time off from my work. Besides, you know what I think of L.A. I can't stand the people, and the air makes my eyes burn."

"I know, I just thought I'd ask."

"What is it?" Rheinhardt asked again.

Stoke shrugged, continued to stare at the ceiling. He stopped tapping on the wall, moved his hand out over his face, wiggled the fingers. His hand dropped to his side, and he turned his head to look at Rheinhardt.

"Got my induction notice." He shrugged again. "They move fast."

Rheinhardt didn't say anything. His heart seemed to stutter a moment, something caught at his breath, drove down into his gut; then it all fluttered away, leaving behind a hollow, numbing ache.

Stoke sat up on the cot, stood, paced around the small open space, then strode to the door, opened it. "I can't breathe in here," he said. He stepped out onto the roof, walked quickly to the edge, began circling the roof. Rheinhardt followed him out of the room, then stood and watched Stoke make several circuits of the

roof before he seemed to calm down. Stoke stopped a
few feet from Rheinhardt, sat on the perimeter ridge,
legs dangling over the edge.

"You don't know what you're going to do, yet, do
you?" Rheinhardt asked.

Stoke shook his head.

"Have you been thinking about it at all?"

"No." Stoke shrugged. "I guess I'll think about the
whole thing while we're down in L.A."

"No you won't."

Stoke didn't reply. Rheinhardt sat beside him, one
leg on the roof, one over the edge. What was there to
say? Nothing.

"What made *you* decide to go?" Stoke asked.

"Nothing." It was a truthful answer, but he knew it
wouldn't mean anything to Stoke. Nothing he could say
would.

"I don't understand."

"I know. I'm not trying to be deliberately vague. I
just can't help you with this one, Stoke."

"I asked you before, to talk to me about it, tell me
what it was like. You said you would."

"I said I might." Rheinhardt closed his eyes, his
entire body growing heavier. "You just can't understand what it takes, even to think about it." He shook
his head. "Shit. Maybe some other time, I don't know.
Right now, though, it's impossible. I barely have
enough energy to keep working. I don't know if I can
even finish this damn thing." He gestured toward the
room.

"I'm sorry, I guess I shouldn't be bothering you
then."

"No, it's all right. This is important, I realize that. It
was important to me. I would have been different if I
hadn't gone. Better or worse, who knows? But different.
You just can't expect me to talk about it."

Stoke nodded, sighed heavily. "Ah, shit, Rheinhardt,
I'm just afraid."

"Of what?"

"Of making a decision. Of making the wrong one."

Rheinhardt's breath caught again briefly, his stomach seemed to fold in on itself. There it is, he thought. The terrible part, that you didn't *have* to decide. That when you didn't, the decision got made for you, by inertia.

They sat beside each other on the edge of the roof without speaking, and waited for the fog to come in.

Rheinhardt paced the perimeter of the roof, faster as the energy of frustration built within him. The morning was cool, but a sweat had already broken out on his forehead, under his arms. He pulled off his sweatshirt, tossed it onto the gravel without slowing.

He could not make himself sit still at the table and work on the sculpture. Crazy, fighting himself as much as he fought the clay. Each time he stopped work on the sculpture—to put in his hours at the shop, to see Terry or Stoke, to go to a club, a party, a movie, even to eat or sleep—it was a bitch to get back to it. It took so damn much energy to bring his full concentration back to the sculpture, as if he had to somehow completely shift worlds to return to the sculpture.

So he procrastinated, just as he was doing now, pacing the roof. He found other things to do. Long walks, coffee on Haight, lost hours in used-book stores, trips to the zoo, the beach, or the buffalo pen at the other end of the park. He felt both pushed and pulled by himself—he intently avoided sitting down at the table, yet felt frustrated and depressed when he didn't work on it.

Rheinhardt stopped pacing, gazed out over the rooftops. He held out his hands, looked at them. They were trembling. That was another problem, or part of the same problem. His hands had been doing that a lot lately when he worked with the clay. For no apparent reason they would start to shake, until he had so little control he could hardly work. The shaking would eventually fade, but it always returned—if not that same work session, then the next, or the one after that.

He *knew* it wasn't neurological; he could see the

connections too clearly, the patterns of when it occurred. But that didn't mean he could do anything about it.

Rheinhardt turned, looked at the room. Through the window he could see the outline of the sculpture, the ruined building that steadily, if slowly, grew atop the rubble. There it was, what kept him going. When he *was* able to work, to sit at the table and call up the energy and concentration, Jesus Christ there was nothing like it. He became completely immersed in the work, oblivious to the world around him, wanting nothing but to work the clay, mold and mark and form it to bring something into existence from his mind and hands that he knew could not be done by anyone else.

But then there were days like today, when it was so fucking hard to do a single thing, and he was afraid, painfully afraid that he would be unable to complete it. And right now it was everything to him.

Rheinhardt walked back toward the room, started for the door, but turned away from it, shouting silently at himself. He stood next to the window, looked in at the sculpture, and began pounding on the outside wall with his fist. After two or three minutes of pounding, Rheinhardt stopped, turned and leaned his back against the wall, bent his knees and slid down into a squat, put his head in his hands. He did not move.

Justinian

Justinian stands on the rocks at the base of one of the Golden Gate Bridge towers, watching a huge luxury liner, brightly lit, plow through the dark water beneath the bridge, headed out to sea. Music, not quite covered by the shush of water swirling against the rocks, floats out from the boat, and figures move about on deck, in and out of shadow. Justinian remains on the rocks, silent and unmoving, watching until the liner is so far away the music can no longer be heard, and then continues watching, for nearly another hour, until not even a speck of light from the boat can be seen.

Justinian walked along the dark corridor on the fifth floor of a Tenderloin hotel. A single light burned at the far end of the hall. At the first two doors Justinian paused and looked closely at the scratched numbers, then continued on until he was halfway down the hall. He stopped in front of a door on the right, knocked.

Almost immediately the door opened, and a tall, thin, gray-haired man nodded at Justinian, backed away from the door. The man wore gray, baggy pants, white T-shirt, and a khaki overshirt with a black and red Lazarus patch on the shoulder. Justinian stepped in, and the man quickly closed the door behind him.

"Hello, Justinian."

"Ake."

The room was sparsely furnished—a twin bed, nightstand and lamp, a chair, a two-drawer chest. Two layers of peeling wallpaper were on the walls, the carpet was worn and stained. There were no curtains over the window.

"Why am I here, Ake?"

The tall, thin man turned away. "Minh," he said. "You can come out."

The door of the tiny closet opened, and a young Asian boy stepped out.

"This is Tay Minh," Ake said. "Minh, this is Justinian." The boy nodded, and Ake turned back to Justinian. "He's Vietnamese. Both of his parents were killed by the police, in the Nam."

"It's not 'the Nam' over there anymore, Ake."

Ake went on without pausing. "He won't tell me how he got over here, or how long he's been. A while, though, he speaks English all right." He glanced at the boy, then back at Justinian. "I found him cruising Polk

Street. He says he's fourteen, but I'd guess twelve. Word
I got, he's only been on the street, here anyway, a couple
of days, so he doesn't really know the story, just knows
it's a way to make some money." He paused. "He's a
good kid, Justinian. That's what my gut says."

Justinian nodded, looked at the boy. "Your gut's
always been good enough before, Ake."

"We turn him over to the authorities, he's back in
Vietnam next week. We let him loose, who knows
what'll happen on the street, what he'll pick up."

Justinian nodded again. "Tay Minh?"

"Yes?"

"You want to get off the streets?"

The boy shrugged. "I don't know. Maybe yes, maybe
no. Depends on where I go."

Justinian smiled faintly. "At least that's an honest
answer. Well, we'll see what we can do, Minh. It'll be
your choice, you want to stay or go, all right?"

Tay Minh looked back and forth between the two
men, then slowly nodded.

Justinian led the boy along the dim, blue-lit corridor,
then into his room, turning on the overhead light.

"For now you can stay with me," Justinian said.
"Until I figure out what to do with you."

"You live here?"

"Yes."

Minh carried a faded black duffel bag, and he swung
it against his leg as he walked about the room, glancing
at the bookcases, the walls, the furniture. Justinian
pulled two brown blankets from a crate, set them on the
overstuffed chair.

"You can sleep on the bed, I'll take the chair."

Minh nodded. He set the duffel bag on the floor
beside one of the bookcases, pulled a book from a shelf
and leafed through it.

"You read English?" Justinian asked.

"No. A few words." He put the book back, turned to
Justinian. "Bathroom?"

"All the way down to the end of the corridor, bends right." He gestured with his hand, waving it. "Second door on the left. Just a toilet."

Minh nodded, went to the door, flipped the dead bolts. He looked at Justinian for a moment, then stepped out into the corridor and closed the door.

Justinian stood in front of the pen and ink drawing of the woman sitting on crates, looking at it with unblinking eyes. He breathed deeply once, then turned away. He went to the cupboard, poured himself a half glass of bourbon, sat at the table, lit a cigarette. He sat and drank the bourbon, smoked the cigarette, gazing at the blank cement wall across from him.

The door opened, and Minh came in, closed the door and threw the dead bolts. He crossed the room, sat across from Justinian.

"Cigarette, please?" he said.

"You smoke?"

"Sure."

"You're pretty damn young. You ever think about quitting?"

"Sure. Tomorrow." He grinned.

Justinian smiled, gave him a cigarette. Minh pulled a box of wooden matches from his shirt pocket, lit one with his thumbnail, then lit the cigarette.

"I had a son once who looked a little bit like you," Justinian said. "His mother was Laotian."

"He live here, in United States?"

"He's dead. He died when he was eleven."

"And the mother?"

Justinian shrugged. "I don't know. Maybe she's alive somewhere, maybe not." He shrugged again.

When their cigarettes were gone, Justinian said, "Bed, I think. I need sleep, and you probably do too."

Minh nodded, got up, went to his duffel bag. He opened it and took out a portable radio/disc player and a couple of discs. Minh took them over to the bed, set them on the floor against the wall, changed discs, started the player. A fast-paced jazz emerged from the tiny speakers. Minh took off his shoes and pants, then got in between the sheets, lay on his back.

Justinian switched on the corner light, then turned off the overhead, bringing tangled shadows to the room. He sat in the chair, sank back into it, wrapped one of the blankets around him. Light and shadow striped his body, but his face was all in darkness.

"You sleep with that light on?" Minh asked.

"You sleep with that music on?" Justinian returned.

Minh didn't say anything more. Justinian remained motionless in the chair, eyes open.

Thirteen

Rheinhardt felt sick. The building was complete, but he didn't even want to look at it. Not for a couple of days, anyway. Put some distance, some time, between him and the sculpture. He'd have to think about getting it cast in bronze so he could work on the top section. Catarina would do it, he'd even have her do the plaster casting, he wouldn't fuck around with any of that himself. Now, though, he just couldn't stand the thought of anything related to the sculpture. He needed to get away.

Sitting on the cot, Rheinhardt didn't want to move. It wasn't physical exhaustion so much as it was the letdown from finishing this stage of the sculpture, letdown coupled with depression from doubting his ability to finish the entire piece. He didn't have much left in him.

He got up and left the room, locking the door. It was early, barely past noon, and he had to get away from the sculpture. He just had to get away.

Rheinhardt walked into Golden Gate Park, went to the Conservatory. The day was hot, a strange summer day without the hint of fog, and he knew they'd probably be misting the plants inside. Just inside the entrance, before he approached the ticket window, he stood and smelled the air, smiled. Even here he could smell the damp heat, feel it in his lungs.

He bought a ticket, and the guy who sold it to him said, "You again. I've seen you before."

Rheinhardt looked at the guy, who did seem familiar,

but he wasn't sure. He took his ticket, walked through the main entrance.

The central hub of the Conservatory was like a tiny enclosed rain forest, the glass-domed ceiling about thirty feet above. The huge, upper leaves of the taller trees brushed at the dome, casting shadows below. The air was dense with the humidity, warm and thick, gently laying a thin coating of moisture on his face.

A dirt path wound through the vegetation, a short run; the cluster of tropical trees and plants was relatively small, but their density and height gave the section a much larger feel.

Rheinhardt walked halfway along the dirt path. Checking to see that no one was around, he stepped off the path and pushed into the dense undergrowth at the base of the trees. Someday, he thought, he'd climb the trees, find a roost high in the branches.

He crawled silently through the broad-leafed plants and ferns, then squatted with his back against the twisting roots of a tree, completely hidden from both the path and the tiled walk that ringed the hub.

A quiet hissing sounded from above. Rheinhardt tilted his head back, gazed up through the foliage, and through small openings saw the misters spraying a delicate cloud of water upon the trees, watched the mist drift down toward him, collect on leaves, drip in heavier drops to other leaves or the damp, rich earth beside him. He sat without moving, then closed his eyes, and tried to clear his mind of all thoughts, searching for some kind of peace. But though he knew he would remain here for hours, he knew also that peace was something he was not going to find.

Terry stood in front of "Placebo Effect," looking at the black and white photograph, the last one remaining on the wall of Deever's Place. Behind her, Wendy was carefully wrapping and packing the other photographs. One of the smaller galleries on Grant Street was going to display the photographs for at least two weeks, maybe longer if the response was any good; Terry and Wendy were due there with the photographs that afternoon.

"I want to buy this," Terry said.

Wendy came up, stood beside her. "I've got other prints," she said. "I'll mat one, give it to you for nothing. You deserve it, all the help you've given me."

Terry shook her head. "No, I can afford it, and I want to buy it. Whatever price you end up putting on it in the gallery, that's what I'll pay."

"Half that," Wendy said. "The gallery gets a fifty percent commission, and we won't be dealing through them."

"Sure, but you ought to get part of that anyway. Say seventy-five percent of the gallery price."

"Sixty percent."

Terry turned, smiled, put out her hand. "Deal."

Wendy took Terry's hand, then pulled Terry to her, gave her a hug. "Deal," she said. She eased back. "Come on, let's get it wrapped up so we can go."

Terry carefully raised the picture and handed it to Wendy, who took it to the table with the others.

Deever came in from the back room, coughing harshly for a few moments, half a burning cigarette in his hand.

"Empty walls," he said between coughs. "I hope they don't stay that way for long."

"Does that mean I can put up more from Warehouse people?" Terry asked.

"Sure. On one condition." Then Deever shook his head. "Scratch that," he said. "No conditions, the walls are yours." He dropped the cigarette to the floor, crushed it with his shoe. "I do have a favor to ask, though."

"Go ahead."

"Minh," Deever called over his shoulder. "Come on out here."

A young Asian boy stepped out from the back room, stood at Deever's side.

"This is Tay Minh," Deever said. "Minh, this is Terry Cassini. An old friend."

Terry and Minh shook hands, the boy nodding.

"Minh's Vietnamese," Deever went on. "Parents dead or missing. He's in-country illegally. A friend found him hustling on Polk, felt the boy was a good kid, worth helping out. Brought him to another friend, who brought him to me. Last couple days he's been staying here, helping out a bit, but that's temporary." Deever shrugged. "I need to live alone. So Minh needs a place to stay, food. I was wondering if you might be able to find enough work for him around the Warehouse, odd jobs, like that, in return for a place to sleep, something to eat. Just enough to get by."

"A kid his age should be in school."

Deever sighed. "What are we going to do? Turn him over to the city people? They won't do anything."

"Except deport him."

"Exactly. *That* he doesn't need."

"You don't want to go back to Vietnam?" Terry asked Minh.

"No, no fucking way. I want to stay here, be American, buy American."

Terry smiled. "You a good kid, like Deever's friend said?"

"Sure." Minh grinned. "What should I say, I'm a mean fucker?"

Terry laughed, looked at Deever. "All right, I'll see what I can do. For now we can put him up, at least for a few days. How's that sound to you, Minh?"

"Sounds, sure. I'll work, too."

Terry nodded. "We'll see about that. And I'll think about what we might be able to do to get him into school somewhere."

"Thanks, Terry," Deever said. "I appreciate it."

"I appreciate everything you've done for us, Deever."

He nodded. "Sure, but do it for him, not for me."

"For both of you," she said. "And you, Minh, you

can start right now, help us take those pictures out to the van. And be very careful."

Minh nodded, went to the table, where Wendy placed one of the wrapped pictures in his arms. Terry turned back to Deever, but he was already headed for the back door. She hurried after him, put her hand on his shoulder as he opened the door.

"I'll take care of him," she said. "Though I'd bet he's probably pretty good at taking care of himself."

"He *is* a good kid."

"We'll see, Deever." She smiled.

He nodded once, then turned and started slowly up the wooden steps.

"What is this place?" Minh asked.

"The Warehouse," Terry answered. But what would that mean to him? Nothing.

They'd come here after delivering Wendy and her photographs to the gallery, driving onto the lot as dusk fell, around the buildings and down the cement ramp to the underground loading dock where they parked the van, pulled the shelter over it. Then they'd climbed the ramp, hiked back around to the front entrance, and now stood before it.

"A warehouse?" Minh asked.

"No. Well, yes, once it was, probably. Not anymore. Now . . ." Now *what?* "Now it's a kind of artist colony." That wasn't quite right either. "Well, it's not a formal colony or anything. On paper—for the city, the state, the feds—we don't even exist. We'd sure as hell be illegal if we did. City health codes, at least. Not to mention zoning." She shook her head. "Artists with no money, they come and live here free of charge, work on their art. It's kind of a street colony, part of an underground, radical art movement."

"Do people know you're here? That people are here?"

Terry nodded. "Sure. It's not *really* a secret. We're not common knowledge to the public, but people do know about us. They just ignore us. The company that owns this land, the building—it's called Solinex—they know, of course, and they let us stay. They take a nice tax loss on this property. They even leave the utilities hooked up for us, as long as we get regular cash payments to them under the table. I think utilities all get metered out of other properties they own around here, so they write it all off anyway." She turned, pointed to a partially lit building down one of the side streets, a block from the Warehouse. "That place, for one. There are a couple of others, I think. They probably make a profit from us." She looked at Minh, smiled. "Do you understand any of what I'm rambling about?"

He shrugged, grinned. "Not really. A little. Artists are living and working here, and they're not supposed to, but nobody really cares too much."

Terry looked intently at him, then turned away. She didn't like the sound of what he'd said. It gave her a strange, uncomfortable feeling in her gut.

"But what about the money?" Minh asked. "You said you had to give money to some people, and money for food and stuff."

She nodded, still looking away from him, out over the cracked asphalt. "Sure, and money for musical equipment, supplies, computers, recording equipment, and stupid fucking radios." She sighed. "There are people who think art is important, people with money. We do have a lot of sources, surprisingly. A lot of money comes from people who you'd think wouldn't . . ." She didn't finish, feeling odd. "Well, we get by okay." She turned and looked at him again. "So, you want to come in, be a part of all this?"

"I don't know. Where else can I go?"

Terry smiled. "Good question." She put her arm over Minh's shoulder. "Let's go on in, see what we can do for you."

She opened the main door, and they entered.

Fourteen

Rheinhardt dragged the large boxes of scrap metal out from under shelves, pulled out the long, narrow rods and strips of metal he thought he might use, pulled out the rods of filler, laid it all out on the workbench. Four holes had already been drilled into the bench top, marking the dimensions of the structure so it would fit into the top of the bronze section of the sculpture. He unlocked the cabinets and rolled out the tool chest, opened it and removed some of the tools—files, metal brush, clamps, wire-cutters and pliers, chipping hammer. Finally he wheeled over the gas cylinders and hoses and torches, set them up in front of the workbench.

Rheinhardt stood beside the welding equipment for a minute, breathing deeply, looking at the tools and metal. Calm down a bit, he told himself. Keep yourself under control here.

Moving more slowly and deliberately now, Rheinhardt put on the dark, heavy work apron, gloves, headcover, and goggles. He placed four steel rods in the holes drilled into the bench, then picked up another steel rod to use as a cross-beam, clamped it between two of the verticals.

Satisfied, he picked up the mixer, opened the acetylene valve, punched the striker at the tip, and the flame sprang to life.

Rheinhardt walked into Mommy Fortuna's on Haight, sat at the only empty table in the place, near the window. The restaurant was small, half a dozen booths, half a dozen tables, a short counter, hanging plants everywhere. It looked like a dump, but the food was good; most of the time there was a wait for tables.

He had asked Terry to meet him here, and surprisingly he was here before she was. He ordered coffee and told the waiter he was waiting for someone.

Terry came in a few minutes later with a young Asian boy. She slid into the chair across from Rheinhardt, and the boy sat between them. Rheinhardt took the boy's hand, shook it.

"My name's Rheinhardt. You Terry's new boyfriend?"

The boy nodded. "Tay Minh," he said. "Yes, Terry's new boyfriend. Want me to find you a new girlfriend?"

Rheinhardt smiled, turned to Terry. "Kid's a smartass. Where'd you find him?"

Terry told him about Deever, Minh's background, what little she actually knew.

"So you're staying in the Warehouse?" Rheinhardt asked. Minh nodded. "You like it there?"

Minh shrugged. "Sure, why not?"

Rheinhardt shrugged in return. "Yeah, why not? How about pancakes? You like pancakes?"

Minh seemed confused at first, then slowly nodded.

"Best pancakes in the city here," Rheinhardt said. "My recommendation."

Minh slowly nodded again, looked at Terry, still apparently somewhat confused.

"Give the kid a break," she told Rheinhardt.

"It's true, they *are* the best pancakes in the city."

"Not that," Terry said.

The waiter came, ending the discussion, and they ordered breakfast—pancakes and bacon for Rheinhardt, pancakes and sausage and bacon for Minh (the kid could eat), a Barbara Fortuna omelette for Terry.

"You look tired," Terry said to Rheinhardt.

He nodded. "I am. Worn out. Just finished the main part of my new piece a few days ago, it's being cast now."

"Bronze?" Rheinhardt nodded. "Catarina doing it?"

"Yes. I had her do the plaster casting as well, didn't want to fuck around with it myself. I did the final retouches on the plaster yesterday, and she'll be doing the bronze casting as soon as she has a chance."

"But it's just part of it?"

"Yeah, you could call it mixed media, I guess. Only about two-thirds will be bronze. The rest will be . . . different."

"I'm a sculptor too," Minh put in.

Rheinhardt turned to him and smiled. "Yeah?"

Minh nodded. He slid a backpack out from under his chair, opened it, and took out a long, twisted piece of driftwood. He held it out to Rheinhardt. "It's a snake."

Rheinhardt took the wood, turned it, looked closely at it from all perspectives. To his surprise, it *was* a snake. Minh had carved the head in great detail, crudely in some parts, but otherwise nicely done, including eyes, nostrils, an open mouth with a suggestion of fangs and tongue. The tail had been tapered, and some sections of the main trunk had been shaved so the snake's body was of fairly uniform thickness. Rheinhardt handed the snake back to Minh.

"You *are* a sculptor," he said.

Minh smiled, and put the snake away.

The food arrived, and Minh started eating immediately, stuffing large chunks of pancake into his mouth. Rheinhardt watched him for a moment, then looked at Terry who smiled and shrugged. "He's only been at the Warehouse a week," she said. "I think he's still making up for his days on the streets."

Minh looked up, mouth full of pancake and sausage. He managed to swallow, then said, "What?"

Terry shook her head, smiling. "Nothing." Minh looked at each of them, then resumed eating. Terry turned to Rheinhardt. "You said you wanted to talk to me about something."

Rheinhardt nodded. "I wanted to warn you. I'm going to be pretty isolated for a while, you probably won't see much of me. I've just started the last part of the sculpture, and you know how I get toward the end of a project."

"Yeah, you get impossible." Terry smiled. "All right, I stand warned. What about your job with Bear?"

"I'm only going to work another couple days, then I'm taking off until I'm finished."

"I suppose that means you won't want to be disturbed."

"If you do, it had better be damn important."

"All right," she said, nodding. "Got it."

Rheinhardt turned to look at Minh, was stunned to see the boy's plate completely empty.

"Jesus Christ, Terry, the Warehouse is going to need a hefty increase in the food budget with this guy."

Minh looked up and grinned at him, and Rheinhardt grinned back. Then the boy's grin instantly faded as the hollow thrump of a dragoncub sounded from above the street, muted by the glass windows. Minh began to tremble, and hunkered down in his seat, leaning back from the window as if afraid of being seen by the dragoncub.

"Minh, what is it?" Terry asked.

Minh shook his head, face twisting. "God dammit metal monster," he whispered.

Then he turned and threw his arms around Terry, burying his head in her chest. Rheinhardt, feeling helpless, watched Terry hold onto Minh as the young boy began to violently shake and cry.

Filler rods melted and flowed, flame burned a hot-cool blue and white, metal glowed and swirled and melded with other metal. Thin, rigid poles rose vertically, sometimes bent and broken, narrow cross-beams webbed a network supporting the verticals, and shards of metal flared in all directions. Sweat flowed beneath glass and metal and fabric, dripped to the ground.

The structure grew.

The sky was clear, the sun high, the day almost hot. Taking a break for some exercise to work out the kinks, Rheinhardt emerged from the apartment building to find Stoke sitting on the bottom porch step.

"So," Rheinhardt said. "Back from L.A."

Stoke nodded. "Yeah, fuckin' L.A." He stood, brushed off his jumpsuit. "Talked to Terry, she said you were in your 'Do Not Disturb' mode, so I thought I'd just hang out until you came up for air. Where you off to?"

"Just going for a walk. Come along, if you want."

They walked up to Haight, then headed west. With the good weather, the sidewalks were crowded, street traffic heavy.

"Aren't you going to ask me how L.A. was?" Stoke asked.

"No."

"I couldn't believe it," Stoke said, ignoring him. "A fuckin' sleaze pit. I mean, I know I have a tendency to overindulge once in a while, but shit. I saw more drugs in two weeks down there than I have up here in a year. And it wasn't just drugs. Man, Rheinhardt, there are a lot of sick people down there. Shit, weird sex is a goddamn spectator sport, I could hardly believe what I was fuckin' seeing. And weird new things, they like to try them. Something called spinal plugs, some people had, jacking into each other or something. And these things called electro-collars, giving themselves a jolt of electricity. And young girls, Jesus Christ, I think eleven and twelve is maybe just a little bit too fucking young."

"Even for you?"

"Even for me. Shit, you know me better than that, Rheinhardt."

"I told you I didn't like the people down there."

"Yeah. I mean I know *everyone* isn't like that, but

shit, sometimes it seemed like almost everyone I saw
for two weeks was fucked up one way or another, and a
lot worse than me. Tell you, I seemed pretty fucking
normal and straight compared to some of those people.
At least I have *some* sense of values."

"You don't need to go on about it, Stoke. I know what
it's like, and I don't particularly want to hear the
gruesome details."

"Yeah, well, I tell you, it depressed the hell out of
me."

"I can imagine."

"Yeah."

They walked for a while without speaking.
Rheinhardt thought about his cousin Tracy who, when
she was living just outside L.A., used to let some guy
she didn't even like fuck her in the ass so he'd shoot her
up with free speed. She was lucky she hadn't ended up
dead.

"You were wrong about one thing," Stoke said.

"Yeah?"

"I did a *lot* of thinking about the army while I was
down there. I got so fucking depressed I'd just about
decided I might as well just go in, it made about as
much sense as anything."

After a long silence, Rheinhardt finally asked, "*Did*
you decide to go in?"

Stoke shook his head and grinned. "Nah. It was just a
temporary bout of insanity. I'm back to normal again,
which means I'm back to having no idea *what* the hell
I'm going to do."

"And back to being afraid?" Rheinhardt asked.

Stoke's grin disappeared, and after a few moments of
silence he nodded.

So am I, Rheinhardt thought. Of different things, but
so am I.

Rheinhardt held the small flame to the clear piece of
glass, the glass held in tongs held by a gloved hand; he
held flame and glass just above one of the lattice

structure's horizontal crossbars. The tip of the glass, glowing red now, began to droop slightly. He kept the flame on the tip, watched the glass slowly drip toward the metal, make contact, flow sluggishly around it. He gradually pulled back the glass, the large droplet breaking free at the flame, then ran the flame back and forth over the bit of molten glass now clinging to the metal. The glass continued to flow, started to drip from the metal rod, and just before it threatened to melt completely free and drop, Rheinhardt pulled back the flame.

As the glass cooled, Rheinhardt cut the flame, set burner and tongs on the bench. He sat back, looking at a tiny, transparent icicle of glass. Yes, that's what he wanted. Rheinhardt picked up tongs and glass, refired the flame, then brought flame and glass together again.

Fifteen

Sparks flew in the darkness, bouncing lightly off horizontal rods, off Rheinhardt's gloves and mask, floating gently to the ground. Light flickered, reflecting off metal and glass, splitting into tiny rainbows, casting thin, elongated shadows in all directions.

The sculpture, and Rheinhardt, stretched up and toward the night sky . . . and nearly reached it.

Rotation date was coming up. Terry sat in the cramped office, reviewing the requests from those Warehouse artists whose terms were due to end and who wanted extensions. Ten of the fourteen due to leave wanted to stay, and most of them didn't deserve to, as far as she was concerned. She had only one vote out of three, though, and with Richmond and Belsen holding the other two . . . shit, most of them would end up staying.

Don Kaspar bothered her most, probably. A multi-media painter, Don had a lot of potential when he came to the Warehouse. Terry had thought he was right on the edge, ready to make a breakthrough into some truly original, innovative work, needing only the opportunity to work with complete freedom to make that final step. Instead, within two or three months of moving into the Warehouse, he had stopped painting entirely. Four months later, when he started working again, he had taken to throwing balloons of paint at large canvases from across the studio, an approach that had become faddish again. The only change Don had made since then was to start randomly pinning the balloons of paint to a canvas, backing the canvas with plywood, then throwing darts at it, bursting the paint balloons and riddling the canvas with tiny holes. Sometimes he removed the broken balloons, sometimes he left them. And the paintings? They looked like shit, but several art magazines had done pieces on him, and he'd sold some of the paintings for decent money. Now he wanted to extend his free ride.

Well, one vote against him from me, Terry decided. Whatever that was worth. Maybe if he was out on his own again something would happen. Sure.

There was a knock at the door. "Yes," she said. The door opened, and Carlton stepped in.

"Andrea's on the radio, calling from the East Bay annex. She wanted to talk to Rheinhardt, didn't know he'd moved out. Said she'd talk to you instead."

"What about?"

"Wouldn't say."

"All right. I'll be right there."

Carlton left, and Terry put the extension requests away, got up from her desk and started for the radio room.

Radio room. She shook her head at the thought. The radio had been another of Richmond and Belsen's defective brainstorms. When the Warehouse got access to a small, abandoned office building a year ago in Emeryville, just outside of Oakland, they set up about twenty East Bay artists in it. Since there were no phones in either building, and no way of getting any lines, Richmond and Belsen decided, in order to maintain communications between the two buildings, to acquire two large, powerful radio transceivers. That way, they reasoned as they outlined their plans to Terry (just before overruling her objections), not only would the two buildings be able to stay in touch with one another, they would be able to coordinate special trans-bay exhibitions that would require communications between the two sides of the bay. Finally, they had the idea that eventually they might be able to add equipment and power to the transceivers, find someone who knew about radio broadcasting, and then jam radio station transmissions, substituting their own to get airplay for the Warehouse musicians. Nothing like that had ever developed, of course, nor had there ever been any "trans-bay" exhibitions, and what they had, essentially, was an incredibly expensive communications setup that was hardly ever used. A complete waste.

The radio room, converted from a small storeroom, was dark except for the glow of the radio displays and the small lamp beside the radio. Carlton sat in one chair, and as Terry sat in the other he handed her a set of headphones, which she placed over her ears. Carlton flicked a switch, pushed the mike toward her, said, "It's all yours." He remained next to her with his own headphones, listening.

"Hello, Andrea? This is Terry."

"Hi, Terry." Her voice was clear and loud. "Rheinhardt's not there anymore, Carlton says."

"He moved out a few months ago. Surprised you hadn't heard."

"I keep pretty much to myself over here. They call me the Emeryville Hermit. Why did he move out?"

"I don't know. Ask him yourself."

There was a brief silence, then Andrea said, "Oh." The silence (not a silence, actually, but a wordless, quiet hiss) resumed.

"Why did you call, Andrea?" Terry asked.

"I wanted to tell Rheinhardt about Gollancz. You know him?"

"Not really. Rheinhardt's mentioned him a couple of times. I've never met him."

"Well, he and Rheinhardt have known each other a lot of years. I guess they were in the army around the same time."

"What is it?"

"He's in the hospital."

"What for?"

"Neurological problems. He's really screwed up, tremors real bad, partial paralysis in his legs, can't hardly talk most of the time. Bad news, bad news."

"What happened? Some kind of disorder?"

"Yeah, disorder all right. Coffin drugs. Apparently he got some really bad stuff with strippers. Probably they won't be able to do anything for him."

"Jesus."

"Yeah. Would you tell Rheinhardt for me? I figure he might want to know."

"Sure. What hospital is he in?"

"Highland General over here."

"Okay, I'll make sure Rheinhardt gets the message. And thanks for giving a call."

"Yeah. Well. I'll see you, Terry."

"Sure. Good-bye." Two clicks sounded, and the transmission ended.

A small sign was tacked to Rheinhardt's door, with dark block letters: DO NOT DISTURB, FOR ANYTHING. Terry stood in front of the door, staring at the sign. The sign meant exactly what it said. No one, and not for anything. She couldn't knock, she couldn't even go around and look into the window or check the lean-to, or he'd get mad as all hell. There probably were a few things she *would* disturb him for, but this wasn't one of them.

Terry continued to stare at the sign. She didn't know when she'd be able to talk to him. He never had put a phone in, just for this reason.

She felt vaguely depressed, wasn't sure why. She took a notebook and pen from her bag, knelt beside the room, and wrote on the first blank page:

R,

Got a call from Andrea. Gollancz's in Highland General, fucked up bad from some stripper drugs.

Maybe you should go see him? I'd like to see you myself. You know where you can reach me.

Love,

T

She folded the sheet of paper, wrote RHEINHARDT on the outside, then wedged it between door and door frame, resting it on the knob. She stood without moving, listening, but heard nothing she could identify. Even the city seemed unusually quiet. Terry turned, went to the trapdoor in the roof, and started down.

Sixteen

A mound of rubble in black bronze. The ruins of a tall,
multistoried building, also in black bronze, rising from
the rubble. Finally, rising from the ruined building, a
skeletal, latticelike structure of various metals, jagged
and twisting, black/brown/copper/silver/rust, dull and
shiny and flecked with melted glass.

"The Winter Gantry."

The bronze mound rose gradually at first, then
steeply to the plateau; a collection of dirt, rock, broken
concrete, charred timbers, shattered ceramics and
glass, wrecked machinery and automobiles.

The building that rose from the plateau had been
constructed of brick and concrete, with glass windows
now cracked and shattered, the brick and concrete
chipped and marred, disfigured; vague hints of interior
destruction could be glimpsed through the windows.
Several stories up, the building ended at a jagged line of
shattered concrete, the ruined floor of that level serving
as an incomplete roof, marked with remnants of walls,
plumbing, elevator shafts.

A skeleton of metal, like a rocket gantry, rose nearly
as high from the upper ruins of the building just as the
building rose from the rubble, the skeleton peaking
with solitary vertical shoots of twisted metal, charred
and split. The horizontal strands of wire and metal
were dusted with glass snow and dripping glass icicles
that reflected light in pale, twinkling colors from different angles, sparkling.

Barely able to stand, he was so exhausted,

Rheinhardt gazed at the finished sculpture, filled with both painful exhilaration and despair. It was *good*, he felt certain of that; more than good, perhaps the finest sculpture he had ever done. But he felt just as certain that it was the last work of worth he would ever create. It had taken so much out of him, *too* much, and he felt there was nothing left.

For weeks now it had taken all his energy and strength to fight everything that strived to inhibit him, to fight everything that threatened to block the creative processes. He did not know exactly what he'd fought against—the outside world? his own sense of futility? —but the forces had been there constantly, never letting up, leaching every bit of his strength and energy until now; and now that he had managed to somehow finish the piece, he was totally drained.

"The Winter Gantry."

Rheinhardt stood gazing at it, exhilarated at what he saw before him, knowing he had created it himself, flushed with an incredible sense of accomplishment. And he stood gazing at it, sick with despair at his future, desperately afraid he would never create again. He felt both incredibly full, and completely empty.

"The Winter Gantry."

Rheinhardt remained motionless, gazing at it, felt the hollow despair rising and swelling in his chest, and silently began to cry.

Initial Descent

Seventeen

Rheinhardt and Terry walked into the Carlatti Gallery on Sutter Street, made their way toward the center of the room, and stopped in front of the showcase piece—"The Winter Gantry." Two other people, a man and woman in business suits, were looking at the sculpture, and another half dozen people wandered through the gallery, looking at the sculptures, paintings, drawings.

"Nice piece of work," Terry said.

The man and woman turned to her, faces expressionless, and didn't say anything at first. Then the woman, plucking at lint on her jacket, ventured, "It's a bit grim, don't you think?"

"Grim?" Terry said.

Rheinhardt stepped back and remained silent, content to watch. He felt certain Terry would provoke them.

"Yes," the woman replied. "Grim. Just look at it, the whole thing is in a state of deterioration. I get the impression the artist, Rheinhardt I guess is his name, is implying that contemporary society as a whole is in a state of deterioration."

Rheinhardt smiled to himself, still said nothing.

"Isn't it?" Terry said to the woman.

"*I* don't think so."

"Nor do I," put in the woman's companion.

"Maybe the artist sees it that way," Terry said.

"Then I guess I'm not really interested in seeing his warped perception of the world," the woman replied. "I'd rather see something real."

"This *is* real," Terry said, voice hardening.

"Look," the man said. "No reason to get into an argument. You like it, we don't, that's all there is."

"Right," Terry went on. "No point having any kind of intelligent discussion about it, no point having any discussion at all."

"Personally, I think it's a piece of shit," Rheinhardt finally said.

Terry, the man and woman, all turned to face him, but nobody said anything. Rheinhardt shrugged.

"Just my opinion," he said.

The man and woman casually retreated without another word, turned to look at a series of watercolors on the far wall.

"Why did you say that?" Terry asked.

"I don't know. Your 'discussion' with them wasn't accomplishing anything. Thought I'd cut it short."

Before Terry had a chance to respond, Carlatti, the gallery owner, came out of the back room and headed toward them, a folder in his hand. He was a thin, well-dressed man, hair almost completely gray. "Hello, Rheinhardt," he said. "Terry."

Rheinhardt glanced at the man and woman, who had turned to look at him.

"Hello, Carlatti," he said. He smiled at the old Italian. Carlatti was about the only gallery owner he trusted, the only one he knew who really seemed to care more about art than money. And he was the only gallery owner who had ever shown Rheinhardt's work.

Carlatti handed the folder to him. "Clippings of the reviews the piece has received. Quite a range. The one on top I thought would interest you in particular."

Rheinhardt opened the folder, Terry moving to his side and reading over his shoulder. The first clipping was from a new city weekly that had been growing in circulation, influence, and prestige among Bay Area conservatives in the last year. The article dealt with several galleries and shows, and Carlatti had marked the relevant section:

Now on display at the Carlatti Gallery on Sutter
Street is the newest work from the local sculptor
who goes by the single name of Rheinhardt.
Earlier works by Rheinhardt, such as "Swimming
Horses," "The Nuclear Garden," and "Three
Smooth Body Transfers," all bronzes currently on
display at Carlatti's as well, showed a promising
talent that often dangerously straddled the fine
line between art and propaganda. With his newest
work, "The Winter Gantry," a mixed-media
sculpture of bronze and welded scrap (or should I
say "crap"?), he has crossed the line completely,
letting a political message take unbridled control
and leaving nearly all artistic virtues lost in its
wake.

The sculpture (see photo) consists of a partially
destroyed office building rising from a hill of
rubble, the building in turn capped by a bizarre,
skeletonlike structure of scrap metal decorated
with bits of glass. Taken with the title, the piece is
clearly a highly critical attack of our current
administration's foreign and military policies,
implying quite emphatically (and quite wrongly, I
might add) that these policies will lead to the
destruction of civilization through nuclear war.

The word "Winter" in the title clearly refers to
the so-called nuclear winter; and "Gantry," from
rocket gantries, is surely a reference to what the
artist sees as the militarization of space. The
melted glass on the upper structure has the appearance of snow and icicles, the melted glass
bringing the connection right back to nuclear war,
a recurring image of which has often been fused
sand or glass.

The bleakness, utter and unrelenting, makes the
message clear—the current policies of defense,
arms buildup, and the militarization of space will
lead inevitably to the destruction of all civilization. Unfortunately, not only is the message terri-

bly wrong and misguided, the artist has resorted
to clubbing us over the head with the message,
subsuming the artistic virtues latent, but unre-
alized, in the sculpture.

Rheinhardt clearly has raw talent, but just as
clearly it is not yet under control; Rheinhardt the
polemicist is in control here, not Rheinhardt the
artist. Hopefully he will mature, and his future
work will eschew politics, and embrace art instead.

"Who the hell is this guy?" Rheinhardt asked. "And
where the hell does he come up with this crap? Does he
seriously believe this is my approach to my work, that I
created this with all those supposed messages in
mind?"

Carlatti shrugged. "Who knows? He's a man with a
hidden agenda. Or maybe not so hidden. He uses
anything for a political forum."

"Just what he's accused *me* of."

Carlatti shrugged again. "If nothing else, he will call
much attention to your work. Already has. We've had a
lot of people in here to look at it after reading his piece.
Even have several offers to buy it."

"Really?"

Carlatti nodded. "I told them what you said, that it's
not necessarily for sale, but that I would pass on all
offers to you. The names and figures are on a notesheet
under the reviews."

Rheinhardt looked under the clippings, found the
typed sheet, put it on top. The offers were in the $1,000
to $2,500 range, except the last, which was for $10,000.

"Ten thousand dollars?" Rheinhardt was dumb-
founded. He'd never sold a sculpture, what few he *had*
sold, for more than $1,200.

Carlatti sighed. "If I were a better businessman, I'd
say take it, but I don't think you want to sell it to him.
He told me, 'off the record,' that he would be willing to
go higher if necessary. He also told me he wanted to

buy it so badly because it was a dangerously subversive piece of propaganda and he wanted to make sure it got destroyed. He thought I would understand."

Rheinhardt didn't say anything for a while, a numbing sensation spreading through his chest. He turned from Carlatti and looked at "The Winter Gantry." The numbness continued to spread, almost an ache, made his breath feel heavy and slow.

"No," he finally said. "I guess I don't want to sell it to him." He turned back to Carlatti. "I don't think I'd better sell it at all."

Rheinhardt hated hospitals. As he and Terry walked along the bright corridor (a nurse padding quickly down one way, a second hurrying down the other, and half a dozen visitors and patients moving slowly up and down the hall), he could feel the beginnings of a panic attack set in—a flushed heat rising in his head, a cramping in his gut, a cold sweat breaking out on forehead and palms and forearms. He wondered if there was a name for hospital phobia; must be, they had names for everything. It was the smell that did it, reminding him of medics and dustoffs and friends dying. Hospitals had never bothered him before the army; now, they did this to him.

"Here's the room," Terry said.

They turned into a small room with three beds, hardly enough space to walk between them. A single TV in the middle of the wall was on, and the patients in the first two beds wore plastic earphones, faces turned toward it. One was a young woman, her face puffy and bruised, her lips ringed with sores, her arms also dotted with sores and deep scrape marks. In the middle bed was a gaunt older man with pasty skin whose hands twisted and clasped at themselves; he stared fixedly at the television screen. In the third bed was Gollancz.

Rheinhardt had put off coming, hoping Gollancz would recover so Rheinhardt could avoid the hospital. But Gollancz wasn't getting any better. The doctors still hadn't been able to figure out exactly what strippers had been in the drugs he'd taken, and still didn't know the full extent of neurological damage.

They made their way past the first two beds to Gollancz's, by the window. His eyes were closed, but most of his body was trembling, especially his fingers; even his head periodically jerked from side to side, almost as if he was having a bad dream. Actually, Rheinhardt thought, his *life* had become a nightmare.

Rheinhardt squeezed between wall and bed, lightly touched Gollancz's shoulder. "Paul," he whispered. "Paul, it's me, Rheinhardt."

Gollancz didn't open his eyes. Rheinhardt stayed at the side of the bed, breathing slowly and deeply, trying to remain calm. There was something familiar about the way Gollancz looked, the way he trembled; it reminded him of someone . . . but who? He tugged at Gollancz's shoulder, called his name a little louder.

"I wouldn't bother." The woman in the first bed.

Rheinhardt turned. The woman was looking at them, the earphones off.

"I wouldn't bother," the woman said again. "He won't be waking up for a while."

"Why not?" Rheinhardt asked.

"He was having some kind of convulsions or something a little while ago, bangin' all around that bed somethin' awful. So the nurses and a doctor came in, gave him a jab of something, put him out. It's real calmed out now, the shaking."

"Do you know what started the convulsions?" Terry asked.

The woman shook her head. "Nothin'. He was watching TV with the rest of us, me and ol' zombie here." She pointed at the man in the middle bed, who hadn't moved at all. "It just happened. The TV show was bad, but it warn't *that* bad." She laughed. "This show's a lot worse." With that she laughed again, turned to the TV, and put the earphones back on.

Rheinhardt stared at Gollancz, bits of memory clicking into place. Gunther. That's who Gollancz reminded him of, Gunther in the field hospital at night, lying by the window, twitching. Rheinhardt had been with him for an hour, and Gunther hadn't said a word. Then clouds had parted and bright moonlight had streamed in through the window, lighting up Gunther's crushed face. "*Mondlicht*," Gunther had said. Then, not another word. In the morning he was dead.

Terry looked at Rheinhardt, raised an eyebrow. "You want to stay awhile, see if he comes around?"

"Not really. I'd rather come back another time. You know me and hospitals."

Terry nodded. Rheinhardt touched Gollancz's arm again, squeezed back out, then they left the room.

Leaving the hospital, they got turned around and ended up coming out through Emergency. Rheinhardt was getting a little panicky again with the heavy smells, and the place was in chaos. Two guards were stationed on either side of the registration nurse and cashier, who sat behind a window of wire-mesh glass. All of the chairs and benches were occupied, most of those waiting obviously from off the streets. Half the people in the Emergency room had tracked arms, and even the necks on several of them were covered with needle marks. The stink of the people almost overwhelmed the hospital smells.

Before Rheinhardt and Terry could get out, two cops came in through the big double doors, dragging a shabbily dressed man between them. The man was unconscious, bleeding from the forehead, his feet dragging along the linoleum; his head rolled from side to side as the cops pulled him along.

One of the techs came out, told the cops the nurse had been called and was on the way, and the cops stopped near the corridor entrance, trying to hold the man up on his feet. The man groaned, his eyes blinked open a couple of times, and just as the nurse came through the door, the man jerked forward and vomited across the floor, spraying it everywhere.

"Jesus fucking Christ!" the nurse said. "Not another one."

Rheinhardt turned away, starting to feel really queasy, and hurried out the doors, not waiting for Terry. Outside, he kept on down the walk until he reached a wooden bench, then sat on it and breathed deeply, trying to get the fresh air into his lungs.

By the time Terry sat beside him, his stomach had settled, the sweating had stopped, and he was feeling better.

"Nice place," Terry said. "You okay?"

"I've been better." He breathed deeply once more. "But yeah, I'm okay." He tried smiling at her. "You should have seen me in a field hospital. It's the smells, really. Blood I can handle, but those smells." He shook his head, stood up. "Thanks for coming with me."

Terry nodded, got up, and they started down the street.

Hands trembling slightly, Rheinhardt unwrapped one of the blocks of clay on the worktable, set the plastic aside. He picked up the clay, immediately dropped it.

Useless. Even if he could work with it, could keep the shaking under control, he had nothing to create. His mind had become a conceptual vacuum, without the slightest hint of an image, without the vaguest outline of form. He had nothing he could do with the clay, he had nowhere to go.

Rheinhardt tried to put everything except the clay out of his thoughts, but it was impossible. He kept thinking about the Emergency room at Oakland County, and the woman in the gallery who did not want to be exposed to a perception of the world different from her own. And then there was that typed sheet of offers on "The Winter Gantry," with that insane figure—$10,000—at the bottom. Ten thousand dollars offered by a man so he could take the sculpture and destroy it.

Rheinhardt made a fist with his right hand, swung it

down onto the clay, denting it. Didn't much matter if
he never created another sculpture again, did it? No
one wanted to see what he had to offer, so what was the
fucking point? He pounded at the clay again, and again
and again, then picked it up and slammed it down onto
the table.

He stood, backed quickly away from the table, paced
around the room, frustration building within his chest,
rising from his gut. He stopped finally, and once more
held out his hands. They were still shaking.

Rheinhardt brought the left hand to his mouth, bit
firmly into the webbing between thumb and finger,
harder until the pain shot through it in jagged waves,
then pulled his hand away and looked at it. It continued
to shake.

Eighteen

Rheinhardt and Terry sat on the roof of his room, watching cars burn in the middle of the street below them, a crowd of people gathered on the sidewalks. Occasionally someone would throw something new into the fire.

"There are times when I'd like to move out of the city," Rheinhardt said. "Move up into the mountains or to a tiny coastal town. There are a lot of small, isolated towns along the northern coast, Oregon and Washington. Retreat and live like a hermit, get away from people, away from this fucked up world." He gazed at the fire, the flames whipping about in a gusting breeze.

"But I can't," he went on. "I just can't walk away from it all. I *know* it's fucked up, and I'm convinced that most people are fucked up as well, but . . . I don't know, maybe this doesn't make any sense to you, but it's *knowing* it that keeps me from walking away. To me it would be . . . sticking my head in the sand. I can't do that. I have to stay *in* the world, live inside it, and do what I can."

"Do what you can."

"Yes."

"Which is?"

He shrugged, held out his hands, slowly turning them over. "Sculpt."

There was a long silence, then Terry said, "You really think you can change the world through art?"

"Don't you? There must be some reason you put so much into keeping the Warehouse going."

"I'm asking *you*, Rheinhardt."

Rheinhardt breathed deeply once, shook his head slowly from side to side. "I don't know if I want to try explaining that one, how I feel about it. Not sure I can anyway." He looked at her. "Funny, that we've never really talked about this before."

Terry shrugged. "Not really. I think the importance of art has always been a given. Just not why, or how."

"I suppose." He turned away and looked out over the fire, at the milling crowd. He'd thought about this a lot, knew it was difficult to articulate, so he spoke slowly, choosing his words with care. "If you want to know if I think any single work of art can have a significant effect on people, I'd have to say probably not. Not directly, anyway. Maybe in a few rare cases." He turned back to her. "But what I *do* believe, is that art as a whole, in cumulative effect, impacts significantly on society. Probably through a whole complex web of subtle influences coming from exposure to it, directly and indirectly. I don't pretend to know exactly how, but I believe it completely. And art as a whole simply can't exist without individuals creating their own pieces of it." He shrugged, shook his head. "Besides, I'm not sure that changing the world is what I'm after. Maybe all I'm trying to do is *live* in it, in a way that allows me to live with myself."

There was a long silence, and he wondered if she understood.

"Rheinhardt, I know you probably don't want to go into this, but I need to talk to you about something."

He lit a cigarette without looking at her, nodded. "All right. What is it?"

"It's about Stoke."

"What about him."

"He's been drafted."

"I know. He told me."

"Do you know what he plans to do?"

"No. *He* doesn't know yet."

"I wish you would talk to him, Rheinhardt."

"Talk to him about what?" He knew, but for some

reason he was going to make it more difficult for her. Probably he was angry at her for bringing it up again.

"Leaving the country, or going underground."

"He's aware of those options."

"I wish you would tell him he's got to *take* one of those options. He won't listen to me, he won't even talk about it with me, but he'll listen to you. He respects you, your opinions, and most of all he knows you were in the service yourself, that you fought in the 'mericas, that you know what it was like, how asinine and insane it all is."

"I can't tell him that, Terry. He doesn't have to take one of those options."

"You want him to get killed."

"Of course not, don't run that kind of shit on me."

"It might be different if there were good reasons to be at war, but all we're doing is fighting a bunch of stupid ass civil wars in other people's countries, and nobody seems to really know why."

"I won't argue with that."

"It's insane to take the chance of getting killed for *nothing*."

"It's not that simple, Terry."

"Are you going to tell me some shit about being a soldier makes a *man* out of a boy? That old number?"

"I just said, it's not that simple, not even that 'old number.'"

"Jesus Christ, Rheinhardt, look what it did to *you*!"

He didn't reply. His chest, his head, went numb, and he wasn't sure if he was still breathing or not, if his heart was still beating. He couldn't move at all.

Terry closed her eyes, put her head in her hand. "Shit, I'm sorry," she said. "That wasn't fair."

Rheinhardt swallowed, breathed in, found his voice. "What did it do to me, Terry?" he asked. But he knew there was no answer to that question, at least not one that she would understand.

"I'm sorry," she said again, barely audible.

"It's all right," he told her. And it was. He reached toward her, took her hand in his, easing it away from her head. She squeezed his fingers, looked at him again. They sat that way for a long time, not moving, holding hands in the dark silence of the night, lit by the fire below them.

Siouxsie and the Banshees blasted through the head-phones as Rheinhardt stood staring at the three hideous blobs of clay. He couldn't work without music, and he couldn't work *with* music; nothing was helping any-more, and Rheinhardt could hardly believe he was responsible for the misshapen monstrosities on his worktable. If Stoke were here, he'd probably title them "Three Piles of Dogshit, Without Cigarette Butts." Fucking hopeless.

> *"We found you hiding*
> *We found you lying*
> *Choking on the dirt and sand*
> *Your former glories, and all the stories*
> *Dragged and washed with eager hands."*

Siouxsie Sioux sang to him with her harsh and beautiful pained voice, but it didn't help him at all.

> *"But oh, your city lies in dust, my friend*
> *Oh your city lies in dust."*

Isn't that the fucking truth, Rheinhardt thought. He pulled off the headphones, cutting off the words and music, flung them into the far corner of the room.

Hands shaking, he lit a cigarette and wandered out onto the roof. The sky was clear, the sun a dark orange, now just touching the tips of the park trees as it descended. He looked back at the lean-to and the clumps of welded metal just as hideous as the lumps of clay inside.

The city was strangling him, just as the Warehouse had. Maybe. Maybe it was people, maybe it was the world, maybe it was his relationship with Terry, which had gradually been deteriorating despite the occasional good days they had together. And maybe it was just him. Perhaps he had nothing to blame but himself, some defect or lack that had finally manifested itself, cutting him off, crumbling the links to whatever it was that, in the past, had allowed him to create. Maybe, maybe, maybe . . .

It didn't really matter what it was, unless it was something he could change; the fact was he could no longer work, and that was going to tear him apart, he *knew* that. There was nothing else in his life that meant that much to him, and he did not know how he would live without it.

But he *would* live without it, somehow, he knew that too. That was one thing he had brought back from those years of fighting in the 'mericas, of watching other people die. Life was worth too damn much to give up.

But Christ, was he lost. And he did not know what to do to find his way again.

Rheinhardt sat on the edge of Deever's roof, waiting for him to close up downstairs. He needed to talk to the old man; Deever was probably the only person Rheinhardt knew who might understand.

Rheinhardt looked up at the moon shining down on him and once again thought of Gunther, and Gunther's last word as he lay dying in the small town hospital: *Mondlicht.*

The night air was cold, fog rolling in from the ocean, and before long it would blanket the sky and hide the moon from view. Rheinhardt zipped up his leather jacket and lay back on the gravel surface of the roof, lower legs over the edge, boot heels slowly tapping against the building wall.

He closed his eyes, opened them briefly to look at the moon, then closed them again. What was it Gunther had said the night before he died? The young German had looked up at the moon slanting down on them through the jungle and said, "I'd like to go to the moon.

Must be awful peaceful up there." And Rheinhardt had known just how Gunther felt. He still knew that feeling.

Rheinhardt opened his eyes, sensing the vibrations of Deever's steps as he climbed the back stairs. The fog had come in enough now so that it partially obscured the moon as it drifted past overhead. He watched the fog and the moon, waiting for Deever.

A couple minutes later he heard the creaking of the roof ladder, then Deever's labored breathing, a hoarse grunt, and finally the crunch of gravel as Deever walked across the roof. The old man stopped next to Rheinhardt, vodka bottle in hand, and looked down at him.

"I'm here," Deever said. He stepped back and sat down, leaning against a round metal chimney that squealed from the pressure. "So, what is it?"

Rheinhardt, still on his back, looked at Deever and shrugged. "I needed to talk to someone who might understand."

Deever didn't say anything. Rheinhardt thought about lighting a cigarette, decided against it, and sat up.

"Stoke's been drafted," Rheinhardt finally said. "He's going to have to report soon, and Terry wants me to talk to him, tell him not to go."

"Sounds like where things were a few months ago."

"Yeah, doesn't it? Only now it's too close for him, and I can't put Terry off anymore."

"So what are you going to tell him?"

"I'm not going to tell him anything. *I* can't tell him what to do, but Terry sure doesn't understand that."

Deever drank from his bottle, coughed once, then said, "Is that what you think I'll understand?"

Rheinhardt shrugged. "Partly." He breathed deeply once, shaking his head. "People expect things I can't give them. Stoke expects me to tell him what it was like down in the 'mericas, he expects me to tell him what *war* is like. And Terry, well, like a lot of other people, she thinks I don't talk much about it because there's something I'm repressing, some traumatic event that's 'scarred me for life,' or something like that. A Central American My Lai or Aswan Dam. Well, there wasn't, though I saw plenty of horrible things, and I was fucked up and scared shitless more times than I want to remember. I don't know, Deever, I guess I just don't think people would understand."

"Understand what?" Deever asked.

Rheinhardt turned to look at the old man, who drank again from the bottle, then belched, staring at Rheinhardt. Rheinhardt didn't know how to respond.

"Look," Deever said. "How can you expect people to understand if you don't even try telling them anything?"

"I *do* try," Rheinhardt said. "Just not with words."

"How, then?"

"I sculpt."

Deever didn't say anything, just slowly nodded. Rheinhardt took out cigarettes, one for Deever, one for himself, lit them with a double match.

"I *could* tell stories," Rheinhardt eventually said. "War stories. I could tell people about a time when one of the guys in our platoon, fucked up on coke and ludes, stripped down to a swimsuit and started running through the jungle screaming at the top of his lungs, drawing enemy fire and nearly getting us all killed. I could tell a story about coming across a village with two dozen people in a pit, buried up to their chests, and finding out they'd done it to themselves, and that they didn't want us to dig them out." He paused, looking up at the moon again which now glowed faintly through the fog. "Or I could tell a story about a guy named Gunther who climbed up to the top of a church steeple while on R and R and took a dive into the street below." Rheinhardt turned back to Deever. "But what the hell would they mean to people? Weird war stories, that's what. The horrors of war. Which is part of it, I suppose, but the stories would never come close to conveying what it all meant to *me*."

"And what did it mean to you?"

Rheinhardt hesitated, looking at his cigarette, watching the ash fall to the roof. "A new way of seeing the world."

He didn't say anything more at first, unsure of how to go on. He watched Deever drink again from the bottle, then drag in deeply on his cigarette. The old man knew some things, Rheinhardt realized, most of them bad.

"When I first got back," Rheinhardt finally said, "I thought the world, all the people, had changed in the two years I'd been gone. But it wasn't long before I realized the world was just the same, that now I was *seeing* it differently. I was seeing things I'd never noticed before, I was seeing beneath the surface, *deep* beneath the surface, and to be honest, what I was seeing scared the shit out of me. Still does."

Rheinhardt paused, breathing deeply once, and crushed out his cigarette. "I have nightmares, sometimes," he said. Deever grunted with a nod, and Rheinhardt nodded in return. "Yeah. Terry thinks they're war nightmares. I guess they are, in a way, but they're not of war in the 'mericas, they're dreams of the war brought home. Here, to this city." He paused, thinking about them. "I dream about helicopters. Helicopters, and sometimes dragoncubs. Fuckin' helicopters, I hated them, they made me nervous. Hell, they made me sick. So now I dream about the damn things." He lit new cigarettes for himself and Deever. "Like I said, not down in the 'mericas, but here, helicopters flying above the city and in between buildings, guns and missiles firing, manned by Americans and firing on Americans. Sometimes I dream they're chasing me through the streets at night. Sometimes I dream they're herding hundreds of people into big open plazas or into streetcar tunnels. Sometimes they're just hovering in the air, dozens of them forming beautiful but frightening patterns in the sky. And once in a while there are no helicopters at all, just mortar fire at night, heavy artillery pounding the hills, trip-wires on the sidewalks." He shook his head, trying to smile. "I'm probably making it sound like I have these nightmares all the time, but I don't. It's just that over the years they add up, and I don't feel like they'll ever completely go away."

"They won't," Deever said. He shrugged and drank again from the bottle.

"So, after I'd been back for a while, I decided I had to try to reach people, somehow, to show them what they couldn't see, or what they didn't want to see, or at least let them know there were other ways of seeing the world around them. And give myself a way of dealing with it. I tried painting, first, did that for a couple of years, but I wasn't very good at it. Then I tried sculpting, and found my place." He looked down at his hands, which were trembling slightly. "Now, though, I can't even do that." He looked back at Deever. "If I hadn't gone to war, I wouldn't be a sculptor now, and I wouldn't see the world the way I do. I'd probably have my head in the fucking sand." He shrugged and sighed. "Maybe I'd be happier, but I can't help but feel it wouldn't be real, and I tell you, I'd never want to be like that. I want to *know* what the world is really like, I want to *know* what's going on around me. I don't want to ignore it, or delude myself about it." He paused again. "Do you understand?"

Deever nodded. "Why do you think I drink?"

"Then do you understand why I can't tell Stoke what to do? It's not that I *want* him to go, I'd never tell him to do that, but I can't tell him *not* to go either."

Deever nodded again. "Sure, I suppose. I might decide different, but I understand."

Rheinhardt drew his knees up, wrapped his arms around them. He felt drained, but relieved at the same time. "Thanks for listening, Deever."

Deever grunted, drank the rest of the vodka, then heaved the empty bottle over the edge of the roof. It shattered on the ground below. Rheinhardt looked up, but the fog was thick now, and the moon was no longer visible.

Nineteen

"Your friend's gone under," Kit said. "Manny, the guy you called Speedo."

"Dead?" Rheinhardt asked.

"Dead."

They were in a cafe on Haight, Rheinhardt drinking coffee, Kit drinking tea. He'd been reading the newspaper when she walked in and sat at his table to give him the news.

"What happened?"

Kit held out her left arm, motioned with her right hand as though shooting up. "He's been riding the Horse the last two or three months. Couple of days ago, got some bad shit. Wham. Straight to his fucking heart. The woman who found him, friend of mine, said he'd never even gotten the needle out of his arm."

"Accident?"

She shrugged. "Hard to say. He'd slipped in with some steely-ass motherfuckers recently. Heard he was having some kind of problems, maybe money, but you never know with that shit. In a way, doesn't matter. Either way, he's just as dead."

They didn't say anything for a while, and Rheinhardt realized he didn't feel very much one way or another about Manny.

"Listen, though," Kit said. "You don't do drugs at all anymore, do you?" Rheinhardt shook his head, and she went on. "Okay, but Stoke does a lot, doesn't he?"

"More than his share, I guess."

"Pass on a warning to him, then. This stuff with

Manny just sort of reminds me. *Could* have been an accident, see. Wouldn't be surprising because a lot of the stuff on the streets right now has some bad shit in it, it's really fucking people over. I've been hearing about it, and I've been seeing it in the hospital, people coming in dying, or already dead." She shook her head slowly. "Bad lines. I've quit mainlining. Fact, I'm not doing coke or speed at all anymore. Enough ways to die in this world without that kind of shit. You tell Stoke?"

He nodded, thinking of Gollancz. "Yeah, I'll pass it on. Don't know if it'll do much good."

They were quiet again for a while, then Kit said, "You weren't very good friends, were you?"

"You mean with Manny?"

"Yeah."

"No, not really. He was always just a little too crazy for me. One time, too, out on patrol in the jungle, he did something as stupid as it was crazy, nearly got us all killed." He paused, remembering. "It's hard to forgive something like that out there."

Kit nodded, and the silence returned. The image of Speedo, fucked up on coke and ludes, running through the jungle stripped down to his bikini swimsuit and screaming at the top of his lungs and laughing, rose in Rheinhardt's mind. It brought back the sound of automatic weapons fire, the crump of mortars, the flicking sounds of bullets tearing through the dense foliage, and the smell of damp earth and rotting leaves as he'd bellied down, trying to bury himself, trying to somehow survive.

No, Speedo's death didn't have much effect on him. He wasn't glad Speedo was dead, but he just didn't care. Maybe that was just as bad.

It was after midnight when the air-raid sirens went off. Terry, lying on the couch and reading, sat up abruptly, her heart pounding. It wasn't Tuesday, and it sure as hell wasn't noon.

She stood, the book still in her hand, heartbeat

crashing against her chest and trying to rise up into her throat. The sirens seemed to grow louder, the wail rising and falling, rising and falling, and for a few moments she had trouble drawing in her next breath.

Must be a malfunction, she told herself, they'll stop in a second.

The sirens did not stop.

Terry began pacing back and forth in front of the cold fireplace, wishing she'd built a fire earlier. A hollow swelling rolled through her belly, pushed up against her heart. She left the room, went through the kitchen and out to the utility porch, opened the door and stepped outside.

The sirens were far louder out here, seemed to surround her, press in from all sides. A malfunction, she told herself again, or some kids screwing around, vandalizing the sirens, something like that. But her body didn't seem to believe it, and, despite the cold, a sweat broke out under her arms, on her forehead, even on her palms.

Is this it?

She felt so helpless, knowing there was nothing she could do, nothing but wait for something else to happen. Please just stop, she silently commanded the sirens. Christ.

Terry was having trouble breathing. Helpless, stuck, she thought. Just wait. She looked at the buildings around her, then up at the sky, but didn't see anything unusual—no strange lights in the sky, no waves of airplanes, no dragoncubs, no lights going on in apartment windows, no people panicking. And no sounds except the sirens, nothing but the sirens. Was she the only one who heard them? Was she the only one who thought they meant anything?

Then the sirens, at the lower end of their wave pattern, did not rise up again, but continued to fall, lessening in intensity, dropping in volume, and slowly, slowly fading, winding down.

When the sound stopped completely, Terry remained

on the back porch, listening, heart still beating hard
and fast, waiting, half expecting the sirens to start up
again. The silence continued, but she did not feel
reassured.

Her heartbeat did gradually relax, the tension in her
chest and gut eased, and she began to shiver from the
cold. If the sirens started in again, what would she do?
Fall apart? But the sirens didn't start up again and, still
shivering, Terry finally turned and went back inside.

Rheinhardt was sitting on the edge of the roof,
watching four or five people huddled around a trash-
can fire in the alley below, when the air-raid sirens
pierced the cold night air. The sirens were loud, oscil-
lated regularly with an almost painful wail.

"We're gonna be bombed!" one of the people below
cried. "The goddamn Russians or somebody's comin'
to blow us all to hell!"

"Shut up, you crazy ole bastard," someone else said.
"It's just a practice or somethin', you'll see."

"No, no, we're *dead*!"

Someone started banging on the trash can with a
stick, and sparks flew up in explosions of red and
orange. A window went up in one of the nearby
buildings, and a voice shouted from it. "Keep it down
out there, for Christ's sake! People sleeping."

"With these goddamn sirens?"

"Jesus."

More windows came up, more shouting broke out. A
scuffle started down near the fire, punctuated with
laughter, something or someone crashed into the trash
can, nearly knocking it on its side, and more sparks
shot skyward. Somebody starting chanting in one of the
windows, "Fight! Fight! Bombs! Bombs! Fight! Fight!
Bombs! Bombs!"

More laughter, more shouting, and people started
banging on the building walls.

"What the *hell* is going on here?" someone yelled.

More sirens cut the air, adding to the air-raid sirens,

but Rheinhardt recognized the difference—police.
"Shit, the cops!" someone shouted from below. The
scuffling ceased, and then Rheinhardt saw, in the
flickering light from the fire, shadows taking off down
the alley away from the street, heard the clatter of metal
and wood and scraping sounds and muttered curses.
Down at the end of the alley, the spinning red light of a
police cruiser appeared; the car braked to a stop, doors
swung open.

Just as the cops jumped out of the car and started
into the alley, the air-raid sirens began to tail away. By
the time the cops reached the trash-can fire, the sirens
had completely quit, and not a voice was to be heard
from any of the buildings, though Rheinhardt could see
that a number of people were still at their open
windows, watching.

The cops wandered about the empty alley for several
minutes, poking through the trash, overturning broken
crates, kicking at clumps of dried weeds, their big
mag-lites sending wide beams back and forth in the
dark. One of the cops spit into the fire, raising a loud
sizzle. Eventually, playing their lights casually up the
walls on both sides of the alley, the cops wandered back
to their car, got in, drove off.

Below, the fire continued to burn in the trash-can,
and Rheinhardt remained on the roof's edge, watching
the orange glow and the bright orange sparks that
occasionally rose up toward him.

Past midnight, and Rheinhardt stood in the wind
blowing across the jetty, scanning the water in all
directions. Gollancz had died that morning. They were
to have made another trip out to Alcatraz soon, sometime in the next few days. There would be no more trips
now. He stared out over the water toward Alcatraz,
though he could see only the vaguest outlines of the
dark island.

Rheinhardt sat down in the shelter of several large

stones and lit a cigarette, still gazing out in the direction of the Rock. Hollow thrumping sounds came from the south, and Rheinhardt looked up to see two or three dragoncubs leaving city airspace in tandem, heading out over the water. He tracked them toward Alcatraz, the pulsing glow marking their rapid flight as they homed in on the island.

For the next half hour, feeling helpless but unwilling to leave, he watched the glowing lights of the dragoncubs dance about the island, occasionally emitting streams of crimson-colored lights which were sometimes answered by red and orange lights from below; listened to the muted cracks of something like gunfire, the hollow booms of what might have been explosions. Then there was silence for a while, and the glowing, flickering dragoncubs shot away from the island, crossed the water, and dropped back into the city.

The bay was empty and quiet now, the island dark again. Rheinhardt felt hollow inside, as if he'd lost something—Christ, he *had.* Water broke quietly against the rocks at his feet. He didn't want to move, but then he really didn't want to stay, either. He finally stood, turned into the wind, and started back across the rocks.

All the clay was sealed in plastic bags; it hadn't been touched or moved in weeks. Rheinhardt sat on the cot, smoking a cigarette and looking at the neglected worktable, the clay and tools and supplies that had become a kind of immobile sculpture by default. Already a thin but solid coat of dust lay over it all, and he could not even bring himself to wipe the dust clean.

He got up and put out his cigarette, left the room, walked around to the lean-to. Workbench, cabinets, crates of metal, supplies he'd left out—everything here was collecting dust as well. The sun, unobstructed by clouds, slanted in sheets through gaps between sections of the lean-to, and as he paced within the shelter, the stirred dust floated and shimmered in the narrow beams of light.

Rheinhardt was afraid. He was afraid to start something new, afraid to touch the clay, afraid to touch anything that might lead to another piece of work. He was afraid of disaster.

Rheinhardt sat on the rough gravel, back against the wall, his legs striped with the sunlight, one beam lancing down his left cheek and eye. He shifted his head slightly, and the narrow beam now ran down the center of his face, along his nose, a thin line of warmth cutting him in half. He closed his eyes and did not move.

Justinian

At dawn, Justinian emerges from the bay, wearing only shorts, staggers up the slope of rock and sand. Two cuts on his forehead are bleeding, and one on his arm. An enormous, blue and purple bruise covers most of his right thigh. He stops above the waterline, dripping water, breathing heavily, and closes his eyes.

For a long time he remains in that spot. When he starts to shiver, Justinian opens his eyes and begins walking inland.

Hidden in shadow, Justinian sat in a crouch on a building rooftop, looking at Rheinhardt two rooftops away, who was standing under the lean-to, motionless. The sun had just set, and darkness was moving in quickly.

Justinian shifted slightly, lit a cigarette, kept his gaze on Rheinhardt. Rheinhardt didn't move for a long time, and soon was barely visible in the growing darkness. Then Rheinhardt's arm moved up, and a light hanging from the lean-to ceiling came on, illuminating him.

Minh came up over the edge of the roof a few feet away from Justinian, walked over to him and stood at his side, looking out toward Rheinhardt.

"Where have you been?" Justinian asked.

Minh didn't answer.

"Where have you been?" Justinian asked again. "You're late."

"What's he doing over there?" Minh asked.

Justinian didn't answer immediately, glanced at Minh. "Nothing," he said. He turned back to Rheinhardt.

Rheinhardt was still motionless, but after a minute or so he stepped up to the workbench, began picking up objects, looking at them, then putting them down again. Fifteen minutes later, he stepped back from the bench, turned off the light. He was just visible, a dark, unmoving form lit by nearby window lights that had come on. Soon he began pacing back and forth across the roof, stopped to light a cigarette, then continued pacing.

"Why am I here?" Minh asked.

"To see this," Justinian said.

"Why?"

Justinian shrugged. "That's a man who's lost, a man who can't create anymore. I thought it might be important."

"Important for what?"

Justinian shrugged, shook his head.

Across the way, Rheinhardt threw his cigarette to the ground, crushed it with his shoe, then went to the trapdoor, lifted it, and started down the stairs, closing the trapdoor behind him.

"Are we supposed to follow him?" Minh asked.

Justinian shook his head. "No." He stood, walked to the edge of the roof, looked down at the streets below. Rheinhardt did not appear.

Twenty

News was on the television in the bar, and Rheinhardt sat at a table close to the set, nursing a beer. The sound was so low, the people in the bar so noisy, that he couldn't hear the newscaster; all he could do was watch the images on the screen, close-ups of the newscasters broken by occasional clips of news footage.

Concentration was difficult. His head felt too large, his throat was scratchy, and body aches were starting to set in—he was pretty sure he was getting sick. He wondered which Asian version of the flu was pumping through the city this year. Why the hell was it always some *Asian* flu?

The beer was soothing on his throat, but wasn't helping his headache much. On the television, footage of stretchers being loaded into several ambulances appeared; in the background, flames were licking the walls of a building, and smoke poured out and into the sky. The woman newscaster's face reappeared, and she mouthed words that Rheinhardt couldn't hear. He didn't really care. Then her face was gone, and a chorus line of dancing electro-charged lipstick tubes came on the screen, tiny stick arms linked together, stick legs kicking; the lipsticks themselves, emitting bursts of silver sparks, slipped obscenely in and out of the tubes. Rheinhardt turned away and drank from his beer.

The bar was crowded now, and two people were arguing at the jukebox, shoving each other. At a big table in the back, a young woman stood up on a chair, pulled down a strap of her tank top, and bared a single breast. "Oh, God, not again!" someone yelled, and the people at the table began laughing. "If I have to look at that one more time I'm gonna puke!" The woman gave someone the finger, pulled her strap back up, sat down to a chorus of cheers.

I *am* getting sick, Rheinhardt thought, turning back to the television. On the screen now was footage of the space station, the gaping, jagged holes in the outer structure; then the footage cut to a close-up of a salvage team retrieving a suited body drifting in orbit, most of one leg missing.

Rheinhardt finished his beer, walked out of the bar, and started back for home and bed.

Night was falling, and Terry stood outside Rheinhardt's room, knocked loudly on the door. There was no answer at first (the room was dark), but as she started knocking again, a hoarse voice answered from inside. "Who is it?"

"Terry."

There was a long pause, then Rheinhardt said, "All right, come on in."

She opened the door, stepped into the dark room. The air was stuffy, smelled of sickness. All she could see were dark shadows, and the glow of a cigarette. Terry left the door open, felt her way toward the center of the room and pulled the chain to turn on the overhead light. The chain clicked, but the light didn't come on.

"Bulb's out," Rheinhardt said. Another click sounded, and a small desk lamp next to the cot went on, giving the room a dim orange glow. Rheinhardt was lying on the cot wearing a sleeveless T-shirt, blanket covering his legs; even in the dim light, Terry could see the sweat on his arms and face.

"You look like hell," she said.

"Thanks." He crushed out the cigarette on the cot leg. "I've been sick, some fucking flu. Actually I'm feeling a lot better now."

"Good, because we've got a play to go to tomorrow night."

"Yeah?" He looked at her with eyes almost closed.

"Yes."

Rheinhardt turned to face the wall, pulled the blanket up. "You go," he said. "I'm staying here."

Terry didn't say anything at first. She looked around the room, saw the dust on his worktable and tools, the twisted blobs of clay, the cigarette butts all over the table and floor, the crumpled sheets torn from his sketchbook. She sat on the high stool, looked at him.

"Listen, Rheinhardt. I know how you feel, I think. I'm not surprised you got sick, the way you've been wasting away up here lately, but sitting around doing nothing isn't going to accomplish a damn thing."

He turned back to look at her, but didn't say a word.

"All right, you're having trouble working, and . . ."

"How the fuck do you know if I'm having trouble?"

". . . and some nut wants to buy 'The Winter Gantry' so he can destroy it, so I think I know what you're feeling, but the world is still out there, and you're still alive."

"Now what the hell is that supposed to mean?"

Terry shrugged. "I don't know. Look, forget all that. The play tomorrow night, at the Taurus Theater, that's why I'm here. It's not just some play. It's a performance piece that Brisk has put together."

Rheinhardt pushed himself up, sat with his back against the wall. "Brisk? He's out of jail?"

Terry nodded.

"And he's got a new play?"

She nodded again.

"And he managed to get a theater to produce it?"

"Not exactly, and that's the problem. At the Taurus Theater, some musical is playing, and that's what everyone who'll be there in the audience will be expecting to see. But Brisk is . . . well, taking over the theater for the night."

"And the theater doesn't know it."

"Right. I don't know how he plans on doing that, and I'll be honest with you, Rheinhardt, I'm pretty uncomfortable with the whole thing. I feel like we've *got* to go.

I really think he might be going too far this time. The piece is called *Hostages*."

Rheinhardt stared at her for a minute, then said, "Shit."

Terry just nodded.

They picked up their tickets at the will call window (Brisk had somehow arranged it), entered the theater. The Taurus was not a large theater, a single balcony, seated around 900. Terry and Rheinhardt were out of place, dressed in jeans; most of the men wore suits or coats and ties, most of the women were in evening gowns. The air smelled of perfume and after-shave.

They found their seats, left side back row, and settled in. They had a view of the entire audience as well as the stage, which Terry was sure Brisk had intended. The air was cool, the air conditioning on, but Terry felt closed in, slightly dizzy, and her intestines gurgled and tightened inside her. Beside her, Rheinhardt sat silently, stiff and unmoving.

Terry could not stop thinking of Brisk's previous plays, what he called guerrilla theater. *The Lunatic Terrorist* had been his first, in which he'd wandered along Market Street at lunch hour wearing what looked like explosives strapped to his chest, and carrying a sign that said—THE LUNATIC TERRORIST: AN EXPLOSION IN ONE ACT. As he'd walked through the Financial District, he had shouted obscenities and threatened to blow himself up. When he'd been surrounded by firefighters and police and a bomb squad, he set off the smoke bombs which *had* been on his chest, laughing hysterically through the smoke. As the smoke cleared, he handed out leaflets to the cops and firefighters and anyone else on the street, explaining that they'd just witnessed a performance piece. He was arrested immediately, though he didn't spend any time in jail.

The last piece he'd performed, over a year before, though Terry and Rheinhardt had tried to talk him out of it, had been called *Sniper*. Although he had distributed explanatory leaflets the day before, most students on the San Francisco State campus did *not* know what was happening when he opened fire on them from the top of the student union. He was shooting blanks, of course, and tiny explosive charges had been planted throughout the plaza which he set off in time with his gunshots, but hardly anyone knew it, and the students and faculty panicked. Brisk was lucky he hadn't been killed by the tactical squads that had overrun the place—three or four shots had actually been fired at him. This time, when he was arrested, he *did* end up in jail. Terry was surprised he was out so soon.

Terry wanted to talk to Rheinhardt, but didn't know what to say. She couldn't relax, and she felt her heartbeat hitting up against her ribs, pulsing at her throat. Rheinhardt took her hand in his and squeezed as the house lights came down.

For several minutes nothing happened. Then a spot came on in front of the curtain, and a few seconds later a figure descended from above, back to the audience, supported by wires brightly lit with strings of blinking red lights. The figure landed awkwardly on the stage and turned. It was a woman dressed in black tights with her face made up to resemble a mouse or rat. She pulled a chunk of cheese from a pocket, nibbled on it, then tossed it aside, wrinkling her nose. "Limburger," she said, and people in the audience laughed.

"That's funny?" Rheinhardt said. Several people shushed him.

"I want CHEESE!" the woman mouse shouted. The curtain pulled back, revealing a dozen men and women dressed in black or white tights and made up as mice; they scampered around the stage, then the first woman-mouse was lifted into the air as she cried out "I want CHEESE!" again. The orchestra began playing, and all the "mice" on stage began singing the play's title song, "I Want Cheese!"

"Jesus Christ," Rheinhardt said. "This is the fucking musical."

Again several people shushed him. Terry squeezed his hand, leaned toward him, and whispered into his ear. "Quiet, or we'll get kicked out."

"We might be better off," he whispered in return.

Terry nodded and sank back in her seat, relief painfully washing through her, and tried to concentrate on the play.

"I don't know," Rheinhardt said. They were outside the theater, watching the people from the audience climbing into cabs and expensive cars. "Sitting through that might have been worse than being held hostage."

"You didn't *have* to sit through the whole thing," Terry told him.

"I thought I should. Now I can talk semi-intelligently about what a piece of crap this thing is that people are spending seventy and eighty dollars apiece to see."

Terry sighed; she had to agree with him. It had been pretty awful, and she had read somewhere that it was setting box office records for the theater, or something like that.

"I wonder what happened to Brisk?" she asked. "I hope he didn't get hit by the cops, trying something in the theater he couldn't pull off. Better if he just backed out."

"I'll try to find him tomorrow, find out what the story is." Rheinhardt put his arm through hers. "Let's go. I believe our limo is waiting for us in the next block."

Terry smiled and nodded, and they started off down the street, leaving the bright lights of the theater behind.

Rheinhardt found out where Brisk was living, but he wasn't at home; neither of his roommates had seen him in two or three days. Rheinhardt tried three of Brisk's regular bars before finding him at a back corner table in the Potrero Arms, a bottle of Anchor Steam Dark in his hands.

"Heya," Rheinhardt said. "Mind if I sit?"

"Be my guest." Brisk picked up the bottle, brought it to his mouth, and tipped head and bottle back. Rheinhardt sat, watched the up and down movement of Brisk's throat as he emptied the bottle.

A waitress came by, and Brisk asked for another. Rheinhardt told her to make it two.

"You were there last night," Brisk said. His breath smelled heavily of beer.

"Yeah. Believe, Brisk, it was a crappy play. I'm glad I didn't have to pay for the tickets."

"Terry there too?"

"Yes. She didn't much like it either."

They didn't say anything for a couple of minutes. Some generic country song was playing on the jukebox. The waitress came by with their beers, left.

"What happened last night, Brisk?"

"You mean what *didn't* happen. Do you realize what it was going to be? What I was going to do?"

"I have an idea."

"I had some people working with me, we were going to take the whole damn theater hostage. Audience, ushers, cashier, cast, stage crew. We had M-16s, M-18s, no live ammunition but plenty of blanks, which were a bitch to get hold of. Live ammunition would have been easier. I had it all worked out, even had two plants in the audience who were going to try running and we would gun them down, blood flying everywhere. It should have worked. Would have held them hostage for maybe half an hour, told them we were making demands, that negotiations were underway." He stopped and drank from his beer, and Rheinhardt lit a cigarette, offered one to Brisk. "No thanks," Brisk said. "I quit two months ago." He shook his head, laughing quietly. He picked at the bottle label, went on. "I figured the first five minutes would be the most crucial. That's part of why the plants, drive it into the audience that this was serious, that they'd better not goddamn move from their seats. And I didn't want to go more than a half hour, figured the longer it went on the greater chance someone would flip out and do something crazy, or someone would try to be a hero. At the end of a half hour we'd start making our exits, then I'd announce to the audience that they had just participated in a performance piece called *Hostages*, the two plants would get up from the ground, and we'd take off, cars waiting for us." Brisk shrugged. "End of performance."

Rheinhardt didn't say anything. Jesus fucking Christ. He shook his head, drank from his beer, hit on his cigarette, shook his head again. His hands were trembling slightly; why? "Shit, Brisk," he finally said. "Don't you think that was just a little extreme?"

Brisk finished off his beer, set down the empty bottle, and stared at it. "That's why I ended up canceling it. The closer it got, the more insane it seemed. And I mean truly, clinically insane. On top of which it was probably way too complicated. The audience would have been easy enough to keep under, all in one room, sitting still. But the ushers, the cast members in all the different rooms, the stage crew all over the fucking place, makeup people, orchestra . . . shit. We never could have pulled it off."

Brisk put his head in his hands, rubbed his eyes, then sat for a minute holding his head, eyes closed. When he started speaking again, he kept his eyes shut.

"Even if we *could* have pulled it off, I was beginning to realize it was . . . insane. Not just insane, but wrong, too. Just plain wrong." He opened his eyes, looked at Rheinhardt. "I want to wake these people up, that's what I've always tried to do with my pieces, try to get them to see the real world, to see outside their nice houses and big cars and resort vacations and gourmet food and private clubs and schools and all that shit, try to get them to understand that a lot of this world is really fucked, and that they're part of the reason. But shit, not like that. I can't do that kind of thing to people, not to anyone, put them through that, terrorize them, even for just a half hour. That's not communicating anything, that's just fucking them over."

Brisk stood up, paced quickly back and forth a few times, pounding at his thigh, banging the wall with his fist. He stopped, ran both hands through his hair, breathed deeply two or three times, sat down again, tried to drink from the empty beer bottle. He slammed the bottle on the table.

"I don't know what to do anymore, Rheinhardt. I don't know how to reach people anymore, I *can't* reach them. They don't want to hear what I have to say, and I can't figure out anymore how to make them listen to me. I just don't know what to do."

Rheinhardt sat looking at Brisk, feeling sick, as if his chest were collapsing. What's happening to all of us? "I can't help you," he said to Brisk. "I don't have any answers, either. All I can do is buy you another beer." When Brisk didn't say anything, Rheinhardt turned, caught the waitress's eye, and signaled for two more.

Twenty-One

Rheinhardt climbed the shaky wooden steps to the second floor of Kit's building, knocked on the door. When there was no answer he knocked again, then tried the door. It stuck at first, but wasn't locked, and the knob clicked and turned; he pushed the door open, walked in.

The room was empty.

All the drapes were gone, and light flooded in through the large windows. Rheinhardt walked slowly through the room, but floor, ceiling, and walls were completely bare, nothing left behind except splotches of paint on the floor and walls of what had been Olden's half of the room. Even the cupboards and shelves were empty and clean.

Rheinhardt went back outside and sat on the top step in the sun, lit a cigarette. He had hoped that talking to Kit, seeing her work, would somehow help, break him loose so he could work again himself. Now, though, finding the place deserted, he felt as empty and hollow as the room.

Terry sat at the desk in her office in the Warehouse, nodding off. The office was suddenly full of people talking and laughing, drinking gin and champagne, all of them ignoring her. She couldn't understand what any of them were talking about, and she tried to catch someone's attention, anyone's, to try to explain something to them about the Warehouse.

Terry's forehead hit the desk, jerking her awake. The office was empty, though the voices and laughter still seemed to drift around in her head. It was late, she was tired; she probably should leave, go home.

A horrible cry came through the wall on her left, from the tiny cubicle where Minh slept. Another cry sounded, even louder, frightened and frightening, followed by bumping sounds.

Terry got up, hurried out of the office, pushed open the door to the cubicle. There was no light on in the room, but the light from the corridor came in through the door, revealed Minh crouched on his cot in the far corner, holding a gun pointed directly at her.

Terry dropped instinctively to the ground, a gunshot sounded, incredibly loud, and she scuttled back into the corridor and out of the doorway as another gunshot exploded, chunks of plaster erupting from the corridor wall. Jesus. She found she couldn't move, could hardly breathe.

There was silence at first, then she heard footsteps approaching from the ends of the corridors, and a few faces cautiously appeared around corners, out of doorways. Terry waved people back, relieved that she could move again.

A few moments later, Minh appeared at the door, the gun still in his hand but held limply now, barrel pointed at the floor. Sweat reflected light from his face.

"I'm sorry," he said. "I had a bad dream, a nightmare, I didn't know where I was." He glanced at the gun, then back at Terry. "I'm sorry."

"Jesus, Minh, where the hell did you get that gun?"

Minh gripped the gun tightly again, held it protectively against his chest. "It's mine."

Terry nodded. "All right, all right, I'm not going to take it away." She struggled to her feet, her legs still a little wobbly, and cautiously approached him. "You okay now?"

Minh didn't say anything, just looked at her with eyes filling with tears. Terry put her arms around him, pulled him tightly to her, and he began to cry.

*   *   *

It took Rheinhardt a week to find Olden. The painter was, to Rheinhardt's surprise, an old man in his seventies or eighties, a mulatto with gray hair and beard, tall and thin and very soft-spoken. The old man lived in the garage of a relative's house in the Excelsior district, a hammock strung in the back corner, two chairs and a TV set on a piece of worn carpet; his paintings were stacked against the garage walls and up in rafters.

Rheinhardt introduced himself, and Olden said yes, he knew the name, Kit had talked about him several times. The painter led him out of the garage and into the small backyard, motioned to one of the folding chairs on the cement patio; Olden sat in one himself, took a pair of mirrorshades from his shirt pocket and put them on, leaning back to face the sun. Rheinhardt sat in a chair facing him.

"Cigarette?" he asked.

Olden shook his head. "Gave 'em up thirty year ago. But go ahead if you like, won't bother me none."

Rheinhardt lit a cigarette, watched the old man, disconcerted because he could not see the painter's eyes through the sunglasses.

"I've been trying to find Kit," Rheinhardt said. "Last week I went by the warehouse you used to share with her, found it empty."

Olden nodded. "I got the boot. Actually, they told me they were tripling the rent." He shook his head. "Shit, they knew I couldn't afford that. Kit had to go, too."

"You know where she went? I tried calling S.F. General, but they said they canned her about three or four weeks ago."

Olden grinned. "That woman never could hold down a job."

"Do you know where she went to live?"

Olden shook his head. "No. Not anywhere in the city, don't think. Last time I saw her, she was getting ready to dismantle that piece she was working on, you know, with the poles and wires and mirrors?" Rheinhardt nodded, and Olden went on. "She said to me, 'Olden, I think I'm gonna leave town.' 'Yeah?' I said. 'Where to?' And she said, 'The desert, somewhere, where it's hot and dry, and there aren't too many people.' Then she gave me a peck on the cheek, and I left. I haven't seen or heard from her since, and I hope she *is* out in the desert somewheres. Do her good." He nodded again, apparently to himself.

Leave town, Rheinhardt thought. Maybe that's just what he should do. "What about you?" Rheinhardt asked. "What are you going to do now?"

The old man shrugged. "I've been thinking about retiring. Taking up a hobby." He grinned. "Like painting." He started chuckling, and Rheinhardt smiled. "I don't know," Olden said. "I'll work something out, always have."

Rheinhardt stood, shook the old painter's hand. "Thanks," he said. "Take care."

"Thank you."

Rheinhardt walked to the side gate leading out to a narrow walk along the garage, opened it, then heard Olden call.

"Hey, Rheinhardt."

Rheinhardt stopped, turned, holding the gate open. "Yeah?"

"I was in Carlatti's Gallery the other day. You do some mighty fine work for a young slick."

Did, Rheinhardt thought. Past tense. "Thanks," he said. He nodded, went through the gate, and closed it behind him.

Stoke was sitting in with an all-black jazz combo, playing the blues. Terry sat with Minh at a table near the stage, watching, though how Minh had managed to get into the club was still a mystery; he wouldn't talk about it.

The band was playing an old Fenton Robinson song, "Loan Me a Dime," the lyrics incongruous with the times, but somehow making the song even more poignant. A dime for a phone call, Terry thought. She couldn't remember if it had ever been just a dime in her life.

But when Stoke started playing the guitar solo, Terry could hardly believe what she was hearing. He was sitting toward the back of the stage, almost completely in shadow, looking not at the audience, but down at his feet, or at his fingers as they moved across the frets, as they picked at the strings. He was playing the blues, all right, and the notes came out of his guitar with so much sadness it was painful to Terry.

"He makes it pretty sad," Minh whispered to her.

She nodded, but couldn't say anything. As he played, his face tensed and twisted with each note, as if feeling every bit of that pain himself. Watching and listening to him made Terry's heart ache, not just because of the sadness in the music, the despair in the notes and in Stoke's face, but because he was so young, he was too damn young to know that much about pain, about *real* pain in life; and it was obvious that Stoke *did* know that pain, and felt it deeply, and was now letting it all come out of him.

Terry turned away, looked into the shadows at the rear of the club so she would not have to look at Stoke, but she could not stop listening to him, and he continued to play, and her heart continued to ache without relief.

Rheinhardt sat on the edge of the roof, looking down at the dim alley below. The sun was setting; he could not see it directly anymore, but it reflected brightly from the curves of the skylight over his room.

Down in the alley, several street people were gathering for the night, most coming into the alley with a stick or two of wood. Constance, whose name Rheinhardt had learned from watching and listening over the past several weeks, stood in her huge overcoat by the old trash can they would use for the fire, and collected the wood; the others combed the alley itself for scrap wood.

The amazing thing was that, though they found and burned every bit of wood in the alley each night, there was always more in the alley by the next evening. He had seen nearby residents toss pieces of scrap wood into the alley from their windows or fire balconies. Rheinhardt had regularly contributed to the stock himself.

The people below had quite a pile now, but they didn't start the fire yet; they'd wait as long as possible, until the cold set in hard. Though it was still summer, a lot of nights got bad, especially with the fog.

Gravel crunched, Rheinhardt turned, saw Justinian approaching. The old man held up a hand, sat on the ridge near Rheinhardt.

"How about a cigarette, my good man," Justinian said.

"You never have any of your own."

Justinian grinned, said nothing. Rheinhardt gave him a cigarette, took one for himself, lit both with a lighter.

"Wondered when I'd see you again," Rheinhardt said. "It's been a long time."

"Yes, it has. But you should have known I wouldn't be able to stay away forever."

"Yeah, I should have known."

"*Hey up there!*"

Rheinhardt looked down into the alley. It was so dark now he couldn't make out faces, just dark forms moving about, but he recognized the voice; it was Constance.

"*You gonna smoke up there, how 'bout sharin' some with your less fortunate neighbors!*"

Rheinhardt smiled. It had become something of a ritual lately. He took a brand-new pack he had ready in his jacket pocket, dropped it over the edge.

"On its way!" he called down.

It hit the ground, and Constance called back up. "*Many thanks!*"

Rheinhardt nodded, though he didn't know if she could see it.

"You're very generous," Justinian said.

"Yeah, I'm just a generous guy all around." He looked at Justinian. "So what's up? You here for a reason, or just to pan cigarettes?"

"I came to say good-bye."

"You going somewhere?"

Justinian shrugged, gave him a strange half smile. "One of us is."

A hard knot formed in Rheinhardt's gut. How could Justinian know what he'd been considering? He couldn't, of course. The old man had to be referring to something else.

"What do you mean?" Rheinhardt asked.

Justinian shrugged again, still with that odd smile, and Rheinhardt wanted to hit the old man. Anger, and a little bit of fear cut through his chest, but he forced himself to breathe slowly, deeply, took a few hits on his cigarette until he felt almost relaxed, under control again.

"All right. Good-bye, then," he said to Justinian.

Justinian remained silent, smoking for a couple of minutes, and the smile gradually faded. Then Justinian nodded, crushed out his cigarette, stood.

"Good-bye, Rheinhardt."

He turned, crossed the roof to the trapdoor, and, without looking back, stepped through it. Rheinhardt was alone again.

Twenty-Two

With the cutting torch, Rheinhardt sliced large sections of sheet metal into dozens of smaller pieces; he warped and bent thick rods with the blue-white flame; then he welded batches of the metal scraps randomly together, one on top of another, intertwined, pieces sticking haphazardly out in all directions.

When the mass of metal was about five feet high and three across, he turned off the flame, pulled the sculpture to the ground, then dragged it across the roof, out of the lean-to and into the open. He removed his gloves, skullcap, and goggles, put on a pair of clear plastic shop goggles, took a large sledgehammer from one of the cabinets, and approached the sculpture.

Rheinhardt planted his feet firmly, gripped the sledgehammer with both hands, then swung it around and down hard onto the sculpture, badly bending one of the projecting pieces of metal. He adjusted his grip on the sledgehammer, breathed in, and swung again.

Pilate Error was on stage, but the crowd in the club was making almost as much noise as the band. Terry had sensed the tension building during the last half hour, people in the crowd yelling at the band, Stoke yelling back at them, which just made it worse.

Terry and Rheinhardt were sitting at a table near the back of the club, against the wall. Though the band was in the middle of a song—"Attitude Problem"—the people in the audience were whistling, shouting obscenities. On stage, Stoke was obviously angry, banging at his guitar and screaming the vocals so they came out harsh and ragged, more than was usual with him. Even Pace, the stabilizing element in the band, was pounding erratically at the drums with uncharacteristic frenzy, not quite maintaining a consistent beat.

The song crashed to a close, and Stoke turned from the mike to adjust his amp.

"Hey!" somebody shouted from one of the front tables. "You're a bunch of wimpy cunts up there, know that?" People around him laughed, and he kept on. "What kind of shit is it you're playing, anyway? Girl-band cotton?" More laughter, and Stoke turned around, held up his guitar.

"You want me to come out there and shove this up your ass, shithead?" he shouted.

"Oh eat me, you fucking pussy mouth."

"Listen," Stoke said. "You don't like it, get the fuck out of here. Here, here's your cover back." Stoke crammed his hand into his jeans pocket, pulled out a few bills, wadded them, threw them at the guy who was yelling at him. "Now go, asshole. Out!" He retreated to his amp again, but this time didn't turn his back to the crowd.

The guy who had been shouting stood up with a beer bottle in his hand, yelled "Fuck you!" then threw the bottle at Stoke. The bottle hit Stoke's guitar, bounced off against the amp, spraying beer across the stage.

Stoke reacted immediately. He dropped his guitar, scrambled for the beer bottle, picked it up, got to his feet, then ran and leaped from the stage directly at the guy, yelling loudly. He landed on the table, bottles and glasses scattering, slid across it and while falling grabbed the guy by his shirt as they tipped over to the floor with a crash. Stoke landed on top of him, straddled the guy, held the bottle over the guy's face, and poured the rest of the beer onto it.

Somebody grabbed Stoke, tried to pull him off, but that was the last Terry saw of him as everyone in the club got to their feet to watch, blocking her view. She turned to say something to Rheinhardt, but he was already up and pushing his way forward through the crowd.

The next few minutes were confusion for Terry. People yelled and shouted, furniture banged and crashed, glass shattered, the bartender stood on the bar screaming at everyone. Twice Terry almost plunged into the shifting crowd, but realized there wasn't much point.

Then she saw Rheinhardt emerge from the press of people, dragging Stoke, who was on his hands and knees, behind him. He pulled Stoke to his feet and they went around the corner, down the dark narrow corridor leading to the bathrooms and the rear exit.

Terry squeezed through people until she reached the corridor, which was now empty, then hurried along it to the back door, pushed it open. The alley ran in both directions, but it was empty as well. She jogged to the right, the shortest stretch to the street, but when she reached the sidewalk, looked around in all directions, there were no signs of either Rheinhardt or Stoke anywhere.

The bar was quiet, the quiet almost tangible after the noise in the club. Rheinhardt and Stoke sat at a small table in a corner, drinking Irish coffees.

"That was Terry came out after us," Stoke said.

"I know."

"So why did we stay hidden?"

"I want to talk to you alone."

"Yeah? Why's that?"

"Tonight on stage, you really ran a number. That guy was a jerk, but shit, Stoke, you were provoking him long before he let loose. You were egging on the whole crowd. What's that old expression, itching for a fight? That's what you looked like up there tonight. And you got one, didn't you?"

Stoke shrugged, drank from his coffee. "You didn't give me much of a shot at it."

"I've seen enough of that kind of stupid shit behavior, I don't need to see it from you. You'll get plenty of chances to jack it up where you're going."

"What do you mean?"

"You've decided, haven't you?" Rheinhardt said. "You're going into the army."

Stoke grinned, sat back in his chair. "Can't run anything past you, can I?" The grin quickly faded, and he looked hard at Rheinhardt. "Yeah, I've decided. And yeah, I'm going in. None of this leaving the country or going underground shit. And jail is out of the question. And I don't need to have you trying to talk me out of it, either."

"Come off it, Stoke. Have I ever tried to tell you what to do about this?"

Stoke shifted in his seat, then shook his head. "No. But I figured Terry might put you up to it. She doesn't want me to go."

"Of course not. She doesn't want to see you get killed for nothing—that's how she sees it. She doesn't want to see you come back . . . changed."

"Like you?"

Rheinhardt sighed, nodded. "Like me."

"Is it for nothing, Rheinhardt?"

"Man, I can't answer that one for you, Stoke."

"Would you go the same line if you had the chance to do it over?"

Exasperated, Rheinhardt clenched and unclenched his fists. "Shit, Stoke, questions like that don't mean a fucking thing. They're worthless, and completely unanswerable. I *did* go into the army, and I fought in the goddamn jungle, and that's what counts. I *can't* change it, I *can't* do it over again."

They lapsed into silence, and when the waitress came by Rheinhardt asked for plain coffee, and Stoke ordered another Irish. They remained silent until she brought them their drinks, left. Rheinhardt took a few sips of the hot coffee, leaned forward.

"I will tell you a few things, though, that maybe you

ought to hear. I don't know. For what it's worth, my personal opinion is we've got no goddamn business in most of the places we're fighting, but I'm not sure that's really relevant. The important thing you have to remember is, it's fucked out there. Doesn't matter where you end up fighting—jungle, desert, mountains, snow —it's no fucking game. Everything is real, even if it doesn't make any goddamn sense, and a bullet in the head means death. The mines are real, the bombs and booby traps and the bullets and mortars and diseases are real. It's war, no matter what name they give it, and you can get killed. As in dead. Don't ever forget that."

Stoke shrugged. "Yeah, well, you can get killed right here in the city, too."

Rheinhardt slammed a fist on the table, then grabbed Stoke's arm, squeezed it tightly. "Don't be a fucking idiot!" he hissed. "It's *not* the same, and if you go with that attitude you *are* likely to get killed, you stupid shit. I'm trying to give you an edge that just might save your ass, god damn it. There's no room for fuck-ups, they just end up dead. What I'm trying to tell you is, you have to watch yourself all the time, *all* the god damn time. Try to remember that. Just fucking try." He released Stoke's arm, tried drinking some coffee, but his hand was shaking too much. Instead, he lit a cigarette, barely managing that.

"I'm sorry," Stoke said. "I am, Rheinhardt."

Rheinhardt nodded, starting to calm down a bit. "I know. It's all right." He thought about telling Stoke about his nightmares, his doubts, try to explain why he was so damn touchy right now, but he decided he probably shouldn't. "How soon do you report?"

"Next week."

"Want me to come see you off?"

"No. I want to go that alone."

Rheinhardt nodded. "Come by and see me once more before you leave? I'll buy you a beer."

"I'll try." He paused, breathed deeply. "You haven't asked me why I decided to go."

Rheinhardt shrugged. "That's your business, Stoke. Besides, if you're anything like I was, you don't really know why."

Stoke stared down at his Irish coffee. "Is it bad that I'm afraid?" He looked back up at Rheinhardt.

Rheinhardt smiled softly, shook his head. "I guess I'd be more worried if you weren't."

There was a long silence, then Stoke nodded, but didn't say anything. Rheinhardt raised his coffee mug, Stoke did the same, and without smiling they brought the mugs together with a dull clinking sound, and drank.

Twenty-Three

Two nights later, Terry got off the bus three blocks from her apartment, tired and depressed. The day at Monterey House had been a disaster, with Cindy Robertson's father showing up with a court order saying he could pull her out of the house and bring her home. Which was crazy, since Cindy only came to the House because her parents had kicked her out in the first place. But Terry could see what was coming. Cindy was due in a few weeks, and though she didn't know it yet, she was going to be in a court fight with her parents for the custody of the child. That was why her parents were forcing her back home, not because they wanted her, but because they wanted the grandchild, and they were going for leverage. The bitch of it was, Terry could do nothing about it, and she knew who would win custody —the grandparents. Cindy was going to get fucked over again.

The porch light was on, and from half a block away Terry could see someone pacing back and forth beneath it. Rheinhardt? She hurried to the building, started up the steps; it was Stoke. She could tell immediately that he was really hammered on something again. In fact, she didn't know if she'd seen him straight at all in the last few weeks, what little she did see of him. It was starting to seriously concern her.

"Hey, Terry!" Stoke shouted. He threw his arms around her, squeezed tightly. "I've been waiting here for . . . I don't know, maybe an hour. No, probably not that long, it just *seemed* like an hour." He released her and stepped back, bouncing on the balls of his feet.

Terry unlocked the door, opened it, said, "Come on in."

Stoke went in ahead of her, bounded up the stairs. Terry followed him, much more slowly. "What's up?" she called. The lights came on as he moved through the apartment hitting the switches.

"I wanted to talk to you about some things," he called back.

At the top of the stairs, she draped her coat over the railing, leaned into her bedroom and tossed her bag onto the bed. She followed the sound of humming into the kitchen; Stoke had the tea kettle going on the stove and was looking into the open refrigerator, swinging the door back and forth.

"I take it you haven't eaten dinner. Want me to fix you something?"

He unwrapped a small piece of cheese, chewed on it. "No, I just want some tea. Mind if I make a fire?"

She shook her head. "No, go ahead. I'm going to make some dinner for myself. You sure you don't want anything."

"I'm sure." Still chewing on the cheese, he left the kitchen, and a few moments later she heard wood being thrown into the fireplace.

Terry started making a salad for herself, got out lettuce, tomato, cucumber, green onions, celery, left-over olives. She'd cleaned the lettuce and had started cutting the tomato when the kettle whistled. Terry turned off the gas, called out to Stoke.

"Your water's ready. What kind of tea do you want?" He didn't answer. "Stoke." Still no answer. Terry put down the knife, walked down the hall. "Stoke, the water's boiling."

She walked into the front room, and Stoke was on the floor in front of the crackling fire, deep asleep.

* * *

In the morning, Terry made hot tea for them both, brought a cup to Stoke who sat at the kitchen table with his head in his hands, then sat across from him. The light coming in through the kitchen windows was a bright gray, only a thin overcast muting the morning sun.

Stoke picked up the ceramic mug, hands shaking, sipped at it, spilling some over his fingers. He set the mug down, looked up at Terry, managed a half smile.

"A little shaky this morning," he said. His voice was harsh, cracking. "But I'm used to it."

"Why do you do this to yourself, Stoke?"

"Hey, I'm just having fun."

"This is fun?" She gestured at his left hand, which still trembled.

He shrugged. "It's not so bad. And yesterday *was* fun. I think." He grinned briefly. "I'm entitled, anyway. I plan to spend the next six days completely blown out of my mind."

"The next six days."

"Yes."

A large mass seemed to rise up from her stomach to her chest, crushing her heart. "Oh, shit, Stoke."

"Yeah, I'm going into the fucking army. I've got to report next week." He turned away from her, toward the window, and his voice got quiet. "That's what I came to talk about."

Terry felt suddenly very tired, and wanted to cry, but there wasn't the anger she expected, though she did sense it deep down inside her, muted and dormant.

"Does Rheinhardt know?"

He nodded, still not looking at her. "Sure. He figured it out the other night, when I jumped on that guy at the Laza Club. I didn't even have to tell him." He shrugged. "We talked about it after, after he pulled me out of there."

"What did he have to say?"

"Different things." He turned to face her. "He told me it was going to be some bad shit, told me to watch my ass or I'd get killed. Told me I didn't have any room to make mistakes, or do stupid things."

"But he didn't tell you not to go."

"Of course not. You just don't understand, do you, Terry. He *can't* tell me what to do. I don't want him to, and even if I did, he just couldn't do it. Can't you understand that?"

"I guess not." She paused, watching him drink more of the tea, his hands still shaking. "I just wish you wouldn't go."

"I know. But I *am* going, and there's nothing you can do to change that."

She didn't answer, and Stoke drank down the rest of the tea, pushed the mug away.

"I wanted to tell you myself," he said. He stood, breathing deeply. "And say good-bye."

"Good-bye? Won't I see you again before you leave?"

He shook his head. "I don't think so. I don't think you'd want to. So better we say good-bye now."

She breathed in deeply, pain in her chest. "Just like that? No time or anything together?"

"Just like that."

Terry nodded slowly, stood. She stepped up to Stoke and hugged him tightly, fighting back the tears. She didn't want to let him go.

"Take care of yourself," she whispered. "And like Rheinhardt said, you watch your skinny ass. I want you coming back, god damn it."

"I'll be back."

She squeezed him once more before kissing him on the cheek and letting him go.

Terry walked with him down the stairs to the front door, stood in the doorway as he descended the porch steps to the sidewalk. He turned, waved once to her, stuffed his hands into his pockets, then started down the street and a few moments later was gone.

The bass line thumped through the headphones, vibrating Rheinhardt's ears, cut through by Tensor of

Desire's vocalist hissing unintelligible lyrics. Rheinhardt lay on the cot with his eyes closed, letting the music take him away—away from his shaking hands, away from his empty, hollow feelings, away from the room and the unused clay, away from the city and away from the world.

An out-of-synch pounding broke in on the bass line, irregular, pausing, then starting up again. Then another voice intruded, distant and grating, and gradually Rheinhardt realized there was someone at the door. He opened his eyes, took off the headphones, sat up.

"Hey, Rheinhardt, you in there or what?" Stoke's voice. "I hear something."

"Just a minute!" Slightly disoriented, he turned off the tape player, got up, went to the door. When he opened it, Stoke stood there grinning, wearing a bright white jumpsuit and a leather shoulder bag.

"What do you think?" Stoke grabbed the waist of the jumpsuit, flapped it several times. "It's the Pete Townsend look."

Rheinhardt smiled. "You're not old enough to know who Pete Townsend is, or what he wore."

"Neither are you, but I've seen the pictures and films, too. This is it, isn't it?"

Rheinhardt nodded. "Yeah. Come on in." He left the door open, feeling a need for fresh air.

Stoke came into the room, went to the worktable, looking it over. He shrugged off the leather bag and set it on the floor, then ran his fingers through the dust on the table, held them up to Rheinhardt. "You haven't been working, have you?"

Rheinhardt shook his head, sat in the chair by the door, lit a cigarette. Stoke sat on the stool, leaning his elbows on the table.

"Is it bad?" Stoke asked.

Rheinhardt shrugged. "Bad enough. Haven't been able to do shit since I finished 'The Winter Gantry.' Lately . . . Christ, lately I haven't even tried."

"Do you know why?"

Rheinhardt shook his head again. "No. Oh, sure, I have lots of ideas, each of which makes as much sense as any of the others, but I don't really know."

"It must be hard."

"It's a bitch, especially since I don't know what the hell to do about it."

"What *are* you going to do, then?"

Rheinhardt tried to smile. "Shit, I don't know. For a while, nothing. And maybe after that, nothing for a while longer. Maybe work my ass off in Bear's shop, try to forget everything. But hey, enough about my problems. What about yours? You leaving soon?"

Stoke nodded. "Day after tomorrow. That's why I'm here." He leaned over, opened his bag, took out two dark beer bottles. "Here." He tossed one across the room.

Rheinhardt caught it easily, the bottle ice-cold still; he looked at the label. "Sapporo Black. Well, Japan's one country you can be pretty sure you won't be fighting in." Stoke had opened his bottle with the opener on a pocket knife, tossed the knife to Rheinhardt. Rheinhardt opened the bottle, held it up toward Stoke, who did the same. "To coming back as screwed up as you are now," Rheinhardt said.

"And with my balls intact."

"That too." He took a long drink, the beer wonderfully cold and bitter.

They sat for a long time without speaking, slowly drinking the beer.

"Does Terry know?" Rheinhardt asked.

"Yeah. We talked about it a few days ago. It went okay, I guess. Better than I thought it would." He smiled. "I think she's madder at you than she is at me."

"That figures."

The silence returned.

"Shit," Rheinhardt said after a while. "I don't really know what to say."

"I know, I've been the same way. I keep thinking I should be saying things to people before I go, but then I

can never figure out what." He sighed. "So let's just talk
when I get back, all right? I'll have a lot more to say
then, I guess."

Maybe, Rheinhardt thought. And maybe you'll be
like me, never want to talk about it, never want to think
about it. But he didn't say anything.

They finished their beers in silence. Stoke got up
from the stool, slung the leather bag over his shoulder.
"I should get going. I've got things to do, still."

Rheinhardt nodded, got up from the chair, and they
embraced in the doorway. Without a word, Stoke
crossed the gravel rooftop to the trapdoor, looked back
once, then disappeared through the opening, pulling
the trapdoor closed over him.

Justinian

Justinian and Deever stood on Deever's back porch,
side by side against the porch railing; they were both
smoking cigarettes, smoke drifting up into the clear
night sky.

"Rheinhardt's drowning," Justinian said. "He's lost
everything, seems completely confused. Maybe even
given up hope."

"Is it permanent?" Deever asked.

The shorter man shrugged. "Hard to say. It doesn't
look good right now. I think he'll take off soon, leave
the city."

"For how long?"

Justinian shrugged again. "I'm not a fucking mind
reader."

"Sometimes I think you are," Deever said. "Frankly
scares the shit out of me."

Justinian shook his head. "You always were superstitious, even in the Nam."

Deever snorted. "And you weren't? You were a god
damn lunatic, you and your fucking talismans."

Justinian turned, face twisting, grabbed Deever's
arm. "The talismans are *real* old man, they have real
power. They're the only reason I'm still alive."

Deever pulled Justinian's hand off his arm, backed
away a step. "You still believe in that shit."

Justinian nodded. "Yes. So let's forget about it. We
all have our . . ." He smiled. "Eccentricities."

Deever breathed deeply, leaned back against the
wooden rail, nodding. "I guess so." He took a hit on his
cigarette, knocked ash over the edge, watched it float
down to the steps below. "About Rheinhardt, though."

"I don't know what else to say. If he comes back to
the city, maybe he'll have a chance of pulling out. If he
stays away, running or hiding or whatever, then I think
he's lost for good. More than ever, now, it's up to him. I
can't do anything else. It's always been up to him
anyway, all I could ever do was nudge, prod, give him a
slap in the face. And I've done all of that I can for now."

Deever nodded, finished his cigarette, flicked it over
the edge of the railing. "I'm tired," he said.

"We're all tired these days," Justinian said.

They remained at the railing, side by side, and silent.

Dawn in the Greyhound Bus Depot was a dark gray.
Stoke showed his ticket to the gate clerk, came through
to the long sheltered boarding area, sat on a yellow
plastic chair, and set his duffel bag on the cement at his
feet. Two lines, each with about a dozen people, waited
at boarding gates in front of two buses, and another ten
or twelve people milled around or sat in the plastic
chairs. The pinging and yelping sounds of video games
emerged from a small enclosed structure near the snack
bar.

Justinian was at the snack bar, came away with two
cups of coffee, two doughnuts. He approached Stoke,
sat beside him, nodding. Stoke nodded back, didn't say
anything.

"Coffee?" Justinian asked. He held out one of the cups.

"Who the hell are you?" Stoke asked.

"My name is Justinian. We're not really strangers, Stoke. We have mutual friends."

"You know me? What friends?"

"Deever. Rheinhardt. Coffee?" he asked again.

Stoke took the coffee, frowned. "They send you to talk to me? What's the deal?"

"No, they didn't send me. They don't know I'm here. I came on my own, because I wanted to see you, give you something. I'm a Namvet, and I know you're headed for the army yourself." He sipped at his coffee, took a bite from one of the doughnuts.

"I don't see a Lazarus patch," Stoke said. He took a small sip from the coffee, then another.

"I don't have one, but I am a Namvet."

Stoke shrugged. "All right. So what do you want to talk about?"

"Would you believe me if I said I didn't know?"

Stoke smiled, shaking his head. "Sure. This entire conversation's been lunatic, that fits right in."

Justinian put his hand inside his coat, withdrew it, held it over Stoke's lap. "Your hand," he said.

Stoke frowned again, then held out his hand, palm up. Justinian put his hand over Stoke's, pressed, then drew it back revealing a metal pendant on a chain, the pendant a dark red and black dragon.

"Wear it," Justinian said. "It's a talisman. It will keep you alive."

Stoke looked at Justinian, silent at first, then said, "You're serious."

Justinian nodded. He got up, threw his coffee cup and partially eaten doughnut into the trash can, handed the other doughnut to Stoke. "Watch yourself out there. Don't fuck up, wear that, and you'll be all right, and I'll see you in a couple of years when you get back." He turned, walked through one of the boarding gates and onto the pavement, went around the corner of the building and was gone from sight.

Justinian dances.

He is in his room, the corner light throwing shadows, the rumble of machinery shaking the furniture and walls and pipes. Barefoot, wearing only khaki shorts, he moves in and out of shadow, almost in slow motion. He bends one knee, leans over it, slides his other foot, straightens and turns, kicks out, toes pointing, in shadow, in light, the beams crossing him as he moves through them. Up, down, spinning slowly again, light and shadow, shadow and light.

Justinian dances.

Twenty-Four

"He's gone," Terry said.

Rheinhardt nodded. He'd been dreading this, but knew he had to face it; he was surprised, though, that she'd asked to meet him here, in Buena Vista Park. They sat on a bench at the lower end of the park, a gray overcast blocking the sun.

"I was a lot angrier when he first told me," she went on. "Angry at him, angry at you." She shook her head. "I don't know, I don't seem to have the energy to be angry anymore. I just feel sad and tired. And I guess a little scared for him." She turned, faced Rheinhardt. "You could have kept him from going, you know. He would have listened to you. If you had told him not to go, he wouldn't have."

"You should give him more credit for having a mind of his own," Rheinhardt said. "He might have gone anyway. But the point is, whether you understand it or not, I simply could not tell him what to do. Listen, we've been through all this before, there's no reason to go at each other again over it. Won't change anything. Like you said, he's gone."

Terry nodded. "I'm really tired, Rheinhardt." She paused for a few moments, then went on. "I've got some things I need to work out, including a few that have to do with you. I think I'd rather we didn't see each other for a while. I need some distance from you."

This was the time to tell her, he thought. Tell her he was going to leave San Francisco, maybe for good, for a long time anyway. But he couldn't do it. Instead, he just nodded. It wasn't fair to her, he knew that. Still. He stood up from the bench.

"He'll be okay," Rheinhardt said.

Terry looked up at him. "Will *we*?"

"I don't know." He tried to smile, thought he managed it. "Probably not." Then he shrugged. "I'll see you sometime."

She nodded. "Yes, sometime. Good-bye, Rheinhardt."

"Good-bye."

He turned and, without once looking back, started down the hill.

Rheinhardt stood on the rooftop beside his room, rucksack over his right shoulder, duffel bag in his left hand. He felt drained and hollow, slightly queasy, but now that he had decided to leave, he could not imagine any other course. He smiled to himself—inertia again.

Everything had been taken care of, as far as he knew. Keys were with Carlatti, and the letter had been mailed to Terry. The sick feeling in his gut intensified when he thought of her, but that was something else he could not change.

Rheinhardt adjusted the rucksack, checked the door, then walked to the opening in the roof and started down the wooden steps.

Terry had a sick feeling go through her when she saw the letter from Rheinhardt, and she hurried into the apartment, up the stairs. In the kitchen she put the kettle on the stove, then sat at the table and carefully opened the envelope, pulled out the single sheet with Rheinhardt's small, neat printing.

Terry,

I know this is a crappy way to tell you, but I just couldn't talk to you about it. I'm leaving San Francisco, should be gone by the time you get this. I

don't know how long I'll be gone, probably months,
maybe years. Carlatti's got the keys to my room,
the outside cabinets, my P.O. box. I told him you'd
take care of the sculptures. All my tools and
supplies and other stuff are boxed, and I'd appreci-
ate it if you would take care of all that as well.
    You want reasons. So do I, and I don't have any.

    Take care.

                                              Rheinhardt

Jesus. Terry reread the letter, then carefully set it on
the table. Why? Damn right she wanted reasons. Jesus,
the god damn bastard. The sick feeling spread through
her, down her legs and along her arms, rose up in her
throat. Stoke was gone, and now Rheinhardt. Jesus
Christ.

Her hands were shaking. She felt as if her world,
everything she had tried to hold together, had now
completely fallen apart.

The water in the kettle started boiling. Terry did not
get up to take it off the stove, and the shrill whistle kept
on, filling the cold and empty kitchen. She remained
motionless at the table, waiting for something to fill the
hollows of her heart.

Nearly midnight, and the Warehouse was quiet.
Terry wandered along the dim passages, looking at the
drawings, poems, and graffiti on the walls without
really registering any of it.

She stopped at the foot of the ladder leading up to
Rheinhardt's old studio, looked high into the darkness
above the mutelights. Nothing was visible, maybe a
patch of darkness darker than its surroundings. Terry
took hold of the ladder, put her foot on a rung, and
started climbing.

Once on the landing, she hesitated for a minute, then
opened the door. More darkness. She walked in, her
footsteps echoing, pulled the chain switch and the

overhead light came on. Terry blinked at the sudden brightness, at the blank walls of the empty room. She made a single circuit of the room, searching for any sign that Rheinhardt had once lived and worked in here. But there was nothing to see, and eventually she turned off the light, bringing back the dark. She left the room, closed the door behind her.

Terry leaned against the platform railing and gazed out over the building, over mostly empty space. If at all possible, she would refrain from putting someone else in the studio, would keep it empty. Not for Rheinhardt's return—if he came back he would never return to the Warehouse—but as a reminder of what was happening here, and in the world around her.

Rheinhardt woke to the sound of rain spattering against the bus window, and the cool dark gray of cloudy skies. He was somewhere in Washington, motoring toward Seattle. The road was a darker gray than the sky, and on both sides of the freeway was the lush dark green of trees and thick brush and more trees.

The seat beside him was empty, though the bus was more than half full. Voices were low, a background murmur as soothing as the gentle rumble of the bus engine and the patter of rain against glass.

Rheinhardt felt hollow; in his chest was the flutter of something that was either fear, or a sense of loss. Maybe both. He shifted in his seat, refolded his leather jacket, lay his head on it again, his forehead against the cool glass. Cool. That's what he wanted, needed, the cold, wet weather of the Pacific Northwest. Cool. Rheinhardt closed his eyes and breathed in deeply, trying to fill the hollow with his breath. But the emptiness remained.

PART TWO

RETURN

Clinical X-Rays

One

Two in the morning, the streets were empty. Rheinhardt emerged from the broken first-floor window of a derelict office building, dropped to the ground. He remained in a squat and scanned the streets, the dark and silent buildings, the starlit sky.

Rheinhardt was dressed in black, his rucksack as dark as his clothes. He wore black leather fingerless gloves, and he flexed his fingers as he searched the darkness.

Nothing moved. The cones of light from the few working streetlamps were motionless, dim, flecked with hovering dust. He could just see the blinking lights of the barricades a few blocks away, and wondered why this part of Emeryville had been cordoned off. All the buildings seemed to be deserted. The only sounds were faint noises from distant parts of the city—indistinct traffic hiss, the muted wail of sirens, a dull, unidentifiable thudding. Rheinhardt stood, and started down the street, his boots nearly silent on the pavement, on the cracked concrete walks.

Rheinhardt kept to the shadows, moved quickly along with one hand on the building walls beside him. Clouds moved in overhead from across the bay, dark and heavy. The cold night air thickened.

He turned a corner, spotted the triangular projection four stories above, across and halfway down the street. Slower now, more cautious, Rheinhardt slid along the building wall until he was directly opposite the triangle, and felt for the doorway.

He was certain the building was deserted, like everything else here, but he knocked anyway. After a pause, he tried the door; it was locked, and didn't budge. A moment later, however, a soft click sounded, and the door slid open. Rheinhardt hesitated a moment, then slipped in through the black doorway. The door clicked shut behind him.

The darkness inside was complete, and the air had a hollow, deserted feel. Ticking sounds filtered down from above, as of cooling metal.

A black upon black form appeared, shuffling footsteps like sand blowing through glass.

"Who is it?" Rheinhardt asked.

A man laughed, said, "You know me, Rheinhardt."

"Justinian?"

The short, stocky man laughed again; a narrow beam of light lanced out, aimed at Rheinhardt's throat. The heat of the needle light tickled the skin just above his Adam's apple.

"You've been gone a long time, Rheinhardt. Five years." Justinian put out his free hand. In the beam of light Rheinhardt could see mottled skin across the old man's fingers and palm. Rheinhardt did not shake Justinian's hand. The light flicked out, and the blackness returned.

"Here," Justinian said. "You'll need this." He pressed the needle light into Rheinhardt's fingers, then shuffled back a few steps. "Stay off the roof, it's wired."

Rheinhardt thumbed on the light, caught Justinian's smile as the floor opened beneath the old man's heavy boots. "See you 'round," Justinian called as he dropped through the opening. The echo of his voice cut off as the floor snapped back into place, solid and secure. The building's silence, punctuated by the steady ticking sounds, returned.

Rheinhardt used the needle light to make his way along the narrow, high-ceilinged corridor. A network of dulled copper wire hung from the ceiling, an impenetrable, patternless mesh from which dangled jagged strips of bent and twisted metal painted in slashes of neon-brite colors. The colors seemed to shimmer and reflect from one another, pulsing as Rheinhardt played the light across them. He wondered who had done it. It reminded him of Kit's work. Maybe she, too, had returned.

At the end of the corridor was the open doorway to the stairs. Tiny, widely-spaced blue minnow lights marked the way, casting just enough illumination to show the steps, the handrail, and some of the graffiti that covered the walls. He glanced at a few of the clichéd outbursts in black and red ink, the crude pornographic sketches, then ignored the rest as he ascended.

The air grew warmer and more stifling as he climbed. He stopped, lit a cigarette. After two or three hits, he tossed it to the ground and crushed it with his boot.

At the top of the stairs, Rheinhardt paused, resting and listening. The ticking sounds persisted, louder now, but he heard nothing else. He pushed open the heavy metal door, entered the corridor.

Darkness again. He flashed the needle light along the hall and started walking. The walls had been painted with layer upon layer of acrylics, giving a raised, three-dimensional effect. The colors were mostly deep greens, blues and grays, with occasional showers of red—a single mural of computer arcades, exploding space stations, domed cities, and vast, densely populated underground caverns. A future that was very near, Rheinhardt thought.

A door near the end of the corridor had been blown off its hinges, the black scars of the explosion still etched into the metal walls, disfiguring the mural. Inside the room, the needle light illumined the radio.

Rheinhardt found a chair, dragged it to the table, and sat in front of the radio. He clipped the needle light to his ear and turned his head as he needed light. Through the blacked-out windows he could just hear the rain begin.

As he waited for the radio to power up, fiddling with switches and knobs, Rheinhardt felt a nervous ache rise in his chest. Christ, why had he come back?

When the radio was ready, he fine-tuned it to a frequency he had not used in a long time, a frequency he could barely remember. Rheinhardt gripped the transmission switch, and began sending.

Tay Minh appeared at the back door, a thin, dark figure emerging from the night and the rain.

Terry saw him from the edge of the party crowd. She squeezed away from several people and went to meet him on the covered utility porch. Minh stood, silent, water dripping from his dark green poncho; his face shadowed, he looked older than seventeen. The music, loud and pounding in the other rooms, was quiet out on the porch.

"Can you come?" Minh asked.

"Problems? Cops or something?"

He shook his head. "Someone on the radio."

"On the *radio*?"

Minh nodded. "Asking for you. Only you."

"Someone. Who?"

"Rheinhardt."

She couldn't say anything for a moment. Then, "Jesus." A knot twisted in her chest, pounded at her ribs for release. "All right."

While Minh waited, Terry returned to the front room and tracked down Ann, her roommate. Ann was trying to smoke a joint and take pictures with a Polaroid at the same time.

"I'm gone," Terry said. "Probably not back tonight."

Ann nodded, took Terry's picture, and grinned, the joint flicking up and down.

Terry went to her room, grabbed her worn leather jacket, put on boots, old flannel hat, and returned to the porch. Minh led the way down two flights of wooden steps, across the yard through the pouring rain, and up over the top of a fence to the next street. In a black, narrow alley he dragged a moped out from beneath a stack of broken crates. Terry climbed on behind him.

"This is new," she said. "You buy it?"

Minh laughed, but did not answer. He push-started the moped, and they shot out into the street and the rain, headed for the Warehouse.

Rheinhardt. Rheinhardt was back. Terry closed her eyes and held on.

Rheinhardt scanned the airwaves.

It would be a while before the call-back came, and he needed to keep busy. He waited, headphones light and comfortable over his ears, and tuned into the voices of the night.

He tried the FM band first, scuttling across the frequencies. Muzak, syntho-pop, generic country—he caught and passed them all. Then a whisper cut through, a defined hiss surrounded by bells, and he brought in a weak station broadcasting ether rock. It wasn't bad. Rheinhardt closed his eyes, let images rise in his mind. In the darkness of the room the tolling bells, the synth-bank whispers, and the smooth, soothing tones of vibes created a subdued wash of color rolling through the air—the blue-green and white of stormy surf. Rheinhardt listened and watched, swimming through the cold surf, riding the wave crests, locking it all in his memory so he could draw on it later for his sculptures. If he ever sculpted again.

Almost unconsciously, his hands moved to the radio and faded the station. When the silence and darkness returned, he switched over to the short-wave bands. Static hissed and crackled, louder as he jacked up the volume. A voice came in, the static dipped, and Rheinhardt made some fine adjustments.

The voice, a man's, spoke rapidly in Spanish, faint but distinct. Rheinhardt could understand only a word or two of each sentence, and never enough to make sense of what the man was saying; strange, Rheinhardt thought, since he had once spoken Spanish fluently.

Perhaps his mind was trying to block out the language along with all the other memories of those times down in the 'mericas.

There was a slight pause, then a woman began to reply. She spoke more slowly, but though Rheinhardt recognized the words, he still could not understand them. "... *flores para los* ..." *Flores*. Flowers?

For the next half hour, Rheinhardt sat in the heavy, hollow darkness, hands softly pressing the headphones to his ears, listening to the voices coming to him from another part of the world. The longer he listened, the more he came to understand, not only the words, but the mood and emotion the voices carried across the charged night air.

Minh slowed as they drove through the south of Market and reached the edges of the Mission. They passed dilapidated apartment buildings and houses, noisy dim bars, corner groceries encased in grillwork, abandoned warehouses only partially demolished. Traffic was light, pedestrians rare. Nearly a third of the streetlights were dark, glass covers shattered. Minh wove his way through a series of narrow streets and dark alleys, and approached the Warehouse from the west. He cut the moped's engine, doused the light, and they glided through the cold rain, pushing off the cracked pavement with their boots.

The Warehouse grounds were unlit, surrounded by high fencing. The main building was an enormous, hulking shadow in the darkness. Above and behind it, another shadow against the night sky, was the old derelict freeway a few blocks away.

Standing at the gate, Terry breathed deeply, looking over the darkened grounds. Rheinhardt had lived and worked here at one time; so had a lot of other talented artists. Not anymore. The radical, cutting edge aspects were gone. In the last few years the people and the creative atmosphere in the Warehouse had gone to shit; the place was stagnating, no longer had any of the life and energy it once did. More than stagnating. Terry felt certain it was dying, and that a part of her would go with it.

She inserted her key card, punched in password and code. Minh pushed the moped through the narrow opening that appeared, and Terry followed. She secured the gate behind her.

Minh took off, pushing the moped toward the corner of the building. Terry walked across the mud and chunks of old pavement of what had once been the parking lot. The main door, for the third time in a month, was unlocked; she wondered if there was any point in spreading the word again. Probably not.

Once inside, Terry could feel the vibrations of music throbbing from below, a deep bass line thundering its dominance. Packer had control of the main sound system again, broadcasting his DeathRock compositions through the cellar hallways. Terry shook her head. He would probably be screwing Lisa or Wilsy, tiny dermal mikes taped all over their bodies, recording transitions for his next demo.

Only the mutelights were on overhead, and Terry moved along the dim corridors, ignoring the few open studio doors she passed. Nearly every square inch of wall and floor space was covered with paint, plaster, light-mosaics, inked or etched poems and stories. Terry rarely bothered anymore to see what was new; most of the new was crap, the percentage steadily increasing, and the trend depressed her. The whole place and everyone in it depressed her now. Maybe she was just getting old. At thirty-five? Maybe.

Terry stopped at the foot of a rope and wood ladder leading up to a room high in the darkness of the building's upper reaches—Rheinhardt's old studio. It was dark now, though it wasn't empty. She turned away and continued along the corridor.

The communications room glowed with the light from computer terminals. Geometric figures rotated on the monitors, but the chairs in front of them were empty. In the opposite corner, Lester, who kept an eye on things at night, sat in front of the radio, eyes closed. As Terry approached, he opened his eyes, looked at her.

"I've heard of this guy," he said.

Terry didn't respond. She sat beside him, put on a set of headphones, and Lester activated the call-back. The light showed that Rheinhardt was calling from the old East Bay annex. She'd practically forgotten it still existed; no one had used it in two years. The next minute was filled with hisses and pops, then a sharp click, and finally Rheinhardt's voice.

"Terry?"

"Yes, Rheinhardt." She turned, stared at Lester until he removed his headset and left the room.

There was a long silence, then Rheinhardt finally spoke again. "Hey," he said.

"Articulate as always." She paused. "It's been a long time, Rheinhardt."

"Yeah."

Her mind seemed blank, unable to think of what she should say to him. "What's with using the radio?" she finally asked.

"Couldn't get into the city. BART's shut down for the night, and the Bay Bridge is closed off completely. Heard something about someone trying to blow up the damn thing."

"Yes, couple weeks ago. Nearly succeeded. Managed to screw up a lot of the roadway, enough so it'll be weeks before traffic can use it again. A hell of a mess for commuters." She smiled to herself. "Breaks my heart."

"I imagine." He paused a moment. "So I couldn't get into the city, and couldn't get anyone by phone. No listing for you, your old number disconnected. No listing for Deever, Stoke, anyone I know. Wondered if everyone was dead or gone."

Some of both, she thought, but she didn't say anything.

"Didn't know what else to do," he went on. "So I came here. The place is deserted."

"Hasn't been anyone over there in at least two years. I'm surprised the radio still works."

"It's a mess over here, actually. Radio's probably the only thing that *does* still work."

Terry closed her eyes for a moment. "It's a mess everywhere."

"Yeah." Rheinhardt paused, then said, "You know how Stoke's doing? He must be back in the city, unless he reupped, and I don't think even *he* was that crazy."

Terry couldn't answer. All the old anger and pain and terrible aching erupted within her, taking her by surprise, and she wanted to scream at him. But her throat was constricted, and by the time she had calmed enough, and was ready to tell him, Rheinhardt spoke first.

"Noooooo . . ." His voice trailed off.

"Yes," she said, nodding slowly to herself. "He's dead, Rheinhardt." She breathed deeply once. "Killed in Honduras. Or maybe Colombia. I got conflicting reports."

There was another long silence. She was afraid to break it, but when it seemed he would not speak again, she did. "Why are you back, Rheinhardt?"

He didn't answer at first, and she wondered if he was still listening, but then his voice, quiet and steady, broke the silence. "Can you meet me in the morning, Terry? Eight o'clock, Cafe Olivia?"

"It's been closed down," she told him.

There was a pause, and Terry expected him to ask her what had happened, but he didn't. Instead, Rheinhardt asked, "How about Cafe Bugatti?"

"I have to work tomorrow morning."

"Can you meet me, Terry?"

Another deep breath, a rising ache. "Of course, Rheinhardt."

Still another silence followed. Too much to say that couldn't be said until they were face to face.

"Terry."

"Yes."

A final silence, then a single click, and Rheinhardt was gone again.

Stoke was dead.

Rheinhardt climbed the four flights of stairs to the roof, rewired the door alarm, and opened the narrow metal door. He propped it open, squatted in the doorway, careful to stay off the roof itself. The rain slanted in with the wind, cold and hard. Rheinhardt pulled a poncho from his rucksack, put it on, huddled inside it.

Cold rain, warm rain, he'd sat through enough of it in the jungles. Twelve years ago. Stoke had done the same. Following in Rheinhardt's footsteps? He didn't think so, but that's what Terry might say. Did she blame him for Stoke's death?

Stoke.

A skinny kid in a green jumpsuit, pedaling furiously through the Financial District on his heavy-duty bike; up on stage, hair shining in the lights as he sang and played guitar in bars and sleazy clubs for free beer and a few bucks and the chance to go home with a warm body. It was why he'd gone into rock 'n' roll, Stoke had told Rheinhardt: "Because it's the only thing I can do worth a damn, and the only way I can get laid." The Kid.

Fuck. Fuck . . . fuck . . . fuck.

Rheinhardt pressed palms to temples, trying to ease the pain.

Stoke.

Stoke was dead, and the night rain continued to fall.

The apartment was quiet, empty but for a vaguely familiar woman curled up on the front room sofa, asleep. The stereo lights blinked at Terry, but no music played. A thumping sounded from the ceiling, then the rapid bumps of running footsteps. The remnants of the party were on the roof.

Terry went out to the utility porch, looked up at the

obscured stars through the open hatchway. The rain
had stopped, the clouds moving east across the bay. She
heard more running, and stifled laughter. After a moment, she climbed the wooden ladder built into the
wall, pulled herself up and out onto the graveled
rooftop.

Half a dozen people strolled about on the wet roof,
dark forms in the dim light. Ann was jumping over
shiny pools of water, laughing, the Polaroid swinging
from her wrist. Someone else had another camera, and
the flash burst, briefly and sharply illuminating the roof
and its occupants. A match flared, and cigarettes were
lit. Ann and the other photographer took pictures of
each other taking pictures, flashes exploding almost
simultaneously. More laughter, stifled giggling.

Terry sat on a stove chimney, the metal cold and
damp. Derek saw her, sauntered over and offered her a
joint. Terry shook her head.

"Thought any more about my offer?" Derek asked.

"Don't be such a shithead, Derek. I gave you my
answer, it's not going to change. Go find some other
body to experiment on. You and your fucking spinal
plugs. And stay the hell away from Dolores, I've warned
you about her before." Derek gave her a half smile and
a shrug. She turned away from him, waited until he'd
wandered back to the others before she let herself
shudder. I *am* getting old, she thought.

An awkward, undefined sensation pulsed through
her. Rheinhardt was back. She didn't know what she
felt, or what she should be feeling. Why was he back?
She almost wished he had stayed wherever he'd gone.

Something brushed against her calf, then pushed
hard against it; Terry looked down at Al, her huge gray
cat who looked back at her with gold eyes and yawned.
Terry reached down, scratched him behind his ears,
under his chin as he twisted and turned his head,
purring loudly.

A tremendous flash of brilliant white lit up the sky; it
dimmed slightly but remained bright, glowing in the

west. Terry turned, saw huge glowing white letters
suspended from the Sutro Tower:

DEFECT

It had to be Defectors. She wondered if they had also
been responsible for the damage to the Bay Bridge.
Defect. Sometimes she felt like doing just that, defect-
ing from the Warehouse, from this city. What was it the
Defectors wanted people to defect from? They never
said. Society, she supposed. The establishment. Sanity.
They certainly had.

Two more flashes went off in succession, from cameras, then everyone on the roof started running around,
splashing water, kicking up gravel, banging on metal
vents and laughing, yelling "Defect! Defect!" Terry
wanted to scream at them, tell them to just shut the
fuck up, didn't they have any respect for the dead? The
dead? Stoke. Rheinhardt. But Rheinhardt wasn't dead,
though she hadn't really known for sure these last few
years, not until tonight. Rheinhardt. Her body ached all
over. Jesus.

But Terry didn't scream at anyone; instead she stood,
stepped across the narrow gap between buildings and,
with Al padding along at her side, began walking from
one rooftop to another under the cold, glowing sky.

Two

Rheinhardt rode a BART train under the bay, standing in a cramped car filled with perfumed and sweating commuters, his rucksack digging into another man's back. He had passed through metal detectors to get into the station; his rucksack had gone through the fluoroscope. Uniformed security guards were stationed at each end of every car, and one at the central doors. Things had tightened since he'd left.

While they were still under the bay, the train shuddered to an abrupt halt, and Rheinhardt could smell the quickly rising panic. The guard at the center doors shifted position, freeing his right arm, placed his hand on his gun. No announcement was made.

No one moved, no one said a word, and the car was silent without even the hiss of recycling air, the atmosphere stifling. He could see people around him breathing more quickly with fear, or deliberately breathing slowly and deeply, trying to relax. The lights flickered twice, then twice more, and though the lights remained steady after that, he could see the increasing tension on the faces around him.

But several minutes later, when Rheinhardt was beginning to think someone in the train would lose it before too much longer, the train finally jerked forward. As it resumed progress the relief was tangible, a stale and acrid exhalation.

Ten minutes later he emerged into the cool air of Market Street, high clouds flowing past above him, obscuring the tops of the taller buildings. Much of the street had been torn up for repairs, but no one was working now; traffic crawled, a single lane in each direction, creeping through mounds of damp earth and broken concrete, past toppled barriers and rusting machinery.

The police were noticeable here in the heart of the Financial District. Looking around, Rheinhardt could see five or six cops within a few blocks, walking casually along the sidewalks. A pair on the opposite side of the street watched him closely as they walked past.

He caught a trolley coach on Sutter after only a ten-minute wait, found a seat in the rear. On the back of the seat in front of him, in dark blue felt marker, was KILL ALL NIGGERS AND FAGS. Below that, in black ink: WHITEY SUCKS MONKEY DICK. Rheinhardt leaned his head against the scratched window, and slept.

When he woke, the bus was nearly empty, and he was two blocks past his stop. It was still early, though, and he stayed on to the end of the line on the border of the Presidio. He thought of going out to the Wave Organ, but instead walked down Lombard, the short stretch at the end with hardly any traffic.

He stopped in front of Cafe Olivia. The sign was still up, but the door and windows were boarded over. How long? He wondered if Martin was still in the city somewhere. He wondered how many of the people he had known were now gone.

Rheinhardt crossed the street, walked past seedy motels and small apartments, then started down toward the Palace of Fine Arts and the Exploratorium. Traffic was light in the direction of the Golden Gate Bridge, heavier headed toward downtown. He crossed Richardson Drive, then walked the two blocks to the edge of the lagoon fronting the Palace of Fine Arts.

Overhead, the clouds were growing darker, heavier, and the lagoon area was deserted except for a few ducks drifting about on the water. The houses fronting the lagoon, large, luxurious, and expensive, did not show the signs of deterioration he'd seen elsewhere in the city, which did not surprise him at all. The sidewalks were clean and well maintained, lawns and gardens immaculate, paint tasteful and solid.

Rheinhardt skirted the edge of the lagoon, walking over damp grass, then along clay and gravel paths and through the parking area, as deserted as the lagoon, to the front of the Exploratorium building. Like Cafe Olivia, the doors and windows were boarded over. There were no signs, no posters, nothing but leaves blowing along the cracked cement in front of the entrance.

A huge sense of loss washed over Rheinhardt as he stood in front of the building, staring at the warped sheets of thick plywood and knotty two by fours. He realized, then, that he had somehow expected the city to be the same now as when he'd left it, as though it would have been put "on hold" while he was gone; as though the continual deterioration of the city would have, through some strange process, been suspended. It was absurd, of course, but he saw now that he *hadn't* expected any changes, though he should have, and he wondered how prepared he would be for whatever others he would see.

Rheinhardt turned away from the building and started back toward Richardson and Lombard, intending to start the long walk to Cafe Bugatti. Instead, as he neared the Presidio entrance, he impulsively checked into one of the run-down motels he'd passed earlier. A neon sailboat sputtered on the side of the building, blue and red.

His room was on the second floor, with a view of asphalt and concrete out front, and broken glass and garbage cans out back. The mattress sagged in the middle, and the carpet was worn through in several spots, but the room was clean, the locks and bolts sturdy and secure.

Rheinhardt stood at the front window and watched the traffic a block away curving past in both directions, headed either downtown or toward the Golden Gate

Bridge. He lit a cigarette and lost himself in the flow of cars and the light drizzle of rain that began to fall.

Rheinhardt was late. Terry sat at a window table in Cafe Bugatti, watching the rain, sipping at a cappuccino. How arty, she thought.

An old, gray-haired man sat at another window table with a sketch pad and charcoal sticks. He did not draw; his hands trembled, clasped together, and he gazed out the window, hardly blinking. On his jacket shoulder was a faded green and red Lazarus patch, reminding her of Deever. There was a lot Rheinhardt didn't know yet, none of it good. The old man by the window probably didn't have much longer to live, and Terry wondered what was killing him.

She wondered what long-term effects would be discovered thirty years from now for the soldiers who fought in the South and Central American jungles, or in the African deserts and jungles and grasslands. Rheinhardt had been back for what, twelve, thirteen years, something like that. Physically he'd been apparently unharmed. Had anything changed in the last five years? What about in another ten?

She turned away from the vet, looked back out onto the street. Several minutes later Rheinhardt appeared, walking up the hill. He still had the bleached tail of hair at his neck, still wore mostly black. A knot tightened in her chest.

Rheinhardt glanced at her as he went past the window. He came in through the door, dripping from the rain, and turned to the Vietnam vet. Rheinhardt gave him an odd extended salute with three fingers and several motions. The old vet returned the salute, slowly and stiffly, then turned back to the window and the rain.

Rheinhardt went to the counter, asked for coffee. Terry watched him, listened to his voice to see if he had changed much. He did not look at her.

When he came to the table with his coffee, he kissed

her on the cheek, then sat across from her. They both remained silent.

"I don't know what to say," Terry finally said. "I don't even know what to *feel*, for Christ's sake. All these years." She shook her head.

"I know." Rheinhardt breathed in deeply, then out. "I don't either." He turned away, and they were silent again. Terry watched him, the knot tightening in her chest, becoming almost painful.

After several minutes Rheinhardt's gaze seemed to lock on something outside. Terry looked out the window. Across the street, huddled in an alcove and shifting from foot to foot, was a short, stocky man. The man gazed back at them.

"Who is that?" Terry asked. "Someone you know?"

"Sure. Don't you?"

"I don't think so. Why?"

"I thought he had some connection to the Warehouse now. He was there last night, in the East Bay building."

"No one's been out there in two or three years. I can ask around, though. Who is he?"

"His name's Justinian. You've never met him?" Terry shook her head, and Rheinhardt shrugged, went on. "He's a little bit crazy. Maybe a lot. I don't know." He paused. "He's okay, though. Sort of. He's a Namvet, apparently never been cleared, never been screened or identified, never been marked." He shrugged again.

"He's following you?"

"I don't know. I don't really care." He turned away, looked at Terry. "He's a friend of Deever's."

Deever. I should tell him about Deever, she thought. The silence returned, and they drank their coffee with quiet, slow movements. The knot of tension in Terry's chest did not ease.

"We should have a lot more to say to each other," Terry said.

Rheinhardt nodded. "We will. It's what you said, that it's just been too long." He turned away, looked out the window again. Terry looked too; the old man was gone.

"Rheinhardt. Why are you back?"

He breathed very deeply once, faced her. "A last hope." He held up his hands, rotated them and flexed weathered fingers. "I have not produced a single sculpture, I haven't done a thing to a block of clay in over five years." He paused, looked away once more. "I'm afraid I never will again."

She was looking at his hands, which had begun to tremble slightly, then looked up at his face. And from the tension in it, the way his brow furrowed, skin tightened, eyes lined, she could see he *was* scared. She reached across the table, put her hands over his. "Let's go for a walk," she said.

Rheinhardt turned to her, and nodded.

They walked out along the yacht harbor jetty, and though the rain had stopped, the gusting wind was damp and cold, rattling ropes and tackle against the masts of sailboats so that it sounded as if there were dozens of wind chimes suspended out over the water. A few people were working on their boats—coiling rope, brushing varnish onto wooden rails, scrubbing walls or decks—and on one enormous motor yacht, half a dozen people could be seen inside the huge cabin, standing around and talking and drinking; the cabin was larger, Rheinhardt thought, than any apartment he'd ever lived in.

"Must be nice," Terry said. "That kind of money. It's like insulation from reality."

"I suppose."

When they were past the boats, and walking over the dirt and gravel path out toward the far tip of the jetty, the wind kicked up even harder, spraying a mist at them that grayed both air and water. Jagged rocks formed the banks on either side, with a few scrawny weeds growing up between the higher ones. Ahead, out near the tip, was a small stretch of wet sand, maybe ten feet long and two feet wide, a tiny beach that would disappear as the tide rose. Small waves hissed at the sand, splashed against the rocks.

"Where have you been all this time?" Terry asked.

"A lot of different places. I spent most of the time in Alaska, though."

"Alaska?"

He smiled. "Yeah, Alaska."

"Doing what?"

"Worked on a fishing trawler for a while. A couple of long stints in a cannery. Went north, worked my ass on an oil rig and made obscene amounts of money, far more than I could spend, and ate the best damn food of my life." He shook his head. "Spent about four months, once, holed up in a place called Barrow, about as far north as you can go."

"Cold?"

"Oh, yeah, cold. Cold and terrible and beautiful."

They reached the tip of the jetty, where the banks had been built up with chunks of granite and marble enclosing the pipes of the Wave Organ.

"Do you know where they got these blocks?" Rheinhardt asked. When Terry shook her head, he said, "Old Victorian tombstones. Where they got *those*, I don't know."

They were silent a minute, standing in the mist. The wind eased slightly. Then Terry said, "Were you there, then, in Alaska, when those people blew up a part of the pipeline?"

He nodded. He remembered feeling at the time that he couldn't even get away in Alaska.

"Why Alaska?" Terry asked.

Rheinhardt shrugged. "I don't know. Isolation, I guess." Like this tiny strip of land, he thought. "And I think maybe I didn't want to be reminded of jungle for a while."

They stood in silence for several minutes; Rheinhardt sensed a growing tension in Terry, and eventually she turned and looked at him. "You feel that way, Rheinhardt, then how could you have let Stoke go? That's exactly where he ended up, in the damn jungle."

"Stoke made his own decision."

"But you could probably have . . ."

"Jesus Christ, Terry," he started, cutting her off. "We went through all that five years ago. I didn't come back here to rehash it all again. We can't change anything now." He turned away from her, looked out toward the Golden Gate Bridge. It was a dull orange, bleak in the mist, yet beautiful still.

Stoke. He wondered what Stoke had looked like in battle fatigues—a strong, wiry kid running through the jungle with music in his ears, pumped up with the shit they gave you out there, especially on night patrols. Light up your eyes, fire up your ears, hype up your brain before they fried it. Rheinhardt hadn't touched drugs once since his discharge, but sometimes his vision still lit up on him, flared out the back of his eyes all on its own. Well, Stoke wouldn't have to worry about that now.

"So, what is it?" Terry asked after a long silence. "Why you haven't been able to work all this time."

What is it? Just what he had been asking himself for five years. "I feel paralyzed," Rheinhardt finally said.

"By what?"

"By the world."

"The world."

He nodded, then shook his head. "I know what that sounds like, but it's the closest I've come to it. I've been doing a lot of thinking, trying to understand just what the hell is shutting me down." He clenched his fists, wrapped his arms around his chest. "Everything is so fucked up, *people* are so fucked up . . . I feel overwhelmed by my own pessimism, and I can't shake it. I haven't done a thing since 'The Winter Gantry.' I don't know. Paralyzed by the world, by a sense of utter futility."

They clambored over the granite blocks and down into a hollow formed by two stone benches and three walls of the blocks, sheltered from the wind; rubber-rimmed tips of several Wave Organ pipes jutted up from the rock, like periscopes. Rheinhardt felt all his pent-up frustrations and anger begin to surface, surge through his gut, pressuring for release. Terry sat on one of the benches, but he remained standing, tensed.

He paced back and forth in front of Terry, and though he opened his mouth several times, he was unable to speak. His hands began to tremble, only slightly at first, then more violently until they shook so much he could not control them. He stopped pacing, faced Terry, held out his shaking hands.

"This," he managed to say. "This is what happens to me, I try to sit at a table with a block of clay, or outside with metal and welder, and my god damn hands shake so much I can't do a thing. I can't handle the flame or hold the metal still, I can't even work with a block of clay without dropping it."

Terry was staring at his hands, and he stared at them with her as they shook and shook without stopping. His throat was dry, and he was only barely able to speak.

"I sit there," he said, "and I keep thinking, what's the point? What is the fucking point?"

He turned away from her and jammed his hands into his pockets where they could hardly move. His arms continued to tremble as he stared out at the gray, overcast bay.

"I think I understand how you feel," Terry said.

The cold mist felt comforting on his face, and he looked out toward Alcatraz, remembering Gollancz. It looked different; the buildings were almost completely gone now, little more than rubble.

"The worst of it is," he continued, still without looking at her, "I haven't even *tried* in the last two years. I haven't even tried."

"I *do* understand," Terry said again. "I've been feeling that way myself."

"The Warehouse?" He turned back to her. His arms had finally ceased trembling.

She nodded. "It's gotten pretty bad."

"It was bad five years ago, Terry. You just couldn't see it. Why I moved out of there when I did," he said. "I was drowning in there, the place was sinking down a hole. Shit, the work people were putting out . . ." He sat beside her, looked down at a tiny green and black crab scuttling along the rocks at the water's edge. "It was choking me, and I had to get out. So I did. But it was too late, or it wasn't enough, I don't know. I barely managed to get 'The Winter Gantry' done, and that was it. I stopped working. I tried, actually, I really tried back then, but I couldn't do shit. I wanted to talk to you about it, but I couldn't, not at all. I felt like I was dying here, and I had to get out, hope I could get started again somewhere else. So I just took off." He paused. "Went to Alaska." Shrugged. "It didn't do any good."

They were silent, gazing out onto gray, choppy water. A single gull bobbed with the swells.

"But you've come back."

"I didn't know what else to do."

They walked back by way of the lagoon in front of the Palace of Fine Arts, and as they walked, Terry watched his movements, the way he carried himself, listened to the way he talked. Now that she observed more closely, it seemed to her that he'd grown thinner, though he looked physically stronger at the same time, muscle delineated beneath fatless skin. There were dark areas under his eyes, and several places in his hair where gray was starting to appear, not quite matching the color of the bleached tail. Up close, he looked older than his age; it was disconcerting, and Terry wondered if she looked older, too.

Rheinhardt waved toward the old Exploratorium building, now just barely visible through the trees. "I went by there this morning," he said. "When did it close down?"

"About two years ago."

"Money?"

"Money."

He slowly shook his head. "Things just keep getting worse, don't they?"

"Seems that way." As soon as she'd said it, Terry wished she hadn't; admitting it aloud added extra weight, extra certainty. They kept on, leaving the Exploratorium behind them. "I should tell you about Deever," she said. "He disappeared, almost a year ago."

"Disappeared?"

"Yes. He was having problems with his place, cops closing him down, confiscating artwork from the walls, videotapes from the tube-rooms. He'd get arrested, get out on bail, then charges would be dropped. He was pretty sick a lot of the time, which didn't help. Liver. About ten, eleven months ago he was closed down again, arrested. I heard he was out on bail, was going to be arraigned, but next thing I saw his building had been boarded up, order of the city. I haven't seen him since."

"Hasn't anyone seen him?"

Terry shook her head. "No one. No one knows whether or not he's still alive."

Rheinhardt stopped walking, closed his eyes, and Terry watched him in silence, his breath deep and regular. He opened his eyes, but didn't look at her.

"I wonder if it was a mistake, coming back," he said.

There was such sadness, such hopelessness in his voice that Terry, too, felt almost overwhelmed by despair. She'd gradually lost more and more hope during the years he'd been gone, though not *because* he was gone, and now his return was making it worse. Look at us, she thought. Two cases of terminal pessimism. Terminal futility. There was a part of him slowly dying, she could see that. Was there a part of her dying as well?

Probably. She almost didn't care anymore.

No, that wasn't true. She did care, and even if Rheinhardt had given up (and she didn't believe he completely had), *she* had not. Not yet. Not quite yet.

Terry put her arm through his, tugged slightly, and they resumed walking. She had no destination in mind, but soon Rheinhardt was leading the way, across Richardson, then a short ways to a small, run-down motel just off Lombard.

"I got a room here this morning," Rheinhardt said. They walked up a flight of cement steps to the second floor, down past a couple of rooms, then stopped in front of a brown door, the paint peeling badly from it. Rheinhardt unlocked the door, and they stepped in.

Terry stopped just inside the room, looked around at the gray walls, the worn green carpet, the sagging bed. "You going to stay here?" she asked.

"For a while."

She nodded. She pulled the drapes closed, and the room darkened. Rheinhardt switched on the nightstand lamp; it cast dim orange light and pale shadows through the room. He lay back on top of the bed, looking at her. Terry sat in the chair by the window. The room was already stuffy, and she reached behind the drape, opened the window. A cool breeze blew in, billowed the drape for a moment. She wanted to go back out into the cold, damp air, walk along a deserted beach or across the clifftops above the sea.

"What are you thinking of?" Rheinhardt asked.

"Stoke."

A slight pause, then, "It's not my fault he's dead."

Terry looked at him, nodded. "I know. But seeing you again makes me think of him." She sighed once. "Seeing you again. Christ." Her hands had clenched into fists, and, surprised at the sudden rush of anger, she banged her right fist against the table beside the chair, then banged it twice more, harder each time. She continued to stare at Rheinhardt, breathing rapidly.

"You never wrote, god damn it! Never wrote, never called, not once in all these five fucking years." She pounded her fist again on the table, wincing. "Why, damn you? Why?"

Rheinhardt sat up, and she watched him, waiting. Twice his mouth moved, and it looked like he was about to say something, but neither time did he say a word, and eventually he just slowly shook his head.

Terry nodded. She pulled off her sweater, unbuttoned her shirt. After a slight pause, she took off her shoes, then stood and unbuckled her belt. By the time she'd removed her jeans, Rheinhardt was sitting on the edge of the bed, undressing.

Neither spoke. Naked, they crawled in between the cool sheets, sinking into the lumpy mattress. They lay still, barely touching, and Terry listened to Rheinhardt's regular breathing.

He reached for her, she closed her eyes, and he pulled her tight against him. His breath was warm on her neck, but his fingers were rough, hesitant, and unsure on her skin. She could hear the rain outside, pouring now, and she pressed her hips into his, not knowing what else to do.

They moved together in the dim orange light, almost struggling, intense but out of synch with one another. Under layers of sheet and blankets the heat increased, and soon Terry was sweating, her skin slick against Rheinhardt's. He raised himself on his hands, she slid beneath him. When he entered her she opened her eyes to see his tensed face in the shadows above her.

A gust of wind billowed the drape, caught her glance, and for some reason made her think of shrouds. She shuddered as the drape fell back.

"What is it?" Rheinhardt asked.

"Nothing." Terry pulled him tightly into her, and closed her eyes. The rain was loud and persistent on the window, and neither of them spoke again.

Rheinhardt lay on the bed and watched Terry dress. It had not gone well. Too many years, too many things still unresolved, they'd been too awkward and desperate. Now, they probably wouldn't try again for a long time. Perhaps it was better that way.

Terry wrote on a small card, dropped it on the bed. "My address, case you've forgotten it. I'm still at the same apartment, still with Ann. But I've got no phone. Damn phone company's cut off my line."

"Why?"

"The Warehouse. I really don't want to run it all right now, but there's a lot of pressure for us to get out, vacate the building. They want to close it down."

"Who? Solinex?"

She nodded. "Their building, their land. Look, Rheinhardt, like I said, I don't want to talk about it now. Later, maybe. Things look bad for the Warehouse, in every damn way you can think of, and that's all I'm going to say." She leaned against the wall, pulled the drape aside and gazed out. "Maybe it's not such a bad thing."

"Looking for something?"

"No." She let the drape fall and turned back to him. "We'll talk later, Rheinhardt. I've got to get to work, I'm already hours late."

"Still with Monterey House?"

"Yes." She opened the door. Cold and rain gusted inside. "Good-bye, Rheinhardt. I think I'm glad you're back."

"I'll see you, Terry."

She stepped out, closed the door behind her.

The room was quiet and cold. Rheinhardt got out of bed, pulled on his black jeans and a gray sweatshirt. He lay back across the bed and gazed silently at the ceiling, listening to the loud rain falling outside.

Terry walked to the bus stop at one of the Presidio gates, stood in front of a slatted wooden bench, thinking about what had just happened.

She felt uncomfortable, sticky between the legs. It had been stupid, in a way, as well as awkward. She had always been so careful, and so had Rheinhardt, and this time neither of them had done a damn thing. Working at Monterey House all these years, she knew as well as anyone that it only took once to get pregnant. Given the time of month, it wasn't likely. Still. Stupid. She wanted to take a shower. Maybe she could squeeze one in at the House if things were slow.

Rheinhardt was back. She still didn't know what exactly she felt about it, besides confused, didn't know what, if anything, she wanted from him. Time, she told herself. It had been too many years, it would take a while.

Terry put her foot on the bench seat, turned it slowly from side to side, then pushed back with it, an ache rising in her chest. She sat on the bench and waited for a bus to come.

A sharp knocking sounded at the door. Rheinhardt jerked slightly, half asleep, sat up on the bed with bits of strange, half-waking dreams scattering. The knocking sounded again.

"Yeah?"

The door knob rattled, wouldn't turn. Rheinhardt stood, still disoriented, walked to the door and opened it, expecting Terry. Justinian stood in front of him, grinning and dripping from the rain.

"What the hell are you doing here?" Rheinhardt asked.

The short old man pushed past Rheinhardt and into the room. "Close the door, damn it, it's cold out there."

Rheinhardt closed the door. Justinian sat in the window chair, unraveled his thick, wet scarf and laid it over the chair arm. "Got a cigarette?" he asked.

Rheinhardt went to his rucksack, dug out cigarettes and matches. After lighting a cigarette for himself, he sat on the edge of the bed and tossed matches and cigarettes to Justinian.

"You following me, or what?" Rheinhardt asked.

Justinian dragged deeply on his cigarette. Two or three days growth of beard stubbled his face, most of the whiskers white. His skin was a carpet of deep, mottled wrinkles. He'd aged a lot in five years.

"Yes," Justinian said. "No. Depends on your perspective. I've been *with* you, not following. Important distinction."

"*With* me."

"Yes. I am your dwarf."

"You're not a dwarf, Justinian. A little short, but not a dwarf."

Justinian inhaled, blew a slow, large smoke ring, popped a smaller one through it. "Didn't say I was *a* dwarf. I am *your* dwarf. Another important distinction."

"And what the fuck is that supposed to mean?"

"Not for me to explain. It's for you to learn."

"Christ."

"I have been the dwarf for others before you, and I will be the dwarf for others after. Don't start thinking it means you're something special."

"You're a god damn lunatic, Justinian." He pointed to the door with his cigarette. "Get the fuck out of here."

Justinian took one final drag, then crushed out the cigarette on the windowsill. "You need an ashtray in here." He stood. "I can leave this room, but I won't be leaving you, Rheinhardt. It's not that easy."

"Out."

The old man wrapped his scarf carefully around his neck. He opened the door, again letting in the rain and the cold.

"It's not hopeless," Justinian said.

Rheinhardt didn't respond. He sat motionless on the bed, watching the old man. Justinian finally nodded, stepped outside, and pulled the door shut.

Rheinhardt remained on the edge of the bed and finished his cigarette.

Three

Dusk was falling, dark with heavy clouds overhead, but there was no rain. Rheinhardt came around the corner, slowed as he looked across the street at Deever's building. The front door and ground-floor windows were boarded or grilled over, and two NO TRESPASSING signs were posted in the yard, one tilting on its post. The front doors on the ground and third floors were both boarded over, doorknobs covered with police security seals.

The streetlights were on, the few in the neighborhood that still worked, and window lights were on in other buildings, but Deever's place was quiet and dark. Rheinhardt crossed the street, went to the side of the building, climbed over the tall fence and dropped into the narrow alley. It was darker than out on the street, and he slowly worked his way by feel through the empty garbage cans and wooden crates.

In the backyard he could see a little better. Two of the back windows were broken and partially covered by cracked wooden slats, but the door, though locked, wasn't boarded over or sealed. Rheinhardt crouched behind the wooden steps leading to the second and third floors, reached up under the third step, felt for the small ring of keys hanging on a nail. He found them, stood, walked around the stairs to the back door. The keys still worked, and he unlocked the knob and both dead bolts, slipped inside and quickly shut the door.

Inside was even darker than the alley. Rheinhardt took out the needle light Justinian had given him, flicked it on. He swept the narrow beam slowly back and forth across the back room, creating thin moving shadows. The stage was empty, the open floor cluttered with tipped-over folding chairs, crumpled sheets of paper, a few broken beer bottles.

He went into the front room, where little seemed to be disturbed. Tables and chairs, covered with a thick layer of dust, were upright, but the walls were all blank, empty—no artwork hung from them, no paintings or photographs or drawings.

Rheinhardt started up the stairs to the second floor, and was halfway up when he realized something else was wrong. He backed up to the railing and ran the light beam over the wall running up to the second floor. It, too, was blank, where before it had been covered with layers of artwork in acrylics, watercolors, oils, felt markers. Roller strokes were visible. Someone had come in and painted over all the artwork.

The walls in the second-floor hallways and rooms had also been painted over, two or three coats of off-white paint sloppily rolled over the artwork, burying it. The whole floor seemed dead and lifeless, almost sterile.

Rheinhardt went out the back door and climbed the final flight of stairs to Deever's apartment, unlocked the door, stepped inside. Though there was dust on everything, nothing looked out of place, the pantry shelves still stocked with cans and bottles. Rheinhardt picked out an unopened bottle of scotch, brought it into the kitchen, set it on the table.

He went through the rest of the apartment, room by room, but besides the thick dust everywhere, all appeared undisturbed, waiting for Deever to return and clean it up, start fresh again.

Back in the kitchen, Rheinhardt opened a cupboard, looked at the glasses coated with dust, closed it. He took the bottle into the living room with him. The drapes were drawn wide, and he stood at the bay window, looking out at the rooftops and lights of the buildings around him. Where *was* Deever? Was he even still alive? Or was he dead, like Stoke? Rheinhardt opened the bottle and drank, the scotch liquid fire down his throat.

He used the sofa cushions to beat the dust from the sofa and from each other, opened the windows to air out the room. When the dust had settled, he put the pillows at one end of the sofa, lay down with the bottle on the floor beside him. Propped up by the pillows, he could look out the windows, see the city glow rising to the dark clouds sweeping past overhead. Rheinhardt lit a cigarette and lay there a long time, moving only to drink from the scotch, and to smoke from his cigarette.

Terry sat in the dim light of the floor-level attic around the corner from her room, the small twenty-five-watt bulb in the back throwing pale shadows through the wooden beams. In front of her were Rheinhardt's sculptures and his earlier drawings and paintings. Behind them was the stock of tools and materials he'd left behind, including all the welding equipment.

She didn't care much for his drawings and paintings, most of them done soon after he'd come back from the 'mericas. They were too angry, out of control. But his sculptures . . . nearly all of them were beautiful. Terry had hated keeping them locked away in the dark, but she hadn't wanted the constant reminders. Now, though, maybe she could bring one out.

No question which it would be—"Swimming Horses." At one time it would have been "The Winter Gantry," but that was impossible now. Christ, she was going to have to tell him about that, too. She glanced into the back of the attic, at the shadows and boxes that hid what remained of "The Winter Gantry." Then she leaned forward toward "Swimming Horses," picked up the tall, thin bronze, and carried it back to her room.

Terry studied the piece as she cleaned it, refamiliarizing herself with all its facets. The sculpture consisted of two very tall and thin sea horses, so thin they were almost skeletal. It was five and a half feet tall, on a base meant to represent the ocean floor, and the sea horses were no more than an inch and a half thick, except the heads which were only slightly thicker, elongated and stretching toward the sky, tiny mouths open. The sea horses were studded with sharp, tiny spikes, and both of their tails were coiled around a hypodermic syringe resting on the ocean floor.

When she finished cleaning it, Terry set the piece on the crate filled with Stoke's letters. She hadn't read through them in a long time, and thought she might never again, but she wondered if Rheinhardt would want to look at them. A few, still unopened and tied together in a separate bundle, had been addressed directly to Rheinhardt. Those, at least, she had to give to him.

Al padded into the room, leaped gracefully onto the bed; he reached out with a paw and hooked Terry's fingers, and she sat on the bed beside the big gray cat, stroked him as she gazed at the bronze statue. Looking at it still made her chest ache. It had been the same when she saw Rheinhardt, even after all this time, even with the way he'd left. That hadn't changed.

But Rheinhardt had changed. Maybe not changed, so much. More like just being eaten away inside. She did not know what she could do to help him.

Probably nothing. She didn't know if she could even help herself. And that was the world, wasn't it?

Yes, she decided. It was. Terry put her arms around the big gray cat, pulled him tightly against her and closed her eyes.

Rheinhardt was abruptly awakened by heavy, thudding footsteps on the roof. He sat up on Deever's couch, glanced around the dark room, looked out the window. Nothing. Above him, the sounds continued, like someone leaping about the roof.

Justinian.

He swung his legs over the edge of the couch, kicked
the scotch bottle, caught it with his hand before it
tipped over. The footsteps on the roof stopped, and he
sat without moving, listening, wondering if Justinian
had gone. After a several-minute pause, they started up
again. Rheinhardt stood, head still foggy from sleep
and scotch, started for the back door.

He opened the door slowly, carefully, tried not to
make any noise, stepped out onto the back porch. Most
of the clouds had blown away, and the gibbous moon
shone through breaks in the few clouds that still
remained. Rheinhardt rolled up his left sleeve, looked
at the thin scar on the inside of his arm, pushed the
sleeve back down. Still silent, he started climbing the
wooden ladder leading to the roof. The jumping sounds
were louder now, accented by the crunch of gravel.

Just as he reached the top of the ladder, came up over
the edge of the roof, all sounds ceased. Out toward the
center of the roof, standing motionless with his back to
Rheinhardt, was Justinian. Rheinhardt didn't move,
breathed slowly, silently.

"Hello, Rheinhardt," Justinian said. The old man
turned and faced him.

Rheinhardt came up and over the edge, stepped out
onto the gravel. "Justinian." He cautiously approached, stopped a few feet away. "What are you
doing up here, calisthenics?"

Justinian shrugged, didn't answer.

"Where's Deever?" Rheinhardt said.

"I don't know."

"I thought you were his friend."

"I was."

Was? That mean no longer friends, or that Deever
was no longer alive? "What happened to him? You're
the one who always seems to know what's going on."

Justinian shrugged again, said nothing.

"Terry said he was arrested, got out on bail, then
disappeared."

"That's all I know," Justinian said.

It was then, somehow (tone of voice?), that Rheinhardt knew Justinian was lying; he also realized the old man would tell him nothing. He felt suddenly very tired. He turned away, started back toward the ladder.

"Where are you going?" Justinian asked.

"Back to sleep. Talking to you is worthless, and to be honest, I don't need this kind of shit, from anyone." He reached the ladder, turned around and started down.

"Rheinhardt."

He stopped, looked at Justinian. "Yeah?"

"Tuesday, around noon, a little after, be downtown. Market Street, Montgomery and Sutter, that block. Near Stacey's bookstore."

"I know where you mean. Why?"

"Something I think you'd appreciate seeing." He paused. "Let's say an exhibition of sorts." Paused again. "I'm very serious, Rheinhardt."

Rheinhardt watched the old man, nodded. "I'll see what I can do." He nodded again, and continued down the ladder.

Back inside he made sure the locks and dead bolts were secure, returned to the living room, dropped onto the couch. He drank once from the bottle, capped it, then lay back and closed his eyes as the thumping sounds resumed above him.

Four

Terry came up the porch stairs, opened the front door, and walked into the foyer of Monterey House. Donna was at the front desk, typing on an envelope. In the background was quiet pop music, smooth and lilting. It was weird, Terry thought, how Donna liked to listen to *exactly* the same kind of music Rebecca had.

Donna looked up, pulling the envelope from the carriage. "Can you watch the desk and phone for a while?" she asked Terry. She folded a sheet of paper in thirds, slipped it into the envelope, licked the flap shut, then placed the envelope atop a stack of others. "I've got to go to the post office, mail all this stuff, then to the bank to make a deposit." She was already up, putting on her coat and stuffing the envelopes into her purse before Terry answered.

"Sure," Terry said. She sat on the edge of the desk, watched Donna cross the foyer, open the front door.

"I'll be back," Donna said, not looking around. She pulled the door closed behind her, and Terry could hear the rapid footsteps descending from the porch.

Terry slipped off the desk, walked around it and sat in Donna's chair, leaned back and turned slightly, looking at the radio. Christ, that's awful music, she thought. She was about to turn it off when a squeal cut through the music in mid-song. After a moment of loud hissing, the static cleared and a voice came on.

"We are interrupting this program to make a special presentation of a new musical work."

At the familiar words, Terry jumped up from the

chair, grabbed one of the blank cassettes she always kept nearby, and popped it into the tape deck.

"The following is an original work, composed and performed by local musicians."

She punched up the power, pressed the RECORD and PLAY panels. Who would it be? Packer? Simmer? She hoped not. Maybe one of those independents that had been popping up. She didn't recognize the broadcaster's voice. And how was it being done this time? A signal jam and sub? She wondered how long they'd be able to maintain control of the frequency.

"We hope you will enjoy . . . 'Artificial Gravity.' Thank you."

After a short pause, a quiet, syncopated percussion line came on solo, with the barest trace of echo. The beat seemed odd at first, almost out of step, then Terry realized it was in 5/4 time. Suddenly the high wail of a saxophone broke in, ran through a rapid, atonal jitter, then dropped out to be replaced by a smooth bass line. Electric guitar joined in, sounding as if it was in pain, climbing up minor chords, halting and jerking with the beat, its initial tight structure coming apart as it rose.

Peg came down the stairs and walked into the front room, a fifteen-year-old who'd been at the House for four months now, and was expecting in a few weeks. She stood, resting both hands on her large belly, grimacing. "What the hell is that?" she asked.

Terry smiled. "Don't know, but I think I like it." She could tell already that no one in the Warehouse had done it. None of them had the talent. Who, then?

"You like that? It's just noise . . . it sounds horrible."

"It's not just noise. I'm recording it, so you can listen to it again later, if you want. It might take a few times to get used to it." Terry figured she'd have to listen to it a few times herself.

"No thanks." Peg sat on the couch, breathed heavily.

Terry leaned forward, smiled at her. "How are you two feeling? Just a few weeks away, isn't it?"

Peg stared at her a moment, then looked down at her

swollen belly, covered her face with her hands, and began to violently cry.

Terry hurried over to the couch, sat beside Peg and held her tightly, rocking the young girl.

"Hush, little one," she whispered. "It'll be all right."

But she knew she was lying.

And Peg continued to cry.

Rheinhardt was perched on a fence railing near the corner of Market and Montgomery, watching the Financial District's lunchtime pedestrian crush. Though there were clouds high overhead, no rain fell, no fog drifted by. The air was still and dry, but noisy from all the people and the crawling lines of traffic and the blasting horns.

The cops were out in force again, and what Rheinhardt noticed this time was the absence of the street people—no one sat in front of buildings or near the metro entrances with their shopping carts or pets or cardboard signs asking for money. The district had been cleaned out; Rheinhardt wondered where all the street people had gone.

Watching the people walk past him, he tried to picture himself in a suit and tie, working regular hours five days a week, taking the same bus or train to work every day at the same time, taking the same one home (the idea of commuting by car and spending hours in gridlock was almost incomprehensible). Just the idea of working every day for years at a time in the same building, the same *room* for Christ's sake, was almost beyond him. Actually, it frightened him, and thinking about it gave him a trapped feeling, because he *could* imagine himself in that kind of life. But he knew he would never do it. It would be his death.

A tense murmur rose from the pedestrians nearby, then several cries. Rheinhardt looked out along the sidewalk, saw shimmers of black and gray appearing above the heads of people who were stopped and staring upward. More cries and shouts rose from across the street as the shimmering forms appeared above the opposite sidewalk as well.

The forms, about a dozen on each side of the street and spaced out along the entire block, coalesced, focused to become distinct holographic X-ray projections that hovered several feet above the crowd, out of reach. Most appeared to be full-body X rays, though there was one across the street that was only a skull, and another that was just a torso. All the projections had holographic plaques beside them with clear white print. Rheinhardt could just read the plaque of the one closest to him:

ANKYLOSING SPONDYLITIS; Marine officer; associated with severe ulcerative colitis resulting from overexposure to (omitted) radiation; incurred in military operation (date, name, and location omitted).

Even from this distance Rheinhardt could see the spinal deformities, the fused vertebrae unnaturally curved into a severe stoop.

Rheinhardt pushed off the fence, started down the street. He had to squeeze his way through the crowd, the pockets of pedestrians that formed around and beneath each projection.

When he approached the second projection he could see that within the skeletal X ray was an organ radiograph. The skeleton itself appeared healthy. Next to the internal radiograph was a small tag that read LIVER SCAN. The contrast fluid was highlighted in dull red, and several spots in what was apparently the liver glowed a bright crimson. Rheinhardt read the plaque hovering beside the rib cage.

ANGIOSARCOMA OF THE LIVER; nuclear reactor worker; exposure to thorium dioxide in minor accident.

Rheinhardt continued down the street, studying each projection for a few minutes, then going on to the next. Although a few of the skeletal X rays showed bone deformities, tumors, or progressive disease conditions of the bone, many of the skeletal systems were healthy, enclosing projections of other diagnostic test results—organ radiographs, CAT scans, simple X rays, bone scans, an angiogram. All revealed debilitating or fatal conditions.

The "patients" were as varied as the testing procedures—chemical workers, industrial accident victims, military personnel exposed to radiation or biological and chemical weapons, even a young child with bronchogenic carcinoma who had lived in an area of heavy arsenical pesticide spraying.

Rheinhardt crossed the street, studied each of the other projections. Were they actual X rays, scans, and radiographs, or highly realistic creations? It didn't matter. They were beautiful. They were horrifying, disturbing, and made him slightly nauseous, but they were beautiful.

He stopped at the next to last projection. It was a simple skeletal X ray, with a number of small, jagged objects lodged in different parts of the spine, and three larger pieces embedded in the skull. Rheinhardt didn't need to read the plaque; he recognized shrapnel. But after a time of staring at it, he did read.

SHRAPNEL; U.S. Infantryman; fragmentation grenade?; incurred in battle (date and location omitted).

Rheinhardt remained motionless, staring at the projection. That could be Stoke, he thought. He wondered how Stoke had died. He rubbed his wrist, which still ached sometimes from the small piece of shrapnel he'd caught himself from a booby trap triggered by another soldier. Who? That old guy, Schofield. Old? Schofield had been twenty-eight; seemed old at the time. He never got any older.

And Stoke. Stoke had been twenty-one.

The projection shimmered a moment, then partially disintegrated. It lost some of its solidity, but didn't disappear completely. Rheinhardt looked around.

Nearby, a fireman was up on a ladder, dismantling a projection unit that had been hidden on a building wall about twenty feet above the ground. Other firemen and police were searching the buildings on both sides of the street. An image above the opposite sidewalk fluttered, and a third of it collapsed from view.

Rheinhardt stayed the rest of the afternoon and watched as, one by one, a piece at a time, the projection units were dismantled and the shimmering figures above the street disappeared.

Five

Terry came up to the porch, put her feet on the first step and stopped, the ache rising in her chest again. Rheinhardt sat by the front door, under the porch light, rucksack in his lap, eyes closed. After all these years, to see him waiting again as he sometimes had before he'd left the city. She resumed climbing, stopped beside him and looked down.

"Have you had dinner?" she asked.

"Yes."

"Good. I've already eaten myself. You want to come in?"

"Of course." He opened his eyes, smiled up at her. Terry unlocked the door, went in, and a few moments later Rheinhardt followed.

Upstairs, Terry made a pot of tea, and they went into the front room. She built a fire with scrap wood she and Ann had collected the week before from a building that was being torn down a couple blocks away. They'd gone in after dark, carting away as much as possible before other people came and joined in; it was the first firewood they'd had in months.

"How's it been, being back?" Terry asked.

"Shitty," Rheinhardt said. "I don't know what I expected, but this hasn't been it." He shrugged, shook his head. "Thing is, I *should* have expected what I've seen. Things falling apart a little more. The world getting to be a crappier place to live in all the time. If you'd have asked me five years ago, that's exactly what I would have said would be happening. Ask me *now* and it's what I would say. So why is it unexpected?"

"Maybe you just didn't *want* it to be this way. Who the hell does?"

Rheinhardt sighed. "I suppose that's possible. Still, it hasn't been completely without hope." He paused. "I saw something downtown today that was pretty damn amazing. Holographic X rays projected above the sidewalks. Diseases, injuries, deformities, all 'man-made,' so to speak."

"I heard about them," Terry said. "Kirin, a woman I know, called me at the House, told me about them."

"They were beautiful. Disturbing, but beautiful. And then the cops tore them all down."

"Kirin didn't say much about beautiful, but she said they sure were effective."

"Any idea who did it? Someone in the Warehouse?"

Terry shook her head. "No. Definitely not someone from the Warehouse. But I tell you, Rheinhardt, there *is* good work being done in the city. Somewhere, no one really knows. Not in the Warehouse, not in the mainstream. Out on the fringes, in every way. Like the X rays. Like . . . listen to this." She got up, went to the tape deck; the tape with "Artificial Gravity" was already in place and she rewound it, then started it. "I taped this off the radio yesterday, somebody jammed the transmission, slipped in this." The announcer's voice came on, then the music started.

They sat without moving, without speaking, and listened. Terry closed her eyes, let the rising progression take her up through the heat of the fire and the darkness of her closed eyes, let it gently break her apart at the peak so she slowly, lightly showered back down through the warm darkness and gradually coalesced, everything coming back together again. Then the upward progression began once more, this time with a different feel, a different color as the saxophone took her instead of the guitar.

Several times the cycle repeated, with variations, each one looser, less controlled and structured than the previous, until the piece itself softly disintegrated in a delicate shower of glittering notes and color.

Terry opened her eyes, looked at Rheinhardt. "What do you think?"

He nodded. "That was terrific. But not connected to the Warehouse or any other group you know of?"

"No." She got up, stopped the tape, turned and looked at him. "This isn't just an isolated thing, a fluke. The last year or so, maybe a little longer, stuff like this has been appearing all over the city. Music played on the radio, videos jammed into TV transmissions, pamphlets of fiction and poetry and drama handed out free. Sculptures and paintings and drawings appearing in public parks, displayed on the streets, tacked up on buses and streetcars. No one seems to know who's doing it, but these people have a lot of talent. The reactions have been intense, too. The sculptures have been torn down and destroyed . . ." She hesitated, thinking of "The Winter Gantry," then went on. "Pamphlets burned, paintings torn up. We get politicians making indignant speeches, calling for police crackdowns on forbidden displays of art or subversive materials, the Board of Supes has drafted new legislation to make free art displays illegal without prior approval from the city."

She paused, realized she had begun pacing back and forth in front of the fireplace, much as Rheinhardt had paced in circuits out on the jetty the other day. She stopped, looked at Rheinhardt. "I'm about to really start up on all this," she said. "I've had a lot building up inside me, thinking a lot the last couple of years, and not too many people I could talk to about it. I could end up talking you out."

"Go ahead, please," Rheinhardt said. "I'd like to hear it."

Terry nodded, breathed in, and went on. "It's why the Warehouse is coming under fire, all these new artists. Some people think it's the Warehouse artists who are doing all this, and those who don't think so, who *know* better, don't care. We're an easy target, a scapegoat. The visible enemy.

"In the last couple of years I've had some growing

suspicions about the Warehouse. I know this is going to sound like paranoia, but I've been seeing some patterns which depress the hell out of me. A gradual decline in the number of good artists in the Warehouse, a decline in the quality of what's being produced there, a decline all the way around. We've always seen ourselves as outlaw artists, a rebel community, but . . . I don't know. Maybe at the beginning. Mostly, I think, it's been self-delusion. And—here's where the paranoia comes in—I've begun to think that all along we've been tolerated, almost encouraged, by the city and the art establishment, whoever, because somehow having these artists all together in one place made them easier to keep track of, easier to control. People almost always seemed to know what we were up to, and though we managed to get shows or displays started, they were almost always cut short, diluted, or canceled altogether. Like when they arrested Wendy and confiscated all her photographs.

"And then I look at what went on with the artists. The first year or two the place was *filled* with talented, cutting-edge artists, or those with a real potential to become so. But over the years the Warehouse got a steady infusion, over my objections, of hacks and frauds, which contaminated the whole atmosphere, and maybe helped undermine the better artists. Trying to look at it as objectively as possible, I get closer and closer to concluding that over the years the Warehouse has actually killed a lot of good art, and ruined a lot of good artists."

"You won't get much argument from me," Rheinhardt said.

Terry nodded, sighing. "Sometimes I wonder if it was all deliberate, if we were being used." She paused, looked at him. "Paranoia?"

Rheinhardt shrugged. "I don't know. Healthy skepticism, maybe. But now you say there's pressure to close it down."

"Yes. Like I said, the people in this city—the Mayor, the Board of Supes, the other politicos—are looking for a scapegoat. Our money sources are drying up, we've been given notices by Solinex to get out on our own, before they have to use force." She smiled and shook her head. "Last we heard from them, they offered to cover moving expenses. Very civilized."

"What do you think will happen?"

"We'll get forced out, eventually. And maybe it doesn't really matter anymore. Hardly anything worth a damn comes out of there now." She turned and stared into the fire, crouched and added a few pieces of wood, careful to avoid the nails. "Still, I don't know. There *are* a few people in the Warehouse who have some potential, if they just had the opportunity. I've been trying to work with them myself, trying to keep them isolated from the rest of the people, get them to use the Warehouse as a place to live and work but without any contact with any of the other so-called artists. Of course, there's practically no money to do anything now." She turned back to Rheinhardt. "Remember my friends Richmond and Belsen?" Rheinhardt nodded. "Well, they're not around anymore. Three months ago, right after we had a heavy influx of donations, they took off with every bit of cash the Warehouse had. I don't even know how I'm keeping the place together." She shook her head. "After all these years, all the time and energy I've put into the Warehouse, I can't seem to give up just like that. I don't *want* to."

"But there are these other artists, the people who did the X rays, 'Artificial Gravity,' the other things you mentioned."

"Yes. Whoever they are."

"I think I'd like to find some of these people, talk to them, see what they're doing."

"So would the cops."

Rheinhardt smiled, nodded. Terry poured more tea for both of them, left the pot on the warm bricks near the fire. She remained near the fire, absently poking at it with a piece of two by four.

There was a scratching at the window, and Terry

crossed the room, opened the far right window. Al bounded in from the adjacent roof, rubbed against her, then shook once. He looked at Rheinhardt, slowly approached and came around the corner of the sofa, stopped about two feet away.

"Who's this?" Rheinhardt asked.

"Al."

"Al? What kind of name is that for a cat?"

Terry smiled. "For this cat, the perfect name."

"He's a big fucker," Rheinhardt said. He put out his hand, and when Al came forward, he scratched the gray cat's chin. "How long have you had him?"

"About four and a half years. Got him from the SPCA when he was a kitten. Had *no* idea he would be this big, but I like it. He's a good cat."

Al quivered once, tail upright, then darted out of the room, letting out a single cry.

"I've got to feed him," Terry said. "Be right back."

She went into the kitchen, poured some dry food into Al's yellow bowl, then returned to the front room. She stood in the doorway, looking at Rheinhardt.

"There are some things I should give you," she finally said. Rheinhardt held his mug in his lap, looking back at her; she could see the flames reflected in his eyes, tiny flickering lights. "Letters from Stoke."

"Letters?"

"He mailed a couple to you, to your P.O. box until I told him you'd left the city. After that he still wrote, sent them care of me. In case you came back or I heard from you. I never opened them."

Rheinhardt stared at her a long time without speaking.

"If you want, you can also have the letters he wrote to me, read those too. I'm sure he wouldn't have minded."

Rheinhardt shook his head. "No, just the ones to me."

They were silent for a while, then Terry asked, "What about all the other stuff I have? Your sculptures, your tools and supplies?"

"I don't want them," he snapped. "What the hell am I supposed to do with it all? I'm living in a goddamn motel, for one thing. And all my tools and supplies, just what the fuck would I want with them?"

She didn't respond, and eventually he put a hand to his temple, closed his eyes.

"I'm sorry," he said.

"I have more bad news," Terry told him. She just couldn't put it off any longer.

Rheinhardt smiled, slowly shook his head; he kept his eyes closed. "Terrific." He opened his eyes, still smiling, looked at her. "Go ahead."

"It's 'The Winter Gantry.'"

His smile slowly faded, but he didn't say anything.

"You remember there was some guy who wanted to buy it from Carlatti so he could trash it?"

"Carlatti didn't sell it to him?"

"No. He didn't sell it to anyone. But about two months after you left, someone came into the gallery, middle of the day, with a sledgehammer, and attacked it. Destroyed the upper structure. Didn't do much damage to the base, the bronzed section, but . . ."

Rheinhardt didn't say anything, he didn't move. Terry watched him, tried to guess what he was thinking, what he felt, but his face remained expressionless, the only movement the occasional blinking of his eyes.

"I've got what's left, even the part that was mangled so badly. If you want to see it . . ."

Rheinhardt shook his head. "I don't think so." His voice was quiet, calm. He put the mug on the sofa arm, stood. "I'd better get back to the motel."

Terry nodded, slowly got to her feet. She wasn't going to ask him to stay. If he asked, maybe, but she would not ask him herself. She didn't know if she was really ready for that yet.

"I'd like the letters," he said.

"Sure."

She went to her room, took the small packet of

unopened letters from the crate, and brought them back into the living room. Rheinhardt had his rucksack open and he took the letters from her, stuffed them inside. They went downstairs to the front door without a word, and she stood in the open doorway as he stepped out onto the porch.

"I'll see you again soon," he said.

"All right."

"Thanks for the letters."

"Sure."

Rheinhardt turned, descended the steps to the sidewalk, and as she watched him start down the street in the light from the overhead lamps, she still didn't know if she was glad he was back, or if she wished he had stayed the hell away.

Rheinhardt sat on the bed with his back against the wall, scotch bottle, glass, ice, and Stoke's letters on the nightstand beside him. The letters were arranged by date. He lit a cigarette, poured a drink. He opened the top envelope, postmarked Fort Lewis, Washington, unfolded the sheet of paper inside, and read:

Dear Rheinhardt,

So, first letter to you.

Basic was fucked, things are only going to get worse, I know that, and I just don't give a shit. Tomorrow I start AIT, which means I'm on the deathline, as they call it around here. The line to war. I don't give a shit about that either. Might as well be here or there as anywhere.

What to say, you've been through all this before. Two guys were killed last week, no one really knows what happened either time, except their bodies came back from the field in bags. Drill sergeant says they were stupid, got themselves killed, but rumor is somebody in charge fucked up. Does it matter? They're dead, and I'm not, but I don't feel

too fucking privileged. I'm going to have plenty of other damn chances, won't I?
  Onward.

All the best,

Stoke

Rheinhardt folded the letter, put it back in the envelope, slipped it to the bottom of the stack. He drank some scotch, but didn't open the next letter. Instead, he turned off the nightstand lamp and sat in the dark, drinking and smoking and trying not to remember.

In the morning he rode a bus, then a streetcar out along the avenues all the way to Ocean Beach. By the time the streetcar reached the beach turnaround, the clouds overhead had opened and rain began to fall.

Wearing his poncho, Rheinhardt walked through the dim tunnel leading under the sand banks and out onto the beach, his bootsteps echoing off the concrete walls. The tunnel walls were covered with graffiti and large, crude pictures. Most of the graffiti was just names and dates sprayed on with black or red paint.

He came out onto a dark gray beach littered with aluminum cans, glass bottles, clumps of seaweed. The sand was damp. Gulls picked through the trash, unafraid of him even when he passed close by, but otherwise the beach was deserted. The number and variety of birds had decreased over the last ten or fifteen years, and Rheinhardt missed the tiny sticklegged birds that used to run up and down the slope at the edge of the waves.

The tide was out, the water far down the slope. Rheinhardt stayed on the soft sand, and began walking north. In the rain the remains of the Cliff House were only dark, vague but jagged forms on the rocks in the distance.

Rheinhardt passed the cold remnants of a beach fire;

next to the charred wood and rocks was a stack of about ten disposable syringes. The metal of the needles was still shiny, glistening with moisture.

The wind picked up, the rain grew heavier. Rheinhardt climbed the grass-dotted slope, found a hollow partially sheltered from the wind. He crouched in it, settled back against a wall of sand and grass, and looked out at the ocean. The surf was rough, almost violent, steel-gray rollers frothing white in the rain.

He hunched forward, lit a cigarette in cupped hands, and smoked it slowly. As he smoked he studied his hands, periodically flexing his fingers, slowly, slowly. They didn't hurt, they moved as well as they ever had, even his scarred wrist, but they would not do what he wanted.

Why *had* he come back here?

Because there was nothing in Alaska, nothing in isolation, not a chance for him; here there was at least the possibility of . . . of being able to create again.

And the hope *was* here. He'd seen it in the X-ray projections, heard it in the musical piece "Artificial Gravity," in what Terry had said about the other artists working on the fringes, felt it in the fog and rain and the vibrations of city machinery and the movement of people trembling the air.

He just didn't know if it was enough.

Rheinhardt finished his cigarette, buried it in wet sand, then leaned back again and watched the waves crashing up the dark and sandy slope.

The Subterranean Gallery

Six

There was going to be a bookburning in Union Square.

Rheinhardt had been surprised, reading about it in the morning paper, but when he thought about it, realized he shouldn't have been. A group called Concerned Citizens for Healthy Minds had applied to the city for assembly permits, applied to the Fire Department for fire permits, and had constructed a huge, Fire Department-approved fire pit in the square, near the spot where the annual Christmas tree was erected. The Board of Supervisors had given it unofficial sanction, since the primary purpose was to burn as many copies as possible of a book that had been freely distributed throughout the city without the Board's approval. The book, titled *Noble Gasses and Others*, contained over a hundred pages of fiction and poetry, photographs and drawings, all of which were termed by one of the supervisors as "pornographic, obscene, immoral, subversive, and downright disgusting."

As Rheinhardt approached Union Square the sidewalks grew more crowded, people spilling out into the street, slowing traffic; horns sounded, people shouted from inside cars or at the cars from the street. Rheinhardt could see smoke, thick and pale, rising above the buildings.

On the sidewalk circling Union Square police paced back and forth, trying to keep order, holding back the small pockets of demonstrators protesting the bookburning. The protesters, trying to march up to the fire pit itself, were pushed back by the police, heckled by the crowds, and had copies of books waved in their faces, some of the books slightly charred or actually burning as people held lighter flames to them until police or firefighters interceded, put out the flames, and directed the bookburners up to the fire pit itself. Somewhere nearby, a gospel group was singing.

Rheinhardt worked his way slowly through the crowd, up the steps, moved by the press of people up and across the gentle slope. He passed a bench, climbed onto the seat, then onto the back, holding a lamppost for support. Several feet above the crowd now, he had a clear view of the fire pit. The pit was rectangular, about forty feet long and twenty feet wide, with brick walls about three and a half feet high. Inside, blazing away, was a large mound of burning books—hardcovers and paperbacks, pamphlets and magazines.

The bench was close enough to the pit so Rheinhardt could read some of the titles, and he could see that the majority of the books *were* copies of *Noble Gasses and Others*, but there were hundreds of others as well. The old standbys were well represented—*Huckleberry Finn, Lord of the Flies, Ulysses, Johnny Got His Gun, Slaughterhouse-5, To Kill a Mockingbird*—but there were others as well, some of which he knew, some of which he'd never heard of before—*Dhalgren, The Awakening, Journey to the End of the Night, Going to Neon, The Dead Father, Zoning Assault, The Last Temptation of Christ, The Female Man, Charred Remains, The Atrocity Exhibition*. He felt sick, watching the books burn, watching as the organizers, whenever the flames threatened to die from too many books thrown upon them, tossed balloons of lighter fluid into the fire until the flames burned high and fresh again, releasing a nauseating stink.

Rheinhardt looked at the people near him, searching for copies of *Noble Gasses*, trying to figure a way to get one. A man in a business suit, carrying a briefcase, passed near the bench carrying a copy of the book, and

Rheinhardt called out to him. It took three shouts before the man turned and looked up at him.

"You mind if I borrow that copy a bit?" Rheinhardt asked. "I haven't seen one, and I'd like to get an idea of what it's about. I'll throw it into the fire myself when I'm done."

The man frowned at him, said nothing, turned away and pushed through the crowd to the edge of the pit, violently threw the booklet into the fire. Without looking back at Rheinhardt, the man drifted away from the pit, carried by the surge of people around him.

"Hey, Rheinhardt!"

Rheinhardt turned toward the voice, scanned the crowd. The voice had been familiar, but he didn't see anyone he knew.

"Rheinhardt!"

It was a man with long, thick unkempt hair and an unruly beard, carrying a cloth bag from his shoulder; like the voice, the face beneath all the hair was familiar.

"Brisk?"

Brisk nodded, smiled, waved him over. Rheinhardt climbed down from the bench, worked his way to Brisk's side.

"Hey," Brisk said. "You're back."

"I'm back."

"Let's get out of here, go somewhere we can talk without all these fucking lunatics. Bookburning. Jesus, can you believe this shit?"

It took them several minutes, jockeying through the unpredictable surges of people in all directions, to reach the edge of the square. The press eased, and once they crossed the street, walking was easier.

"You hungry?" Rheinhardt asked. It seemed like a safe enough question; Brisk was thin, far thinner than when Rheinhardt had last seen him.

"Sure," Brisk answered. "But . . ."

Rheinhardt shook his head. "I'm buying. I'm doing fine with money. Want to eat Chinese?"

"Sure," Brisk said again. He smiled with yellow teeth.

They were in a small place just off Stockton Street, at a window table on the second floor, and had just ordered. Rheinhardt poured tea for them both, sat drinking the tea and gazing down at the noisy, crowded sidewalks below, thinking about the lynchings years ago, the tension that had been in the streets.

"How long have you been back in the city?" Brisk asked.

"Just a few days." It seemed like much longer. "Have you seen this book they were burning? *Noble Gasses and Others*?"

"Sure. You want a copy?"

"Yeah, you know where I can find one?"

Brisk opened his bag, pulled out one of a half dozen copies of the book, held it out to Rheinhardt. "Keep it. I've got plenty."

"You some kind of radical distributor now?" Rheinhardt asked.

Brisk smiled, said nothing.

Rheinhardt took the book. It was thin, printed on surprisingly decent paper, the cover simple. NOBLE GASSES AND OTHERS, it said in large black letters. Then below, in smaller print: A SELECTION OF WRITTEN AND VISUAL EXPRESSION BY BAY AREA ARTISTS. Inside, the table of contents listed the titles of stories, poems, drawings, and photographs with the author names clearly pseudonymous—Argon Cat, Xenon 777, Man of Neon, etc.

"How is it?" Rheinhardt asked.

"Pornographic, immoral, subversive, and downright disgusting," he said. Smiling again.

"I think you forgot 'obscene.'"

"Oh, right. Obscene. Actually, some of it's not so good. But most of it *is* good, and some is pretty fucking terrific."

Rheinhardt set it on the chair beside him, so it wasn't

visible. "So, how are you doing, Brisk? Last time I saw you was after the *Hostages* thing."

"I wasn't doing too well then, was I? Yeah, well, I went through some bad times, believe. I didn't even try to write for a couple of years. Or maybe three. Kind of lost track of time. I had a hell of a time finding jobs I could stand, jobs I could hold for more than a fucking week or two." He tapped nervously on the table with his right hand. "Don't really want to talk too much about all that, though. I *have* started writing again, *that's* worth talking about. I've been working on a new play for the last few months. A real play, like for the stage. Done a few rewrites, managed to get some actors I know to do a staged reading for me a couple of times, worked more changes from those. It's a long one act called *The One-Way Mirror*. But don't even ask me what it's about, I can't talk about something like that, not when I'm still working on it. Not even when I'm finished, that matter." He shrugged.

"What about production? Any possibilities?"

"Yeah, actually. Still working on that, the actors who did the staged readings are trying to help me out on it, and we have some ideas. We'll see."

"Let me know if something happens, all right?"

Brisk nodded. "No worry, I'll let you know. Can I get in touch with you through Terry?"

"Yes. Or at this motel I'm staying in. Shit, I can't even remember the name of it, though. It's off Lombard, near the Presidio. Has a neon sailboat or something like that on the outside. How about where I can find you?"

Brisk shrugged, looked uncomfortable. "Don't laugh, but right now I'm living in an abandoned Volvo on 15th Street, in front of the old Weber Manufacturing warehouse. You can't miss it, kind of rusting blue-gray, no tires, engine stripped, a little blue flag on what's left of the antenna." He shrugged again. "The back seat's damn comfortable." Then he looked away, out the window.

The waiter brought the first two dishes, pot stickers and war won ton soup. Although Brisk was apparently trying to control himself, after he scooped a bowl of the soup he practically attacked it, spooning it rapidly with shaking hands into his mouth, dripping some onto his beard, onto the table.

"Hey," Rheinhardt said. "Slow down, or you'll get sick."

Brisk looked up at Rheinhardt, paused, then shrugged once more and smiled. "Sorry, I haven't eaten in a while."

Rheinhardt smiled back. "Don't worry." With chopsticks he picked up one of the pot stickers and took a bite as Brisk, more slowly now, resumed eating the soup.

The midday sun was bright, not a trace of cloud or fog in the sky, so Terry took Peg and Dolores to Buena Vista Park for lunch. Dolores was fairly new at the House, had shown up three weeks before after being beaten by both her brother and her father. Terry suspected she'd also been raped by one of them, or both, but Dolores refused to talk about it. She was sixteen, five months pregnant, with huge brown eyes so dark they were almost black like her hair; the bruises gone now, she was, Terry thought, quite beautiful.

They'd brought sandwiches, oranges and apples, and a large thermos of ice water, and they sat on the grass of the lower park slope. With the good weather there were quite a few people in the park, eating lunches or walking along the cement paths, or just sitting, some on the grass, some on benches. At the bottom of the slope was the bench where she'd had lunch with Stoke so many times.

"Did you hear about the bookburning they're having in Union Square today?" Peg asked. "It was in the paper."

Terry nodded. "It's really depressing." She shook her head, not knowing what else to say.

"Why?" Peg asked. "They're just burning illegal books, the paper said."

"Yeah," Dolores put in. "Stuff by illegal artists, that they said was pornographic."

"Have either of you actually seen this book?" Terry asked.

Both girls shook their heads.

"Then don't make judgments until you have. And even if it *is* pornographic . . . bookburning, Jesus. They'll be burning a lot of other books, too, count on it. And it's just crap about 'illegal' books and 'illegal' artists, anyway. Utter *crap*. There's no such thing as an illegal artist. And as for illegal books, these laws about forbidding free distribution or displays are so fucking repressive, not to mention unconstitutional, it makes me sick." Both girls were looking at her as if they didn't have the vaguest idea what she was ranting about. "I know you're both young," she resumed, "but you better look at the world around you with open eyes. You're both going to be bringing children into this world, so you'd better know what it's really like, what you'll have to face as parents, as adults."

"But I don't even *want* to have a baby," Dolores said.

Terry sighed, nodded. "I know. But it's like the world, Dolores. You don't really have a choice, so you have to do the best you can with it." She tried smiling. "We'll work it out."

"I've heard there's ways," Dolores said.

"Ways of what?"

Dolores patted her belly, which was only barely starting to show. "Taking care of this. Derek was telling me."

Terry stopped smiling, felt her chest tighten. "Don't talk about that, Dolores. Don't even *think* about it. Jesus. You're worried about illegal, well, these 'ways' are not only illegal now, most of them are dangerous. Too many goddamn butchers out there, is the problem, and you haven't got the money to make sure you've got a safe one. So forget about it, all right? And keep away from that asshole Derek." She paused, and when Dolores didn't say anything, Terry again said, "All right?"

Dolores nodded without saying a word. Then Peg whispered something so quietly Terry couldn't make it out.

"What did you say, Peg?"

Peg looked as if she was about to cry, and when she spoke again, her voice was still little more than a choked whisper. "I said, *I* do. I *want* this baby." And then she did start crying.

Terry moved closer to Peg, put her arms around the young girl, and hugged her tightly. "I know you do, Peg, I know. And you will." She closed her eyes. "And don't worry, it'll be all right." Then she opened her eyes and looked at Dolores, who was slowly shaking her head, and Terry wondered why she was still lying.

Rheinhardt sat in the chair by the window of his motel room, curtains drawn wide, looking through *Noble Gasses and Others* by the bright afternoon light. He had skipped over the poetry, but had read the first two stories in the book. One, called "Red Rain," was a mildly effective mood piece about a dissatisfied businessman who, one day while walking through the city (San Francisco, it seemed, though it was unnamed), found the world around him gradually changing, metamorphosing into a dark, almost gothic world of somber pale blues and greens, black overcast skies, and a blood-red rain falling from the clouds above.

The second story, though, titled "The Man Inside My Mouth," was a daring and brilliant piece about a woman who woke up one morning to find that there was a tiny man inside her mouth, about the size of one of her teeth, who spoke to her by echoing his voice through her sinus cavities. Rheinhardt was amazed at the story's energy, its life, and it was so real that both the woman and the tiny man became incredibly believable.

The middle section of the book was printed on high quality, glossy paper, reproducing the work of two photographers. But when Rheinhardt saw the first two pictures, credited to Xenon 777, he *knew*, though he had not seen those particular pictures before, that it was Wendy's work.

Rheinhardt felt a rush of elation, seeing the photographs, knowing that she was still working, and that she was doing *good* work. He went through the photographs slowly, more certain with each one that he wasn't mistaken, that it *was* Wendy's work. All the pictures were black and white, and there was something in the slightly askew angles that was familiar; but more than that was the subject matter, the melding of human beings, technology, and death in horrifying, beautiful and painful ways—a man flying off a downtown building with coils of wire and glass rods emerging from his bare chest and back; two naked women, back to back inside a shimmering metal cage, huge cables snaking around it, and a spike of lightning-like electricity arcing toward them; and more.

Then he turned the page and stopped breathing a moment, stunned.

The picture took up both pages, and Rheinhardt's first thought was that it was an impossible photograph, and he wondered how the hell she had taken it.

It was a close-up, multiple exposure of a dragoncub, apparently in flight in the night sky, faint stars visible in the background. The craft's outlines were silver, distorted waves, each exposure giving it a slightly different shape; strange reflections of varied shape and brightness came off the surface material, and toward the rear of the craft, at what must have been its propulsion system, was a series of warping vortices of light.

But what was most disturbing about the photograph was toward the front of the vehicle, at the cockpit which should have been completely opaque. A single image came through, barely recognizable from the pattern of shadows and faint smudges of light—a face, the pilot's face, staring out toward the camera with features twisted in agony, eyes wide, and mouth open in a silent scream.

Dear Rheinhardt,

I leave tomorrow, fly to L.A., then on to Tegucigalpa. Maybe. They seem a little vague around here, seems to be deliberate, they don't seem to understand that most of us don't care about the specifics. Wherever we go we'll be going farther.

I'm scared, which doesn't surprise me, but I'm looking forward to it at the same time, like I can hardly wait, which does surprise me.

Funny thing, no one even tries to tell us exactly why we're fighting, what's at stake, no one says shit. They've taught us how to kill, fuck have they ever taught us that, but no whys. Most of the other guys don't really care, they just want to get to it. We know we might be fighting Cubans, we might be fighting the Nicaraguan rebels, we might be fighting the Mestizos, we might, might, might . . . Shit, someone says they might turn around, ship us down farther south and put us against the Cokers.

My head feels funny a lot, Rheinhardt. I've been straight most of the time, smoke a little duke once in a while, nothing major, but we've all done these night patrol numbers they give you, and man, that's some weird shit. Little explosions in my eyes, tiny fucking fireballs flying through the air, everything alive like glowing electric bodies, even the rocks and shit. The come-down is fucked, and I hate to think about what that'll be like out in the jungle instead of here.

Lots to look forward to.

Like I said, we learned a thousand and one ways to kill, which gives some of these assholes around here a weird power trip thing, but me, I just think how it means there are a thousand and one ways for me to get killed.

I'm staying straight tonight. Most everyone else is getting wasted, or laid, or both. I just can't.

Shit, I don't know what else to say. Terry says you've taken off, so maybe you aren't ever going to read this. If you are, though, I guess it means you're back. If you are, I hope . . . shit, I don't know what I hope. Watch your ass, and I'll watch mine.

Boyo.

Stoke

Seven

The Warehouse was a lifeless, black mass in the night. Terry stood at the gate, looking through the diamonds of the cyclone fencing. She'd come from Monterey House when her shift ended, intending to do some work, talk to a few of the artists she was trying to work with, but she now realized she couldn't face it, not tonight. Just walking in through the door would depress her too damn much.

She looked around her, the buildings on all sides as dark as the Warehouse, the amber streetlights providing the only illumination. There was no traffic, there were no people, no sounds but distant rumbles. Deserted cities of the heart. What was that from? An old song, she thought.

She started off down the street, at first with no specific destination in mind, just the need to get away from the Warehouse, but before she had gone more than a few blocks she thought of Macy, who lived just a mile away. Terry hadn't seen her and her daughter in two or three months. Lisa was almost five now; or had Terry missed her birthday? She couldn't remember. She wondered if things were any better now for the two of them; they sure as hell couldn't get much worse.

As she got closer to Macy's apartment building, the night grew louder, and Terry thought she could hear crashing sounds, and shouts, and before long there were sirens as well. Soon, she was smelling smoke, and she picked up her pace, looking up at the sky. Yes, there were slight flickers of pale red and orange glowing above the buildings.

She turned a corner, and suddenly the sidewalks and streets were filled with people milling about, talking and shouting and pointing. Two or three blocks down, flames were visible, waving halfheartedly from windows in a tall building, and three streams of water poured onto the building from the street. Terry thought it was the same block as Macy's apartment, but on the opposite side of the street.

More sirens cut the air, a fire truck followed by an ambulance drove past her toward the fire, and Terry broke into a jog. Two cop cars came around a corner in front of her, the first almost hitting a group of onlookers out in the street, lights flashing and sirens wailing.

When she reached the block of the fire, Terry could go no farther. Cops and firefighters had cordoned off the street, were pulling people out from it while trying to hold back those already behind the barricades. Terry climbed the porch steps of a building, looked down the street. Three fire trucks were in the street, and now several streams of water from hydrants and the trucks were washing across the burning building as well as those on either side of it. She thought she also saw streams of water coming from behind the building, from one street over, and the wail of more approaching sirens filled the air.

The fire *was* on the same block as Macy's apartment, but Macy's building, across the street and half a block down from the main fire, looked safe enough. Terry wondered if there was any way she could get to the building, wondered if the buildings had been evacuated; she didn't see anyone looking out at the fire from windows across the street, which she would have expected, so maybe they all *had* been cleared out.

An explosion sounded, followed by shattering glass, and flames erupted from the building adjacent to the one already burning. Two more explosions rocked the air, and showers of glass fell on the street, scattering the firefighters. Then, out of all the chaos and confusion, she heard her name called.

"Terry! Terry, over here!"

Terry scanned the crowd, trying to lock in on the voice which continued to shout her name. Finally she saw Macy, Lisa in tow, squeeze free of the throngs watching from behind the barricades and hurry toward her. Lisa, tiny legs working frantically, could barely keep up with her mother. Macy slowed, took a firmer grip on Lisa's hand, and pulled her up the stairs as she joined Terry on the porch.

Terry hugged Macy, then picked up Lisa and gave her a hug, the little girl's chubby arms clasping around Terry's head and covering her ears.

"Hi, Terry," Lisa said. "A house is burning down, where Consuela lives."

"A friend of Lisa's," Macy explained. "What are you doing here, Terry?"

"I was on my way to see you, actually."

"Consuela isn't burning up, is she?" Lisa asked.

Macy took Lisa from Terry and nuzzled her cheek. "I already told you, I don't think so, I think they got everyone out, honey."

"What about Mr. Pesto?"

Macy turned to Terry, smiling. "Mr. Pesto is Consuela's kitten." She turned back to her daughter. "I think Mr. Pesto's probably fine, Lisa."

They stood on the porch and watched the fire spreading through the second building, and Terry wondered if the entire block would end up burning to the ground.

"Any idea how it got started?" Terry asked.

Macy shook her head. "Haven't heard anything."

"Maybe someone was making a fire to keep warm," Lisa said.

"It's not that cold, hon," Macy replied, tousling her daughter's hair, shifting Lisa's weight in her arms. Lisa gave an exaggerated shrug. "So you were coming to see us," Macy went on. "Any special reason?"

Terry shook her head. "No, just wanted to see you, see how you're doing. It's been a while."

"We're doing okay, I guess. No regular job, yet, but I got a temp last week, cash, doing inventory in a warehouse. Six days work, yesterday was the last day. Least got the landlady off our backs."

Suddenly several loud, successive bursts of shattering glass erupted, not from the direction of the fire but from behind them. There was more breaking glass, splintering wood, the banging of metal against metal, and Terry turned to look down the street. She didn't see anything at first except people running, but as the crowds scattered, she saw them.

"Oh, shit."

A dozen or so figures approached on foot, now about two blocks away, all wearing red crash suits that glowed brightly in the night, heads encased in sealed riot helmets, visors lowered. Some were carrying clubs or metal pipes, and as they walked along swung them at the windows they passed, shattering glass and wood frames, or bashed them against parked cars. Others carried rifles and would occasionally shoot at windows three or four stories above ground level.

"Defectors," Terry said. "We've got to get the hell out of here, *now*."

Already the crowd in front of the barricades was starting to break up as word spread, people running down the side streets, some overrunning the barricades and plunging down the street toward the fire.

Terry grabbed Macy's hand, hurried down the steps from the porch and headed to the right, away from both the fire and the approaching Defectors. The Defectors had probably started the fire themselves, Terry realized, to pull in the cops and firefighters for confrontation.

"Don't run," Terry said, "especially carrying Lisa. We'll walk fast, get out of here, but for Christ's sake don't run, easier to fall and get hurt, stuck, trampled or whatever, all these people."

And, as she finished talking, they were nearly overwhelmed by a mass of panicked people rushing past
them. Terry kept the three of them at the edges of the
crowd, against the buildings, hugging walls and fences.
Out on the sidewalk and in the street, people stumbled
and fell, remained on the ground struggling to get up as
others ran over them.

After they'd gone a few blocks, though, the crowds
thinned out, the noise decreased, and though gunfire
was more frequent (the Defectors had probably reached
the barricades by now and were battling the police and
firefighters), it was muted. A series of hollow thrumps
shook the air around them, and Terry glanced up to see
a pair of dragoncubs pulsing toward the fire.

"Where are we going?" Macy asked. Lisa, hanging
desperately to her mother's neck, was crying now, tears
forming dusty streaks down her face.

"We'll go to my place, you can stay the night. We'll
see tomorrow if you can go back to your apartment."
Terry stopped for a moment in an alley, searched her
pockets and counted her money. Enough for a cab, if
they could find one out here, or get one to stop. She
stuffed the money back into her pocket, and they
started off again through the dark streets.

Rheinhardt, on the roof of Deever's building,
watched the flames of burning buildings rise into the
night. The fire was two or three miles away, but the
small hill on which Deever's building sat was just high
enough to give him a fairly unobstructed view. Occasionally he even caught a touch of the odor of smoke.

He lit a cigarette, watched the match burn all the way
down to his fingertips, dropped it to the roof. Smoke
curled up from it for several seconds. Was that how the
fire had started? Carelessness? More likely, it had been
deliberate.

The roof was quiet, deserted. He had come up here
expecting, hoping, to see Justinian. He needed to talk to
the old man, for some reason, ask him some questions.

What, he wasn't sure; he knew only that questions waited to be asked. But Justinian wasn't here.

Someone began shouting on the street below. Rheinhardt stepped to the edge of the roof, looked down. On the other side of the street, half a block away, a man was staggering down the steps from a second-floor apartment, carrying something in his arms. A woman stood in the open doorway, shouting down at him.

A baby began to cry—the bundle in the man's arms—and the woman broke into hysterics.

"What? You got the baby?!" she screamed. She started running down the steps after him; the man was on the sidewalk now, staggering down the street. "You fucking bastard!" the woman screamed. "You can't take her, she's mine!"

The man didn't answer, continued down the street, weaving from side to side. The woman reached the sidewalk, hurried after him, came up from behind and started pounding on his back with her fists. The man stopped, hunched over and keeping his face turned away from her, but the woman swung around in front of him, grabbed at the bundle in his arms.

"Give her back, damn it, you can't take her!"

The man said something Rheinhardt couldn't make out, and Rheinhardt knelt at the edge of the roof, wondering what the hell he should do. The baby began crying louder, and the woman started in again.

"Yeah? How you know you're the father? Maybe you aren't, ever think of that?" She pulled hard, the baby came into her arms, and the woman staggered, caught her balance. "And don't come back!" she shouted at the man. "I don't want you no more."

She started back toward the apartment, rocking the baby against her shoulder, and the man sank to his knees, dropped his head into his hands. He began to moan, rocking back and forth, side to side, and the moaning gradually grew louder.

At the foot of the stairs the woman hesitated, looked

back at the man. He remained on the ground, his moans wavering as he rocked back and forth. She shook her head once, turned, started up the stairs.

When she was halfway up, the moaning ceased. The man raised his face from his hands, looked up into the night sky, opened his mouth and began to howl, loud and bellowing. An ache rose in Rheinhardt's chest, there was so much pain in the man's voice.

The woman stopped again, pressed the baby tightly to her neck and shoulder, turned to look at the howling man. She sat down on the steps. The man continued to howl, weaving from side to side, pounding at his thighs with clenched fists.

After two or three minutes, the woman stood, slowly descended the steps and walked down the street to the man. She touched his shoulder with her free hand, ran her fingers along his face, through his hair, leaned over him, perhaps to say something.

The man's howling subsided, returned to a low moan. He struggled to his feet, holding onto the woman for balance, and they started back along the sidewalk. Side by side, they climbed the stairs, the man still moaning and shaking his head and holding onto her for support. Then they went into the apartment and the woman closed the door behind them, returning the street to silence.

The sun awakened him.

Rheinhardt shifted in the sleeping bag, and a draft of cold air entered. He blinked several times against the glare of the white sun, turned his face away, looked at the rooftop gravel dully reflecting the morning light. Stove chimneys cast long shadows across Deever's roof.

His clothes, rolled up at his feet inside the bag, were almost warm. Rheinhardt dressed quickly, pulled on boots, and stood, looking out over the city. He was sore in spots; the foam rubber mat hadn't been quite thick enough, and he'd felt the gravel through it all night.

Looking out toward the west, he could see the faint

traces of rising smoke; the fire, apparently, was out.
How many buildings had burned down, how many
gutted? How many people had died? And did whoever
was responsible even care?

Rheinhardt turned and gazed at the Financial District buildings, the tall jagged structures flanked by the
spires of the Bay Bridge on one side, rolling apartment-
covered hills on the other. He stared hard at the bridge,
but could not see where the damage was; hidden,
perhaps, by Treasure Island.

Islands. The Financial District was an island in this
city. Isolated from and ignorant of (by choice, surely)
most of the rest of the city, connected by narrow land
bridges to the hills—Nob, Russian, Telegraph—and
parts of the Marina, Pacific Heights, connected by the
Golden Gate to the nice streets and houses of Marin
County, connected by BART and, usually, the Bay
Bridge to tiny pockets of other isolated islands, pro-
tected suburbs scattered along the freeways to the east.

You can't change it, he thought. You can't change
shit. So what *could* he do? He still didn't know, but he
was still looking for an answer, certain that, if one
existed, it would be here in this city.

Dear Rheinhardt,

*First firefight today. I can't really tell you exactly
what happened, cause I have no idea. Platoon was
marching along the side of a mountain, headed
toward some ridge, all of a sudden everything goes
fucking nuts. Something exploded, gunfire started,
and then everyone was in the dirt, crawling, yelling, at least I was, trying to bury myself. A bunch of
other explosions, I think, can't be sure, more
gunfire, I heard someone on the radio, then the guy
in front of me gets up, starts shooting into the trees,
this way, that way. I don't know, all of a sudden I
was up and shooting too, firing at God knows what,
I wasn't seeing or hearing anything, I was just*

*holding that fucking trigger, letting that gun shake
me around. Then, just like that, it was over, the LT
screaming at us to hold our fire.*

*I was just standing there for a while, holding my
rifle, looking into the trees, my heart pounding and
my body all shaky from this fantastic rush. I felt
like, I don't know, hard to explain, like something
had got into my bloodstream and just, wham,
cleaned it all out in a flash, blasted it out in all the
sweat I was dripping. Instant purge. Kind of like
sex, I guess, that feeling right after you come, those
first few seconds, only intensified. I suppose you
know what I'm talking about.*

*I guess it felt good. I wasn't so scared for a while.
But tell you true, Rheinhardt, when I think about
it, I could do without.*

*That's all I can write for now. Still a little shaky,
get shaky thinking about it. Whooeee.*

Bye.

> *All the best,*
>
> *Stoke*

They were stopped by two cops as they came around
the corner of the block where Macy lived. The streets
and buildings were a disaster—ruins from the fires,
rubble and broken glass in buildings in all directions,
cars with shattered windows and flat tires. Broad stains
of dried blood were visible on the sidewalk.

"This street's restricted access," one of the cops said.
He was older, hair graying. The other was young, early
twenties. "You'll have to go some other way."

"I *live* here," Macy said, pulling Lisa closer, up
against her legs.

"You do?"

"Yes." She stepped to the side, pointed to a building.
"There."

The two cops looked at the building, back at Macy,
then at Lisa. "This your sister?" the older one asked.

"She's my daughter."

"You can't be serious, girl. How old are you?"

"Nineteen."

"It's her daughter," Terry said. "And why are you hassling her? She told you she lives here."

"How about you?" the cop said to Terry. "You her mother, or what?"

"I'm a friend. Now, will you let us go? You've got no cause to keep us."

"There was a fire here last night. Arson. And a riot with Defectors."

"We know," Terry said. "That's why they stayed with me last night. And now they'd like to go home. I'm sure you can understand that."

"Can we see some identification, from both of you."

Terry showed her driver's license, Macy showed her state ID. The cops looked back and forth between faces and pictures. Lisa kept hidden behind her mother, gripping tightly to Macy's jeans.

"She does live here, Sarge," the younger cop said. He turned to Macy. "You *are* just nineteen."

The other cop turned, looked at the ID. "Then how can this be your daughter? She's what? Four years old?"

"Five," Lisa whispered between Macy's legs. The younger cop smiled.

"I was fourteen when she was born, that's how she's my daughter."

The cops returned the identification.

"You can go," the older one said to Macy. "You and your daughter. Doug here will go with you, make sure you do have a key to what you say is your apartment. You have to understand, we've had looters, we have to make sure." He turned to Terry. "But you're going to have to stay here, you're not a resident, and this part of the street is restricted."

"But she's a friend," Macy said.

The cop shook his head. "Doesn't matter. Maybe tomorrow, or the next day, but not today."

Terry turned to Macy. There was no way the cops

would let her through. "Will you be all right?" she
asked. "Do you want to come back to my place until
this is all cleared up?"

"No." Macy shook her head. "We'll be okay. I just
want to go home."

Terry nodded. She took a small wad of folded tens
she'd prepared, tucked it into Macy's front jeans pocket. "Something to help you out," she said. She put her
hand gently on Macy's lips as the girl tried to protest.
"Please, I know you can use it. Can't you?"

Macy reluctantly nodded.

"Take it, then. I'm all right, I can afford it. Okay?"

Macy nodded again. "Thanks," she said. She put her
arms around Terry, hugged tightly. "We'll be okay."

Terry watched as the younger cop, Doug, escorted
Macy and Lisa down the street, up the four steps to the
building's front porch, and then through the door.
Doug followed them inside.

"Move along," the other cop said to Terry. "Nothing
else for you to do."

Terry stared at the cop, wanting to scream at him, but
kept silent; she turned away, and started down the
street.

Eight

The Terminal Zone was packed.

It was "No-cover Night," and all the tables were occupied, the dance floor jammed. Lines of people squeezed their way back and forth between the tables, the bar, the dance floor, and the bathrooms. Clouds of smoke hovered in the air, people shouted at each other, bottles and glasses clinked against wood or other glass, and through it all the White Monkeys were playing on stage, banging their way through "Knife in the Head."

Terry sat at a table against a wall, drinking beer and watching the band. She could just barely see Pace, arms flailing wildly, partially hidden behind the drum kit, the smoke, the club's support pillars, and the other band members.

"Knife in the Head" was a new song, one Terry hadn't heard before. It wasn't bad. If nothing else, it had energy, and there was a lot to be said for that.

The song crashed to a close. The vocalist announced a twenty-minute break, and there were scattered boos mixed with applause. The band left the stage, but the noise level didn't drop much.

Pace came off the stage and headed for Terry's table. He grabbed the back of a nearby chair, then dragged the chair over and sat in it across from Terry. His black T-shirt was soaked with sweat, and more sweat dripped from his arms, face, the tips of his dreadlocks. He took off his glasses, wiped the sweat from them, rubbed eyes and brows, then put the glasses back on.

"What you think of the new song?" he asked.

"'Knife in the Head'? It kicks, anyway. Gets the blood pumped."

"Yeah, it does that. Watley wrote it. Took the title from some old German film, he say. *Messer im Kopf*. Kind of like it, I think." He looked at her, smiled. "Hey, we got radio play few days ago, one of our demos."

"Really? Which one?"

Pace laughed, shaking his head. "The sleaze song."

"No. 'Seven Nights in a Cheap Hotel'?"

Pace laughed again, nodded. "Got a decent response. Lot of sick people in this city."

"It figures." She finished her beer, signaled Mindy behind the bar to bring two more.

Pace lit a cigarette. "Glad you come to see me, the band," he said. "Haven't seen you a while."

Terry breathed deeply. "Yeah, well. I wanted to talk to you." She paused, looking at him. "Rheinhardt's back."

Pace nodded slowly. "I heard."

Mindy brought the beer, told them it was on the club. Pace drank down a third of the bottle, breathed deeply as he set it on the table.

"So, how he doing? Changed much?"

Terry shook her head, then shrugged. "He's Rheinhardt. I don't know, he's got some things tearing him up inside."

"Stoke?"

"No. Maybe a little. It's his work, the sculpting. He's having problems with it."

"He know about 'The Winter Gantry'?"

Terry nodded.

"So what you want to talk about?" Pace asked.

She smiled, shook her head. "I don't know. I guess mostly I wanted to talk to someone who knew him before. No serious questions. Just wanted to talk about him being back, with somebody who would know what that means."

"You glad he's back?"

"I don't know. I think so. I was used to him being

gone, I guess." She shrugged, tapped at her bottle. "Yes, I'm glad the bastard's back."

Pace tipped his head forward, looked at her over the top of his glasses. "It been hard, has it?"

Terry smiled. "It's been a bitch."

Pace nodded once, drank again. He glanced up past her, gaze fixed on the club entrance. He motioned toward it with the bottle, and Terry turned.

Rheinhardt was headed toward them, working his way through the crowd. When he reached the table he shook hands with Pace.

"Hey, Pacemaker," he said.

"Hey, Rheinhardt. Been a long long time."

"Yeah, it has." He paused a long time, looking at Pace. Then he said, "Will?"

Pace shook his head, and Rheinhardt slowly nodded once.

"You part of this band?" Rheinhardt asked after a short silence. "White Monkeys?"

Pace nodded.

"You guys any good?"

Pace smiled, shrugged. "Stick around, find out." He stood, drained his beer. "Take my chair. We'll be starting next set a couple minutes." He set the bottle on the table. "You need to talk, Terry, you know where to find me?"

She nodded. Pace turned and headed for the stage, and Rheinhardt sat in the chair.

"How did you find me?" Terry asked.

"Ann told me. *Are* these guys any good?"

"They're not bad."

Rheinhardt looked at her, breathed deeply once, then said, "I want you to take me to the Warehouse, Terry. I need to see what it's like for myself."

Terry sighed. It had to happen sometime, she'd known that. She nodded. "All right. But not 'til the next set's over."

"Sure." He picked up the empty beer bottle, looked at it.

Terry turned away from him and gazed at the stage.

She really did not want to go to the Warehouse tonight.
Shit, she *never* wanted to anymore, not tonight or any
other time. Well, she guessed it was time for
Rheinhardt to see what it had become. She drank
deeply from her beer and waited for the music to start.

They walked through the rain and the dark, the
streets quiet and deserted. The night air was cold, and
they had not spoken since leaving the club. They turned
a shadowed corner, and the Warehouse came into view.
It had been a long time, but it looked the same to
Rheinhardt. They slowed as they approached the gate,
then stopped.

"You sure you want to go in?" Terry asked.

"No."

They stood silently for a few minutes, the rain's hiss
the only sound.

"Doesn't look like it's changed much," Rheinhardt
said.

"Not on the outside. Inside, it's just disintegrating."

"Like this damn city. Things have gotten worse since
I left."

Terry nodded, but didn't say anything. He mentioned the bookburning, and Terry nodded again, saying, "I heard."

"So why the hell am I here?" Rheinhardt said,
waving his hand at the dark building. "So I can get
more depressed?"

"I don't know. You want to forget about it, go back to
my apartment, talk, something? We haven't had much
time to talk since you've been back. Not as much as we
need."

"No, we haven't had much time. But tonight . . ." He
shook his head. "I don't know why, but I feel I need to
see it. Just as well do it now, get it over."

"All right."

She keyed open the gate, and they started across the
muddy ground to the building.

Inside was as familiar to Rheinhardt as outside. The
artwork on the walls had changed, but the layout was

the same, still fresh in his mind, all the halls and rooms and stairways.

He could feel music vibrating the floor, rising from the cellar studios. They walked along the main corridor, the way lit by dim, multicolored lights suspended from shining wire. They hadn't gone far when a teenage Asian boy dropped out of the rafters in front of them.

"Hello, Rheinhardt," the boy said.

Rheinhardt stared. "Minh?"

The boy grinned, nodded. He'd changed a lot in five years. "Talk later, Rheinhardt. Terry, you have to come quick. We've been trying to find you. Just sent someone to the Terminal Zone."

"What is it?"

"You know a girl named Dolores? Says she's from Monterey House."

"Yes. Is she here?"

Minh nodded. "Tuck was coming in, found her on the ground outside the gate. She was having some kind of seizure."

"A seizure? She's not epileptic. I don't think."

"I don't know. We brought her in. She's bleeding, too. From here." He put his hand between his legs. "About every ten minutes she has another seizure."

"Oh, god, I wonder what . . . ? You've got her in the sick room?" Minh nodded. "All right, let's go. Rheinhardt, you coming?"

He shook his head, thinking of hospitals. "You can take care of it. I'm just going to wander around, take a look at things. Find me if you need help, or when you're free."

Terry nodded, then ran down the corridor with Minh right behind her.

Rheinhardt gazed up into the rafters. Slashes of light emerged from some of the cubicles in the upper reaches of the building, glanced off ladders, pegpoles, makeshift stairways.

He made his way toward the far corner, shifting from one passage to the next, passing rooms and studios, some with open doors. He didn't recognize anyone he saw.

At the far corner he climbed the rope and slat ladder to his old studio, pulled himself up onto the narrow landing in front of the door. Light leaked out from under it. Rheinhardt knocked.

There was no answer, and he knocked again, louder. Still no answer. Rheinhardt pushed open the door, stepped inside.

The room was silent. A bright light was focused on a canvas propped crookedly on an easel. There were two broad streaks of vivid blue near the bottom, but nothing else.

In a corner of the room was a single bed. Lying on top of the bed, naked, were a man and a woman, both asleep. Or passed out. An elaborate, electric water pipe stood on a table beside the bed. Next to it was freebasing equipment. Two empty Old Crow bottles had been converted to candle holders.

The walls were covered with canvases, most of them large. The artist, whoever it was, was big on primary colors, phosphorescent paints. The paintings reminded him of an old punk rock song, "The Day the World Went Day-Glo." Who had done that song? The X-Ray Spex, he thought.

"Pretty fucking pathetic, isn't it?" a voice said from behind him.

Rheinhardt turned. Justinian stood out on the landing, half in shadow.

"You again," Rheinhardt said.

"Me again." He shook his head, looking around the room. "Makes me sick, I see this crap. The work *you* did in here . . ."

"How is it you keep showing up on Warehouse grounds? Terry says she doesn't know you, that you have no connection with the Warehouse."

"Not officially, no. My connections are more tenuous, but they do indeed exist. Like my connections with you."

Rheinhardt just shook his head. He didn't want to get into another discussion like this with Justinian. Instead, he pointed at the bed and asked, "Which one's the artist?"

"Neither. You call that art?" The old man shook his head again. "They both are. They're a *team*."

Neither of the two people on the bed had stirred. Rheinhardt looked again at the paintings on the walls. What was worse? he wondered. Being unable to create anymore? Or producing crap like that?

"Come, Rheinhardt," Justinian said. "Forget them. Forget all this. Rheinhardt?"

Rheinhardt turned, looked at Justinian. The old man seemed suddenly very serious.

"Follow me down, Rheinhardt. I have something to show you. It's important."

Justinian *was* serious, almost grave. Rheinhardt nodded.

Justinian turned and began to descend the ladder. Rheinhardt walked out of the studio, closed the door, then followed him down.

Once they were on the ground floor, Justinian led the way to one of the narrow stairwells going down to the cellar studios. As they descended, the wall vibrations increased, and bits of music from the basement sound studios could be heard.

At the bottom, instead of stepping into the main corridor, Justinian circled around and behind the stairs. He pushed in at a blank, solid wall, and the wall moved, swinging inward to reveal a narrow opening. Justinian and Rheinhardt squeezed through, and Justinian worked the wall closed behind them, bringing complete darkness.

Justinian flicked on a needle light. They were in a corridor no more than three feet wide, the ceiling just an inch or two above Rheinhardt's head. Justinian moved forward, footsteps nearly silent, and Rheinhardt followed without a word.

The corridor ended abruptly. Justinian cut the light.

For several moments Rheinhardt could see and hear
nothing, then a faint click sounded. Justinian took his
hand, guided him forward.

An opening had appeared in the floor, with metal
rungs leading straight down. Justinian went first, and
Rheinhardt followed into the darkness.

Dolores was a mess. Tuck and Wilsy, who were still in
the room, had put her on the wall couch, a pillow under
her head. She was in the middle of what *did* look like an
epileptic seizure, her head and limbs frantically twitching. Her dress was soaked with mud, rain, urine, and
blood.

"How long has she been here?" Terry demanded.

"About an hour," Wilsy said.

"An hour? Jesus, she should be in a hospital."

"We couldn't call an ambulance," Tuck said. "All the
problems we've been having, trying to kick us out? This
comes out, we'd be forced out of here for sure, and it
doesn't even have anything to do with us."

"Right," Terry said. "Better she dies. Christ." She
knelt beside Dolores, helpless. Until the seizure
stopped she really couldn't do anything. But the seizure
did seem to be letting up a bit.

"We talked to Packer about it," Tuck said. "He
agreed we shouldn't call an ambulance."

"Packer, my ass. That fuckhead doesn't give a shit
about anyone but himself. Jesus. Wilsy, under the sink
in the bathroom is a box of pads. Bring them to me.
And Minh, go get the van, drive it around to the side.
We've got to get her to a hospital, fast. No time now to
wait for a goddamn ambulance. Jesus."

Minh and Wilsy hurried out of the room. A minute
later Wilsy was back with the pads, and Terry pulled a
couple out of the box.

The seizure quickly dissipated, the tremors settling
out, fading, fading, until they ceased completely.
Dolores became nearly motionless, eyes closed, the
only movement her heavy, irregular breathing. Terry

cut away her dress and underwear, set to work on the bleeding. She really didn't know what to do besides use the pads, pack them in tight and hope.

"Get blankets, towels, some water," Terry said to Tuck and Wilsy. "You're going to have to help me get her into the van, so when you bring that stuff back, *stick around.*"

They nodded, and left the room without a word. Terry was alone with Dolores.

She couldn't tell if the bleeding had slowed or stopped, there was so much blood everywhere. The silence in the room seemed heavy and stifling. Terry could feel her own heart hammering against her ribs, thought she could actually hear it.

After a couple of minutes Dolores opened her eyes and began quietly talking.

"There are angels dancing in my head, dancing on glass," she said. "I've never seen such . . ." Her voice faded out, but she didn't close her eyes.

"Dolores, you awake? How are you feeling?"

"Terry, is that you?"

"Yes. How are you doing?"

"I feel . . . wonderful. There's glass in my head, and angels dancing on it, I feel . . ." She paused. "Is it gone?"

"Is what gone?" Knowing what Dolores meant.

"The baby."

"Yes, I think so."

Dolores visibly relaxed, smiled. "He said it would work."

"Who said? Who did this to you, Dolores?"

"Derek."

"Jesus, I told you to keep away from him."

"But he said he knew how I could get rid of it."

"What did he do, Dolores?"

"Gave me spinal plugs."

God damn that bastard. God fucking damn . . .

"He said the electricity surges would do it."

"So he plugged into you?"

"Yes.".

"And I suppose he screwed you, too?"

"He said that was a part of it."

"I'm going to kill him," Terry said. "I'm going to kill the fucking bastard."

"No, no, you don't understand. It worked, didn't it? It was incredible, Terry, it felt like, I don't know, fantastic, like I was floating up into outer space, my whole body just . . . just . . . I don't know. It was the best, the *best*." She opened her eyes wide, staring at Terry, smiling. "And it worked, didn't it?"

Terry nodded. "Lay back, Dolores. Relax. Yes, it worked all right." She eased Dolores onto her side, peeled back more of the dress, exposing the new plugs implanted at the base of her spine. Christ. It was hack work. Derek might even have done it himself. Jesus Christ. No wonder she was having seizures, her entire nervous system was probably all screwed up.

Minh came into the room, breathing heavily. "The van's ready," he said.

"Where the hell are Tuck and Wilsy?"

As if on cue Tuck and Wilsy stepped into the room with bundles of towels and blankets, and a large basin of steaming water.

"All right," Terry said. "Let's get her wrapped up and into the van, we'll try to clean her up on the way."

As they lifted Dolores from the couch, she smiled again and grabbed Terry's wrist. "Angels, Terry, angels dancing in my head."

Yeah, angels, Terry thought. She *would* kill that bastard. She'd rip the damn plugs out of his spine with her bare hands.

They carried Dolores out and into the rain, then laid her down on the carpeted floor of the van. Terry and Wilsy sat on either side of her. As Minh pulled out of the grounds and onto the street, the next seizure began.

The blackness gave way to dim blue light as they descended. The air cooled, and Rheinhardt heard water dripping below. The walls were stone and concrete, and as they went lower, the echo of their footsteps grew louder.

"The sewers?" Rheinhardt asked.

Justinian didn't answer. When they reached the bottom of the ladder, they stepped onto wooden planks crossing a shallow stream of water. A round, concrete tunnel extended in both directions, the ceilings lit by widely spaced blue phosphor lights. Justinian set off upstream along a ledge just above the water. Rheinhardt followed, the tunnel high enough so he didn't have to stoop.

"Always a little leakage," Justinian said. "Specially when it rains. Can't get complete seals on all the diversions. Actually, most of what you're seeing is our own drainage."

"What diversions?"

"We've got this whole area, under three blocks, walled off, solid diversion set up so all the sewage and drain water gets shunted by through alternate routes. We've got a lot of dry space down here."

"Who's this 'we'?"

"You'll see."

Up ahead, light fanned out from side openings in the tunnel. They reached the first, a small cave with its floor above the water level. Rheinhardt stopped and looked inside. A young woman sat at a drawing table, her work space lit by a single lamp hanging from the low ceiling. She was drawing with silverpoint on a black surface, and did not look up from her work. On the floor was a slab of foam rubber and a stained sleeping bag. A few books were scattered about, there was a pile of clothes in a plastic milk crate, and several folios were stacked neatly against the far wall. Two large, framed drawings in silverpoint, both of a space station undergoing demolition, hung on the wall. Justinian touched his arm, and Rheinhardt turned away. They continued along the tunnel.

They passed caves and rooms on both sides, most of

them lit and occupied, all of them small and cramped. Rheinhardt saw painters, sculptors, glassworkers, writers typing on nearly silent keyboards or writing longhand, and two or three people working with equipment and tools he didn't recognize.

The noise level gradually increased as they went on, though never becoming loud. The light, too, brightened, and as they came around a gentle curve in the tunnel, a circle of white appeared. A minute later the tunnel opened out into a large chamber.

The chamber was about twenty feet wide, perhaps twice as long, and the ceiling was nearly twenty feet above the floor. The floor was a wooden platform supported on cement blocks two feet above the cement so water flowed freely beneath it.

A dozen people were in the main chamber, sitting at tables and talking or eating, a few lying on cots. Several cubicles were carved out of the chamber walls. Inside the cubicles were people working with musical instruments and headphones, recording decks, video and film equipment. Each of the cubicles had a glowing space heater. No one paid much attention to Justinian or Rheinhardt. As he looked around, Rheinhardt saw sinks and faucets, three stoves, and in one corner were two refrigerators and a freezer.

"Who are all these people?" Rheinhardt whispered. When he received no answer, he turned around. Justinian was gone.

Rheinhardt slowly wandered through the chamber without approaching anyone. His first impression was that they were fairly well equipped, but as he paid closer attention he saw that the tables and chairs were makeshift, the cot fabric patched, the porcelain chipped and gouged, and the appliances looked like they were ready to fall apart.

Bits of music leaked out of the cubicles where recording and overdubbing was taking place. The studio equipment looked high quality, but he noticed there was no redundancy—there was only one of each piece of equipment, unlike the Warehouse where everyone had their own.

A woman at one of the tables called out to him. "Hey, your name's Rheinhardt, isn't it?"

"Yes," he said. "Do I know you?"

The woman shook her head. "No. Didn't you do a bronze a few years ago called 'Nuclear Garden'?"

"Yes."

"And 'The Winter Gantry'?"

"Yes."

"That was good work." She turned her attention back to her two companions, and Rheinhardt walked on.

When he'd passed through the chamber, Rheinhardt entered another tunnel, and kept on. He passed several more occupied rooms, then came to a side passage on his right.

The passage was dimly lit and filled with slowly rotating mirrors of various sizes and shapes. Fragmented images flashed at him, sharp and bright, but never complete. Some of the mirrors were mounted on the walls, some jutted from the floor, others were suspended from the ceiling. On the walls were photographs, drawings, light paintings, shiny bits of metal.

The mirrors stopped rotating. Brighter lights came up, dimmed for a moment, then came up again. The mirrors remained motionless, but Rheinhardt saw movement toward the rear of the passage. He waited and watched as someone came forward. Glimpses of dark blonde hair, faded jeans, bare arms, and tennis shoes flickered at him from the mirrors. After several minutes, a woman emerged from the maze.

It was Kit.

Dolores was dead fifteen minutes after they got her to S.F. General.

She'd gone into convulsions in the van and almost

immediately the hemorrhaging stepped up. There was nothing Terry could do to stop it, and by the time they pulled into Emergency, she knew it was hopeless.

She endured the questions from the physicians, the interrogation and harassment and threats from the police, until they finally let her go, making it clear they would be talking to her again.

Minh, as usual, had remained out of sight so no one knew he had anything to do with either Terry or Dolores, and Wilsy and Tuck had gone back to the Warehouse long before. When Terry came out of the hospital, Minh was waiting for her. They walked in silence to the far section of the parking lot.

"Where to, boss lady?" he asked, trying to make her smile.

Terry just shook her head. "Give me the keys to the van," she said. "I've got places to go."

"No, I always drive," Minh said. "I'll take you home."

"You're not old enough to drive, you slant-eyed dink. Give me the damn keys."

Minh jumped into the driver's seat, unlocked the door for her, and started the engine. Terry nodded, and sighed. She climbed in and sat beside him, too tired to argue, too depressed to do anything but acquiesce.

"Home?" Minh asked.

"No. Let's go back to the Warehouse. Rheinhardt's still there. Then I'll go home."

The rain was much lighter now, little more than mist. As Minh drove through the dark, slick streets, Terry leaned her head against the window and watched the mist drizzling all around them, like video snow . . . endless, relentless video snow . . .

She woke as Minh drove onto the Warehouse lot, the van bouncing among the potholes. She didn't think she'd actually slept, but she couldn't remember anything since they'd left the hospital. Minh dropped her off by one of the side doors, then drove off for the underground car port.

Terry stood in the rain, unwilling to go in yet. Her legs and arms felt heavy, her heart sluggish and drained. The light rain was cool and soothing on her face, the darkness reassuring. She wanted to cry, but couldn't.

Minh appeared at her side, ghostlike in the rain.

"Let's go in, Terry. Getting wet won't help."

She smiled at him, put her hand on his shoulder. "It *does* help. But yes, we'll go in. See if you can find Rheinhardt, will you?"

Inside, while Minh went searching for Rheinhardt, Terry wandered along the halls and passages, past open rooms and studios. People said hello, or tried to talk to her, but she ignored them and continued through the building; she felt like a slow-motion steel ball from the old pinball machines.

After half an hour, no one had been able to find Rheinhardt. Minh was certain he was no longer in the Warehouse at all.

Terry climbed the swaying ladder up to the corner studio that had once been Rheinhardt's. Without knocking, she pushed open the door, looked inside. As usual, Lester and Penny were passed out. She looked at the canvas on the easel. Just as well.

She closed the door, stood on the landing and gazed out over the huge building, over the shadows and fragmented lights. Then she leaned over the rail and yelled as loud as she could.

"RHEINHARDT!"

There was no answer. She sat down, her legs hanging over the edge, and at last started to cry.

Kit bedded down in a six-by-six cubicle just off the main tunnel a few yards down from the passage of mirrors. She plugged in a hot pot, got two cups to make tea. Rheinhardt sat on a wooden crate, his back against the concrete wall, and Kit sat on the edge of her cot.

"Got a cigarette?" she asked.

Rheinhardt smiled, lit two, handed one to her. After

two drags she started coughing. She hacked loudly for
more than a minute before she brought it under control.

"You don't look or sound too healthy," Rheinhardt
said. Besides the cough, Kit was gaunt and her skin was
pale.

"I'm *not* too healthy. I don't eat for shit a lot of the
time, and it gets damn cold down here."

"Why not get out? Or do you think suffering's some
kind of prerequisite for great art?"

"Jesus Christ, Rheinhardt, you think I live down here
by choice? You think any of us do?" She shook her
head. "Sure, it's a *choice.* I could maybe get a job,
maybe, find a nice little apartment, get a credit card
and kiss off the art altogether. But shit, Rheinhardt,
you know me and jobs. I've tried. Down here's the only
place I can live and work for practically nothing. No
fuckin' free ride like those primas up in the Warehouse."

"I'm sorry. Bad question."

"There you've got it." The water was boiling, and she
made two cups of tea with a single bag. She handed one
to Rheinhardt, gazed steadily at him. "And yeah,
before you ask, I know what I've probably got." She
turned away, sat back down on the cot. "How'd you
find us? Word's not out on the street, is it? That's all
we'd fuckin' need."

"No. Justinian brought me."

She nodded. "Crazy old man. Hangs out down here a
lot. Saw him the other day. Told me he's your dwarf."

"That's what he tells me, too. Any idea what the hell
he means?"

"Like I said, he's a crazy old man. He could mean
anything. Or nothing. I'd forget about it, I were you."

Sure, he thought, but she wasn't. The old man
worried him sometimes.

He sipped at the tea. It was weak, and he wondered if
the bag had been used before. "Did you know Deever?"
he asked Kit.

Kit nodded. "Sure, the old Namvet. The one who disappeared."

"You haven't seen him, then? I thought maybe he might be down here?"

"No, haven't heard a thing about him."

"How long have you been down here?"

"A year, year and a half maybe. Since coming back from the desert. I don't know, time gets a little funny underground." She shrugged. "Everything's a little funny."

"From what I've seen, this place isn't that organized."

"No. You come down, find an empty place that's livable, and move in. Run your own water and electricity, though the people down here who know that stuff will help you get set up. We leech power and water from the Warehouse, mostly. They're a perfect front for us, and they don't even know we exist. We even sneak in, haul as much of their food down here as we can without getting noticed. Lately it hasn't been that difficult."

"I'm not surprised."

"You thinking of moving down here to work?" Kit asked.

Rheinhardt shook his head. "No." He didn't say any more, and they were silent for a minute, drinking the weak tea and smoking their cigarettes. Kit had two more coughing fits by the time she finished her cigarette. She crushed out the butt on the floor.

"These damn things are gonna kill me," she said. "Got another?"

Rheinhardt gave her one, lit it for her.

"I saw a display on Market Street the other day," he said. "A series of holographic X rays, organ scans, radiographs."

Kit nodded. "Effective, wasn't it? Powerful stuff."

"Yes. That done by somebody down here?"

"Oh yeah, that was Artaud's work. I helped him set up the projectors, camouflage them. Took us over a week, working nights."

"How about a break-in piece I heard from the radio a couple of days ago, called 'Artificial Gravity'? That someone from here too?"

"I think so. I don't keep with the musicians much, but I think I heard something about it. Mostly I've been busy with my own project."

"The tunnel with the mirrors?"

"Yeah. I'm making the final adjustments now. It's an active participation work. A lot of the mirrors move, you saw that. The participant goes through them, like a maze, except there's a laser cursor projected from the mirrors that guides the person through. It's mostly visual, with lights, photos, collages and slides and other things, but there's some music, too. I've got it running from two different power sources—the Warehouse lines, for one, and Artaud helped me link into a main city cable, so if one source goes, it'll still run on the other. When I'm finished, I'd like you to run through it. It's called *Mirrors of a Forgotten Future*."

"Sure. When will it be done?"

"Tomorrow. Maybe the next day. Come down anytime after that. I'm real close on it."

"All right, I'll come back."

Kit nodded, started coughing again. She looked bad, but he knew there was nothing he could do for her.

"You hear about Stoke?" she asked after a long silence.

"Yes. Terry told me."

Kit nodded again, looked at her cigarette. Another long silence. Suddenly it seemed to Rheinhardt that they had nothing more to talk about. It shouldn't have been that way. It hadn't been like that five years ago.

A shuffling sounded in the main tunnel. Justinian appeared.

"Time to go," he said.

Rheinhardt nodded once, slowly rose to his feet. "I'll see you, Kit. Take care of yourself."

She looked up, held out what was left of her cigarette. "Spare another before you leave?"

Rheinhardt took the pack from his pocket, handed it to her. "Keep it," he said.

"Thanks." Kit placed it under the cot, then leaned back against the wall, smoking, no longer looking at him.

Rheinhardt turned away and followed Justinian down the large, echoing tunnel, headed back into darkness.

Rheinhardt,

Sometimes I think the old man was right. Justinian. He said you knew him. Before I left he came to see me, gave me the Dragon. For protection. Never thought much about it before, always wore it, though, and I think maybe it saved my life today.

Another firefight, this morning, just after dawn. Fucking ambush, looked like, didn't know what the hell was happening, felt something hit me, I was falling and staggering around, crashing through the brush, next thing I knew I was laying on the ground with the Dragon in my hand, fingers squeezing it for life. All around me was gunfire, some explosions, leaves kicking up, something going off my helmet, I don't know, I just hunched up and closed my eyes and waited it out.

When everything was over, and the squad found me, I hardly had a mark on me. We lost two guys, dead, three more wounded, but me? Looked like my helmet had been grazed twice with bullets, and two pieces of shrapnel were stuck in it. A bullet had torn through my boot heel, more shrapnel in the soles of both my boots, and another bullet had gone through my shirt, leaving a hot red and black streak across one of my ribs.

Don't know how I lucked out alive. The Dragon. A talisman, Justinian called it. Whatever you want to call it, I think today it saved my fucking life.

Stoke

Nine

Dusk, and dark forms gathered in the empty lot across the street—men and women dressed in jeans, sweatshirts, worn denim or leather jackets, torn T-shirts. They clustered together, quiet, carrying thick sticks, sledgehammers, baseball bats, lengths of pipe and two by fours, crowbars, a pickaxe. Ages seemed to range from late teens up through forties, maybe even fifties. It looked to Rheinhardt as if they were waiting for something.

Rheinhardt stood in the shadowed alley between two concrete buildings and waited, watching. A young woman carried a soundblaster, but wasn't playing any music on it. Two men stood back to back in the gutter, watching the street.

The man on the right raised his hand, the other turned around. Rheinhardt, too, turned and looked down the street to his right. Two blocks away was a large dark car slowly approaching without lights. It came closer, and Rheinhardt heard the purr of its engine, made out the lines and hood ornament of a Mercedes-Benz sedan. It was a newer model, immaculate, dark metallic brown, four doors. An indistinct figure sat behind the wheel, steering with one hand.

The Mercedes slowed as it approached, turned and drove up the curb and into the lot, the group of people moving aside to give it room. The car came to a stop in the middle of the lot. The engine stopped.

A woman stepped out of the car. She held up her

hand, dangled a set of keys from her fingers, then flung the keys into the dirt and trash in the far corner of the lot. No one made a sound.

She reached into the car, withdrew a length of metal pipe about three feet long with an elbow on the end, slammed the door shut. The group stepped back from the car, leaving a few feet of space all around it, and the woman climbed first onto the hood, then up onto the roof, stood facing the front of the car. She raised the pipe above her head, then with both hands swung it down with a shout, smashing through the windshield, spraying glass into the car. Twice more she swung the pipe, shattering most of the windshield. She turned, took a few steps, stood above the back window. Again with a shout she swung the pipe down, shattering glass.

The woman continued smashing the car's windows, moving from one to another until nearly all the glass in all the windows had been shattered, sprayed into the car's interior, or scattered on the dirt around it. The woman stood atop the roof of the car, breathing heavily, looking out over the people surrounding the car, then nodded. Music, loud industrial metal rock, erupted from the soundblaster, and the group closed in on the Mercedes.

The woman seemed to lead the assault. She remained on the roof, banging on the metal at her feet with the pipe, while others attacked the rest of the car. There were too many people, so they took turns at the car, and at first they just beat at it with the pipes and heavy sticks and bats, one man putting holes into the hood with each swing of his pickaxe. The noise was incredible, nearly drowning out the music.

Tactics changed. Doors were swung open, bent too far with two or three people pushing at them, hinges pried at with crowbars, door frames pounded at with sledgehammers and steel pipes. The trunk was pried open, emptied, and someone exchanged their heavy stick for the tire iron. The hood followed, smashed and bent and pocked with holes from the pickaxe, and soon Rheinhardt saw pieces of the engine—hoses, belts, air cleaner, distributor cap, wires, even the battery—thrown or heaved across the lot. One of the car doors finally ripped free, and two people dragged it away to an isolated part of the lot where they pounded at it, ripped leather and fabric, broke handles.

Someone apparently had regular tools, because eventually several people were pulling the two bench seats out of the car. They carried the seats away, then set on them with knives and sharp tools, ripping out the upholstery, digging out the padding to scatter it around the dirt. The woman with the tire iron was using the jack to pump up one corner of the car, preparing to remove the wheel.

Darkness had fallen, but streetlights came on, one directly across from the lot, illuminating the scene.

What fascinated Rheinhardt most as he watched them demolish the Mercedes was that none of the people seemed to be enjoying themselves, no one seemed to take any pleasure in what they were doing. He expected laughter, or smiles, joking or small talk, but they were all too serious, involved, appeared to be enraged with the car itself, intent on destroying it completely in some bizarre act of revenge. This was not a game, obviously, not a night on the town, but Rheinhardt didn't understand just what it was, or what it meant to these people. Maybe it *was* revenge.

Two hours later, little remained intact on the Mercedes. The interior was gutted, the roof had collapsed, the hood, trunk, and all four doors had been ripped free of the car and lay bent, gouged, and mangled nearby. Pieces of the engine and all four tires and wheels were scattered all over the lot.

The music and the crashing sounds of metal against metal ceased, bringing a strange, ringing silence to the street. The men and women stood motionless near the car, or staggered slowly about the lot. Even from across the street Rheinhardt could hear the rasp of heavy breathing, coughs, and dry spitting sounds, could see the glistening sweat reflecting light from arms and faces.

Without a word, clearly drained and exhausted, the men and women slowly dispersed in all directions, no one running, no one in a hurry, but no one staying behind. Within minutes they were all gone, and nothing remained but the silent ruins of the car.

Dear Rheinhardt,

Crazyass war. Who we fighting? Why? Don't ask me, got no idea. We just go where they tell us, shoot at anything that moves, that's what it seems like.

Things seem to be changing all the time over here, that's what the older guys say, the guys in their second tours, even the guys in the second year of their first, they say already things are different than last year, and the second tour guys say last year was different than the year before. They all say things just keep getting weirder, the patrols and objectives make less and less sense, and they say our commanders are all hexed by some kind of magic so they don't know what they're doing anymore. And that, Rheinhardt, makes as much sense as anything.

And me? I'm just trying to stay alive. That's the hardest thing, realizing I don't have a lot of control over that. The smart, good soldiers get killed just as easy as the stupid shits stumbling around like assholes. Sometimes it's the stupid shits that get the smart ones killed. Only consolation is the stupid shits go too.

But I'm still alive, and I plan to stay that way. Dragon is doing its job, watching my ass. And I've got some other help—the jungle. I'm learning to tune in with the jungle, Dragon helps me do that, and I try not to take the fucking pills they give us, and these new poppers, at least not too much.

Crazy, huh? Me, who used to take anything and everything. But I melt in with the trees and the rivers and the grass, that's how I stay alive, and I can only do that when my head is clean. Maybe someday I'll melt into the mountains, live on forever as a part of them, and float out over to see you.

Till then,

The Stokeman

Ten

Terry and Rheinhardt sat at the kitchen table in Terry's apartment, drinking coffee. Rain spattered against the window, and Terry watched Rheinhardt gazing out into the gray morning. He seemed far away.

Something had happened to him that night at the Warehouse, but he wouldn't say where he'd gone when he'd disappeared from the building. Terry had told him about Dolores, but he hadn't really responded. She was pissed off at him—for just taking off that night (though that wasn't new for him), for not listening—but she kept it in. She had questions to ask him that would probably make his depression even worse. She had no choice, though, and finally she couldn't put it off any longer.

"Did you ever kill anyone when you were fighting?" she asked. "In the jungles?"

Rheinhardt turned from the window, looked at her. At first he didn't say anything, then he nodded. "Yes. I think so." He paused, breathed deeply. "I'm fairly certain."

"Have you ever *wanted* to kill someone, really wanted somebody dead?"

"I don't know. I don't think so. Maybe the second LT I had." He tried to smile, but couldn't quite pull it off.

"I'm serious," Terry said.

"I know." He paused. "Why are you asking, Terry? You think you want somebody dead?"

"Yes."

"Who? Derek?"

"Yes." So he *had* been listening to her.

Rheinhardt slowly shook his head. "You don't really want to kill him."

"How the hell do you know what I want? The bastard deserves to die."

"I won't argue about all this with you, Terry. What do you want from me, anyway? My approval? You won't get it." He started to turn back to the window.

"I want you to tell me how to do it."

Rheinhardt looked up sharply, stared at her. His eyes became hard, like ice, his face tight. For a moment she thought he was going to explode, shout at her. Instead, a violent shudder shook through him, and he turned away from her to gaze out the window again.

Terry looked down at her coffee cup, a knot of tension in her chest. It *was* a terrible thing to ask him. She sipped at her coffee. It was cold.

She got up, went to the stove, brought the pot back to the table, and poured a fresh cup for herself. "You want some more?" she asked.

"Sure."

She filled his cup, put the pot back on the stove. "I'm sorry," she said.

"It's all right." But he did not look at her, and he continued to watch the falling rain.

A few minutes later the doorbell rang. "I'll be right back," she said. He didn't nod, didn't answer at all.

At the front door was a bike messenger, a thin young woman nearly lost inside a huge, brilliant red raincoat. "You Terry Cassini?"

Terry nodded. The woman handed her a letter, and Terry signed for it. Although there was no return address, she knew it was from Solinex. She carried it back to the kitchen; Rheinhardt was still looking out the window, but now he was smoking a cigarette. Terry sat down, opened the letter, and read it.

Dear Ms. Cassini,

This is a final notice. We have been extremely patient, but that patience has run its course. You

and all your colleagues have until 1:00 P.M. this
Friday to vacate the premises. At that time police
and security squads will forcefully evict anyone
who remains in the building or anywhere on the
grounds. At 8:00 A.M. Monday morning following,
demolition of the building will begin.

The letter was unsigned. Terry handed it to
Rheinhardt. He read it, set it on the table.

"Well?" he said.

Terry shook her head, suddenly very tired and relieved. "I don't care anymore," she said. "I really
don't."

Rheinhardt reached the bottom of the stairs, moved
around and behind them. He pushed at the solid, blank
wall. Nothing happened. He tried to remember what
Justinian had done, and pushed again, first on the right,
then on the left. The wall moved slightly, and he leaned
into it, pushing off the floor with his boots. The wall
turned, stopped, then jerked forward again and slid
open.

Rheinhardt slipped through the opening, pushed the
wall closed. The darkness was complete, and he hadn't
brought any kind of light. He remembered his matches.

He lit one, which cast a dim orange glow along the
narrow corridor. Rheinhardt thought he could see the
end of the passage, another solid wall. There were no
obstructions, so he blew out the match and started
forward in the darkness.

Rheinhardt felt he needed to get underground. He
wanted to talk to the people living below, warn them of
what was happening in the Warehouse. He didn't know
what the effects would be. If nothing else, with the
demolition all the utilities would be cut off. They
needed to know.

Rheinhardt stopped, suddenly unsure in the blackness, no longer confident that the way was clear. He put
a hand out to his right, touched the side wall. He lit
another match.

The end wall was just a foot away. The walls and floor appeared smooth and seamless. With the light from one match after another, Rheinhardt searched the walls, the floor, the ceiling, looking for a button, switch, or depression, some break in the surface. He ran his free hand over the wall, hoping to catch something by feel. He saw nothing, he felt nothing.

Giving up on the matches, he tried pressing on different parts of the wall with both hands, digging at the floor with his boots, but nothing happened.

He gave up and sat on the floor in the darkness, his back against one side wall, his boots against the other, knees sharply bent. The air smelled of sulfur. There was a slight vibration in the floor for a moment, then it passed. There were no sounds except his own breathing.

He lit a cigarette, dragged deeply on it. He realized he *didn't* need to get underground. They would be all right. They could take care of themselves. Maybe he'd try another time.

Fragments of the music piece, "Artificial Gravity," surfaced in his mind: a blast of saxophone, the rhythm of the percussion, the cyclic ascent of the guitar near the beginning. He pictured a twisted, helical structure, tight and symmetrical at its base, then loosening, unraveling, its integrity disintegrating as it rose.

Rheinhardt suddenly wanted very desperately to hold a block of clay in his hands.

He remained in the darkness, smoking. He felt he was beginning to understand some things.

Descent/Ascent:
Artificial Gravity

Eleven

There was no Volvo on 15th Street.

Rheinhardt stood by a white, rusting Chevy, its interior gutted, the engine stripped; all four tires, though flat and bald, remained on the wheels. A half dozen other abandoned vehicles were on the street, parked against the curbs in front of the old Weber Manufacturing warehouse, but there wasn't a Volvo in sight. Few people were around, and traffic was nonexistent. The street had a deserted, uncomfortable feel.

Brisk had left a message for him with Terry, asking Rheinhardt to meet him. Since the message hadn't said when or where, the Volvo had seemed his only option.

Across the street and down the block, a man and woman dressed in heavy coats watched him from the back seat of a derelict Toyota. The Toyota window slid down, the woman put her head out, shouted to him. "You looking for someone?"

Wary, Rheinhardt crossed the street. He approached the Toyota cautiously, stopped a few feet from it, out in the middle of the street.

"I'm looking for someone named Brisk," he said. "He told me he was living in a Volvo here, but . . ." He shrugged.

"What's your name?"

"Rheinhardt."

The man said something he couldn't hear, then lay out along the seat, putting his head, presumably, in the woman's lap.

"The Volvo got towed away a couple of days ago," the woman said. She pointed down the street. "Brisk's moved around the corner, sharing a VW van with two guys until he can get a better place."

Rheinhardt nodded, said "Thanks." He turned and headed for the corner.

The van was about fifty feet down the next street, and Rheinhardt could hear the slow, irregular clacking of a portable typewriter. He went around the back of the van (no tires, two wheels, the van on blocks), stepped up to the back window, which had been propped open. Brisk crouched just inside, typing in the light from the window; he was seated on a block of wood, the typewriter on an empty cable spool tipped on its side to form a table.

"Hello, Brisk."

"Hey, Rheinhardt. Glad you could come."

"Your message didn't say you'd moved."

"Oh yeah, shit, I forgot about that. But you found me."

"I found you. What's up?"

"Just a sec." Brisk crawled toward the front of the van, opened the side door and stepped out onto the street. "Let's go have a seat."

They crossed the street to a cracked cement bench in front of a former bus stop, the yellow markings painted over with gray.

"I hear you've been underground," Brisk said.

"What do you mean?" Rheinhardt asked, knowing.

"The sewers. The artists. Where Kit is."

"You know about it, then."

Brisk nodded. "I work with some of them. I help them out, they help me out. A couple of people down there are going to act in my play, and they're working on arrangements for a production. Looks like it'll come off in about a month, month and a half, something like that."

"But you don't live down there."

Brisk shook his head, gave an embarrassed smile. "I'm claustrophobic. I can't even go down there to talk to people, they come up and talk to me, I've got a kind of arrangement with a couple of them."

"Listen," Rheinhardt said, remembering. "The Warehouse is being closed down. Maybe you should let everyone down below know."

Brisk shrugged. "They know. Doesn't matter." He shrugged again, waved his hand. "The reason I wanted to see you, though, was that I have a huge favor to ask."

"Ask."

"A *big* favor, Rheinhardt. You said you had money. Did you mean a lot?"

"Depends on what you mean by a lot."

"I need six hundred dollars."

"That's a lot. What do you need it for?"

Brisk shook his head. "That's part of it. I can't tell you, I *won't* tell you. Not something I'll be able to tell you later, or that you'll even find out, probably. You won't ever know. You have to trust me that it's worthwhile. And I don't know that I'll ever be able to pay you back. Chances are I won't, so it's got to be six hundred dollars you can do without. Like I said, it's a damn big favor, and I understand if you can't do it, or don't want to. But I need it, Rheinhardt."

Rheinhardt looked at Brisk. They had known each other a long time, and all that money he had earned in Alaska, what else was he going to do with it? He had more than enough to get by for a long time.

He nodded at Brisk. "It's yours," he said. "When do you want it?"

Terry and Rheinhardt waited in darkness for Packer to appear. They were in one of the Warehouse's two storage sheds, and rain clattered on the metal roof above them, spattered gently on the windows. Terry stood by a window and gazed out into the night. The dark shadows of the derelict freeway overpass blocked out most of the city lights. Rheinhardt sat a few feet away, silent and invisible in the dark.

Terry knew why Packer had asked for this meeting. Terry had read the letter to everyone in the Warehouse, told them to leave, but Packer didn't want to go. He wanted to stay and fight the eviction, and he wanted their help.

The outside door opened, letting rain and cold in around Packer's silhouette, then he stepped inside and slammed the door shut. He flicked on an overhead light for a moment, a bright and painful glare, then switched it off.

"We can't just walk out of here without a fight," Packer said.

"Sure we can," Terry answered. "It's the only option that makes sense anymore."

"No. We need to fight back. We have to do whatever's necessary to stay here, and we need your help." He paused a moment, then, "You, Rheinhardt. You fought in the army, in South America or someplace, right? In the jungles."

Rheinhardt didn't answer. Terry's eyes had adjusted to the dark, and she could dimly make out both Rheinhardt and Packer, the two watching each other in the darkness. Packer waited, silent.

"Someplace," Rheinhardt finally said.

"Then you know about weapons. About ambushes and booby traps and ways to fight back. Help us. You lived and worked here once, you understand what's at stake. Tell us what we need to do. Lead us, if you want."

"You want my advice?" Rheinhardt said.

"Yes."

"Get out. Find some other place to live and work. There's no point in fighting. Why do you want to get killed?"

"We don't want to get killed, but everything we believe in is at stake. We're fighting for our art . . . and that is worth dying for."

What crap, Terry thought. The only thing at stake for Packer and the rest was their meal ticket.

"Bull shit," Rheinhardt said, as if on cue. "All you're really fighting for is your fucking free ride. I won't help you get killed for that."

Packer didn't say anything, but Terry could sense the

tension swell and fill the shed. Finally Packer turned away from Rheinhardt and faced her.

"What about you, Terry? *You've* got to stay and help. If nothing else, you've got to talk to people here. Most of them are backing down, planning to leave, they haven't got the guts to stay and fight. If you talked to them, told them to fight back, that it was important, more of them would stay. They'd listen to you, Terry."

She remembered her own words, talking to Rheinhardt about Stoke all those years ago. *He'll listen to you, he values your opinion.* She felt she understood Rheinhardt a little more.

"No," she said. "I won't help you."

There was silence for a minute or two.

"Then fuck you both," Packer said. "I'm not giving up. I'm going to fight it all the way."

And die for nothing, Terry thought. But she remained silent.

Packer slammed his fist on a crate, yelled "Fuck you both!" again. He stormed out of the shed, left the door open as he stomped away through the mud and the rain.

Dim light came in with the rain and wind, and Terry could see Rheinhardt sitting on a box, staring out through the open door.

"What do you think?" she asked.

"He's an idiot."

"What do you think he'll do?"

Rheinhardt shrugged. "I don't know. And I don't really care." He turned to look at her. "Does it matter what he does?"

Terry stood without moving, looking at him, then slowly shook her head. Rheinhardt nodded once, then turned back to look out at the night and the rain.

Following the meeting with Packer, Terry had told Rheinhardt she had something to show him, then picked up the van and drove them downtown, into the heart of the Financial District. He asked her what it was she wanted to show him, but she wouldn't say anything about it.

It was after midnight, and the streets were nearly deserted. They passed one large office building with a catering truck parked in front, and janitorial crews outside buying food, or sitting on the stone steps, eating, drinking; but other than that, they saw practically no one.

After parking the van, they walked two blocks to Montgomery Street just a block up from Market, where a public works crew was digging up the street. Several large pieces of heavy machinery were stretched out along the block, most of them running with loud grinding noises, and two giant machines were pounding away, kicking up dust and tearing up huge chunks of pavement. The work site was lit by bright, silver-blue lights mounted on portable tripods, and the stretch of road was blocked off to all traffic.

Terry and Rheinhardt sat on a marble bench across the way from the work crew, watching; they were far enough from the noise that they could talk.

"This is what you wanted to show me?" Rheinhardt said.

Terry nodded.

"Why?"

She turned to him, smiling. "These people don't work for the city," she said.

Rheinhardt looked back at the road crew, unsure of what she was getting at. The barricade signs all bore markings of the city's Department of Public Works, and the work vests and hard hats on the workers all looked like city issue. He turned back to Terry, said, "I don't understand."

"They don't work for the city," she repeated. "They don't work for anyone."

"Then what are they . . . ?" He didn't finish, some vague ideas forming. He tried to put them together as Terry went on.

"They're going to dig up this entire section of the street, all the asphalt, haul away the sand and dirt beneath it, maybe do something with water or power lines. They they're going to leave it."

"Leave it," Rheinhardt said. "And not come back?"

Terry nodded. "That's it. They'll put up city barricades so it'll look legit, then go tear up another section tomorrow night, maybe a few blocks away. And they'll keep doing it, night after night as long as they think they can get away with it. They'll probably have warning when the city wakes up to what's happening, and then they'll disappear."

"Leaving behind large sections of torn-up roadway."

Terry nodded again. "Right in the middle of the Financial District."

Rheinhardt looked at the work site, imagining the Financial District with half its streets torn up. "How did you find out about this?" he asked.

"You remember that barbecue a few years ago at Monterey House, before you left?" Rheinhardt nodded, and Terry continued. "There was a woman there, Sika, and her daughter, Lindy. Lindy was really shy, but she wanted you to make her a cat or something, so Sika asked you for her."

"I remember."

"Couple years ago, Sika met this guy, Stefan. Nice guy, they got married last year. He used to work for the city, then got laid off." She nodded toward the workers. "He's one of the people on the crew out there."

Rheinhardt started to ask Terry why, but then realized he already understood; he thought of the group of people who had destroyed the Mercedes.

"You know," Terry said, "the funny thing is, seeing this, knowing what they're doing . . . I don't know." She paused, shaking her head. "It makes me feel *good*. I don't understand why, really. Maybe just because it's someone fighting back, in a crazy sort of way." She shook her head. "I don't know."

That, too, Rheinhardt thought he understood. They

were silent for a few minutes, watching the street being slowly, but steadily, dug up and loaded by the shovelful into trucks. After a while, seeing the holes and pits getting deeper, Rheinhardt began to think about the artists down in the sewers beneath the Warehouse. He decided he should probably tell Terry about them, and somehow this seemed a good time.

"I've got something else that might make you feel good," he finally said.

"What's that?"

"The artists you've talked about, the ones you don't know, who did the holographic X rays, 'Artificial Gravity,' the book that was being burned the other day, all those other things you were telling me about."

"Yes?"

He breathed in deeply, then said, "I found them."

Rheinhardt sat on the edge of Deever's roof, watching the lights come on all over the city. The city was beautiful at night, especially from above like this, when you could see nothing but the lights and the dark forms of the buildings and the moving white and red lights of cars, trucks, buses. But there was a beauty to it during the day, too, even if there was so much shit, even if it seemed to be slowly disintegrating.

Gravel crunched behind him, and he turned. A dark form appeared, walking toward him from the ladder. Justinian. The old man approached, sat beside Rheinhardt.

"I'm getting sick of seeing you," Rheinhardt said.

"I'm not so crazy about seeing you either. Your pessimism is depressing. Melancholia, that's what you've been suffering from." Rheinhardt didn't say anything, and Justinian went on. "Of course, you seem to have turned the corner."

"What do you mean?"

"You're not getting worse. You might even be getting better. There's hope for you, that's what I mean."

"I'm very encouraged, old man."

"You should be."

"I don't want to talk to you, Justinian. Not unless you're willing to tell me what happened to Deever."

"I told you before, I don't know any more than you do."

"Right."

"You don't believe me."

"No."

"It's the truth."

This time there was something different in Justinian's voice, and Rheinhardt looked at him. Maybe he *wasn't* lying. But did it matter? Probably only to Justinian.

"Why are you here, old man?"

Justinian shrugged. "Company."

Company? Rheinhardt thought. *His* company? He slowly shook his head. "Christ, old man."

Justinian nodded, and sighed heavily.

Rheinhardt shook his head once more, and they stood side by side for a long time, silently watching the lights of the city.

Rheinhardt,

Saw seven guys get killed today. All in about ten minutes, we got fucking destroyed. Miller. Stretch. Bridger and Spence. Needles, shit, even fucking Needles who we thought could never be killed. Blinky and Weasel. My rucksack got shredded by shrapnel, but all I got was a few nicks. Dragon, again. I'm in tune, I was melting into the trees and the earth, staying alive. So how come I don't feel so good about it? Seven guys. Jesus.

Got no more to say, no more energy.

I feel like shit.

Stoke

Twelve

Terry didn't know what she was going to say to Derek, what she was going to do to him, but she could not just let it go, she could not just ignore him, forget what he had done to Dolores. She could not sit back and do nothing.

She stood in front of his apartment building, looking up at the second-floor windows. The metal gate was open and she stepped through it under a stucco arch, climbed the cement, spiral stairs to the second-floor landing. She knocked loudly on the solid door. There was no answer, she knocked again, then, without waiting, rang the doorbell; she could hear it ringing inside, an obnoxious sound. Still no answer.

There was an awful smell coming from the apartment. Terry couldn't quite tell what it was, but it brought her close to gagging, and she could feel her stomach and chest tighten. She tried the door, the knob turned, and she pushed it open.

The stench was overwhelming, and she had to turn away, back up for a minute—a mixture of vomit, urine, shit maybe. She took a handkerchief from her back pocket, held it over her mouth and nose, and stepped inside.

She went quickly through the apartment. The front room and kitchen were empty. The door leading from the kitchen to the wooden stairs and the garbage cans below was open, but she didn't see anything or anyone in the stairwell. She moved down the hall, caught the first quiet whimpers, walked into the back bedroom.

Derek lay twitching on his side on the hardwood floor, naked, with long, thin cables trailing from his spinal plugs and ending in a tangle connected to a large black metal box with dials and buttons and a flashing red light, which was in turn plugged into the wall socket. He was whimpering, his contorted face in a spreading pool of vomit, and on the floor near him was smeared feces and urine soaking into the floorboards. He convulsed violently for a few moments, then settled back to the twitching, and Terry backed quickly out of the room, ran into the bathroom, and knelt in front of the open toilet.

She remained there a long time, breathing deeply, the gag reflex kicking in every minute or so, but she didn't throw up. There was a rushing sound in her ears, but she thought she could also hear the sounds of flesh slapping against wood. When she felt more in control, she got up, ran cold water on her face, then returned to the bedroom.

Derek was still twitching, and he seemed to be reaching out to her with one hand.

"H-H-He-He . . . m-m-me," he managed. Tears streaked his face, and his mouth opened and closed like a fish out of water.

Terry crossed the room, widely skirting Derek, and unplugged the black box from the wall, but it didn't seem to do anything. Derek did not stop twitching, and once more he began to convulse. It lasted a few seconds, subsided to the twitching again.

"B-B-B-Br-Br- . . ." he whispered.

"What?" Terry said.

But he couldn't manage any more, just a low, whimpering cry, eyes clamping shut.

"I'll get you help," Terry said.

She backed out of the room again, went into the kitchen, and, with shaking hands, picked up the phone and dialed 911. It took her twenty minutes to get through.

* * *

Rheinhardt walked through the gray drizzle, through narrow streets and alleys, across abandoned building docks, over chain-link fences, avoiding the police barricades. It was already past one, and he was late, but he was really in no hurry.

He was within a block of the Warehouse now, but two police cars blocked the alley, and he didn't know if he could get any closer. He wondered where Minh was. They were supposed to meet in one of these alleys, and Rheinhardt thought he'd been through them all.

"Hey." It was a harsh, loud whisper from above. "Rheinhardt." He looked up, saw Minh's face in a broken window three stories up on his right. "Go back out the alley," Minh whispered. "Turn left, first door unlocked. Stairs down the left hall." His face vanished.

Rheinhardt backed down the alley, followed Minh's directions, and a few minutes later was at Minh's side in an empty, dusty room with a clear view of the Warehouse. The Warehouse grounds were surrounded by police, a couple of fire trucks, an ambulance. It looked like several policemen were preparing to launch tear gas, while others stood nearby, armed and wearing gas masks.

"How many are inside?" Rheinhardt asked.

"Fifteen, twenty," Minh said. "One cop's already talked to them, bullhorn thing, told 'em to come out, no arrests, no nothing. Says if they don't come out, cops'll gas bomb the place."

"Any response?"

"No. No one came out, no one inside said or did anything. Packer, he's kind of crazy anyway, who knows what he'll do."

A cop from somewhere nearby came on the bullhorn again, giving the people inside a final warning. After a moment a single gunshot was fired from inside the building, but there was no return fire from the police.

"Terry's not coming to watch?" Minh asked.

"No. Says she's had it with Packer, with the Warehouse. Says she's had it with the whole damn thing.

And she said she had some other things to take care of, someone to see."

Minh nodded. "Derek."

"She was going to see him?"

"Yeah."

"Shit. Wonder what the hell she's got on her mind."

Minh shrugged, and they remained silent, waiting. Then someone, somewhere, must have given an order because the cops started firing tear gas into the building.

Windows shattered on all sides of the building; only a couple of canisters missed and bounced back off the walls. The sick-colored smoke began billowing upward, first from the canisters on the ground, then a few moments later from out of the broken windows.

There was no response from inside the Warehouse, and everyone outside waited. The police seemed patient and unconcerned. If Packer and his friends were smart, Rheinhardt thought, they'd hole up down in the basement studios, force the cops to come in.

When several minutes passed with no response, the police set up to fire a second round.

Just as the fire order was given, and the next volley began, one of the building's front doors opened, and a rifle was thrown out. A second gun was tossed out and onto the ground, cries of "Don't shoot! Don't shoot!" came from the doorway. Through the clouds of tear gas, a line of choking figures with hands and arms upraised staggered out of the building. At the front was Packer.

"Mr. Hero," Minh said, grinning. "First one out."

Rheinhardt didn't say anything. It wasn't so easy. Tear gas was bad stuff, and there really wasn't much you could do without masks. Still, it *hadn't* been much of a fight. Not for something Packer had said was worth dying for.

As the police approached Packer and cuffed his hands behind his back, Rheinhardt turned away from the window, feeling very tired, and started out of the building.

* * *

Minh had followed him out of the building, had insisted Rheinhardt come to the room he was renting in a house a couple of miles away. He had some things he wanted to show Rheinhardt, he had said, and some questions to ask.

In his room now, Minh began to take objects out of his closet, set them on the bed, the chest, his desk. They were sculptures in different media—a few wood carvings, some pieces done in clay, some carved directly from plaster, a few of hand-twisted metal without welds. Most were figures of animals, but there was also a demolished automobile, a tree with a rope ladder, and a strange wheeled vehicle that could only have come from Minh's own imagination.

Rheinhardt looked closely at the figures, surprised at the talent that showed through, and dismayed at the crude execution, the lack of technique. Not Minh's fault, entirely, he obviously just didn't know how to handle some of the materials; he was stumbling along, learning by trial and error. Rheinhardt knew what that was like, knew it would take Minh a long time to make significant progress that way, a terribly long time.

"I told you I was a sculptor several years ago, remember?" Minh asked.

Rheinhardt smiled, nodded. "I remember."

"I want you to teach me, Rheinhardt."

Rheinhardt looked at him, sighed heavily and shook his head. "You can't teach art," he said.

Minh shook his head in return. "I'm not asking that. Technique. How to use the clay, why it does one thing when I want something else. How to carve, how to make molds, what plaster does and what it won't do. That kind of stuff. There's a lot you *can* teach me, Rheinhardt, I know it."

It was true, that was exactly the kind of thing he *could* teach someone, could teach Minh. But now was impossible. Six, seven years ago, maybe, but no longer. He shook his head again.

"I can't, Minh. Terry must have told you, I can't even do my own work anymore. Haven't in five years. I can't do anything now, not even for myself. There's just no way I can teach you." He paused. "I'm sorry. I really am."

There was a long silence, then Minh nodded. "Sure, Rheinhardt, I understand." He smiled. "Later, then, maybe. When you're working again."

"When I'm working again," Rheinhardt said, softly. He shook his head, thinking about sitting in the darkness of the passage below the Warehouse, wanting clay in his hands. He was afraid to think about it. "I don't know if that will ever happen again."

"It will, Rheinhardt. It's what you are." He nodded once more, and began to put away his pieces.

Terry woke to a cold, clear morning. The bed was warm only if she didn't move, so she remained motionless, staring at the ceiling and wishing she wasn't alone. Al lay at the foot of the bed, but that wasn't the company she really wanted, so she wished clouds would return, and rain would fall again.

She finally got out of bed, showered and dressed, put bread in the toaster. The apartment was empty, quiet; felt almost hollow. Ann had met a guy in a bar two nights before, probably wouldn't show up at the apartment for a week. The Warehouse, too, must be empty now, one way or another. She didn't even care what had happened.

Terry put a tape in the deck, cranked up the volume, trying to fill the hollow rooms with music, trying not to think about Derek and what had been done to him. The thump of bass vibrated the walls, shook the mirrors. The tape was a recording made off the sound board at a local club of a band that played a kind of dub-jazz fusion. Antic Revival. They were long gone, without a single record.

She went to get the newspaper. When she opened the front door and stepped out onto the porch, Justinian appeared on the sidewalk below, the newspaper in one hand, a large, empty duffel bag in the other. He smiled at her.

"Good morning, Ms. Cassini. Your paper." He took two steps up, held out the newspaper, but it wasn't within her reach.

"What do you want?"

"My name is Justinian."

"I know who you are."

He climbed another two steps, still holding out the paper. Terry did not reach for it.

"What do you want?" she asked again.

Justinian came up the last three steps and onto the porch. He gave her the newspaper.

"Rheinhardt asked me to come by, pick up some of his clayworking tools and supplies."

"He's going to start working again?"

"He doesn't know yet. Maybe."

Terry looked into the old man's face, into his steel-gray eyes. For a moment the old man, especially his eyes, reminded her of Rheinhardt. "He doesn't even know you're here, does he? He didn't ask you to pick up anything for him."

Justinian grinned. "No."

"Then why?"

"I'm not going to steal anything. I *will* give it all to him. I just want to have it ready. When he needs it."

Terry didn't know why she trusted this crazy old man, but she did. "All right, come on in."

She led him to the attic room, opened it and turned on the light.

"I can find everything," Justinian said. "I know what I'm looking for."

I'm glad *you* do, she thought. She stood in the doorway and watched Justinian rummage through the boxes and bags and piles, picking out individual items and putting them in the duffel bag.

It *was* a little crazy, letting him go through Rheinhardt's things. But she didn't care anymore. She was tired, and the old man was Rheinhardt's problem. Just so he didn't take any of the paintings or sculptures.

Justinian emerged from the stacks of supplies, the duffel bag stuffed full.

"Got everything?" she asked.

"For now. I thank you." He bowed slightly.

She walked with him out to the front porch, and as he started down the steps she called to him.

"Is it true what they say about you?"

Justinian stopped, turned back to her and grinned. "What?"

"That you fought in Vietnam with Deever."

The grin vanished. He stared at her for a few moments, then turned away and headed down the street without a word.

Thirteen

Rheinhardt stood across the street from the house where Stoke had lived. The house was more run-down than ever; almost a ghost, it had such a deserted feel. He crossed the street, went slowly up the weed-lined walk, stepped up onto the porch; he hesitated a long time, then pushed the doorbell. Silence. He pushed again, ear against the door, but there was no sound, so he knocked several times. A moment later he heard approaching footsteps, and the little brass plate over the square opening in the door swung in. An eye looked out at him. It remained there a minute, watching, then the brass plate swung slowly shut, and Stoke's mother opened the door for him.

"Hello, Mrs. B."

She nodded, stepped back. "Hello, Rheinhardt. Come on in." She looked old and tired, her hair half gray, loose and unkempt, strands in her eyes. Her face was lined, the skin under her eyes dark.

Rheinhardt stepped inside, and Stoke's mother closed the door. They remained silent in the hall, looking at each other.

"I don't really know what to say," Rheinhardt finally said to her.

She gave him a half smile. "Nothing to say. It's been a long time now." Her smile faded. "We tried to find you, when we first heard. We couldn't, and Terry said you had left the city, that she didn't know how to contact you."

Rheinhardt nodded. "I've only been back a couple weeks."

"Then you just heard?"

"Yes."

She opened her mouth to say something, then closed it, looking pained. Breathing deeply, she started toward the kitchen, and Rheinhardt followed. "Can I get you something to eat, drink?" she asked.

"No, thanks anyway. How's Mr. B.?"

Stoke's mother shrugged. "He took it harder, I guess. You know, the proverbial straw? He still isn't working, all these years. He hasn't even looked for work since Stoke was killed." She stopped at the counter, stared out the window into the backyard. "You want to see him, he's out in the back. He's always out there, now."

"I think I will."

He walked out of the kitchen, down the hall, into the family room, stood at the big sliding glass door, looking out into the backyard.

Stoke's father sat in a padded redwood deck chair, gazing out over the scum-covered pond, glass and bottle on the metal table beside him. A shredded umbrella was open over the table, light coming in through the rents so Stoke's father was crisscrossed by jagged, irregular strips of light and shadow.

Rheinhardt slid open the door, walked across the cement. Stoke's father didn't move until Rheinhardt was right next to him, then he looked up, silent. His eyes were dull, like scratched glass marbles.

"Hello, Mr. B.," Rheinhardt said after a minute.

Stoke's father didn't say anything at first, just looked at Rheinhardt with those lifeless eyes. Then he finally nodded once, said, "Rheinhardt."

Oh Christ, Rheinhardt thought, remembering what ~~oke~~ had said more than five years ago—that the time ~~worry~~ about his father would be when he didn't get ~~angry~~ anymore; it looked like there wasn't a trace of ~~anger~~ left in the man. You've given up, he ~~thought~~, ~~Stoke's~~ father.

Rheinhardt didn't know what to say. Giving up. Was this what *he* would be like, if he ever completely gave up on the art? If he never did anything again? He wondered how close he was. It frightened him.

Stoke's father picked up his glass, drank from it, set it back on the table. Then he looked away, gazing at the tall weeds engulfing the back fence.

"Rheinhardt?" It was Stoke's mother, standing in the open doorway. "I have something for you."

He nodded, turned to Stoke's father. "Good-bye, Mr. B. See you later."

Stoke's father nodded once, said, "Sure, Rheinhardt," his voice as dull and lifeless as his eyes.

Rheinhardt turned away and walked back to the house, went inside with Stoke's mother. "Is he always like that?" he asked.

She nodded. "Day after day, he just sits out there. If it rains he sits under the overhang, but still just sits out there. Doesn't even watch the tube anymore." She shrugged. "Sometimes I wish he'd go back to hitting me once in a while. I don't know which is worse."

She held out her hand. In it was a pendant on a chain. The pendant, dark red and black, was in the shape of a dragon. Dragon.

"It was in his personal effects," Stoke's mother said. "I'd never seen it before."

"Someone gave it to him," Rheinhardt said. "Before he left." He paused, then said, "A friend."

"You can have it, if you like," she said. "If it means anything to you."

"Yes, it does, actually." He picked it up out of her hand, held it. "Thanks, Mrs. B."

She nodded. They stood silently for a long time, looking at each other. Then she put her arms around him and hugged him, and Rheinhardt could feel her shaking against him. She made no sounds, and he held her tightly until the shaking subsided. Rheinhardt released her and she looked away, out through the glass door and into the backyard.

"Good-bye, Rheinhardt." Her voice was a whisper. "Thank you for stopping by."

"Good-bye, Mrs. B.," he said. He carefully put the pendant in his pocket, and left.

Fourteen

Rheinhardt,

Life sucks.

S.

That was the last letter.

Rheinhardt lay on the motel bed, smoking a cigarette, watching the smoke drift up to the ceiling where it hovered above him as it slowly dissipated. Everything was packed; he was ready to leave.

He just didn't know where to go.

He picked up the black and red dragon from the table beside the bed, held it by the chain and let it dangle in front of his face. Talisman, Stoke had called it. Or Justinian. He understood. With his free hand he fingered the bleached tail of hair at his neck. He had grown it and bleached it down in the 'mericas, and had gotten superstitious about it—*his* talisman. When he got out alive, he determined to keep the tail, and he always had. But the dragon hadn't kept Stoke alive.

He put the pendant in his shirt pocket, breathed deeply. His fingers itched, so that they almost hurt. Was he really ready to start work again? Rheinhardt sat up, stared at his hands. He was afraid to try; afraid he would fail again. He didn't know how many more failures he could handle.

He thought of Stoke's father.

Where was the rain? He missed it. Outside, the day was clear.

It was time to go.

There was a knock at the door.

"Come in, Justinian," Rheinhardt said. "It's unlocked."

The door opened, and Justinian walked in, held his hands above his head.

"Caught," he said. "How did you know it was me?"

"Who else?"

"Terry."

"No," said Rheinhardt.

"The motel manager?"

"In this dump? I'm paid up through tonight, he's not about to put in an appearance."

Justinian looked around the room. "Through tonight? It looks like you're packed up to leave right now."

"I am. It's checkout time." He stood, shouldered his rucksack.

"Where are you going?"

"I don't know. But it's time to leave this place. I've had enough of it. I've had enough of you."

The old man nodded. He looked almost sad. "You're just about right," he said. "You won't have me much longer."

Rheinhardt smiled. "Am I going to miss you, old man?"

"Probably not." Justinian shrugged. "But I don't think you'll forget me. You do, you'll have more problems."

"I won't forget you, Justinian." He took the key out of his pocket, held it in his hand. Another useless talisman. "Let's go."

Rheinhardt went to the door, opened it, let Justinian leave first. Then he stepped out of the room, tossed the key onto the chair inside, and closed the door behind him.

* * *

Terry sat at the kitchen table with Al asleep on her lap, drinking coffee and looking out at the clear skies. It was her day off from Monterey House, and she didn't know what to do. With the Warehouse gone, there was an empty space in her life she hadn't adjusted to yet. She still had too much to think about, things she didn't know what to make of, issues left unresolved—Rheinhardt being back, and all he was going through; Derek and what had happened to him; what it meant to have the Warehouse gone.

The doorbell rang, startling Al who jerked up, hit his head on the edge of the table and dug his claws into Terry's legs before leaping off and onto the floor. Terry got up and went downstairs, the bell ringing constantly. "I'm coming!" she called out, hurrying down the steps.

Donna was at the door, and a cab was parked in the street behind her, engine running.

"Jesus, what is it, Donna? Something wrong?"

Donna smiled. "No, for a change. It's Peg. She's gone into labor, and they've taken her to Mt. Zion. She said you promised to be with her for the birth. Since you don't have a phone I couldn't call you, so I splurged for the cab, came over to pick you up. I assume you want to come."

Terry felt her heartbeat quicken, felt energy kindle in her limbs, purging the fatigue. She grinned. "Of course I'm coming."

She pulled the door closed, locked it, and ran down the steps with Donna toward the cab.

Peg cried out, and Terry gripped her hand tightly, squeezing Peg's fingers. A shudder passed through Peg, fresh sweat broke out on her face, then she sank back, panting. She turned to Terry and smiled, the sweat dripping down her cheeks. Strands of wet hair stuck to her forehead and temples.

"God that . . . hurt," she managed to say. She tried to keep her breathing regular. "But I . . . don't care."

The OB, gloved and masked at the foot of the bed, shook his head. "Too late now for an anesthetic. I don't understand why you wouldn't take one before."

Peg continued to smile, shaking her head, and squeezed Terry's hand. "Maybe I'm . . . crazy . . . but I . . . want to . . . *feel* it . . . I want to . . . feel it all . . ."

The doctor and nurse both shook their heads, and Peg turned to Terry, still grinning.

"I'm . . . so glad . . . you're here," she said.

Terry smiled back. "I promised. I wouldn't have missed it." She wiped the sweat from the young girl's face with a damp cloth. For the first time in days she felt fully alive, on an edge with renewed energy flowing through limbs that had been dragging, heavy and limp. Now, though Peg was doing the real work, Terry was exhausted, but the adrenaline was pumping through her.

The next contraction came, and Peg bent abruptly forward, grimacing.

"Push!" said the nurse.

What the hell do you think she's doing? Terry wanted to ask. But she kept quiet.

Peg's breath burst from her with another cry, and she fell back, breathing quickly and heavily once again.

"I . . . never . . . thought it would . . . be like this," Peg said.

"What did you think?" Terry asked. "That it would be harder, or easier?"

"I don't know . . . Neither. Just . . . I don't know, I . . ." She was grinning again. "You know . . . Terry . . . I really, I . . . couldn't have . . . made it . . . without you."

"You'd have been fine, Peg." She ran the cloth over Peg's face again.

"No, no . . . I wouldn't have. You were . . . you . . ."

The next contraction began and Peg leaned forward again, fingers clawing, tightening.

"Push!" The nurse again. Terry wanted to strangle her.

Once more Peg cried out before falling back. This time, as she rapidly panted, she did not try to talk for a minute. She looked intense, perhaps a little frightened, but clearly ready. Eventually she turned to look at Terry.

"It's . . . it's going to be . . . pretty hard for me . . . isn't it? Trying to . . . to keep the . . . baby myself."

"Yes," Terry answered. No more lying. "But I think you'll be all right, I really do."

Peg nodded once, smiled. Then her eyes widened, and she hunched forward again with the contraction, face going red. Her fingernails dug into Terry's palm.

"Oh . . . ah . . . I . . . oh, god, I . . . I think . . . I . . . I think it's . . . coming!" She tilted her head back, sweat pouring from it, and her entire body trembled and shuddered. Her eyes were wide, her mouth open.

Fascinated, and awed, Terry turned and watched as new life slowly, fitfully, but incredibly emerged from the young girl squeezing her hand.

Rheinhardt went back to Deever's place one more time. Justinian came along with him, but Rheinhardt didn't care; he realized he still had questions for the old man.

They wandered through the deserted building, their footsteps the only sounds, beams from needle lights the only illumination other than faint slashes of gray leaking through the boarded windows. They walked through the ground floor first, then up the stairs and through all the rooms on the second floor. Then it was outside, up the steps, and into the top floor. After going through the entire apartment, they ended up in the back room at the bay window, looking down at the yard. Rheinhardt lit cigarettes for them.

"You really don't know what happened to him?" Rheinhardt asked.

"What do you think? I've told you I don't know."

"The first time, I thought you were lying. The second time I asked, it seemed you were telling me the truth." He looked at the old man. "It can't be both."

"No." Justinian breathed deeply. "I *want* to know

what happened to him. I don't, but I feel I should. If nobody else knows, at least *I* should."

"You can't know everything, old man."

"I suppose not."

Rheinhardt took out the dragon pendant, held it out toward Justinian. "This didn't work either."

Justinian stared at the pendant. "No, I guess it didn't. I don't understand, it should have." He paused, looked at Rheinhardt. "Unless he gave up."

Gave up. Like his father. Rheinhardt thought of Stoke's last letter. *Life sucks.* "That's probably exactly what happened," Rheinhardt said. Justinian looked at him, but didn't say anything. "Here," Rheinhardt said. "You gave it to Stoke, you should have it back."

Justinian hesitated, then took the pendant, looped the chain over his head, tucked it in under his collar. "You going to stay here, Rheinhardt?"

Rheinhardt shook his head. "No. This place's time is gone. I've got somewhere to go, and this isn't it." He was thinking of Terry; it was time to see her again. It was time for a lot of things. "And I think I'll be going."

Justinian nodded. "I think I'll stay here awhile."

"Good-bye, old man."

"Good-bye, Rheinhardt."

Rheinhardt went out the back door, glanced over at Justinian standing at the bay window, then started down the stairs.

Fifteen

Rheinhardt brought the bottle and Terry brought the glasses. They sat on a rooftop, four stories high and half a block from the Warehouse, where they had a clear view of the building and grounds. The air was cold, and clouds rolled past overhead, but it wasn't raining yet. Dressed in heavy coats, they sat in the hollow of a ventilation shaft just back from the edge of the roof, sheltered from the wind, their backs against cold metal.

On the Warehouse grounds stood several pieces of heavy equipment—squat, treaded vehicles, dump trucks, two bulldozers. Half a dozen workers walked about in the mud, and others were inside the building.

Rheinhardt poured Jack Daniel's into both glasses, set the bottle between them. Terry picked up her glass, held it out toward him. They clinked glasses, drank.

No toast, Rheinhardt thought. What *was* there to toast? Nothing, he would have said a couple weeks ago. Now he wasn't so sure.

Watching the demolition crew wandering about the Warehouse, Rheinhardt lit a cigarette. The air was so cold even the cigarette smoke felt cool in his lungs. Not as cold as Alaska, though. And the Jack Daniel's warmed his throat and belly, kept his mind going.

"You ever going to quit smoking those damn things?" Terry asked.

"Probably not. It's never seemed worth the effort."

"When you're fifty and coughing your lungs out, you'll think it would have been worth it."

"Probably." He dragged in deeply on the cigarette.

They were quiet for a while, watching the demolition crew at work, then Terry said, "You were right."

"About what?"

"About Derek. About not really wanting to kill him." She shook her head. "When I saw him the other day, lying there on the floor, helpless, Jesus, so incredibly fucked up . . . All my anger and hate just sort of crumpled up and disappeared." She paused, drank from her glass. "I thought maybe it would come back, and in a way I guess it did, but not really. Not the same." Paused again.

"I went to see him in the hospital," Terry continued. "Still so completely fucked up. They don't have any idea what happened, whether he was doing something himself that went wrong, or if someone else did it to him. He can't talk at all, or at least not enough to make any sense. The doctors said they don't know if he'll ever get much better."

She turned to look at him. "And you know what? I actually feel sorry for the son of a bitch. I still hate what he's done, and I still think he's a miserable human being, but . . ." She gave Rheinhardt a half smile. "I feel sorry for him, I really do." She shook her head. "I don't completely understand it, but . . ." She shrugged.

"You do seem . . . different. Not quite so resigned. Something."

She nodded. "Yeah."

"From seeing Derek?"

"I suppose that's part of it. You know how it is, usually it's not just one thing. But another part of it is, a bigger part . . . One of the girls at Monterey House, Peg, gave birth to a boy yesterday. And I was there, with her, helping her, watching it happen. I know, sounds real hokey, but I tell you, Rheinhardt, it was incredible. The whole situation's screwed up, the girl and the baby are going to have a hell of a rough time making it on their own. But the birth itself, seeing that blotchy, funny-looking little thing coming out from inside another person . . . I don't know, Rheinhardt." She was smiling and shaking her head. "Just . . . incredible."

Rheinhardt nodded. He didn't know what to say. He could sense the changes in her, small and subtle, but significant, it seemed. He'd been feeling some changes himself recently, but didn't yet really know what they were, or why they were happening, or quite where they were going. He felt right on an edge, ready.

Glass shattered in the Warehouse building, and a piece of machinery was thrown out through the window and onto the ground. Two men leaned out the window, tossed out a few more smaller objects, then retreated into the building. More glass shattered, apparently from behind the building.

Rheinhardt picked up the bottle, poured more Jack Daniels into each of their glasses. He guessed that Terry felt she needed to see the final act, to see the Warehouse physically come down, so that's why they were here. He watched her in silence, slowly smoking his cigarette. It seemed to him that, though she was still in some pain, she had also found a lot of peace.

"What do you suppose will happen to the artists under the Warehouse?" Terry asked.

"I don't know. When I asked Brisk about it he didn't seem too concerned. I'm sure they'll be fine, one way or another."

"Will you try to find out? Try to get down to them again?"

He waited before answering, then said, "Probably."

The air went quiet for a few minutes. The work crews congregated in front of the building, most of them talking and smoking.

Terry crept forward, crouched at the edge of the roof, watching intently. Rheinhardt wondered if something should be said, to mark the event somehow, to catch this moment for Terry. But there was really nothing to say. One more thing whose time was gone.

"I don't understand," Terry said. "Where's the wrecking ball? I don't see a crane, nothing like that."

"No wrecking ball here," Rheinhardt answered. "Maybe downtown they'd use one, but not out here. They'll just dynamite the place."

Terry remained on the edge of the roof and nodded. "Appropriate, somehow. Just blow it all to hell." She continued nodding for a moment, then turned to Rheinhardt. "It's really going," she said.

"Yes," he answered.

They watched in silence, waiting. The workers backed across the cracked and potholed asphalt, stood looking at the building. One of them gestured toward the right, and a few seconds later the explosion rocked the air.

The left half of the Warehouse blew out sideways, sending glass and metal and splintered wood spraying out across the asphalt, over the fence, and into the street. Most of the right half remained intact.

Rheinhardt started laughing, pointed at the workers scurrying for cover behind the machinery. "They fucked it up," he said. "They really fucked it up."

Terry turned to him, smiled. "I'm glad we were here to see it." She paused. "And it's good to see you laugh again."

When all the dust and glass and wood from the explosion had settled, the demolition crew moved cautiously away from the machinery, and some of them started yelling at each other. After several minutes of shouting and discussion, a few of them loaded up supplies and went back inside the building.

The air was cold, the whiskey warm. Rheinhardt and Terry remained on the roof, huddled together for warmth, and waited for them to try it again.

Terry woke to Rheinhardt stirring beside her. It was still dark outside, and Terry could see nothing in the room except the luminous digits of her clock. 5:04 A.M. Rheinhardt's skin was warm, and she cupped her body around his, held him.

"You awake, Terry?"

"Yes."

He didn't say anything more for a minute, then he turned to face her. "I have to get up. There's something I need to do this morning."

Her eyes had adjusted to the dark, and she could see his face now, his eyes and mouth. She nodded. He kissed her lightly on the cheek and rolled out of bed, letting a pocket of cold air into the sheets.

Rheinhardt stood at the foot of the bed and quickly dressed. In the darkness he was only a tall, thin shadow, and for a moment it reminded her of Stoke. Terry's chest began to ache.

She remembered watching Stoke on stage, playing guitar and screaming out lyrics with his lousy voice, laughing and having a good time and then going home with a groupie from the audience, not caring how old she was, or what she looked like. Terry remembered all-night sessions, talking and listening to music, sometimes with Rheinhardt, sometimes just she and Stoke, alone. And she remembered him sitting in with that band, playing the solo on "Loan Me a Dime" with so much pain.

The ache continued, steady. All right, she thought. Stoke was dead, and Dolores was dead. But *she* was alive, Peg and her baby were alive, Macy and Lisa, and Minh. And Rheinhardt was still alive, standing there at the foot of her bed. And that counted for something, she realized. That counted for a lot.

Rheinhardt came around, sat on the edge of the bed at her side.

"I'll see you, Terry," he said.

"Will you be back?"

"Today, I'm not sure." He smiled. "But soon, yes, I'll be back." He leaned forward, kissed her, then stood.

"Good-bye, Rheinhardt."

He nodded, stood there a moment, looking down at her. "Terry," he said.

"What?"

He said no more, just stood there watching her.

"You still can't say it, can you?" she finally said.

Rheinhardt smiled, then slowly shook his head. Then, "I'll see you soon." He turned and left the room.

Terry remained in bed for an hour after he was gone, blankets pulled tight around her to keep warm, and watched the gray light of morning make its way in through the window.

Rheinhardt stood among the ruins of the Warehouse, the fog thick around him, the light a dim, dim gray. The roof was gone, and most of the walls; piles of shattered brick, crumbled concrete, and broken timbers littered the ground. A few jagged pieces of metal protruded from the rubble. Much of the cellar, though open to the air, was intact.

The stairs he'd used with Justinian were gone, and the narrow corridor behind them was exposed. Rheinhardt worked his way carefully over the splintered lumber, checking the footing with each step, then lowered himself into the corridor. He had a pair of needle lights with him now, and he used one to light up the walls and floor.

He had to clear away chunks of stone and pieces of broken wood. The needle light was far brighter than the matches had been, and after a few minutes he found, on the right wall, what he had not been able to find a few days before. He dug at the tiny depression with his fingernail, and the floor dropped away just in front of him, exposing the metal ladder. Rheinhardt turned off the light and climbed down the ladder by feel, resetting the floor above him.

The tunnels were completely dark, completely silent except for the occasional dripping of water. He used the needle light to locate the planks at the bottom of the ladder, then to show the way to the ledge running along the trickle of water. Rheinhardt started upstream.

He shined the light into the caves and rooms as he passed them, playing the thin beam across the walls and floors. The rooms were empty of personal belongings, but most of them contained one or two pieces of artwork, done, presumably, by the former occupants and, again presumably, deliberately left behind. He saw welded sculptures and painted canvases, framed photographs and charcoal drawings, delicate networks of glass and blocky statues carved from wood or marble, pamphlets of written work wrapped in plastic and mounted sheets of poetry. The variety seemed endless.

Rheinhardt entered the large central chamber, now empty and hollow and loudly echoing each of his footsteps. All of the electronic equipment was gone, but in several of the cubicles were audio or video tapes, spools of film, all laid out carefully on stands, each clearly labeled. The entire underground network had become a vast subterranean gallery.

He passed through the chamber, entered the far tunnel. The rooms off this tunnel were the same, empty but for one or two pieces of art carefully displayed in each.

As he approached the side passage that had held Kit's mirrors, Rheinhardt became apprehensive, afraid that they would be gone, or that she hadn't completed the project. He kept the beam of light on the side wall and walked slowly, afraid he would somehow miss it.

A flash of light glared back at him, then several fragmented reflections appeared. He turned the light to the ground until he reached the passage entrance. The mirrors were still there.

Taped to the main tunnel wall next to the entrance was a sheet of paper. At the top, in bold letters, was MEMORIES OF A FORGOTTEN FUTURE. But . . . didn't Kit say it was called *MIRRORS* OF A FORGOTTEN FUTURE? He couldn't remember now. Directly below that it said:

INSTRUCTIONS FOR USE

1) With your right hand, press the tab on the wall just inside the passage, three feet up from the floor. The unit will activate.

2) A green laser cursor will appear at eye level in
the first mirror. Follow it through the mirrors,
moving toward it when it blinks, stopping
when it glows steady. It will lead you through.
3) Thank you.

Rheinhardt found the tab with the needle light,
turned off the light, then pressed the tab. A pale glow
appeared in the front section of the passage, faintly
illuminating the first few mirrors; they did not yet
reflect anything but concrete, light, and Rheinhardt's
own image. The green cursor flashed on, remained
steady. After a minute it began to blink, and
Rheinhardt started forward.

He walked directly toward the first mirror, headed
for his own reflection. Just before he reached it, the
cursor stopped blinking and he halted. He stared at his
reflection for a minute, maybe two, then the cursor
shifted to the left and began blinking again. Rheinhardt
turned and followed it.

Peripherally, he noticed mirrors rotating on all sides,
shifting positions and reflections, rotating at different
rates. Incomplete images flashed at him as he moved
along, disappearing too quickly to identify. He felt
slightly dizzy, a little off balance, but he pushed on.

Rheinhardt moved slowly among the mirrors, following the cursor, starting and stopping at its direction.
He was turning constantly, and at times he felt he was
backtracking, or retracing his own path, but nothing
ever looked quite the same.

Sometimes a complete image would appear in one of
the mirrors and hold for a few seconds, but it would be
out of focus so he still could not identify it. At other
times an image would appear that was *too* clear, hurting
his eyes, overwhelming him somehow so that, at least
consciously, he could not register the picture in his
mind.

Reflections of paintings appeared, of photographs
and carvings, collages and hanging mobiles of strange

figures, table displays, wiring diagrams and chip lay-
outs. In a few spots he was seeing reflections of film or
videotape being projected either directly onto the mirrors or onto hidden, multicolored screens.

It was all so strange, because nothing concrete ever
quite registered in his mind, yet he was certain that was
the intent. He literally did not know exactly what he
was seeing. He was barraged by a steady stream of
shifting, fragmented images as he twisted and turned
among the mirrors.

After a time he noticed fragments of music playing in
the background, broken by irregular periods of silence.
But, like the images in the mirrors, the bits of music
were too brief and disjointed, and though often vaguely
familiar, they never quite coalesced into melodies
before breaking off.

Rheinhardt thought that even the light intensity
changed as he moved through the mirrors, though he
could never be sure because he could not seem to
remember from one moment to the next what the light
had been like in the previous few seconds. It was as
though his short-term memory had stopped working
right.

Rheinhardt continued to work his way through the
mirrors, his time sense slowly disintegrating until he
could not even guess at how long he'd been in the maze.
Fifteen minutes? An hour? Three hours or four? All
day? He glanced at his watch, but found he could not
read the markings.

Then, abruptly, the green cursor faded from sight.

Rheinhardt stopped, looking straight ahead. Directly
in front of him was a blank stone wall. A pale, diffuse
light shone on him, and he looked around, disoriented.
After a few moments he realized he was back at the
starting point. He glanced at the mirrors, which had
stopped rotating, then at the printed instruction sheet,
half expecting a new set of instructions. The words were
the same.

The light went out.

Rheinhardt stood in the darkness without moving. Flashes of the fragmented images came up in his mind, flickering quickly past. He thought he remembered seeing . . . seeing . . .

. . . a clear glass sea horse.

. . . an anemonelike metal structure on the moon.

. . . a flash of exploding metal.

. . . a flaming ball high above the earth.

. . . a metal snake.

. . . stars seen through a port window.

. . . a computer monitor flicking in and out of existence.

. . . ocean waves crashing over layers of human bodies.

. . . a long, dark tunnel with a figure at its entrance outlined in flame.

He turned on one of the needle lights and, images still occasionally rising up in his mind, walked up the tunnel to Kit's room; he reached it and shined the light inside.

Justinian sat on a wooden stool, a large duffel bag on the floor beside him. There was a table on his right, and on the table were several blocks of clay and a basin of water.

"What are you doing here?" Rheinhardt asked.

"Waiting for you." He pulled a chain, and a bulb hanging from the ceiling went on. "It's hooked into the same power source as the mirrors."

Rheinhardt nodded. He looked at the clay on the table. How could the old man have known?

"Where are they all?" Rheinhardt asked. "Everyone who was living down here."

"Gone."

"But to where?"

"No one place, Rheinhardt. They've scattered. They weren't a community or an organization. Some are still in the city, some have left. Who knows? It doesn't matter where they've gone."

"No, I guess it doesn't." He looked at the clay again,

then down at the duffel bag. "What's in the duf, Justinian?"

The old man lifted the duffel bag onto the table, unzipped it, and started taking out the contents. First was a box of Rheinhardt's best clay knives. Then came other boxes of wood and metal scrapers, bundles of stiff wire, rags, and wooden blocks. When Justinian stopped, the bag was still half full. He set it back on the floor.

"Plaster, casting materials, other stuff you might need," he said. Justinian rose, walked out of the room and stood beside Rheinhardt in the main tunnel. "It's yours," he said.

Rheinhardt stepped into the room, then sat on the stool in front of the table, looking at the clay, afraid to touch it. He heard Justinian take a few steps, and called to the old man.

"Are you leaving?" he asked.

"Yes," Justinian answered. "I am no longer your dwarf." He raised his hand, gave Rheinhardt the vet salute. When Rheinhardt returned it, Justinian turned away and started down the tunnel. His footsteps echoed from the walls, fading. But the strange thing was, the footsteps became light and bouncy, patterned, and it sounded as if Justinian was dancing his way down the tunnel. The rhythmic sounds continued to fade, and then were gone, and Rheinhardt could hear nothing but the quiet sounds of water dripping nearby.

Rheinhardt turned his attention back to the clay on the table before him. Once again sections of "Artificial Gravity" played through his mind, and the image returned of the rising, helical structure that he had imagined in the darkness of the corridor a few days before.

He held out his hands, watched them. They were calm and steady, without the slightest tremor.

Rheinhardt reached forward, hesitated just a moment, then firmly picked up the block of clay.

Epilogue

Brisk's play was due to start in ten minutes. Rheinhardt and Terry waited in the lobby of the small theater, watching people go through the curtains. Several cops strolled about the lobby, periodically looking through the curtains.

"He got the manager to rent him the theater for a dollar a night," Rheinhardt told Terry. "Nights when nothing else is scheduled. The ten-cent admission is to get around city regs about free performances."

Terry gestured toward the cops. "They here to try to close the show?"

"Probably. But Brisk was saying that, unless there's nudity, or 'lewd and lascivious' acts on stage, they can't close it down on the spot. If they think there's something subversive or obscene in the content, they have to record it and present it to a judge. Brisk says he should be okay, though."

Someone began coughing behind them, loud . . . and familiar. Rheinhardt turned to see Kit in the back corner, leaning against the wall, smiling. He and Terry walked over to her.

"Hey, Rheinhardt. Terry."

"Kit." He smiled back. "I didn't know you were still in the city. Thought maybe you'd gone back to the desert."

"No." She shook her head slowly, still smiling. "I'm not going anywhere."

"Got a place to live?"

"Sort of. If it becomes permanent, I'll let you

know." She paused. "There's a rumor drifting about, that you're working again."

Rheinhardt nodded. "Rumor's true. Slow going, still feeling my way along, but yeah, I'm working again."

"I'm really glad to hear that."

"So am I. How about you? You been doing anything since the mirrors? Which I did go through, by the way."

"I have, too," Terry said. "Rheinhardt brought me down, had me go through it. Pretty amazing."

"Thanks," Kit said. "Yeah, I'm working on a new piece right now. You both know Wendy Burke, don't you?" Rheinhardt and Terry nodded. "I'm working with her, using photographs and video segments she's putting together. *Long* range project, take us maybe a year, maybe longer." She smiled. "And I'm not the only one."

"What do you mean?"

"A couple of weeks ago, in Seattle, a book called *Noble Gasses and Others* was distributed all over the city."

Rheinhardt smiled. "Really?"

"Really. And two days ago, in Washington D.C., on the street in front of the Capitol building, a series of holographic X-ray projections appeared about ten feet above the sidewalks. You won't have heard about it because the press isn't reporting things like that."

"Artaud?"

"Artaud."

They remained silent for a minute, looking at each other.

"We're doing okay," Kit said.

Rheinhardt nodded. The lobby lights flickered once, and they went into the theater to watch the play.

As Rheinhardt came around a bend in the tunnel, he saw a glow of light emerging from Kit's old cubicle, and stopped. He was certain he'd turned the light off when he left.

He approached cautiously, reached the room and looked inside.

Minh sat at his worktable, smoking a cigarette and looking at the clay and wire structure that Rheinhardt had been working on these past few weeks.

"How did you find this place?" Rheinhardt asked.

Minh looked up. "I've always known about it. From when they first started coming down here." He shrugged. "I knew this was where you were working." He pointed at the clay. "You *are* working again."

"Yes."

"Then teach me, Rheinhardt."

Rheinhardt didn't answer at first, looking at the clay that was gradually becoming an oddly helical structure, looking at Minh and remembering the crude sculptures the boy had shown him. Boy? Young man, now.

"Teach me," Minh said again.

Rheinhardt nodded. "All right, Minh, I'll teach you." He nodded once more, and stepped up into the room.